CRITICS PRAISE JOHN EVERSON AND *THE 13TH*!

"John Everson's *The 13th* is one of the creepiest and most compelling novels I've read in years. It's a brand new genre: 21st Century Gothic that has street smarts and scares in equal measures."

—Jonathan Maberry, Bram Stoker Award–winning Author of *Patient Zero*

SACRIFICE

"*Sacrifice* is not for the timid or weak of heart, it is a full frontal assault on your senses. It is a dark, brutal, bloody, and terribly frightening book. Everson went deep into some dark abyss to bring this book to the light of day. . . . I highly recommend *Sacrifice*."

—Famous Monsters of Filmland

"Everson is in full form. The action is quick, brutal, and visceral. In many ways, *Sacrifice* is like that "slasher flick" we know we shouldn't enjoy but do anyway."

—*Shroud Magazine*

"If you like your horror with healthy doses of blood and sex, this is the book for you."

—Fear Zone

"This is a novel that begs to be finished in one night, and likely will be."

—Horror World

"Everson demonstrates genuine skill. . . ."

—Bookgasm

"John Everson manages in *Sacrifice* to dispense buckets of blood, provide edgy perversity, and walk the tenuous tightrope of horror and sex without falling: it's rather an amazing feat."

Notes

"John Everson is br   world of horror."

eview

COVENANT

"*Covenant*—now available as a mass-market paperback—won Everson a Bram Stoker Award back in 2004, and after reading it, you'll agree that this tight, gripping story was definitely worthy of the distinction."

—*Rue Morgue*

"I've waited four long years to read *Covenant* and it was well worth it. Everson has taken a classic genre plot and given it his own spin. This is how horror is done RIGHT."

—The Horror Fiction Review

"You might even begin to wonder with writing this good, if Everson agreed to his own covenant in order to create this devilishly dark and terrifying tale."

—*Pagan Pulse Magazine*

"Truly entertaining no-frills horror, which is a damned good thing."

—Horror World

"Equal parts dark mystery and supernatural horror, *Covenant* is a white-knuckle reading experience that will keep you guessing and gasping."

—Creature Feature

"Everson allows the storylines to unfurl, carefully layering each of the individual character's arcs as he crosses genres ending up with a nice blend of mystery and horror."

—*Dark Scribe Magazine*

"John Everson has written a powerful tale as readers wonder whether it is a coincidence, the supernatural, or a serial killer behind the suicides."

—*Midwest Book Review*

THE NIGHT OF THE RITUAL

The invitation had arrived two days ago. Even now, Alan couldn't believe he held it in his hand. How long had he waited for this? Half of his life. He'd barely been nineteen the last time someone had tried to invoke The 13th. And that had ended very, very badly. He could still feel the warmth of the blood running fast between his fingers, the sensation of the guiding spirit running violent hands through his hair as he had laid the bodies of the Eighth and the Ninth to final rest on the floor of the old hotel.

Now he was forty-five, and the invitation shook in his fingers. Actually, *he* was the one who shook; the invitation was neutral. It only said one thing:

THURSDAY NIGHT, 11 P.M.: THE 13TH.

Someone not in the know might have pointed out that Thursday was not, in fact, the Thirteenth. But to Alan, those words could only mean one thing: the hotel was alive again. . . .

Other *Leisure* Book by John Everson:

SACRIFICE
COVENANT

THE 13TH

JOHN EVERSON

LEISURE BOOKS NEW YORK CITY

A LEISURE BOOK®

November 2009

Published by

Dorchester Publishing Co., Inc.
200 Madison Avenue
New York, NY 10016

ISBN 10: 0-8439-6267-4
ISBN 13: 978-0-8439-6267-3
E-ISBN: 978-1-4285-0746-3

ACKNOWLEDGMENTS

Bars are great places to write; you settle in for a night in a cozy booth, people bring you Newcastle when you're dry, and if the DJ knows best, there are no distractions. This novel started at a Chicago shot-and-a-beer joint called Trinity tended by a perky girl named Christy. It spent a couple nights brewing at Fado's in Washington, D.C., and Chicago, enjoyed an artist-in-residence stand at Dublin Square in San Diego, unveiled a few key scenes at The Liberties and Johnny Foley's Irish House in San Francisco, and wrapped at Quigley's and Rizzo's in my hometown of Naperville. If only my publishers had picked up the tabs!

Special thanks to Don D'Auria and Dave Barnett for supporting this twisted vision, and to Geri and Shaun for indulging my world tour of Irish bars. Thanks to Bill Breedlove, Bill Gagliani, and Rhonda Wilson for improving my besotted command of the English language; and to my "first fans" Kathy Kubik and Paul Gifford who have never failed to inspire and encourage. Thanks to my Street Team for so much help—you guys are amazing! Thanks to my Polish connection, Robert Cichowlas, Mateusz Bandurski, and Alina Ciejka for helping my words cross the ocean and a language barrier.

Thanks for constant encouragement to my Dark Arts "Sirens" Loren, Maria, Bel, Christa, Jade, Martel and Whitney; and to Dave Benton, Audrey Shaffer, Jen Vickers, TigerLady, Terri Beirness, Sheila Halterman, Jess Kaan, Peg Phillips, Sheila and Joan, Lauren and Brenda, John Palisano, Louise Bohmer, and Giovanna Lagana.

This Dark Dream is for you!

THE 13TH

PROLOGUE

Twenty-five Years Ago

The room would have felt closed in and dark . . . if not for the Christmas lights. They trailed in long sparkly strands across the shadows, white globes illuminating the horror on the floor like gently oscillating spotlights. They would have been cozy warm . . . if not for the hell they revealed. Some of those long white globes were speckled in dark spots. And some of those spots were clearly, nauseatingly, crimson.

Beneath those swaying holiday orbs ran drying rivers of stagnant red.

"Oh my God," breathed the officer on duty, just before turning his mouth to the side and retching into the darkness. Maitlin was young, only a few months on the force in Castle Point. Up to now, the most disturbing thing he'd probably witnessed was the diaper of a newborn. His horror at the current scene was audible in the quiet room . . . and the gagging smell of his fear melded with the raw iron stench of blood that soured the room.

The captain choked back his own disgust, but soldiered on, urging Officer Maitlin to follow. "There may be survivors," he said, though his voice did not sound hopeful.

"Of this?" the rookie gasped, looking up from the shadow of his weakness.

"No matter how bad it looks," the chief said, "there is always someone left."

Just then, Maitlin's toe stopped dead on the rebound from something soft. Something spongy.

He bent down, and in complete disbelief, reached down to retrieve the object of his toe stop.

The captain's eyes bugged out as Officer Maitlin lifted the disembodied limb from the red goo of the floor like a soiled party favor.

"Do you think so?" the rookie asked, brandishing a stiff arm in his grip. He pointed the gory piece where a shoulder should have been at the face of his boss. From another vantage point, it might have looked as if he were shaking hands with the corporeal appendage of the air. The tips of glossy, long red fingernails seemed to grip his wrist.

"No, sir," Officer Maitlin said, his voice filled with the hysteria of "last straw."

The captain looked at the severed arm for a moment in the shadows of the hotel basement and shook his head slowly.

"Yeah," he said. "Me either. Let's get out of here."

But just as the two turned to leave, a moan came from behind.

"Oh shit," the captain mumbled, and turned toward the sound. The corridor in the back of the room was pitch-black; they hadn't investigated what charnel secrets lay behind the veil of darkness there. They really, really didn't want to. But they couldn't ignore a victim in pain.

Officer Maitlin's hand slid to the holster and his fingers toyed with his gun. He'd never used it, except in target practice at the academy. But he was ready to now. They'd gotten the anonymous telephone tip that people had been butchered at the old hotel an hour ago. Nothing could have prepared them for what they'd found when they'd walked through the half-open front door of the building.

The moan came again, and the captain motioned him to follow. He fingered a cigarette lighter and held it in the air to light the way. The feeble light flickered off surfaces that seemed to ooze with wetness. Maitlin thought it looked red in the orange glow of the flame. But he didn't dare lean in closer to see if his supposition as to its nature was true. He'd seen enough in the long basement room.

"This place is a slaughterhouse," he breathed.

At his words the moans grew louder, and the captain suddenly dropped to his knees.

The source of the moans lay on the floor, naked and crumpled against the wall. Maitlin saw the whites of her eyes before anything else; they were staring in terror at something just beyond his left shoulder. As he joined the captain, she shuddered, and the red glistening mess that had once been her belly opened wider. Too wide.

The rookie turned away, his gorge rising as the woman's insides turned out.

"Who are you?" the captain whispered, putting a calming hand on her forehead. His fingers stuck to the drying blood in her long matted hair.

The dying woman's eyes flickered, and for just a second, focused on the captain's sympathetic face.

"The Twelfth," she whispered, and then her eyes went wide once more.

This time, they didn't close again.

CHAPTER ONE

David Shale pushed a foot toward the ground with an audible gasp. Then he did it again, with the other. "Sheeeit!" he yelled, and stabbed a foot down again, struggling to keep a steady rhythmic drive on the pedals that had been steadily slowing as he and his Triomphe climbed a summit of Crossback Ridge. The trees surrounding the narrow, snakelike road didn't answer, but a humid breeze slipped across the back of his neck like an intimate breath. When he'd left the sleepy town of Castle Point he'd been a well-oiled engine, feet rising and dipping with the precision of pistons, steadily adding speed and distance to his ride. But now, twenty minutes later, the sweat dripped from his forehead like a bad leak and his legs were on fire with fatigue. You didn't fast-pump your way across the ridge. At least, normal folk wouldn't. But David wasn't interested in normal. David was interested in the Olympic cycling team. And after leading Boston University's cycling team for two years and then washing out at the Olympic tryouts, David was definitely not interested in a normal training regimen. Training "normal" was cool for college. It didn't cut it for where he wanted to go.

So this summer, when he'd come to stay with his aunt for break, he'd decided to use her backyard as the course. Nobody biked Crossback Ridge. Hell, most people wouldn't hike it.

"*Fuckin'* shit!" he added for emphasis, and pumped an impossible pedal down toward the potholed and much-patched asphalted surface that this backwoods county called a road.

Something *like* a tear squeaked out of the corner of his left eye and he pushed his other foot down with a moan. If you'd called it a tear he would have punched now and asked what you meant later. David Shale was no sissy. It was something else that definitely was not a tear. "Fuuuuck!" he screamed in a voice that echoed back across the ridge like a moose call. "Damn, damn, damn," he huffed, slowly picking up speed again.

It was going to be a long summer.

The climb ended without warning. One minute, David was straining to keep the wheels creeping forward, standing hard on the pedals for every inch. The next, and he was above the ridge, high on the plateau, looking out over a drop of hundreds of feet of emerald green. The roadway was cut into a limestone rock face behind him, and at the top, a lone tree hung like a slanting bonsai over the cutback. But as the road continued, it disappeared around the bend of the ridge and down at a breakneck drop. Here, for a few yards, was the only flat surface he'd seen in the past hour.

David stepped off the bike and gently laid it to the gravel. He stepped to the edge of the ridge, and took a deep breath, crouching down to ease the strain in his legs, which currently felt something like unbendable iron rods. The air was clean, rich in the scent of . . . life. For miles all around, the landscape was blanketed in trees, riddled with hidden creek beds and broken by clearings full of wildflowers. This was unspoiled wilderness. "God's country." *This is the feeling I've missed since I've been away from* . . . Something caught in his throat as his mind choked on the word . . . *home*. He didn't know where home was anymore, which was why he was spending the summer with his aunt. Since the fire, David had been on his own, always with a roof, but never a home. But still, he'd spent plenty of time visiting these hills over the years, and so in some way, it was a homecoming. Point was, air just didn't smell like this anywhere else.

As his panting slowed to a semblance of normal respiration, David noticed a small plume of smoke from a spot just a little way down the ridge. He followed it to the ground with his eyes and squinted, then crooked an eyebrow. The smoke was coming from the old Castle House Lodge!

His stomach lurched. What if the place was burning down? Castle House had been closed for most of his life. Even as an outsider who came up here to visit once in a while, he knew the stories. It was the local equivalent of a haunted house—an old mansion from another era, fallen on hard times and long boarded up. Before the depression, the place had been a private resort hotel for the turn-of-the-1900s rich. And unlike a lot of big-money kinds of resorts, the place had survived the '20s and '30s and staggered on as a destination for families with names like Rockefeller into the '50s. But then the whole ridge changed. The rich and famous stopped going to the hill country for vacations, and the minor industry that kept the nearby town of Castle Point afloat found itself trumped by river port towns with cheaper labor and easier transportation. The sleepy little outback got more tired.

Castle House Lodge had closed and the level of clientele that crossed the ridge took a turn for the blue-collar. The lodge had reopened a handful of times to steadily decreasing success, and sometime in the Reagan years there had been the murders there—a grisly, horrible episode—and the place had been boarded up and abandoned for, what the town had assumed was, good. Since then, it had slowly descended into the realm of legend. It didn't take long before there were ghost stories attached to the place. The cries of disembodied infants echoing out through the windows of the old hotel to carry over the ridge. Spirits glimpsed furtive and faint in the surrounding woods at night, moaning at ethereal pains. Bloody Mary inhabited the top floor. A ghoul dragged the unsuspecting into the catacombs of the cellar.

Kids snuck out here sometimes late at night and dared each other to enter the place, armed with just a flashlight or a candle. Wet crotches frequently ensued when a bat or a night bird exploded from a rafter, its privacy disturbed.

David had kind of grown up with the legends of Castle House. So it was not surprising when he realized that the place was not burning, but in fact was apparently inhabited again, that he stood up from his crouch, put a hand across his brow and said aloud, to no one in particular, "What the fuck?"

He'd been intending to turn around at this point and take the long coast downhill back home as a prize for a hard ride of sticking it out . . . but now he picked up his bike and aimed it downhill in the wrong direction . . . away from home and toward the entry road to Castle House. He'd come this far, and had to see what was going on down there . . . Was someone opening up the hotel again? Who in their right mind would take a plane into Castle Point and then rent a car to cross the ridge just to have a vacation in the hills in this day and age? Spas were a dime a dozen, and most were easier to access.

David shook his head, and kicked off down the hill.

You could see it from the road as you coasted down . . . the trees obscured it from some angles, but as the asphalt twisted, you could catch glimpses of the yellowed gables and green shingled cupolas of what had once been a grand castle of a building. As the road curved to turn off into the drive to the old building grounds, David braked and stopped. He stood for a moment, looking down the shadowed roadway. Once it had probably been a stand of proud, sculpted trees guiding travelers to the up-scale Gothic-spired mansion at its end. Now it was an overgrown tunnel, branches hanging low across the road to form a seamless canopy over the broken asphalt in between.

David hesitated. You could just barely make out the start of the resort grounds at the end of the dark road. Should he pedal his way in and check it out? It was getting late in the afternoon and it was going to be a long, hard drive back, without a side trip. Did he need to add an extra mile onto his aching thighs' odometer?

He shrugged and pushed his jeans back to the seat. "No pain, no gain, right?" he mumbled aloud, and kicked the bike into motion again. He was curious.

In the back of his head, he heard the unspoken reply.

Curiosity killed the cat.

Christy Sorensen gunned the engine once more to punch the Olds up the last jog of the hill. She knew the turnoff was just ahead, but the old '78 was not firing on all cylinders these days. Or something. "Piece of shit," she murmured, and pushed her foot to the floor hard, kicking the back tires out for a second. The resulting swoosh and sway of the back end made her grin.

"Still something to be said for rear-wheel drive," she added. And then swore.

"Fuck me!"

The turnoff to the Castle House was . . . NOW.

Christy pulled the steering wheel hard to the left, felt the rear end slide on loose gravel and saw the trees that should have been on the side of the car loom dead in front of her. She corrected and yanked the wheel to the right, pulling the car out of imminent collision with the forest and fishtailing back onto the road to the old lodge. And found a reason to swear yet again.

"Jesus fuckin' Christ!" she screamed and yanked the wheel back to the left. A biker was pedaling down the center of the road, and her radiator was aimed right at his ass.

The car was still shimmying from her poorly executed turn and Christy couldn't pull it out in time. The biker looked up at the last second, and she saw his eyes widen as the grill of the Olds kissed the rubber of his rear wheel.

Her heel pushed the brake to the floor and her shoulders screamed as she slammed the wheel to the left, but it wasn't enough. The bike shuddered and collapsed at the impact and the guy lost his grip on the handles and for a brief, kidney-clenching moment shot sideways through the air. His flight came just in time as the front wheels of the car crunched over the rear wheel and vacated seat of the bike before hitting the ditch to the left and stopping finally, the air echoing with the screech of brakes and rattle and roll of a hubcap that left the car when it left the road, and proceeded to twirl around and around like an old tin cup on the pavement.

Christy looked up and saw the brown of the tree trunks inches away from the car's front bumper, and took a deep breath.

"Shit, shit, shit," she whispered, and clicked the release on her seat belt. How the hell was she going to report this?

CHAPTER TWO

David heard the roar of an engine just behind and looked up in time to see two headlights bearing down like a death sentence. His surprised eyes caught just a hint of two equally shocked brown eyes behind the windshield, and then he was no longer *sitting* on his bike. The green of tree branches and long grass filled his mind and then a smash of dirt filled his mouth as he connected with the ditch and rolled. He felt something hot flash in his back, and then his forehead smacked against something that, had he remained conscious, he would have described as something not unlike the business end of a fraternity brotherhood paddle. You never want to experience the business end of one of those, if someone else is swinging it.

There were white stars.

There were screams. Probably his own.

There was darkness.

And then there was a dull, persistent noise. "Ruuull-rriiiite. Shhhhhthshhhht. Rullllrriiitte?" It repeated itself several times before he realized what it really said.

"Are you all right?" he finally made out through

the haze. When he opened his eyes, there was first a flash of green, and then a woman's face peered over him. Looking up at her was like seeing someone through the water of a bath—if you were on the bottom of a deep tub.

David tried to rub the blur from his eyes and realized he couldn't feel his arm. He wanted to ask the woman where his arm was. He could see a wisp of frightened hair hanging down over her nose as she bent in closer, asking him again, "Are you all right?"

He wanted to say, "No, there's a rock in the back of my head and someone pulled my left kidney out and stomped on it."

But he didn't ask about his arm or complain about his head. Instead, he said, "Guh?"

To which the woman replied, "Jesus fuckin' Christ."

David took that as a good cue to go to sleep.

When he woke up the next time, the woman's face was gone. In its place were two deep-set blue eyes, and a mouth carved from pink granite. A close-cropped goatee accented the pale color of his skin. "He's waking up now," the man said.

David's first intelligible words after the accident were somewhat academic.

"What hit me?" he murmured.

There were white fluorescent lights behind granite lips, and then those were obscured by an already-familiar pair of brown eyes.

"I did," the voice that went with those soft eyes said. The voice seemed a little harder than the eyes. Like maybe the eyes worked in a soup kitchen but the voice had kicked back a couple shots of Jack before deigning to speak to him. That wouldn't be the first time that it had taken a little Jack to convince a girl to look his way.

David tried to sit up, but a pain like a crowbar to

the base of his spine convinced him that a prone position was exactly the pose he wanted to model for the brown-eyed girl and the granite-mouthed man.

Instead, he looked past them to the white walls, and saw a poster with two human figures detailed in spread-eagle fashion with arrows and diagrams highlighting various points of anatomy. The poster hung above a pink counter and aluminum sink. The room seemed very clinical, he thought, and then realized that granite lips wore a white coat beneath his chin, and as a hand came into view, rubber gloves.

"Where am I?" he managed.

The man smiled, and leaned down to pry open David's left eyeball. He peered into it a moment, nodded, and then let go. He nodded again.

"Welcome to Castle House Asylum," he said. "I'm Dr. Rockford. You've had an accident, but there doesn't appear to be a dangerous concussion. Nothing is broken. You're going to be fine."

David let that sink in for a moment.

The woman stood at the doctor's side, brown eyes wide with concern, and . . . something else. She looked from the doctor to him, and then asked in a small, but tight voice, "How do you feel?"

"Been better," he said. David looked at Dr. Rockford. "Asylum? This place used to be a hotel."

"What better setting for an asylum?" the doctor answered. "We have lots of rooms, a big kitchen, exercise rooms, consultation offices and lots of privacy, given the location. We're still renovating the place, but we've taken in our first patients."

"Who would they send all the way out here, to the middle of nowhere?" David asked. "Who are you treating, serial killers?"

Rockford shook his face and smiled, a little sadly. "No, nothing like that. These patients wouldn't hurt a fly. Let's see if you can sit up, shall we?"

The doctor pressed a hand to David's back, and gingerly, he sat up. His head throbbed and the room swirled just a moment when he got all the way up, but otherwise, he felt okay.

"Can you stand?"

David slid his feet off the examining table, and let himself down to the floor. The doctor held his elbow to steady him, but aside from some throbbing spots on his left shoulder and right calf, which he supposed had hit the dirt hard on his roll from the bike, he didn't hurt too badly. Not as bad as he would have thought after being run over by a skidding car, anyway!

"Let's take a walk," the doctor said. "I'll give you both a little tour of our facility, and see how your legs are working after your spill."

The doctor led them through a white door and into a slate-floored corridor. Paintings of hilly country interrupted the yellowed walls every few feet. David supposed they were artists' renditions of the countryside surrounding the old hotel.

"These paintings are all vintage pieces," the doctor offered. "Many of the guests of the old resort hotel were artists, and they left some of the work they did while they were here to the owners."

At the end of the corridor, the rich tapestry of fall and summer trees turned abruptly to a frame holding a kaleidoscope of color. David stopped and looked at the piece, trying to ascertain what, exactly, it depicted. There were arcs of red and shadows of orange. An explosion of magenta and yellow lit the top right corner, as if a bomb had lit the night sky in a grove of apples.

"We've tried to continue the tradition," the doctor said. "One of our patients used to paint before she . . ." His voice trailed off, and he motioned them into a wide foyer. In the middle, two women in blue hospital gowns sat cross-legged on the black floor. Both had long hair, one with straight blonde bangs hanging half over her eyes, the other with dirty bronze curls slipping down her shoulder to drape her chest. Their feet looked white as bone against the glossed surface. David thought they were staring at him. Staring, and yet, their eyes were blank, empty.

Another woman walked into the room from a different hallway. She seemed to float along like a ghost, silent and slow. A wraith in azure with silent eyes. When she reached the center of the room, she went down on one knee, almost in slow motion, preparing to sit next to the other two women. Her belly looked thick, and David wondered if she was pregnant. He shook his head and guessed not. They couldn't drug a mother the way she obviously was, and not harm the baby.

She hung there, one knee in the air for a good minute, and then finally slipped to the ground with the blonde and the bronzette. And then, as she settled, cross-legged like the others, her face rose like a crane moving an unwieldy hunk of concrete and steel. Stark cheeks raised centimeter by centimeter until her gaze evened out with the others.

And there were three women now staring, blankly, at David, and Dr. Rockford, and the woman who had nearly run him over.

"You see, these patients are no danger to anybody," the doctor said softly. "This is a home for women. Women who have been pushed beyond their limits."

"Battered women?" asked the woman who'd run him over.

"Some," the doctor said. "Not all. Sometimes people lose their way. For no reason we can even tell. The brain is an unpredictable organ. But we try to help them. And we need the privacy of a place like this to do that."

David looked at the women and suddenly forgot the ache in his back. The hair on the back of his neck rose. He shivered as he stared back at three sets of empty, unblinking eyes. The blonde put a hand on her stomach and began to rub herself in slow, circular motions. A low hum issued from her lips and she rocked forward and back, fingers kneading her breasts before slipping inside the part in her thin robe to touch places unseen. The woman beside her only continued to stare straight ahead. Straight at David. Her eyes never seemed to blink. David felt the blood rush to his face, as he recognized the naked eroticism in the movement of the other woman's hands, which now disappeared with clear intent below her belly. A soft moan escaped her lips as she rocked.

"What is she doing?" he whispered.

"Feeling," the doctor said. "This is a good sign. She's in touch with the sensations of her body. These are difficult cases and sometimes the treatments leave them so numb they can't recognize sensation for months."

David shifted his legs, embarrassed at the reaction of his body to the spectacle. The pain seemed to slip away in favor of a strange, urgent heat. His hands ached to reach out to someone, anyone, to . . . touch them. Next to him, color also crept into the female driver's cheeks and she crossed her arms over her breasts to hide her own obvious arousal.

"My God, what do you do to them?" David whispered, watching the zombielike patient blatantly rub herself to orgasm.

The doctor frowned, seemingly oblivious to the obscene actions of his patient and the discomfort of his unexpected visitors. "We treat them, of course," he said. "We're here to help."

CHAPTER THREE

Billy elbowed TG once in the ribs and yelled, "Slow it the fuck down, asshole." Only he couldn't stop laughing as he threatened.

TG responded by stepping on the gas and the Mustang shot through the next bend with a slalom that sloshed enough beer around in Billy's stomach that his kidneys threatened to void.

"You wanna spend the night in the drink?"

"Hell yeah, I wanna spend the night in the drink." TG grinned. "Guzzling one pitcher after the other."

"Yeah, well, y'all keep up the lead-footin' and we're either gonna be at the bottom of the valley, or we're gonna be playing Five Card Draw in a cell next to Chief Maitlin's work boots for the next eighteen hours. He ain't forgot that night he caught you with Stacy in the park, and he sure ain't gonna miss the Bud on your breath if'n he pulls us over after clockin' an eighty-five in a forty."

TG grinned, then turned to spit a long stream of brown juice out the window of the beat-up 'stang. One strand disappeared over the edge of Crossback Ridge to slap with a wet plop on a tree branch forty feet below the road. The other slapped back on TG's neck, and he absently rubbed it off and onto his jeans.

"Yeah," he admitted, turning his attention back to the blurring, winding mountain road. "Chief wasn't too happy with me when he caught my mitts in his daughter's pinks, but that Stacy, she was worth it. And she was a screamer too. Fine poontang there, I'm a tellin' ya!"

"Fine or foul, he ain't gonna show us any slack if he's got you drunk and fifty miles over the limit. So slow the fuck down! We got us a job to do tonight—cain't afford to be hanging in the Trinity jail. I need the green, Kemosabe!"

"Lighten up, Billy. I need it too. But, if yer gonna be a pussy . . ."

TG stomped on the brake and the car shimmied to a stop, halfway into the intersection at Ridge Road and 190. The stop sign seemed pointless out here, but TG made the token stop before letting off the brake and sliding past the valley intersection, on their way back up the ridge away from town.

"Chief don't bother coming out this way during the day, believe me, I've checked. He's making the rounds in town. But we can slow it up. We got a couple hours to kill anyway. Cain't do this job 'til dark, or we *will* be spending the night with the chief. And the next month or two!"

"We pullin' this one in town then?" Billy asked.

"You wanna drive fifty miles around the switch-back to Oak Falls?"

"Not really."

"Then we're working local. So it's time for a little picnic 'til dark. Anyway, we need to get that shit out of the trunk. We need room."

"There's a whole keg back there, Holmes. Whaddya thinkin'?"

"Keg's staying here," TG said, as he ripped the car to the left and they pulled up a steep dirt road that bent up and around a stand of old pines. In seconds, the mountain pass was out of sight and they were in a small clearing next to a beat-up

A-frame cottage. Well, shack was really more like it. Cottage would imply some kind of vacation spot. This piece of graying fractured wood was absolutely a shack. But the black electric line that hung through the trees to latch onto a panel on the side of the building showed that the place wasn't just an abandoned bit of decaying planks. This shack was still alive, and TG laughed and slid the car up as tight as he could to those graying timbers, dust clouding the air all around as the car coughed itself silent.

"We need to fill the fridge 'fore we fill the trunk," he said.

Billy rubbed his crotch suggestively. "We ought to *fill* what we fill the trunk *with* before we take her down the mountain."

TG grinned and slapped his partner on the shoulder. "See, that's why I like to work with ya, ya dipwad. I likes how you think. Only one problem. How do we turn over the merchandise if she's screaming 'rape' over and over again?"

Billy shook his head and faked a yawn. "You telling me that every girl you took up to Fallback Point was fully cog-nigh-sant of where's you was drivin' her?"

TG rolled his eyes and shrugged. "No?" he asked with false innocence.

"Damn blotto-babed-right the answer is no," he said. "We need to find us a chicky tonight who wants some 'shine. Time we got some payment *ahead* of the green."

"Let's just get that keg on ice," TG said. "I'm thinking we's gonna have us a party tonight."

"A party's where you find it," Billy agreed.

"I think I know just where to find *her*," TG said, poppin' the trunk.

"Think she'll remember in the mornin'?" Billy asked.

"Not if my tire iron has anything to say about it." TG grinned, holding up a rusted rod from the trunk.

"Oh, this is gonna be a fun time."

"My brother, would I pull you into a business that *wasn't* a good time?" TG asked.

Billy shook his head.

"I'm glad you think so. Now let's get this fucker in the house."

Together, they hoisted the keg out of the trunk and up the peeling gray-painted steps to the mountain shack.

A lot of people would have been a lot happier if Billy and TG had drained the keg and forgotten about the business of the evening.

But they didn't.

CHAPTER FOUR

If Brenda Bean hadn't spent so much time trying to get that one pink strand of hair to tuck in "just so" behind her ear, she probably would have caught the #190 bus into Oak Falls and not ended up spending the evening with the hicks at the Clam Shack. A lot of things might have been different if Brenda had caught the #190. But while she may have been a punk, Brenda was still firmly a girl, and so she *did* lean over the sink again and again, first wetting the strand, then blow-drying it out, then pasting it with some gel, then shaking her head in disgust, rinsing it out, and starting all over.

When she left the bathroom and saw the time,

she swore out loud. The bus only ran this route every couple hours and the next one would be too late. Her mom heard the *F* word from down in the kitchen.

"Brenda! You know what I told you about using foul language."

"Sorry, Mom," she answered, and then did a double take on the stairs. She was wearing the ripped black T-shirt her mom hated, and she really didn't feel like dealing with a lecture on *that* at the moment. Brenda didn't know what her mom hated more about it—the fact that it was two sizes too small and showed very clearly that Brenda hated bras, or the sayings that middle-fingered the world on front ("Fuck You If You Can't Take A Toke") and back ("Virgins Do It Behind Your Back"). She slipped back into her bedroom and pulled her dad's old khaki button-down off the doorknob. He had dropped the shirt in the basement on the rag pile a few weeks ago, but she'd instantly retrieved it.

"Why would you want to wear that?" he'd said the first time she had appeared in it, untucked shirttail hanging way below her butt.

"It's a cool color," she'd said. "And it's cool to wear a guy's shirt."

Her dad had grinned and then shrugged. "Suit yourself. Just as long as it's not some other guy's shirt. Because then I'd really have to ask why you were wearing it."

"And I'd just have to tell you probably 'cuz he forgot it when he climbed out of my bedroom window this morning after sleeping over last night," she'd teased, and ducked when he threatened to cuff her.

"Kidding, Dad!" she'd laughed. "I'd never make him climb out the window. He'd just have to wait 'til you left for work."

She ran out of the room at that one, khaki shirt flapping behind her like a pauper's gown.

The shirt was ratty, but looked too-too comfortable against her faded denim jeans, and it effectively hid the offensive T-shirt from her mom's eyes as she breezed through the kitchen on her way out of the house.

"Gonna be late?" Dorrie Bean asked.

"Not as late as I'd planned," Brenda moaned. "I missed the 190, so I'm staying in town tonight."

"Good." Her mom nodded. "I hate you taking that bus home from Oak Falls so late. You never know what kind of loser could be on that bus."

"Same losers who are everywhere, Mom. The bus doesn't have a lock on lowlifes."

"Yeah, well, the freaks come out at night. I'm not too fond of you hanging out at the Clam Shack either. Talk about asking for trouble."

"Mom, everybody hangs out at the Clam Shack. If you don't head into Oak Falls, where else IS there to go?"

And that was the truth. As Brenda stepped out onto the sidewalk and headed down the hill toward Main, she saw a couple other heads bobbing along the streets below, moving in the same direction. You could always find someone to talk to at the Shack, because it was the only watering hole for at least twenty miles in any direction. You could also usually find someone there to go home with after last call for the same reason. The running joke at the Clam Shack was that you could eat your clam and take it home too. And the more you drank, the better your catch.

Brenda didn't want to catch anything at the Shack tonight . . . she just wanted to get buzzed. She was bummed about not going into Oak Falls, because the conversation there was always more interesting. Here, well hell, everyone in town already knew everybody else's business . . . What else was there to talk about? Ron O'Grady's latest scheme to start an Internet porn site with high-school girls . . . Well, cops'd nipped that one right quick. Or how about Sheila Halterman's latest recipe for holiday eggnog—with just a hint of that secret spice she'd never reveal? Oh, the talk went from sinfully perverse to diabolically dull in the span of a heartbeat at the bar. And most of the time, she'd heard it all before anyway. But, it was still better to hang at the bar than to sit in her room or downstairs with the parents all night.

The breeze kicked up the back of her dad's shirt, and Brenda unbuttoned the front, setting it free to billow like a cape as the wind slipped deliciously around her cleavage like the most tentative lover. She felt her nipples harden instantly, and she shimmied just a little, letting the cotton and the cool dusk wind work together to remind her breasts of how close freedom lay.

Brenda giggled to herself and threw back her head, taking in a deep breath, and letting it out with a slow whistle. She felt good tonight. Maybe she would catch something at the Clam Shack tonight, she mused. Only it wouldn't be a clam. No way. Bring on the sausage, hold the fish!

CHAPTER FIVE

It was still early, so he had his pick of the perches. When David slipped one leg over the bar stool at the Shack he groaned as the aches from the accident reminded him of why he was here and not out riding.

"Slow night," he said, but Joe, the bartender, only grinned.

"Give it an hour," he said. "And you won't be able to leave that stool to hit the head or you'll lose it. And don't even think of asking someone to save it for you. There is no honor during happy hour!"

"Sounds dangerous," David laughed. "I'd better prepare myself. How 'bout a Lite?"

Joe hadn't finished pulling the beer when the door rattled open and shut, and two more stools were quickly claimed. As Joe delivered the beer and then turned to the newcomers to say "What'll you have?" the door rattled again, and the inside screen slammed shut with a crack.

"Really oughtta fix that, Joe," a feminine voice said over his shoulder. The woman slid onto the stool next to David's.

"Yeah, yeah, yeah," Joe groused. "I'll fix that right after I repaint the siding, reshingle the roof, dig out the weeds from that thing they used to call a flower bed out front and rod out the plumbing in the men's John so it quits overflowing every night just before close."

"Fixing the door would be a lot easier than the rest," she suggested.

"Holding the handle an extra second so that it doesn't hit you in the ass on the way in would be even easier," the bartender shot back.

"Blah blah blah," the woman said. "Just set me up."

"You drinking vinegar on the rocks, or straight up?"

"You get tips with a mouth like that?"

"Only from *pretty* girls." Joe turned away to pull a Guinness and a maraschino cherry hit him on the back of the neck. "Starting out spunky tonight, heh," he said, flicking the fruit to the floor.

The woman shrugged off a dingy old shirt and slipped it under her jeans on the bar stool. David saw that the equally beat-up T-shirt beneath it was tight enough to be a crop top, and as mouthy as the girl who wore it. The creamy small of her back was clearly visible between the hug of the lower end of the shirt and the chain-cinched jeans beneath. "'Virgins Do It Behind Your Back,'" he read on the back of the shirt, and snorted.

She heard him, and turned to raise an eyebrow. "Something funny?"

"Like your shirt," was all he could think to say. Instead of skewering him though, she only smiled and puffed out her already well-defined chest. David realized the front held an even more offensive saying than the back, but he couldn't focus on what it said, because his eyes were reading what was beneath the thin cotton.

She shook a mass of shoulder-length raven hair, and a hot-pink strand slipped out from where it had been slicked back behind her ear to trail across her cheek and the black neckline of the tee. "If you're done, I'm going to have my beer," she said, and David felt the blood rush to his face. He had been staring, and not even trying to conceal it.

"Sorry," he said, and then took a deep breath before venturing, "How 'bout I pick up that tab for you, to make up for being a horrible male pig?"

She snorted and rolled her eyes. They looked dark in the dim neon glow of the bar, but he wasn't sure if they were gray, green or brown.

"Only if I pick up the tab on yours," she said. "But I won't pay good money for that swill you're sipping. Don't you have any self-respect?"

"I don't drink much," David admitted. "I'm usually in training."

"If you're going to spend the night drinking you need some training on what to drink. And putting Lite in your gut is just asking for a gunshot ache in your head and a shitty taste in your mouth tomorrow morning."

"So what would you suggest?"

"Guinness always starts the night good for me, or, if you can't handle that, you might go with a Sam Adams. They're kinda hoppy though."

David shrugged and kissed the morrow good-bye in his head. He caught the bartender's eye and laughed as he said, "I'll have what she's having . . ."

CHAPTER SIX

TG stretched one beefy arm behind his neck and with just a slight jerk, popped a vertebrae loud enough to be heard around the corner of the shack. He groaned a little, and then grinned as he let one rip from his other end. Call it the yin and yang of stretching.

"Oughtta get that looked at, man," Billy said, huffing as he threw an armful of rope, duct tape and a cooler into the trunk of the black Mustang. "Necks shouldn't make that kinda sound."

TG shrugged. "I've made a neck sound worse."

"Okay." Billy grinned. "Necks on a livin' human being shouldn't sound like that, not iff'n that human bein's gonna keep on living any length of days."

"Nothin' a couple quarts of 'shine don't fix. You ready yet?"

Billy slammed down the trunk and nodded. "Yeah, man, but . . ." He stopped short of saying that he didn't want to do the run this time. Though he really didn't. It'd kept him up lately, thinking about these poor girls they were pulling off the street and hog-tying and throwing in the backseat or trunk. And delivering to God knew what kind of fate. He'd done a lot of things he wasn't proud of to make a buck in his life, but he'd never thought that being the middle link in a chain of . . . what? White slavery? . . . would be his claim to fortune if not fame.

"But what?" TG barked. He buttoned up a blue-checked flannel shirt to hide the stained white T-shirt beneath. You going out on the town, you try to show a little decorum (never mind that the flannel had grease and a small bloodstain on the left shoulder). "You gonna go chickenshit on me?"

Billy shook his head. "No, man, you know I'm with you. And we need the cash bad right now."

"Damn right we do. If we're gonna buy the old Hanson place and set up that bar yer always yammering about opening, we need a stack a green." He nodded at the car and then rubbed the roll of his gut. "And the kegs and gasoline to keep these machines running ain't cheap neither."

"I just wonder what they're doing to those girls, is all," Billy said quietly. He felt unusually empathetic today.

"Whaddya care?" TG said, smacking Billy on the

shoulder and pushing him at the passenger's door. "Ain't like any of 'em are ever gonna drop drawers for you."

The two men slid into the Mustang, and in seconds the rev of the eight-cylinder engine echoed across the canyon as TG slipped the car into gear and gunned it down the twisted road and toward town.

Night had fallen, and as most people were already home from a day's work, finishing the dinner dishes and tucking the kids into bed, TG and Billy had only just begun their day. After an afternoon of steady drinking, they were going to work.

The Mustang shimmied like a snake as it hit the asphalt of Crossback Ridge.

"Yee-ha!" yelled TG, waving one arm out the window.

Billy didn't answer. He was staring down the ridge at the tiny lights and the small plume of chimney smoke from the place that paid their admittedly unusual salaries.

Castle House Asylum.

CHAPTER SEVEN

Christy Sorensen stripped off the leather jacket and the shoulder holster hidden beneath it, and angrily hung both from hooks in her locker. She slammed the door with a metallic crash and didn't look back to see if it latched or not.

What a fuckup. Her first "undercover" gig and she manages to hit a stupid biker. Nothing like blowing your cover before you even start. She'd had no choice but to take the kid into the asylum to seek any medical attention he might need immediately. But that also meant that there'd be no casual snooping from Castle Point's finest (or at least, youngest!).

"Fuck, fuck, fuck," she hissed to herself as she stalked through the station. Chief wanted to see her as soon as she got in, and he wasn't going to like what she heard. Not that he hadn't gotten most of it already over the radio.

"Close the door," he said when she stepped into the closet he called an office. The place was so tight she could practically feel his breath when she squeezed into the chair wedged in front of his desk.

She complied, and crossed her arms over her gray T-shirt. Then she realized that the motion only accentuated her cleavage, and that probably wasn't the right message to be sending at the moment. She dropped her hands to her lap, where her fingers insisted on intertwining, and cracking knuckles.

"The kid is okay, is that right? He's not going to sue the department?" His voice came in a low rumble, chimney-smoke thick and deep.

She nodded.

"And you are okay?"

"No bruises, Chief," she said. "No physical ones anyway."

The chief had a way of letting his silver-rimmed glasses slip down his nose so that he could peer at you over them, light blue eyes glinting with almost electric light over the metallic frames. Those stares could last for minutes at a time, as his hands continued filing papers, or reaching for the phone, or any number of other independent tasks. His gaze never wavered. It could be unnerving to the uninitiated, but Christy was ready for it.

"It happens," he finally said. "That's not an excuse—you weren't careful enough. But it happens. Don't let it happen again."

"I won't," she promised, and popped a knuckle. Bad nervous habit.

"What did you see while you were there?"

"Not much," she admitted. "I took the guy in and a nurse helped us into an exam room. The doc checked him out, said he was okay, and then showed us a couple of their new patients on the way out."

"And . . . ?"

"And nothing, really. Couple of thorazine flyers buzzing about the color of the air, I think. Hospital gowns and tranquilizers . . . that's about all I got before we were out the door again."

"And the kid?"

"I put his bike in the car and drove him home. Gave him a couple twenties to cover any damage to the bike, and gave him my number in case he had a problem. I don't think I'll hear from him though."

Chief puckered his lips a moment, and looked at a corner of the ceiling populated solely by cobwebs. Then he stood up and pulled a drawer open from the three-drawer file tucked in the corner directly in front of the door. When it slammed shut, he held a manila folder in hand. The chair complained as his 6'2", 290-pound bulk crushed its cushion back toward the ground, but he squeaked it back toward the desk and passed the folder.

"You're still on this one," he said. "You can't do it undercover anymore, but maybe we don't need that. For now, we're just keeping an eye out in that direction. There's something not quite right about this guy's operation out there, I can feel it."

"What do you want me to do, Chief?"

"Just keep your ears open, for now," he said. "Take some drives out to Crossback Ridge when you can. And read the folder. It'll give you the history of the place, and a couple notes I found regarding our new owner."

"What do you think's up, Chief?"

"I wish I knew," he said. "Maybe nothing. But I always trust my gut. And my gut says otherwise."

He nodded, indicating her dismissal, and he had already picked up the phone to make a call before she'd risen to leave.

"Hey, Harry," he spoke into the receiver, voice a full octave above the plateau of the immediately preceding conversation. "What would you say to heading out to Autumwa this weekend and laying some lures on a few bass?"

Christy slipped out of the office, glad that she'd escaped with so little censure, but still pissed that her first big investigation had stumbled right out of the gate.

"Hey, Sorensen," someone called. She glanced around and saw Matt Ryan grinning like he'd swallowed two thirty-eight double-Ds and just taken a short break for air.

"Yeah, Matt."

"You know when they say fifty points for a biker, they're not really serious."

"Ha, ha, ha." She grimaced.

"Did you at least smack him good with the car door?"

"No dents, sorry," she said.

"So what's the deal with Castle House? They really turning the place into a crazy house up there?"

" 's what it looks like. Chief has a feeling about it though. So I'm on surveillance duty for a while."

"You know what they say—if you go looking for trouble . . ."

". . . It'll find you. Yeah. Well I'd say it *did* find me today."

Christy sat down at the booking desk and logged in to the computer. She had to file a report on the accident before she went home. She opened up the form and started to type . . . but stopped after only a sentence. She hated reliving her stupidity.

Abruptly she rose from the desk, and walked over to Matt's desk. He was holding down the call desk tonight, but the phones were mercifully quiet.

"Did you ever hurt anyone in the line of duty?" she asked.

Matt was a lifer on the Castle Point force (though *force* may be overstating the case a bit—Castle Point's police force consisted of the chief, Matt, Christy and a night-call operator. The three officers traded off every three nights). Matt and the chief had patrolled the town since before Christy was born. If there was a skeleton in anyone's closet, they knew about it. And Matt, in particular, loved to talk about them. Christy had answered the recruitment ad during her last month at the police academy, and Matt had been the first to interview her.

"Did you ever meet a man with three testicles?" he asked during their first conversation. She'd gaped at him, shocked both at the inappropriateness of the question, and at the oddity he described. She shook her head no.

"We got one here in Castle Point." He grinned. "Lives up the ridge near the crossback. Then there's the guy who lives down near Smythe's Grocery who thinks that when he shaves and puts on a wig and a pair of panty hose and a dress that nobody recognizes him when he goes shopping. We pretend not to. Got a lot of weird shit here. You'll get to learn it all by and by."

Christy had grown to like Matt over the past couple months. He was older, but he never treated her like she was a kid. And he needled her like an older brother. Now though, as he looked at her face and saw how troubled she was by the day, he got serious. Matt stood, and put both hands on her shoulders.

"Listen," he said. "I was just kidding before. We all screw up once in a while, sometimes because we're not careful, and sometimes because we can't help it."

His long fingers squeezed her arms in reassurance. "I've never hit anyone with a car on duty, no, but I had to shoot a guy once."

Her eyes widened at that. While it was a daily possibility that you'd have to pull a gun while on police duty, she knew that in a tiny town like this, it rarely happened. His eyes held hers, and his chin nodded, just once. For the first time, Christy really looked hard at Matt's face, and saw the crow's-feet rippling there around his eyes, and the amount of silver that salted his close-cropped hair. On the surface, Matt barely looked forty, but a closer inspection revealed someone who'd been here for the long haul. He was weathered, but still hale.

"It's not something I'd care to repeat," he said. "I've fired plenty of rounds into the sky, but we had a holdup down at the gas station one night a few years back. Stupid kid—wore the ski mask and everything. I was actually just a block away when the clerk pulled the alarm, and so I was out in front of the door on foot before the kid could get to his car. He took off running, and I yelled for him to stop. He did. But then he turned toward me, reached into his pants, and pulled out a gun. He'd tucked it right there at his belt buckle when he left the store.

" 'Back off,' he yelled, pointing the piece right at me. I was shitting my pants, I'm not ashamed to say. This guy's got a gun on me, the first time that had happened in something like twenty-five years as a cop. I pulled my own and yelled for him to drop it.

"He just laughed, raised the gun in the air and then aimed it at me again and yelled, 'Bang, bang, you're dead.'

"I fired. He didn't. And when I got to him, he was shaking and crying on the ground. I picked up the 'weapon' . . . and it was a kid's cap gun. I pulled the hat off and saw he was just a kid. High-school kid. I'd tried to shoot him in the arm, but I'd hit him right in the chest . . . He was bleeding all over and coughing."

Christy gulped as she saw the pain that crossed Matt's steel blue eyes. The humor normally so much a part of his every motion was completely erased.

"That was the worst day of my life," Matt said, and then gave her a little shake and a pat on the back. "Bad shit can happen to you, whether you're a cop or not. You screwed up today, but in the scheme of things, it wasn't bad. Now get out of here, sleep on it and forget it."

He grinned then, finally, though his eyes still looked sad.

"C'mon. Tomorrow there'll be more bicyclists to run down."

She slapped him in the shoulder and shook her head. "Nice. And for just a moment there, I was feeling bad for you."

"Sympathy will only get you ulcers," he said.

Christy grabbed a cup of coffee from the kitchenette, dosing it heavily with sugar and creamer. She liked it black in the morning, but by nightfall, a cup was more like dessert. So it should be sweet, right?

She sat back down with the Styrofoam cup and banged out the quick summary of the accident and visit to Castle House Asylum, hit save and logged off. Tossing back the last gulp of stale java, she gave the peace sign to Matt, who had two feet up on the desk while reading this week's *People*, and headed for the door.

"Night, Chief," she called, and thought there was an answering rumble from the back office.

There was nothing quite like the air of a fall night in the hills, Christy thought, as she fished for her keys. She'd grown up in the suburbs of St. Louis, and the air there had smelled like rubber and decaying tenements, but never like heaven.

Here . . . she took a deep breath and savored it while staring up at the stars that sprinkled the sky as thick as shells on a Florida beach. It was crisp and clean, and sometimes redolent with the faint scent of lavender or roses or some type of sensually extravagant flower. The brush that struggled to cover the limestone outcroppings jutting from the sides of Crossback Ridge was riddled with wildflowers, and Christy couldn't identify most of the colorful blossoms, but she loved to see them. And smell them. There might not be a lot of choice in guys or bars here, but Castle Point did have some advantages.

She keyed open the Olds, and slid into the cool but well-worn seat. She'd bought the car in her second year of college for $500. A boyfriend had helped her pour an equal amount of money into it over the next six months to get it running dependably, but since then, except for oil changes, the car had run like a rusty dream. Sooner or later she was going to have to do something about the clouds of blue smoke it coughed up when she started it, but not yet. She had student loans and an apartment to finish furnishing. She patted the dash and whispered, "Stay with me, buddy."

Then she gunned the engine and shot out of the police lot like a bullet.

She'd not become a cop because she liked to uphold the speed limit.

Christy took Main through the center of town,

and noted that the Clam Shack was already packed for the night. She hoped Matt wouldn't be getting called down this evening to break up a fight. That was usually about the only action that happened in this one-bar town, and it was the one thing she still felt a little apprehensive about dealing with. Blue uniform and nightstick or no, a twentysomething blonde who didn't even stand five and a half feet tall and barely weighed enough to tip the 120 mark on the scale didn't exactly engender fear in the hearts of drunken loggers and mechanics and fishermen . . . or gypsies, tramps and thieves, her mental voice sang with a silent smile.

Physical intimidation was never going to be her strong suit in law enforcement. Nevertheless, she could handle herself. She'd worked hard in the academy to learn all the moves she could to turn her slight size to her advantage in hand-to-hand combat, and she'd gotten damn good at dropping 180-pound guys without breaking a sweat. They were always stunned to find themselves lying faceup on the wrestling mat. The dumb ones always wanted another go.

Christy left the Shack behind and wished Matt a quiet night. But then, instead of taking the left at Arbor Street and heading up the short street to her apartment, she threw her signal on and took the next right.

If the air in town smelled sweet, the air that settled over Crossback Ridge after dark was nectar. Christy rolled both windows down as she eased the car up to sixty miles an hour and took the curves around the ridge like a jittery roller-coaster ride. As she came down the stretch just before the turnoff to the old hotel, another car came barreling down the road in the opposite direction. A black Mustang. She caught a glimpse of the unkempt faces of two laughing men in the glare of her headlights as the cars whooshed past each other in the dark. For a second, she considered pulling a U and going after them. She didn't have a radar gun, but she knew they had to be doing twenty over, if they were moving at all.

Then she shook her head and looked at her own speedometer.

"Off duty," she murmured.

But a voice in her head said, "Then why are you driving up the ridge to spy on the asylum?"

"Maybe I've just got a thing for crazy people?" she answered the voice.

"Well, you *are* talking to yourself."

She shook her head and hit the brakes. The asylum was just down the ridge from here. Christy found a section of road with a wider shoulder than most of the route, which dropped off a hundred steep feet at the edge of the white line. She killed the lights, but left the car idling, and stepped out on the gravel. From the backseat, she pulled out a pair of binoculars that she'd bought for bird-watching up here in the hills. Then she rested her butt against the trunk, and stared through the darkness at the tiny lights below.

The breeze rustled the leaves around her, and she shivered just a little in the night air. Otherwise, it was quiet. Deathly quiet. That was one thing Christy hadn't yet gotten used to about the ridge. Every other place she'd ever lived, the air had reverberated with the distant vibrations of something— factories, cars, trains, music—something. Here . . . there was only a void at night. And the faint whisper of the wind.

She shivered slightly, and shook her head, looking away from the binoculars and out at the faint snake of the road winding up and away. What did she think she was going to find here? What made the chief suspect there was anything odd about this new business?

Christy was just about to get back in the car and head home when the bend in the ridge suddenly lit with twin beams of yellow light. Unconsciously she shrunk down, closer to the trunk, and put the binoculars back to her eyes.

The vehicle was some kind of van, she saw. White. It slowed before it reached her cutoff, and instead turned onto a side road.

The side road.

She watched as it made its way down the gravel path to finally pull up in front of the twin lights that marked the front door of the asylum.

A man got out, but she was too far to tell anything about him. He was just a dark smudge against the side of the van for a moment. And then the back doors opened and closed, and the man walked up to the asylum. The door opened before he even raised a fist to knock, and in a heartbeat he was inside.

Christy turned the binoculars back to the van, and struggled to read the block lettering stenciled on its side.

INNOVATIVE INDUSTRIES it read. And below that, in smaller type, TAKING THE FICTION OUT OF SCIENCE FICTION.

After a few moments, the man reappeared at the door of the asylum and carried some kind of package to the back of the van. Then he slammed the door, got back in the cab and pointed the vehicle back up the ridge.

Christy slipped back into her own car, in case the van opted to exit in the opposite direction that it had come, but by the time she'd sat down and looked back over the seat, the van was already nothing more than a pair of red lights in her rear window.

Hrmmph, she thought to herself. Medical supplies? Delivered at eight o'clock at night? Was it really a suspicious delivery, or was she just inventing suspicion?

Pursing two very pink lips together, she eased the car back onto the road, and followed the van back toward town.

CHAPTER EIGHT

"Let's take a walk," Brenda said.

David nodded. "Yeah, I could probably use a little air to clear my head. Guinness is not Lite."

"Thank God," she laughed and steadied him with her hand as they walked out the door of the Shack. The door cracked like a rifle behind them and from inside Joe yelled, "Just hold the door, all right?"

They'd been talking and drinking for the past three hours now, and Joe had lost track of how many times his glass had been refilled. Brenda seemed none the worse for the alcohol, which only made David feel more of an idiot as he stumbled against her as much from the booze as from the aches from the accident earlier that day. The stars were doing a slow, hazy dance, and Brenda led him around the side of the bar. When they got to the far side, away from the parking lot, she pressed him against the cinder block wall and said, "Stay here. I need to pee."

"Out here?" he slurred. "Are you nuts?"

She laughed, and squatted down a few feet away

in the shadows. He could see the pale skin of her thigh presently, but nothing else.

"I'd be crazy to pee in the john inside," she said. "That place stinks like a three-day-old used tampon."

"Are you trying to make me get sick?" he asked, not totally kidding.

"Nah," she laughed. "Just sayin'. You might want to take care of your business too, while we're here."

David frowned at the idea of unzipping when a woman was just a few feet away. But then the pressure in his bladder caught up with the slow motion in his brain and he said, "Yeah, maybe I will."

"Just don't point it this way!"

They both laughed, and then were silent for a minute as nature took its course. When Brenda made her way back to David, she took his hand, and pulled him away from the building. "There's a path over here," she said. "And I think you should walk a little."

"Couldn't hurt," he agreed, afraid to say much more since his lips seemed to have turned to rubber.

There was indeed a path behind the bar. A small rut of dirt that looked like a biker's route. They followed it for a few minutes as it led up a short hill and then down again and around a small copse of oaks before it disappeared from view. The starlight gave everything an eerie, fairy glow. Or at least, David thought it was the starlight. But then he considered, maybe it was the Guinness?

He laughed at that, and Brenda stopped, looking up at him. She took his other hand and pulled him to face her. "What's so funny, drunk boy?"

Her face was angelic in the night glow, white and perfect, with softly jutting cheeks and deep, dark eyes. Her hair hung in long black waves behind her, and he struggled not to follow the pink strand, which slid down across her T-shirt, away from the rest.

"I just was thinking how beautiful the night was," he said, trying to speak very deliberately so as not to slur like a drunk. "Thank you for bringing me here."

"Hey, I don't want it on my conscience if you fall and crack your head open on the way home," she said. "It's my duty to sober you up a little."

David found himself staring at the tiny reflections of sky in her eyes, and the crinkle of humor in her forehead. "You're beautiful," he said, without thinking.

"Shut up and kiss me, you moron," she laughed, and pulled him down to her lips.

David closed his eyes and the cool breeze of the night slipped across his neck as her arms wrapped around his back and slipped down to cup his ass. The warm flicker of her tongue in his mouth made his knees go weak, and he clutched her tighter, pressing her chest to his. His hand slipped under her shirt and he ran his fingers up along her bare shoulder blades, feeling the gentle bump of vertebrae, and slipping to the side to caress the soft, silky slope of a breast. When she broke the kiss, gently, he actually staggered backward a step, and gasped.

"Um, wow," he said.

She wiped the moisture from her lips and winked. "Not bad for a drunk."

Then she took his hands and put them on her chest, holding them there with her own. "I think this is what you were avoiding, isn't it?"

"Yeah, I guess." He gulped, paralyzed. He wanted to knead and clutch at her breasts—they had looked perfectly lush through the black tee, and now they felt like warm, wanton velvet pillows beneath his fingers. But instead he only left his hands where she placed them, enjoying the lusty feel of her slipping slightly beneath the thin cotton.

"Not tonight," she said, gently moving his hands around her waist again. "But if you're still interested tomorrow, when you're sober . . ."

She leaned up and kissed him again, but just a peck this time.

". . . I might be interested too."

Then she pulled him back the way they'd come. "C'mon, I want one more before last call, and I think you could use a pitcher of ice water."

The door to the Clam Shack slammed hard behind them and Joe shot a dirty look at Brenda, but she only smiled sweetly. "You should fix that, Joe."

She settled David in a booth and went to the bar to order another beer and an ice water. When she settled again, she opened her purse and wrote down her number on a scrap of paper. Then she slipped it into the chest pocket of his shirt. "Don't forget to look for it before you do wash again," she said.

He downed the water in one long gulp, and then chewed a cube of ice.

"Your eyes are really bloodshot," she said. "Put your head down for a minute. I'm going to go get you another water."

At that moment, the door to the Clam Shack opened again, but this time, it didn't slam, and with the noise of a couple dozen conversations buzzing in the air, nobody noticed. Two men sauntered in slowly, the larger of them in a blue-checked flannel. He surveyed the crowd, head moving from side to side like a bank camera, slowly, deliberately.

"Sit down," the big man said, and pointed to a single empty stool near the bar.

"You want a beer?" his partner said, sliding a pair of dirty jeans onto the stool. The bartender hadn't noticed them yet; he was talking to a dark-haired girl in a black T-shirt a few feet away.

"No," he said, eyes fixed on the pink streak that shot like neon across the side of the dark-haired girl's head. "We're not going to stay long."

David didn't fight it when she told him to rest his head. It was throbbing with a dull buzz and his eyes felt like two poached eggs. He knew the hangover was going to be something spectacular. He could feel the pulse of his temple against his forearm, and relived the long kiss of just a few moments before. Just thinking about it made something stir beneath his belt, and he smiled and slipped deeper into the memory. So deep, in fact, that he dozed off.

In his dream, Brenda skinned the T-shirt over her head and this time, instead of pressing his hands to her chest, she pressed his lips between a pair of breasts that he could only describe as spectacular. Full and soft and white and tipped with pink buds that begged for sucking, he lost his eyes and cheeks against her flesh, rolling his face back and forth across the sin of her flesh. He could feel her hands running up his back and into his hair, stroking him and driving him deeper into her mystery.

But then the gentleness of her hands changed, and she was pulling at his hair. He cried out, and she rapped a knuckle against his skull, again and again with increasing force. Finally he pulled away from her, and found himself blinded by the glare of a bald electric light and a neon bar sign screaming BUDWEISER in Christmas red.

"That's it buddy, time to go," Joe said, standing next to his booth. "You all right?"

David blinked, and found the throb behind his eyes was no longer dull. It was drill-sharp.

"Um, yeah, yeah," he said, pushing off the seat

unsteadily, and taking a couple steps toward the door. There were only a couple other people left hunched over the bar, talking in low tones.

Joe held the door open for him, but just before he stepped through, David panicked, and looked back inside.

"Wait," he said. "The girl I was with . . ."

"Brenda?" Joe said, and gave a sad smile. "Sorry friend, I haven't seen her in at least an hour. Ain't gonna happen tonight."

David frowned, but moved out into the night, focusing his meager abilities on setting out on the right path home. The sky was a fog, but the sidewalk shambled on, crack by crack, toward home. He wondered why she had just left him there, and then mentally kicked himself. She'd done what she could to sober him up, but after that . . . She wasn't his babysitter. Just a mouthy chick who'd split a few beers with him. What did he expect?

Ten miles away, wedged in the back of a tight trunk, Brenda squirmed and screamed beneath the duct tape that crossed her lips and bound her wrists together. The floor bounced and rocked with a steady muscle-car hum, but then slowed until it finally came to a stop. Brenda stopped trying to scream out when she heard the key in the lock. Instead she stared at the black spot just beyond her forehead, and waited for the trunk to open.

CHAPTER NINE

There was a jackhammer pounding away some-where just outside of the covers.

Or no. It was inside the covers. It was in his pillow.

Or no.

It was in his head.

David rolled to his elbow and began to sit up and then promptly collapsed back to the heat of the mattress.

"Oh God," he moaned. His mouth tasted like shoe leather, and he could feel the alcohol evaporating in waves from every pore of his body. The red LED on his clock radio read 11:13.

"And she said Lite was bad," he mumbled. The sound of his voice hurt his head, and he decided to keep his thoughts to himself for a while.

Slowly he eased his way out of bed and into the bathroom, because while his head didn't want to go, other things did. Once relieved of the baser needs, he shakily pawed through the medicine chest for a bottle of Motrin, popped four, and turned on the shower. Somehow he had to face his aunt today, who would no doubt be amused at his discomfort.

"Oh God," he moaned again as the water pum-meled his temples, before he remembered that he wasn't going to speak for a while. He rested his head against the cool tile above the spray and let the water dance down his chest and thighs.

He considered that the world was not a wonderful place to be.

But even as he cursed his existence, he thought again of Brenda's kiss just hours before. The hangover was absolutely worth that. Anything was worth that.

The thought of her lips at the top of his mind, David eased the shampoo cap open and began to massage it into his hair. He would live through this. Toast and the Motrin might have him stabilized by mid-afternoon, he hoped. And when he was, he intended to dig out that number from his shirt pocket. Assuming he hadn't just dreamed that she'd put it there.

It wasn't a dream. After many painful minutes in the shower, and twice as many painful minutes hobbling his way into underwear, socks, fresh jeans and a T-shirt, David fished the scrap of paper from the shirt that lay rumpled in the corner of his room, and took himself and the number downstairs.

His aunt was waiting in the living room, watching television with a cup of coffee in hand. "Well, the cat dragged something in, but I'm not quite sure what it is," she poked. "What time did you get home last night?"

"Dunno," he said, and slipped into an easy chair next to her.

"Guessing you won't be riding today," she mused.

"Um, no."

She stood up and lightly touched his shoulder. "I don't believe in hair of the dog, but I do have a cure. How 'bout a bit of French toast to sop up the sauce?"

It sounded awful to him at that moment, but David knew the bread probably was the best thing he could eat. He nodded, and slipped deeper into the chair.

Everything hurt. His leg was stiff as a plank from where he'd taken the fall yesterday. After the hours at the bar last night, the accident and trip to Castle

House earlier in the day seemed a year away. Quite a day, he thought. Bike the ridge, get run over, wake up in a haunted house populated by crazy people and then meet the girl of your dreams in a bar and hang on the hurt-ing-est drunk *ever.*

Another twelve hours like that, and he'd be dead.

He fingered the paper tucked in his jeans pocket. He was supposed to be here for one purpose this summer: training. All pain, lots of gain. In between, he'd promised to help Aunt Elsie around the house with some painting and to reengineer the deck out back, which bowed and creaked whenever you walked across it. He guessed not much was going to remain but the posts once he started stripping away the rotten wood.

He didn't have time to blow, not on a girl. Even if she did have amazing breasts and a kiss that would melt the metal off your old silver fillings. One thing he knew about sports was that single-minded train-ing and losing yourself in the smile of the opposite sex did not mix. Pretty soon you were consuming lots of high-calorie dinners and spending precious time pumping on the couch instead of pumping iron and pedals in the pursuit of the ring.

And after all, hadn't she abandoned him at the bar in the end? The smell of cooked butter sizzled into the room, and presently his aunt called from the next room.

"David, drag yourself in here and get some of this in your gut while it's hot!"

He pushed off the chair, and felt queasy for a mo-ment, clutching the arm hard. Then he shoved the scrap of paper deep into his pocket, and vowed to eat. And then, somehow, to ride.

No pain, no gain.

CHAPTER TEN

David pressed his foot to the pedal and stifled a moan. While his entire left side was stiff and painful, the leg *really* ached to put pressure on it. And then there was his head. And his stomach. He felt nauseated and gimpy and he was pedaling a bike up a steep, curved hill for no good reason.

Clearly he'd lost his mind.

And it wasn't even his bike. The cop had bent the back tire of his Triomphe with her crappy old car, and now he was borrowing his aunt's Huffy ten-speed. Who knew how much it was going to cost to fix racing wheels. They didn't keep parts for Triomphes at your local Wal-Mart.

Aunt Elsie had laughed when he'd pulled on his riding shorts and limped to the garage after lying on the couch most of the afternoon.

"You've got to be joking, Davey," she called from the kitchen. "French toast can only do so many wonders. You have to let time—and a lot of tap water—do the rest."

Impatience was one of his virtues . . . or so he defended. The fastest way to work the stiffness out of his leg was to pedal. The fastest way to get past the hangover was to burn off all the poison.

But he wasn't a complete idiot. Rather than take the 190 out over the ridge again, he rode down Main and took the cutoff to Brookstone. The view there wasn't as breathtaking as the ridge, but it did raise an eyebrow. The little subdivision only had four streets, but the homes were all mini-mansions. This was the rich part of Castle Point, and many of these homes were only occupied part of the year. It was hard for David to look at the brick archways and rich oak entry doors and garages and imagine that someone could not only afford to live there, but keep a presumably larger domain elsewhere.

His aunt's style of living was more along the lines of what he thought of as normal. She had a three-bedroom Cape Cod a couple blocks from Main, on Second Street. It lacked a basement and most of the rooms measured no more than a dozen feet wide. The front room was just big enough to put a couch, an easy chair and a TV in, and she used what was probably supposed to be a fourth bedroom on the main floor as a second family room where she kept her sewing machine and a couple bookcases. David liked staying there despite its closeness, because Aunt Elsie slept on the main floor in the largest bedroom, which meant he had both upstairs bedrooms and the bath there to himself.

He looked at a country-style three-story on Culligan Street and just shook his head. The upstairs master bedroom had floor-to-ceiling windows and a walk-out balcony. You could probably fit most of Aunt Elsie's house in those peoples' bedroom!

David pulled off the subdivision's paved route and onto a dirt trail that ran up a hill and down to merge with Park Street just behind the Clam Shack. The late-afternoon heat beating off the asphalt was starting to get to him, and he considered stopping along the forested path to rest.

A squirrel darted out in front of his bike and froze. At the last possible second, but before David could brake, the animal took off into the brush, leaves rustling behind it. Close call.

That would be a good one. Yesterday get hit by a cop, today get hit by a squirrel. He opted not to stop—once he did, his legs would stiffen, and he didn't want to tackle the incline between Main and Second with a charley horse.

In minutes, he was gliding down the dirt trail where he'd kissed Brenda the night before. He recognized a huge log decomposing at the side of the trail, and then he was at the Shack's back parking lot. Where he'd peed in front of a girl too.

Oh man. No wonder she'd blown him off last night. Who cares if she was dropping trou . . . he should not have followed that lead. What if she saw his stuff and thought . . .

He pushed the thought from his head and circled the bar, noting the beat-up red siding and ripped screens all around. The white soffits had been painted recently, but aside from that, the building looked as if it was slowly moldering into the earth. Even the red neon sign looked forty years old in the daylight; at night all you could see was the flickering call to all barflies within a twenty-mile radius.

David took a long pull from his water bottle and realized that his head was pounding a little less in sync with his pedaling, and he hadn't felt like puking in at least a mile. His eyes still felt sunken and fried, but a night's sleep would solve that. Tomorrow he intended to be back out on 190 across the ridge. Today was just a reminder ride.

He pulled up the hill on Park and gasped as his legs slowed. It was like running up steps that never ended. Finally, just as he thought he couldn't stomp his feet toward the pavement anymore, the familiar brown brick of Aunt Elsie's house came into view, and he turned the corner and pulled into her cracked asphalt drive. That was one of the projects he'd promised her this summer—the drive needed a strong dose of crack filler and sealant.

There was a police cruiser parked out on the street, but David didn't think much about it until he ditched the bike in the garage and walked in the kitchen door.

"David, is that you?" his aunt called from the front room. "There's someone here to see you."

Now? David cried mentally. He could barely walk, he was puffing like he'd run a marathon and sweat was pouring in torrents down his temples and across his cheeks. He grabbed a hand towel from the kitchen drawer and solved the latter issue, and then walked into the living room.

"You!" was the first word out of the blonde policewoman's mouth.

David blinked twice when he saw her. While her outfit was regulation—navy pants, black belt and medium blue shirt buttoned to the neck, there was no mistaking the wavy curls of honey blonde hair that cascaded across her shoulders and sent unruly wisps out to straggle across her cheeks. Yesterday when she'd run him over, Christy had looked casually sexy. Today she looked like a sultry coed who'd donned a uniform for a costume party. The uniform couldn't constrain or contain the organic ease of her attraction.

"Um, yeah," was all he came up with. He wiped his face once more with the towel and wondered how deep the sweat stains around his pits had leached. He wondered if she could smell him across the room.

"David, this officer wants to talk to you about a girl you were with last night?" his aunt said.

"We've met," Christy said.

Aunt Elsie looked confused.

"This is the woman who sideswiped me yesterday," David explained.

His aunt suddenly put folded two arms over the orange hibiscus flowers of her housedress and looked suitably perturbed at the cop.

David put a hand up to calm her. "It's okay," he said. "It was an accident."

He looked at the formal uniform again, and gestured at the couch. "Do you want to have a seat? Can I get you something to drink?"

Christy shook her head. "I just need to ask you a few questions about last night." She looked pointedly at his aunt, who got the point.

"I'll be in the kitchen," she volunteered, and then slipped from the room.

"What's up?" he said.

"You look none the worse," she said, sizing him up.

"Best way to get over a spill is to get back on the horse."

"Last night, you spent some time with a girl at the Clam Shack."

"And this is a crime?"

Her dark eyes flared at him in disgust. "Don't be cute. Who was she? How well do you know her?"

David felt uncomfortable suddenly. Why were the police concerned with whom he'd been talking to in a bar?

"Her name was Brenda. I met her last night and we talked a while. What of it?"

"Her parents called the police because she never came home last night."

"Yeah, well you can ask my aunt—she didn't come here."

"Well, when was the last time you saw her?"

David wiped his face again; he could feel the

blood still pulsing in his temples, and he couldn't stand any more. "If you don't mind, I'm going to sit," he said.

She followed suit in the chair across from the couch. David couldn't help but notice when she flicked a strand of almost amber blonde hair back across the uniform blue. He'd been too shocked yesterday to appreciate it, but . . .

"Tell me about last night," Christy prompted.

"Look, after you knocked me around, I went to the bar to drown my sorrows a bit. Figured I wouldn't be training anymore this week after that and I was going to lose time."

"Obviously you went out today," she countered.

"Figured it was the best way to burn off a hangover," he laughed. "But I wouldn't call it training. Just a ride.

"Anyway . . . I met her while I was at the bar. She said her name was Brenda, and we got on pretty good. Talked for about three hours, and she kept buying me Guinness and got me so drunk we had to walk around the bar outside."

"So you took her outside alone?"

"Yeah, but we went back to the bar after, so I could have some water. I chugged the first one, and when she went to get me a second glass, I laid down on the table to rest. That's the last I saw of her. Next thing I knew, Joe, the bartender, was shaking me and tossing me out. Not much of a story."

Christy nodded and jotted down something in a small notebook. "Jibes with what Joe told me," she said. "Just wanted to check it out."

She rose to leave.

"She seemed really nice. I hope she's okay," David said.

Christy shrugged. "She may be sleeping it off at someone else's house. Are you all right with coming down to the station to give a formal statement if need be? We'll see if she turns up in the next twenty-four first."

"Sure," he said.

"Thanks," Christy said, and then looked him hard in the eye. "Watch yourself," she said. "You seem to be in the wrong place at the wrong time lately."

CHAPTER ELEVEN

The fuckin' piece of shit Nova. Carrie slammed her hand down on the dashboard and then swore when it stung from the impact. She turned the key five more times to hear five more clicks, and then got out and slammed the door behind her in disgust.

She walked back to the trunk, changed her mind and walked to the hood, then turned again to look through the driver's window at two empty seats.

"Fuckin'.

"Piece.

"Of.

"Shit."

She pronounced each word clearly and distinctly, sending her damnation of the car out to anyone in a five-mile radius. Unfortunately, there most likely wasn't anyone within a five-mile radius of where the Nova had opted to summarily quit. You could sit for hours overnight on the crossback and not see a soul.

That's why Carrie thought it was her lucky day (well, night) when the headlights broke over the ridge heading in her direction—toward Oak Falls. It was at least another twenty miles, and she did not want to attempt walking it. God knows what might pick up her scent from the hills and choose her as an easy dinner. There were bears, wolves, even a mountain lion or two up in those hills. She stood halfway in the oncoming lane and waved both hands frantically. The car slowed, and pulled in right behind hers.

A black Mustang.

Two men got out of the still-running car and started toward her. The driver, a big man in a lumberjack flannel, waved a broad hand. "What's a matter, ma'am, you stuck?"

"Fuckin' piece of shit Nova just quit, just like that," she said. "I just had it in for a tune-up a month ago."

"Mechanic probably left a screw loose," the big man said, finally reaching her and extending a palm. "I'm TG," he said, and nodded at the smaller man, who wore dark clothes to match his shadowed eyes. His nose was long though, giving him a birdlike look in the harsh shadows of the Mustang headlights. "This is my partner Billy. We can take a look under the hood if you like, and if we can't fix it, we can at least drive you into town."

"Thanks," Carrie said, trying unobtrusively to straighten her blouse and hair as the two men moved to the front of the car.

"Go ahead and pop the hood," TG said.

She opened the driver's door and leaned down to find the latch that released the lock on the front hood. It was just a small handle, but she'd never had a problem finding it before (not that she opened it much, but every now and then she added wiper fluid to the car herself). Naturally, now that two guys were waiting on her, she couldn't seem to find it. Her fingers flitted through invisible space, grasping at nothing and coming up with . . . nothing.

"Let me help you," the smaller man's voice said from behind her.

Carrie jumped, just a little, and she pulled up
from her crouch to flash the man a nervous smile of
thanks. But the look froze on her face and trans-
formed into something that wasn't very thankful at
all. Because the hook-nosed man was not there to
help her. He was definitely there to *hurt* her. The
blade that suddenly pressed cold and sharp against
the underside of her throat said that her car was
not going to get fixed tonight.

She was.

"Fuckin' piece of shit," she whispered for the third
time that night. Only this time she wasn't talking
about the Nova.

"What do you want?" she whispered. "I don't have
much money. If I did . . . I wouldn't be driving this."

TG's face peered over Billy's shoulder. He wore
a grin that showed yellow teeth and an unsympa-
thetic mean streak. "Well, for starters," he said,
"you could unbutton that blouse. That ought to be
worth a buck or two."

Deep inside Carrie's stomach, a pin pricked. And
that pinprick opened a hole that grew and grew, as
ice water cascaded from somewhere deep within
her worst nightmares and filled her belly with terror. She suddenly knew without a doubt that she
was not going to get back to Oak Falls tonight, or
probably ever.

With trembling, clumsy hands she released the
buttons on her blouse, exposing the white lace bra
beneath.

TG approved. He reached into his back pocket,
pulled out a beat-up leather lump of a wallet and
pulled a dollar bill from it. Then he made a big show
of folding it in half long ways before reaching past
Billy's knife and slipping it across her right breast
to lodge under her bra. His hand lingered a moment
before he pulled back.

"Well," he said, plucking the blouse away from her, "you're not dressed for strippin', but that ain't half bad. Billy, back up. Let's see if the panties are a match. I hate it when a girl wears droopy drawers and a sexy bra. Just not right neglecting the other half, you know what I mean?"

"Please," Carrie said, flattening her back against the cold metal of the rear car window. The tip of Billy's knife followed her as she stepped out of the trap of the driver's-seat entry. "I'll strip if you like. I'll do whatever you want. Just please let me go home afterward?"

"We'll take you home," TG said. "I already promised you that." He gestured at her jeans. "Now let's see about the other half."

"You some kinda lingerie conn-o-saur now?" Billy mumbled.

"Just having some fun," TG said through gritted teeth. "Lighten up and you might have some too."

Carrie undid the belt buckle, all the while frantically trying to remember what color briefs she'd pulled on this morning. She had matching Victoria's Secret sets, but had she worn one? In the insanity of the situation, she honestly couldn't remember. She held her breath and dropped drawers in the cool night, exposing a pair of lean runner's thighs, and a pair of white panties edged in the same lace as the cup of her bra. She breathed her own sigh of relief as she saw them.

"She's organized," TG pronounced. He moved forward, and ran one knuckle down her cheek, neck and across the exposed top of her cleavage.

"I like that in a woman."

She shivered at his touch, but forced herself not to move away. But when his fingers slipped beneath the lace, she cried out.

TG didn't miss a beat. He belted her one across the jaw, never letting go of the bra. The result was a suddenly freed breast, nipple angry pink in the dark, and constricted by the half-yanked-down bra cup.

TG leaned down and took the nipple between his teeth. Carrie pushed at his shoulders, but it was as effective as swatting at a swarm of flies. In a flash his hands were all over her, yanking hard on her undies and ripping and tugging at the clasp on the back of her bra.

"Jesus," Billy yelled. "We talked about this. You can't be doing this here."

"Yer right," TG said, pulling his face away from the woman's chest. "Spot me down here in the gulley. I've got some organization to tend to."

He dragged the girl away from the car and down the slight decline away from the road in the dark. Presently, he said, "Oh yes, she's very organized. Neat and tidy and trim. I like that in a woman, yes I do."

Billy just hung his head and paced near the back of the Mustang, praying no headlights slipped around the bend. But the noises in the ditch soon died down, and TG reappeared, dragging the struggling, screaming naked girl by a hank of blonde hair up the incline.

"Duct tape," TG demanded. Soon the screeching subsided to muffled whimpering.

Then, "Rope."

Then, "Tire iron."

And then there wasn't any noise at all.

The Mustang pulled away from the Nova without any pretense of civility. Gravel flew and tires screeched. And TG gave out a buoyant "yee-ha" as the car fishtailed onto the asphalt and sped back toward Castle Point.

"I thought we were going to have to actually walk the bar scene in Oak Falls again," he laughed. "You know how much I hate that. But here, right here on the road, we get a little vixen just sitting here waiting for us. A gift," he said.

"You shouldn't a fucked her," Billy complained.

"Why, because you didn't get to? You want me to pull over and you can have your turn?"

"That's not it," the other man said. "We're supposed to be delivering her for testing and experiments. We don't know if she's going to be back on the street in a week, and if she is . . . we're fuckin' toast, man!"

"You know Billy, you worry too much," TG said. "How you gonna run a bar, where shit happens virtually every night in the bathroom or the brawl room, if you're such a worrytit? I mean . . . think about it. The doctor, he's paying us to deliver him healthy, young females, ain't he? And he's PAYING us to pick them up, tie them up and deliver them to him. Do you honestly think these girls have a chance in hell of getting out of whatever the hell he's doing to them? Shit, Billy, what I just did for that girl is a *favor*. Probably the last good time she's going to have. You need to lighten up."

"Pull up to the back," Billy complained, as TG powered down the Mustang at the front door of the Castle House Asylum. "The doc said to bring 'em to the back."

"I know what he said," TG growled, ripping the gear shift into park with an audible crack. "But I'm going to let him know we're here. It's late, and I'm not sitting around the back of this haunted house throwing rocks at the windows and hoping someone hears."

TG left Billy in the car and stomped up to the

twin torchlights that framed the oak door of the asylum. They were the remnants of another era, not the sort of entry that you'd expect at the crazy house, but someone had obviously polished and pimped them up to serve again. TG tried the knob before knocking, but it didn't open.

So he pounded a few raps with a beefy fist and waited. In a moment, the door cracked open, a chain obviously still securing it to the frame. Billy couldn't hear what was said, but a moment later TG was back in the car and throwing it into reverse.

"We're going to the back," was all he said.

Billy didn't ask questions. It was best that way.

The back of Castle House was dark, except for a single light high up on the third floor.

"They could at least put on a light," Billy said. The darkness stretched unbroken from just beyond their car headlights to probably the outskirts of Castle Point, almost twenty miles and several steep bends away.

"It's right here," TG said, and aimed the car toward a small white door set amid the brown brick. There was a gravel path that led past the door and opened to a circular parking spot in front of an old metal shed.

"Utility entrance," TG said. "C'mon, help me get her out of the trunk."

TG reached in and hefted her half out of the trunk by her legs, while Billy reached in to hoist the rest of her out by her armpits. They shuffled toward the door, but when he felt something warm on his arm, Billy cried out.

"Jesus, man, you hit her too hard. There's blood all over me."

"She'll be fine," TG promised. "They got a doctor in the house."

But the bigger man could see even in the slight illumination from the third floor that the girl had blood all over her head. Maybe a tire iron hadn't been the best blackjack.

"Bang your heel on that door and let's get her in."

Three quick kicks was all it took to get a reaction from inside. The white door opened and a woman in a white smock went wide-eyed when she saw the cargo. The door opened wide and she demanded, "Come in, come in. What's happened to her?"

She led them down a short hall to an exam room, and motioned for them to lay the body on the paper-covered table.

"Where's the doc?" TG demanded. "Did you call him like I asked?"

"He's on his way," she said, but refused to meet his eyes. She wet a towel in the stainless-steel sink across the room and then used it to clean the blood away from the back of the unconscious woman's skull.

TG stood at the girl's feet, arms crossed, frankly just enjoying the view. The chick was stacked, and she kept the bushes pruned too. There was good reason he'd taken this one to the ditch. They'd lucked out on the drive tonight. Saved a trouble-some full trip into Oak Falls AND found a sweet peach to boot.

Billy wasn't so calm. He paced in and out of the exam room doorway as the nurse cleaned Carrie's wound. And he visibly jumped when the doctor strode confidently past him into the room and barked, "What the hell did you do to her?"

TG didn't flinch. "Found her on the side of the road, Doc. Thought you'd want a piece of her."

The doctor brushed the nurse out of the way and examined the wound, holding back the thick clumps of sticky hair to trace the ragged flesh beneath. "Looks more like you had a piece of her," the doctor said without looking up. "Please tell me, why is she naked?"

TG shrugged. "Wanted to make sure she was healthy for ya, Doc." He couldn't stifle the chuckle at the end.

The doctor straightened up and glared at the men. "Two things I demand from here on out," he said. "You don't fuck the girls, and you don't touch their heads. You just messed with the two reasons I need these women. Now tell me . . . where are her clothes?"

"I threw them in her car," Billy said softly.

"And the car, where is it?"

"Out on the crossback, where it stalled," TG answered.

"Great," the doctor said. "So her clothes, covered with your hair and probably semen and sweat and a hundred other sources of DNA, not to mention her car, which you also probably put your fingerprints all over, is sitting there in the open waiting for the police to pick up on all the evidence and ID you. And then, when they've picked you up and thrown you in a cell, you'll point the finger at me. Not that that will save *your* asses from a long stretch in jail!"

Billy turned pale. Even TG blinked an extra time or two.

The doctor straightened up to his full six feet and pointed a blood-smeared finger at them both. "Listen to me, morons. You get out there, and you get that car off the road someplace where nobody's going to find it. You burn her clothes and anything else you put your fingers on. Do that, and IF this girl recovers enough for me to use her for what I need, then we can talk about payment."

"Whoa, Doc," TG began, putting two beefy hands in the air. "We need cash if we're gonna keep doing this."

"Get your dipshit asses out there and get rid of the evidence you left sitting around in full view of the first cop who gets a missing persons report and we'll talk," the doctor said. "Git! I need to help this poor girl."

TG and Billy were a mile down the road from the asylum when Billy finally got up the courage to say it.

"I told you not to fuck her."

TG didn't take his eyes off the road. But his voice was sharp as glass. "Just for that, you're getting under the hood of her piece of shit Nova and figuring out what the hell's wrong with it. That, or you're pushing it all the way back to the shack."

Billy thought it best not to answer.

CHAPTER TWELVE

The lab coat folded very neatly after he creased and laid it on the counter. Barry Rockford appreciated a good crease. He knew it was just a sign of a mental fixation that begged to become an obsession, but frankly, my dear, he didn't give a damn.

There was a reason Barry—that's Barry Rockford, MD, PhD, thank you—had taken his family inheritance and a silent siphon of offshore investor funds and moved out here to lab-rat land. And obsession had a lot to do with it. But it wasn't an obsession with fabric folding.

After twenty years in a lab at MIT, his focus was on more organic problems. Barry Rockford had published dozens of papers on his research in the pages of journals like *Science* and *Genetics*. His paper on in vitro stem-cell mining had generated the largest avalanche of mail the *New England Journal of Medicine* had ever received. It had also gotten him barred from ever submitting another paper there. Which was laughable, since, after all, weren't they the ones who'd agreed to publish his research in the first place?

He didn't care. The stem cells were just the means to an end. And more and more, the end was just the beginning.

Barry pulled out the chart on the girl in room seven. The dipshit boys had brought her in two weeks ago from Oak Falls. She'd been a little roughed up when she'd gotten here—apparently the boys hadn't expected her to pull a knife when they cornered her in a parking garage. But the bruises were finally starting to fade. Amazingly, the Neanderthal hadn't broken a rib or her jaw, but it would be a couple more weeks before the evidence would be completely gone.

No matter. The patient wouldn't be fully conscious for the foreseeable future to complain.

The chart read, "Diagnosis: extreme psychosis. Dangerous to self and others. No next of kin identified. Treatment recommended: long-term sedation and therapy."

His lips turned in a slight smile as he skimmed the description and the subsequent notations on her "treatment" since arriving. The diagnosis would certainly have been news to the girl who had no doubt been leading a typically unsatisfied life of unfulfilling relationships and insolvable debt before being set upon by two thugs in the dead of night. Although, she had proved adept with a knife, as the dressings on Billy's chest would attest, if he admitted to anyone that they were there.

He read the last notation in the chart and grinned.

It was time to start on the next phase of her treatment. Her cycle had begun again.

Dr. Rockford stood, and called down the hall for his head nurse.

"Amelia!"

She appeared in a heartbeat from the exam room.

"Yes, Doctor. The new girl seems to be stabilized."

"I read your notes on room seven. Shall we begin tonight?"

"If you are ready, Doctor," Amelia said. There was a slight glint to her eyes as she said it. As if she was baiting him.

"I'm always ready," he said. "Bring the restraints and we'll begin."

CHAPTER THIRTEEN

The room was pitch-black and the bed sucked. Those were the first two thoughts that entered Jackie Meyer's head when she blinked open her eyes. The room swam before her, like she'd downed an entire bottle of vodka before slipping beneath the sheets. But . . . she didn't drink when she was 'tending. And she didn't remember going home with anyone.

She tried to clear the fog from her head and think.

Had she worked Teehan's Irish Bar last night? Was it Saturday or Sunday, and little Jack was sleeping over at Becky's so she could work the weekend shift and clear the good tips? Fuck, where was she? And who was she with?

She tried to move her arm to feel the other side of the bed but it wouldn't budge. It was as if her body were a block of ice. Melting away the sleep, but still solid as iron.

Damn it. She'd made rules for herself: no drinking on the job, and no dates on the spur. She had a son to take care of now, and the days of waking up in strange rooms were over.

So where the hell was she?

She felt strange. Not really drunk. Not high . . . She couldn't describe it. Her brain was tripping into gear but the rest of her might as well have been tied to a rack. And the response when she tried to move anything, even her eyebrow, was a fuzzy burn of blue in the back of her head. Like dull sparks that didn't light the fire.

Jackie found she could move her tongue.

That was one muscle that responded. She licked the inside of her gums and grimaced. Her teeth felt like mossy stones. Ugh. And her mouth felt hot. Dried out.

What had she done last night?

Focus.

Think.

Remember.

What was the last thing . . .

There was Jack . . . She remembered leaving him with Becky. His ice blue eyes had opened wide and he grinned with wet pink lips and gave her a kiss. "Night night, Momma," he'd said, a warm lump of a boy in his blue dinosaur one-piece. "Night, kiddo," she'd said, giving him a big hug and thanking Becky who stood behind him, arms crossed and waiting to take the boy to his weekend bed.

Was that last night? Last week? It all seemed strangely distant. But it was all she could pull up. Work at the bar. Yellowed lights blearing over fifty bottles of booze . . . rowdy customers . . . a college kid buying shots of Jaeger for his girlfriend . . . a stubbled regular slurring, "I'm all right, I'm okay," over and over while holding out his glass for more . . .

The memories were a blur, almost overshadowed in sepia, as if she were watching someone else's old film. But they seemed like the last things she could dredge out of her memory.

There were pins and needles in her arm. Damn it.

She hated that. Especially since she couldn't seem to move a muscle to calm them. One, two, three, she counted mentally . . . and threw herself to the side.

Her body didn't move.

But maybe her finger did. She tried again.

One, two, three . . .

Her arm flopped. And, oh shit did the pins and needles come on then. She opened her mouth to cry out and then thought better of it. She didn't know who she'd be waking yet, and it seemed oddly important that she remember that.

She tried again to piece together the night before, but instead of bar scenes, she found herself seeing the eyes of a man looking down at her. He wore a white lab coat or smock—as if he was a doctor.

"Relax," he told her. Something pinched her arm, and his eyes drew in very close to hers. "Everything is going to be all right now."

There was a cold sensation in her arm, and something tugging at her waist. The doctor pulled at something by her thigh, and cold washed over her as her coverings slipped away. Then his hands were on her, rubbing the places that hurt, and the places that felt good. She could feel sensation returning all over her body in a wash of pricks and feather tickles.

"Everything is going to be all right now," he said again. And then a nurse put a hand on her brow. "Just lay back and enjoy it," the woman suggested.

Enjoy it?

Something cold pressed between her legs, something slimy and cool. She flinched, but the nurse again rubbed her brow. And then something definitely *not* cold pressed itself there, something warm and fleshy and she fought to stop its entrance, but then she realized that her arms were strapped and her legs were strapped and the doctor was leaning over her, grinning, ice blue eyes like daggers stabbing their poison into her soul, as his wide, thin lips bent down to touch her own . . .

"Oh shit, shit, shit," she moaned again. The pins and needles had gotten worse and she could make a fist. Where am I? Who was that man?

She tried to think again about the night she'd left Jack with Becky and the people she'd served at the bar. It all seemed a very long and foggy time ago. But then she did remember one thing. At the end of the night, near last call, two hicks had come into the bar. They'd pulled up stools and ordered beer . . . but had seemed half trashed already. When she'd told them it was last call and that they'd have to drink fast, the bigger one had grinned and said he could do it fast, could she?

Then what?

She struggled through the fog to remember.

She saw the doctor, big chin and scary eyes looking over her.

She saw the hick, laughing at two A.M. and staggering out the door with his buddy in tow.

She saw a big hand cupped across her face as she tried to put her keys in the lock of her car. "I told you I was fast, didn't I?" he said, and then there was a cloth over her face and a smell like turpentine and then . . .

She was able to move her arm and she reached her hand across the bed and confirmed what she suspected.

The other side of the mattress was empty, but she already knew that. She hadn't gone home with some loser after last call, and she hadn't gotten drunk on the job.

Some asshole had kidnapped her. But why?

She ran her arm up and down the mattress, and then massaged her face. It felt thick, and weird. Almost like someone else's. She touched her other arm, and massaged the biceps for a while until the needles began and left, and she could raise it. They both felt feeble and weak, but she ran them down her ribs to her hips. Something wasn't right.

She was thicker than she'd been yesterday, and this wasn't water weight. Slowly she slipped her hands across her abdomen, and stifled a gasp when she reached her belly button.

Jackie wasn't just bloated.

Jackie was pregnant. Majorly pregnant.

And when she'd left little Jack at Becky's, she'd not only *not* been knocked up, but she hadn't been with a man in something like six months.

She moved her hands across the definitely distended belly and her eyes welled up. *Oh my God,* she thought. *What did they do to me?*

And then a scarier thought interjected: *And where's Jack?*

Light suddenly flooded the room as the door swung open, and Jackie blinked, trying to make out who was there. She could barely hold her eyes open, but there was a fuzzy man at her bedside just like that. And a stern, black-eyed woman.

Hands stroked her head and she heard a voice say, "She's come up."

"So soon?" the woman answered. "She's had a heavy dose."

"After a few weeks, the body adjusts," the doctor said.

Weeks?

"Time to do a little harvesting," he continued. "Let's take her back down. I don't want her jumping in the middle of the procedure."

Jackie reached her arm toward the fuzzy pancake of the doctor's face and tried to grab on. She slapped against something warm, but then her arm was flat on the bed, and the nurse whispered in her ear.

"This won't hurt a bit."

Then something stabbed her in the shoulder, and it did hurt, more than a bit, but she really didn't have the strength to scream. Or to talk for that matter.

She remembered suddenly, sitting with another woman on a couch. They both wore light blue and flower-patterned cotton robes, and they both just sat there on the couch, happy to be out of bed. They stared at a white wall. The white wall made them feel good. Complete. She remembered the white wall was all she ever wanted to look at.

Jackie felt everything slipping away, as if her consciousness were a sink of water, and the drain had just been opened.

Someone poured Drano in my head, she thought as her eyes closed.

There was a pain in her belly then. Something sharp. It slipped inside her and pricked and poked, and she hoped it stopped soon. She wanted to cry, but her eyes had died.

"That's it," the doctor's voice said. "That's just what we needed."

Then the pain slipped away. And so, for a long while, did Jackie.

CHAPTER FOURTEEN

"Helloo Castle Point," the woman said on the other end of the phone. Christy smiled, and said simply, "Hello" and "What can I do for you?"

"This is Marie from the Oak Falls PD. Who's this?"

"Officer Christy Sorensen, Castle Point. What's up?"

The other woman sounded nice, and certainly exuberant, but there was an edge to her voice.

"We're a little concerned up here, I guess you'd say. Thought we should check in with our neighbors. Is Chief Maitlin around?"

Christy shook her head, though the other woman couldn't see it. Why talk to an underling if the "real" sheriff was in town. Well . . . at the moment, he wasn't!

"Sorry," she said. "Chief's out grabbing some lunch. What can I help you with?"

"Don't know that you can," the woman said. "Just wanted to see if you've been running into any odd cases lately."

"Odd how?"

"Well . . ." The woman paused. "We've had a half dozen missing persons reports over the past three months. Two of them in the past two weeks. And so far, not a one has popped up. We weren't too concerned at first 'cuz they were just transients . . . kinda folks who come and go without warning. But . . . over the past month, we've had a couple disappear who just don't meet that description at all."

"What do you mean?" Christy pressed.

"Well, last night, someone reported that the owner of a hair salon didn't come home."

"One-night stand?" Christy asked.

"That's what I would have said. If there weren't so many other cases to consider. But . . . here's what's really making this look scary."

"What's that?" Christy asked.

"Every one of these missing persons is over eighteen but under forty, and was last seen at a bar," the woman said. "And every one of them has been a woman. We've got a snatcher I think. But God knows what he's doing with 'em. No bodies have turned up."

"Damn," Christy said. "We've not really seen anything like that here . . . though there was a woman reported missing last night. But she's been the only one since I've been on the force."

The other woman got a condescending tone. "And how long's that been, hon? I don't think we've talked before."

"Just eight weeks. But the point is, we've not had a rash of body snatchers in Castle Point."

"Well," the other woman drawled. "I'd guess you might want to be on the lookout for those. Let the chief know I called, huh?"

The line clicked.

Christy swore under her breath. It was hard enough making it as a woman cop without another woman cutting your legs out. Bitch.

She hung up the phone and leaned back in the chair, enjoying the slowly ascending creak as it bent backward.

She would tell the chief about the call when he got back, sure. But she had a feeling that he would point in the same direction she was in her head now. It was the end of summer, and people came and went this time of year. But not usually without warning.

On the other hand . . . what was new in the area?

Castle House Asylum. The place that had the chief's gut in an uproar. The place had opened just a month or two before Christy had started, and that would jibe with right around the time of the Oak Falls disappearances.

And hadn't the doctor said it was a home for one particular type of lunatic?

Women?

Christy picked up the phone and dialed the Oak Falls PD. She hadn't been a good cop on that call. After all, how could CPPD do anything if they didn't know what or whom they were looking for?

"Hi, Marie," she said as a now-familiar voice picked up the line. "About those missing persons you've had. Can you give me their names, and some more information . . ."

When she hung up the phone, she had a list of names, ages and dates. With a little help from Google, she soon had photos to go with those statistics courtesy of MySpace and Facebook and other social networking sites. It was amazing the kind of stuff people posted in the public domain, she thought, after skimming through the photo album of an Oak Falls grade school teacher who'd posed grinning lasciviously for the camera while clad only in a snake.

Armed with photo printouts of a bunch of missing women, Christy decided it was time to take a little drive back to Crossback Ridge. If she couldn't spy on the asylum undercover any longer, she might as well stroll in without compunction through the front door.

The front door was opened by a woman straight out of a business-magazine ad. She was tall, thin and had a mass of long dark hair pulled back in a bun. She wore black-rim glasses that wouldn't have been out of place in a black-and-white Spencer Tracy film. Christy thought she put on her lipstick and rouge too red, but then inwardly slapped herself for being uncharitable. She personally preferred not to wear makeup at all, if possible, so who was she to judge?

"Hi, I'm Officer Christy Sorensen, from the Castle Point Police Department," she said extending a hand. The other woman shook it making the least possible connection between their palms.

"Yes," the woman said. "We've met. I'm Nurse Spellman—you might not recognize me since I was in uniform last time you were here. To what do we owe the pleasure?"

Christy kicked herself mentally. Of course! This was the woman who'd assisted the doctor with the biker kid. "I remember now," she apologized. "I'm so sorry!"

She stepped inside without waiting for an invitation, and gestured around at the marble pillars that framed the gorgeous entryway in white. "I was here the other day to make our welcome visit to the asylum when our accident sidetracked things a bit. We try to stop by all of the new businesses in town during their first few months of operation, just to say hi, get to know the owners, see if you have any questions . . . things like that."

Nurse Spellman raised a thin black eyebrow and then slowly shook her head. "Don't think we've got any questions," she said. "We're pretty self-sufficient here. Have to be when you're running an institution like this—we have to stay pretty separate from the outer world for the patients' sake."

Christy put on her sweetest smile. "I understand completely! Which is even more reason for us to have a good relationship. If anything ever did happen out here—a break-in, or break-out—it'd be good if we knew how you did things here, where things were, you know—the lay of the land. Care to give me a quick tour while I'm out here?"

The nurse looked visibly ill at ease. "I don't know," she began.

Just then a male voice echoed into the broad entry hall. "Amelia? Do we have a visitor?" he said. Heels clicked across the glossy granite tile, and Christy confirmed that it was, indeed, Dr. Rockford.

His lips split into a knowing grin as he extended a hand. "Officer," he said. "We meet again so soon. What brings you to our little center? Nothing traumatic, I hope? Our biking friend, is he okay?"

"He's fine," she said, gripping his hand. "Saw him just this afternoon, in fact."

"Officer Sorensen came for the tour," Nurse Spellman offered.

The doctor pursed his lips. "I suppose that could be arranged. Though there's not much to see." He laughed then and put his hand up to point at the crystal chandelier dangling from the ceiling covered in murals of astrological figures. "I mean, this looks grand and all, but once we're inside the regular halls, it looks just like any other hospital or ambulatory care facility really. White walls, fire doors, crash carts . . . We've been inspected and certified by the state, you know? So it all is up to speed, and probably, to an officer . . . fairly boring."

She shrugged. "Honestly, I'd just love to see what you've done with the old hotel. The place was basically a haunted house for the last twenty or thirty years from what I hear."

"So they say," he agreed. "All I know is it was plenty dirty and run-down, and we've only salvaged a part of it so far. But sure, I can walk you through the part we use."

He gestured for her to follow and led the way across the grand entry to a hallway that instantly dropped the "grand" quotient. The carpet looked old—a dull brick red shot through with random twirls of faint gold. It remained thick—the only sound as they walked was of their breath and pant legs rubbing together. The walls had recently been painted a calming cream.

"This area wasn't too difficult to clean up," the doctor explained. Then he pushed open the door to an exam room. Christy was sure it was the same room they had taken David to. "But rooms like this," he added, "we had to strip to the studs and remove and replace the tile so that we could meet all the health code standards. Took us all spring."

He flipped the light off, and walked through a shadowy corridor filled with paintings. "I think you were here the other day—this was an old wing of the hotel dedicated to art from its patrons, and we've kept it intact."

Christy noted one piece that was obviously new to the collection. Its frame was cheap black metal instead of classic mahogany, and instead of a lush outdoor scene, this one seemed luridly chaotic. A mass of orange and red and yellow paint, with swirls of deep emerald and factory blue, the picture reminded Christy of an explosion. Still, she looked back over her shoulder at it as they passed. It almost seemed as though there was a face peering out of its insane collage. She found herself staring deeper into its abyss, and a warmth began to grow deep in her abdomen, a familiar tingling. The last time her chest had ached like that was when her last boyfriend at the academy had pressed his mouth inside her uniform to . . .

". . . and here is the main O.R., should we need to perform any procedures," Dr. Rockford said, flipping a light on quickly and gesturing toward two emergency patient tables on wheels in the center of the long room. Scalpels and other instruments were arranged on a tray between the tables, covered with some sort of protective plastic.

He flipped the switch off again and led Christy up a wide flight of stairs that curved to the right and around in a spiral. She tried to shake off the strange feeling that had literally made her knees weak, and clung to the stair rail, forcing her attention to admire the intricate carving of the balustrade, made of some rich, almost glowing hardwood. While this place may have been abandoned for years, clearly some of its original beauty had remained unharmed. She crossed her arms over her strangely aroused nipples and pinched the skin of her inner arms, hard. After a moment, the erotic wave passed, and she began to look around at the subject of the tour once more.

The second story of the old hotel was bright and airy—tall windows cloaked by gold gilt draperies opened the world to the hallway every few feet. Here the carpet truly showed its age, as the light gave it no chance to hide. Worn patches and wide faded stains marred its once rich surface.

On the left side, a series of white doors lined the corridor. Small placards had been posted beside each entry, labeled simply ROOM 1, ROOM 2, ROOM 3.

"These are the patient rooms," Dr. Rockford said. "We have about a dozen with us right now, but we're hoping to triple that by the end of the year."

"What size staff do you have?"

He chuckled. "Astute question. It's just me and Amelia right now, with a couple part-timers helping to run the phones and handle odd jobs. We're actually looking for a groundskeeper right now. We don't need a lot of staff with this small of a client base, but we will certainly be looking to hire some qualified personnel from town once more patients arrive."

They passed rooms six and seven, and then turned a corner where the numerical series continued to climb. Christy swore inwardly as none of the doors were open. "Where do you get your patients from, Doctor?" she asked.

"We're a private facility, so it's via referrals only," he said. "I worked with MIT and a number of other institutions for many years, so there are many great physicians out there who know my specialty and will send me patients who fit what I do."

"And what is that, Doctor? What *do* you deal with?"

He paused, and turned to face her. "Officer, if you're worried about the safety of people in Castle Point . . ."

She put up her palms. "Not at all, Doctor. I was just wondering what you specialized in. Why put all this effort into setting up a facility out here in the boondocks like this? It must have cost you a fortune just to modernize it."

Rockford nodded. "We had a private grant, but yes, it was expensive. But the privacy was necessary, and I'd appreciate your force's help in maintaining it. Our specialty, if you'd like to call it that, is helping mentally disturbed pregnant women. Often these are women who have been violently raped or brutalized by their lovers, and have reached the point of catatonia at least once. I've worked over the past several years in developing a sedative treatment regimen that is both safe for the unborn child and yet keeps the mother distanced from the demons that could lead her to harm herself and her baby."

As the doctor said the words "pregnant" and "rape," Christy felt a tinge of warmth begin again between her thighs. She grimaced at the feeling. What the hell was wrong with her?

"It seems very quiet," Christy said, surreptitiously pinching herself again. "Are there patients in the rooms we've been walking past?"

He nodded. "This is the first and main wing, and it's quiet because this is a sleep period for our patients."

They turned another corner and Rockford pointed out the view. The windows faced the downslope of the ridge, and a lush curve of deciduous oaks and elms and others mixed with the occasional spike of pine filled the horizon.

"I have to say that this was one of the reasons I really wanted this property. The countryside is just gorgeous. Perfect for helping our patients relax."

They rounded another corner and Christy noted that the rooms here were no longer labeled. The walls also were a dull orange, paint faded and cracked from years of neglect. Cobwebs clung to the corners of the ceiling. "I take it you've not worked on this yet," she said.

He shook his head. "This is our next project. That will finish the first quadrant of patient rooms. This hotel has four quadrangles, you know. We haven't needed this space yet, so it's not been a priority. But we're getting close to needing it now, so it won't be long. Know any good painters? We brought our last crew in from the coast. I'm not paying for that again."

Christy grinned, in spite of herself. "I'm sure you can find some good painters cheap in town. There are plenty of people in Castle Point looking for a job. Any job. Boondocks doesn't exactly mean strong industry."

"Unless you're a logger," he suggested.

She shook her head. "None of that out here. Nobody would allow them to ruin these hills."

"Good," he said. "Natural beauty should be preserved, not mined."

He gestured for her to descend the stairs that they came to just ahead. "These lead right back to where we started," he said. "Call it the back staircase."

Like the last hall, these stairs had not been cleaned and polished to reflect the prosperity of the entryway. When they reached the bottom, there was a dark alcove to the right, and a shadowed hallway leading away. Christy looked at the door in the alcove, an old beat-up wooden door, which had something scratched into its surface. She stepped to look closer, when Rockford grabbed her arm.

"Old basement entrance," he explained. "You don't want to stick your head down there, trust me."

Just him saying that, of course, made Christy *absolutely* want to stick her head down there, especially since it looked like the wood had been scored by a knife or some other sharp object. She'd been looking closer because the mark seemed to be in the shape of an *X*.

She vowed to come back again and see just what Dr. Rockford's basement held, preferably without his guided assistance.

For now though, except for a brief glance over her shoulder at the darkened door, she followed him back to the main reception area in the front of the building. He didn't offer her coffee, or any further company at the end of the tour; both he and Amelia quietly escorted her straight to the door and waited for her to leave. In truth, she was fine with that; she was still battling inexplicable bouts of . . . well . . . horniness! And she really just wanted to get back to her apartment now and . . . take care of it. Apparently, it had been too long since she'd attended to her baser needs. Christy thanked them and stepped out of the silent whispers of the fledgling sanitarium and into the warm whispers of summer on the ridge.

She took a deep breath, held it, and then let it go to take another, trying to clear her head. Then she walked down the short steps to the parking lot and opened the door to her car. The folded notes and photos of the missing persons she'd hoped to look for still rode heavily in her breast pocket, and she frowned at the thought of her mission gone sour. She hadn't seen a single patient there today.

That's two strikes, she thought. Disgustedly, she slid into the car and revved the engine. In her head, she vowed that the third try would not end in a strike. She was going to come back to the lodge. After dark. With hardly any staff in evidence and a complement of patients who were apparently comatose most of the time, it should be fairly easy to move through the asylum undetected, if she could just slip inside. And the police had plenty of ways to gain entry to locked buildings. A smile grew across her deceptively innocent-looking face. Next time, she was checking out the patients, she thought. And, perhaps, the basement as well!

The silk curtains at the border window to the front door of the lodge didn't fall back in place until Christy's dust was safely downhill.

CHAPTER FIFTEEN

The car turned out to be fairly easy to get rid of. Billy had gotten under the hood and banged around with some wrenches trying to get it started again, while TG paced along the gravel shoulder, looking out for any distant headlights. But the car wouldn't start. And at four in the morning, TG had no more patience for the business. He'd finally grabbed Billy by the shoulder and pulled him away from the engine.

"C'mon, Billy, we don't want to be driving this piece of shit Nova back to the shack anyway. It'd only connect the bitch with us if the chief ever got his head out of his daughter's ass and actually came snooping around our place. I've got another idea."

"You wanna tow it?" Billy asked. He looked confused. "Where we gonna get a tow truck at this hour? Can't hook it onto the Mustang."

TG cuffed him on the side of the head. "No, you dipshit, we're gonna use Mother Nature. Get that extra gas can out of the back of the trunk. Doc said we needed to burn off any evidence, and I've got the perfect way to do it."

While Billy grabbed the gas, TG put the car in neutral, and rocked it back onto the road. With Billy's help, he lined the car up with the edge of the road, and then they coated every surface of the car with splashes of gas. TG dropped Carrie's clothes on the front seat and doused those with the last dregs from the can, and then laughed. "Let 'em try to pull a print out of this fireball."

Then he rolled up the car window, lit a match and tossed it onto the pile of clothes. The flame was instant, orange and hot. He slammed the door shut before it caught the outside, and then yelled, "Let's go!"

He and Billy both pushed hard as linemen against the back fender, and as the inferno enveloped the inside of the car, they got it rolling slowly toward the edge of the road's shoulder. It was a huge drop down after the gravel—hundreds of feet.

"Harder," TG yelled, as the glass cracked on the driver's-side window and black smoke began leaking out, followed by a thin tongue of reddish flame.

"The outside's gonna go any second!"

With two grunting, screaming pushes, they rocked the car past the edge of the roadside, and the front end dipped over the edge into space. The flames did escape the cab then, and suddenly the entire frame of the car was enveloped in a blue fire runner, followed by a crackle of orange heat.

The two men fell back on their asses away from the car as it continued to creak forward and then went over with a crack of broken brush and hungry flame.

A handful of smashing sounds followed, and by the time Billy and TG were back on their feet and to the edge of the cliff, they could see the entire car engulfed like a flaming meteor crumpled against some boulders far below.

"Get the can and let's get out of here," TG said. "Probably nobody will see that smoke at this hour, but you never know. Either way, by the time anyone comes around, that fire should have gotten rid of any traces of our prints. If someone finds the car, they'll wonder what happened to the driver, but they'll assume it was an accident—the car just went over."

The Mustang tore away from the site of the "accident" as an orange glow rose from the rocks below. There was only one thing they hadn't noticed, and that lay on the gravel of the road's shoulder, where it had fallen off the edge of the hood of the Nova.

Billy's large, pitted, yellow-plastic-handled Phillips screwdriver.

CHAPTER SIXTEEN

"I didn't like the way that cop was snooping around here this afternoon," Amelia said.

Dr. Rockford shrugged. "The only thing to do there was give her what she asked for. Let her poke around and see nothing. If you'd turned her away cold, she'd eventually have come back again, probably with some trumped-up warrant to search the place—strictly to ensure our safety, of course. You know what a *dangerous* building this is."

The nurse laughed. "I don't think they have any idea."

"I hope not. Or we will be getting some more visits. But I don't think the Castle Point PD has any real appreciation for the history of this place."

Amelia used a disposable pad to swipe alcohol across the belly of a woman who was nine months pregnant, and then handed a needle to Dr. Rockford. The woman on the table was Angela Kirtch, a former manager of a dry-cleaning business, and a former resident of Newton, West Virginia. She was twenty-eight years old and when she'd last walked out of the dry cleaners after a late night getting orders ready for Monday's customers, she'd been neither involved with a man, nor pregnant.

But now she was hundreds of miles away, and, as she had been for most of the past nine months, out cold. She'd been one of their first recruits, and they'd harvested dozens of vials from her by now. Well, not her exactly. Her unborn baby. Regardless of how seamlessly a child healed in the womb, Dr. Rockford had no doubt that this child was extremely deformed by this point in the pregnancy. They'd gone to the well too often.

But that was okay. This child was never meant to come out of the well. Not alive anyway. Not for long.

"This may be our last session with Angela," he said, as he stabbed the needle into the eye of the pregnant woman's belly. The drugged body jerked, just a little, as the eye of the needle slipped through her belly button, poked through the amniotic sac and bit down into the soft, tissue-thin flesh of the unborn infant inside her. Dr. Rockford drew the stopper back, sucking fluid from the child out of the womb and into the vial in his hand. When it was full, he slid the long needle back out, and laid it on the sterilization tray in Amelia's hands.

"I'll miss her," he said. "She's been a model patient."

Amelia nodded. "She has been a perfect donor," she agreed. "But once we take her downstairs, our real work can finally begin."

Rockford put a hand on Amelia's waist and drew her close, careful not to upset the tray in her hand. He bent to brush his mouth across hers, and then with his tongue, traced moisture across her swollen pink lips.

"I know you're impatient to begin," he said. "But it's close now, I promise. The first of our children is almost ready."

She sighed and nibbled at his ear, whispering, "I want to put on the robes, at last."

"You'll have thirteen chances for that," he answered, running a wide palm along her back, before squeezing her hip firmly. "Now c'mon, we have some other work to do first, or we won't be ready when this one is."

Rockford clicked off the light switch on their way out of room two, and pulled the door shut behind him.

On the bed, Angela Kirtch shivered as tremors rippled across the stretched skin of her abdomen. In her head, she saw visions of a gnarled child, with blackened skin and long needle teeth, climbing her from calf to thigh to middle. The creature had three eyes, though one of them hung useless from its melted face, an orb that blinked milky white blankness. The thing ripped open her thin robe and bent with its yellow dagger teeth to suck from her breast.

"Momma," it growled. "Hungry."

In her mind Angela cried at the pain and the warm spray of blood that dappled the sheets and ran in tiny rivers down her ribs. "Not me," she moaned. "Not me."

CHAPTER SEVENTEEN

David slapped some more black goop down in the cracks of Aunt Elsie's driveway. The July sun was out in furnace fury, and he could feel his back turning red. Still, he left the shirt on the front porch. Cancer warnings be damned; he intended to come back from this summer break both in shape, and deeply tanned. Maybe there wasn't really time for girls in an athlete's life during the on-season . . . but he wanted to at least provoke the opportunity to say no. Or yes. Who said he wouldn't break the rules?

He used the dandelion-pulling tool his aunt had kept in the shed to dredge some more weeds out of the furrow that ran and branched across the bottom half of the drive. David liked to see results fast, so he'd gouge out a section, take a breath, and then fill it with tar before moving on to the next area for weeding. He guessed the exercise was going to take the entire afternoon. Elsie had a short driveway, but it sure had a lot of cracks.

Again his mind slipped back to the girl with the pink hair. Brenda. And the visit from the cop. At first he'd assumed Brenda had ditched him, but over the past couple days he'd realized that something else had happened. Something far more sinister.

After the cop had left, he'd called the number Brenda had given him, and on the fourth ring, it switched over to voice mail.

"Hey," a bored-sounding girl's voice drawled. "You got the Bean. But the Bean's out bopping somewhere else. Or more likely, I'm asleep. So leave me yer action and I'll get back to you after the dream is over. Or not. Girl's prerogative, right?"

The phone clicked and David left his message, just saying he was the guy she'd helped walk it off the other night, and to give him a call.

When he hung up, he had, inexplicably, felt like crying.

Now as he scooped gunk from the bucket and filled up the cracks, he again saw Brenda's semi-obscene T-shirt, and the spark in her eyes as she poked fun at the bartender, and him.

"Where did you go, Brenda?" he whispered. Maybe it was the fumes of the tar, or the heat of the sun, but at that moment, David vowed that he was going to find out.

It was early at the Clam Shack, and a Wednesday to boot, but there were already a few cars in the lot as David chained his bike to a water pipe on the outside of the bar. Some kids were trail-biking in the lot behind the bar, and their laughter echoed across the night. David felt a surge of melancholy in his heart as he watched them use the hills to accelerate on their way to a plywood ramp at the base of the trail.

He remembered when riding had just been for fun. He'd spent hours every day on trails like those, jumping ramps, nearly breaking arms and legs in bad landings. He'd ridden for miles on empty asphalt and taken to mountain biking for a change in adventure. But somewhere along the line, biking had become competition and work, not so much fun.

"Cool it, jag-off," he chided himself. "You're just trying to get out of riding tomorrow. And tomorrow, it's time to get back on the ridge."

Tonight, however, he intended to try to get some answers about what had happened the other night.

The screen door slammed shut behind him, and Joe looked up from behind the bar, an instant look of annoyance on his face. Then his features relaxed. "Oh, it's you again," he said, wiping a place clear at the bar with a dirty-looking white rag. "Come for another dose of Guinness, have ya?"

David sat down on a stool near the spot Joe had cleaned. "Actually yes, I think I will. But tonight I'm not drinking a gallon of it. That shit'll kill ya."

Joe winked. "Lightweight," he said, pushing the pint of impenetrable stout across the bar. "That Brenda Bean drank you right under the table."

"That's what I came to talk to you about actually," David said. "The police say she's disappeared."

Joe's face lost its humor. "Yeah, I know," he said. "They were already here. I told them she was here drinking with you. Sorry if that was a problem."

David shook his head. "I didn't expect to have to face the cops with a hangover the size of Montana, but no, it's fine that you told them. You know I woke up alone at the table. But I'm trying to find out who she might have talked to while I was out. You know, before she left the bar that night."

"I've already gone over this with the cops. It was busy that night, a lot of people going on. I lost track of you two after the first hour or so. Wasn't 'til closing that I realized you were passed out over there. Brenda? No idea who she talked to that night."

"Can you at least remember some of the people who were here? Maybe some of them would remember something."

Joe laughed. "Yeah, sure I can," he said. "But it's not going to do you much good. Half the town was here that night, and you don't know the names from Adam. If the cops can't make tails of the list, you certainly aren't going to be able to. But I already told them the folks I could recall, and my memory was a lot sharper about that night a couple days ago than it is now. I know that Hank Fellers was here and Rhonda Beam. Jason, Brill and Brian all came down after the grocery closed, and Jill Sornholt and Betsy Taylor were on the make as usual. I think old man Briller stopped in at one point, and I remember the Terror Twins making a swing through. Then there was Maggie, Pete, John Jr., and Arnie Jenkins over in one of the booths, and I remember a coupla guys came in from Brookstone, though I don't know their names."

David had tried to scribble down as many of those names as possible on a pad he'd carried in his pocket, and he put up his hand to slow Joe down.

"Wait a minute," he begged. "Do you know the last names of Jason and Prill and Brian?"

"It's Brill," Joe said, "And no. But they're all stockers at the grocery. Easy to find."

"What about Maggie, Pete and John?"

"Maggie Sawyer," Joe said. "Pete's her husband. Don't ask me how John fits into things. He lives with 'em though." The bartender winked at that.

"I don't want to know," David said. "Who are . . . the 'Terror Twins' did you say?"

Joe rolled an eye. "So-called. Coupla losers from out on the ridge. They've got a shack down the little road just before the cutoff for the Castle House Lodge. They come in here every week and roll out with a keg. Don't know how they put away that much shit all the time, but then again, they don't *do* anything else 's far as I know."

The door rattled behind him, and Joe waved. "Here are a couple of our regulars, if you want to check things out with them. But I'll warn you, don't get too close, or you may wake up with a very funny feeling in your stomach when your drunk wears off. It's called, 'Oh my God. What did I eat last night?'"

"Clam Shack special?" David asked.

Joe winked, and then stepped over to greet the newcomers and put on a completely gracious smile. "How can I help you ladies? Stoli and soda?"

A haggard brunette slapped the stool next to her and said, "Sure Joe, and how about your ass on this seat."

"Working, Jill, you know that."

The other woman, who looked to be packing about 180 pounds around a five-foot frame moaned. "Oh c'mon Joe, you say that every night."

"That's 'cuz every night I'm working," he answered and slid their vodkas across.

David took a deep breath. Was it worth this? Then he slipped off his stool and repositioned himself next to Jill.

"Hi," he said.

"Mmmm, fresh meat." Jill grinned, taking a sip of her drink, but not taking her eyes off of him. With one finger, she stretched the front neckline of her V-neck T-shirt a little lower, making sure that he could catch a glimpse of the ample cleavage there.

"Look," David said, "I was here the other night with a girl I think you might know. Brenda Bean?"

"Yeah, yeah, I know her," Jill said, holding up a hand to stop David from going any further. "And I already told the police I don't know where she went that night. They talked to just about everyone they could find who was at the Shack the night Brenda disappeared."

"Did you at least see who she might have been talking to?"

"Look sweetheart, keeping my eyes on the young sluts isn't what I'm about when I'm here, okay? I don't play that team, and usually, we're working different fields anyway. I know she was here that night, and now that I see you, I seem to remember seeing her with you a couple times. But that's all I know."

David backed off, thanking them, and drained the rest of his Guinness before putting it back on the bar.

"Getcha another?" Joe asked, instantly materializing to take the empty.

"Naw," David said. "I got what I came for."

CHAPTER EIGHTEEN

It was nighttime at Castle House, but the asylum was not sleeping peacefully. On the first floor, Amelia was running barefoot down the thick-carpeted art-wing hallway. The moans had started an hour before, and she'd ignored them at first, but they'd redoubled in the past few minutes.

She'd finally gone upstairs to check on Angela Kirtch, and realized with one look at the woman's pain-etched face and arched back, that the time was NOW. She took the stairs two at a time, turned the corner and reached the door with the red *X*, panting. She threw open the door and called down the stairs. "It's time," she cried out into the darkness. "Barry, do you hear me? Our first baby is coming. Right now. We have to hurry."

In seconds, Rockford's face emerged from the shadow, and he vaulted up the stairs. "I was just getting the crèche ready," he said. "Do you have the instruments laid out?"

Amelia nodded. "Everything is ready."

"Then let's begin."

Together they hurried up the stairs to room one.
When they reached the room, Amelia flipped the
lights on as Barry went straight to the bedside. He
put a wide palm on Angela's distended belly, slowly
moving it around and gently pressing, as he stroked
her forehead. Then he lifted the thin cotton robe,
and eased her legs outward in a V so that he could
examine her. The bed was already slick with blood,
and he shook his head.

"She's already crowning," he said. "Let's get her
downstairs, now!"

Amelia ran about the room, disconnecting heart
monitors and propping open the door. Then she took
the wheel locks off the bed with her foot and helped
Barry shove the bed through the door and into the
hallway. There was an elevator just around the corner. On the bed, Angela's entire body tightened, her
fingers clawing into the mattress. Even though she
was still deeply tranquilized, her breathing quickened, and as the contraction peaked, she screamed.
Her eyelids fluttered open, but Amelia could only
see the whites of her eyeballs.

Barry opened the elevator as Angela screamed
again, and when the doors slid open, he stepped
inside and pulled the bed after him. Then he pulled
a key out of his pocket, slipped it into the lock on
the elevator controls and turned it, before pressing
the button marked simply, B.

Angela moaned. "Oh God, it hurts," she slurred.

"And so it begins," Barry answered.

Brenda woke to the distant sound of screaming. She
didn't know that's what it was at first. Because the
first thing that crossed her dazed and reeling consciousness was that she seemed to be paralyzed.
She swam out of oblivion slowly, amid an echo of
people calling her name. Then she became aware of

the dark around her, a palpable heavy darkness that swam across her vision like a relentless widow's veil.

"Who's there?" she tried to ask in the black, but all that came out of her mouth was a thin hiss.

Her body felt encased in amber, taut and immovable. She breathed, and when she forced her eyes to stare hard in the dark, she could see tiny motes of dust glowing and pinwheeling in the abyss.

Her heart began to pound as she struggled to move her fingers, her arms, her legs, and nothing happened.

"Oh my God," she tried to say. But all her body did was whisper, "Gawwww."

In her mind, she slapped herself. "Cool it, calm down," she said. "You had a bad night, probably drank more Guinness than you shoulda, and maybe someone spiked it, who knows? But you'll sweat it off. Chill out."

She closed her eyes and concentrated on feeling her body. Everything seemed warm in a fuzzy, nerves-rubbed-raw kind of way. But she didn't hurt. Just felt . . . sensitive. God, what had she done last night? And where was she? This was definitely not her bedroom. It didn't smell right, for one thing. The air here seemed to taste . . . old . . . in her nostrils. And this bed did not have the dent her butt had worn in it over the last ten years. She'd gone home with someone . . . but who?

She remembered the kid at the Shack . . . David, his name was. She vaguely remembered getting him water from the bar, 'cuz the Guinness had knocked him on his ass. She remembered thinking how sweetly pathetic he looked, passed out on the table, arms flat out in front of him, mouth half open. And then some lug had come up to hit on her, and she'd brushed him off. But after that . . .

Then she heard something cry out in the darkness. Something far away . . . but not outside the building, she thought, whatever the building might be.

It happened again, and she knew without a doubt that it was a muffled, but painful scream. Someone else was here. And someone was hurting her.

Was she going to be next? Brenda tried to keep calm, but she couldn't help but think of scenes from the movies *Saw* or *Hostel*. She felt sure now that she hadn't gone home with someone for a one-nighter. She'd been too tied to David for that, and there's no way he took anyone home that night. So where was she? Who had taken her home?

And what was he going to do to her when he got here?

From far off, she heard the scream again, only this time it didn't seem to end, only ululating in descending and then reascending waves of pain.

Oh shit, Brenda thought, and redoubled her attempts to move her arms and legs.

Officer Christy Sorensen cut the engine of the smoking, rattling '78 Olds on the side of 190 just before the turnoff to Castle House. She stepped out of the car and pressed the door shut as quietly as possible, forcing the lock to catch by thumping it with her hip.

Christy took a deep breath to steel herself for what was to come as she stared down the dark path that led to the asylum. Tree branches swayed in the gentle night breeze, and somewhere, an owl shrieked. Whether it was from frustration or victory at having swooped an unsuspecting mouse, she didn't know. Right now she wondered if she was about to become predator or prey.

She hadn't envisioned police work as walking down a dark road toward an asylum after dark, *that*

was for sure. Her heart beat double time as she
started down the path, trying to walk softly, but
cringing when twigs snapped beneath the soft rubber soles of her gym shoes. She'd worn her old running shoes, along with dark jeans and a black
T-shirt. At least while she was outside, she hoped it
would help her blend into the scenery if anyone inside was looking out a window as she approached.

When she neared the building, she slipped to the
side of the road, trying to walk as close to the tree
line as possible to stay out of sight.

There were only a few lights on in the old building as Christy crept up on it. One of the rooms over-
looking the ridge was lit and she saw what she
thought was the shadow of a figure crossing back
and forth inside. A couple windows on the main
floor burned bright, though the shades were drawn.
She could see the faint glow of light emanating from
the window wells around the foundation as well, so
someone was in the basement.

Christy crouched at the edge of the tree line and
considered the building. She could see the old ivy-
covered front brick and wide-stepped entryway to
her left. She was not going to just walk in the front
door, that was for sure. She needed another entrance.

Still crouching, she ran down the length of the
side of the building and came around to the back of
the old hotel. Long-abandoned gardens—now just
circles of cracked red brick and flagstone edging
filled with towering bushes and weeds—dotted the
clearing there that sloped down to disappear into a
forested gully. Nearer the building were some kind
of small garage or gardener's shed, and a wide
paving-stone patio. A large two-door back entryway, covered by a green awning, led out to the patio.
It was a possible entry point, but Christy worried

that it still might open into someplace too public inside the asylum.

Her eyes continued to peer down at the far end of the long mansion, where a gravel path wound around the building to end in a turnaround near another nondescript white door inset in the building. This one had no awning or adornments of any kind. Some kind of rear delivery entrance, she surmised, and darted across the patio and gravel turnaround. When she reached the door, she dropped to all fours with her back to the asylum and looked around as she caught her breath. The night remained still. In the distance, the faint purple skim of the sunset still colored the horizon, but just barely. The stars had clearly inherited the sky, and the heavens were pinpricked with a million tiny lights. The moon hadn't yet risen, but the stars gave enough illumination that Christy could see the tops of the trees all the way across the gulley and up the other side where the hills climbed back to 190.

As she reached up to grasp the doorknob, Christy froze.

From somewhere inside the building, someone screamed. She didn't move a muscle, though her chest felt gripped in a vise. The noise came again, a long, pitiful cry. And again. Then it grew shrill, an extended *"eeeeyiiiiahhhhooooooh"* of someone in horrible pain. Christy stayed hunched by the back door for several minutes as the series of short screams ignited into one long crescendo of misery.

All of her police instincts told her to force her way inside and rescue the poor soul from whatever torment she was being subjected to. But she squelched them. This was a place of medicine, and theoretically, the doctor inside was helping the crying woman. For Christy to barge in without cause would not only blow her cover for the night, it would put the doctor firmly on guard against the Castle Point police, and likely earn her a suspension if the doctor decided to pursue a wrongful trespass suit.

Without warning, the crying muffled, and then disappeared entirely. Christy counted to a hundred, holding her back to the door, and then pulled out her lock-pick case from a back pocket. Time to slip inside and see what the hell was going on in there.

She tried the easy way first, slipping a skeleton key into the old knob. Gently pushing and jittering the key in the door, she pushed it to the right and tried turning the knob slightly at the same time. It stuck the first time, refusing to budge. But then she pulled the key back a hair, twisted it again, and something clicked.

Easy as pie, she thought, and smiled to herself. Pressing her shoulder and hip to the door, she pushed it open, but as slowly as possible, in case someone was nearby, or the door hinges squeaked.

There was a slight squeal as the door arced inward, and Christy gritted her teeth. Nothing she could do about it. She quickly pushed open the door, slipped inside, and then gently pushed it shut.

She was in a small black-and-white-tiled foyer. Two hallways branched off of it, one going straight ahead, the other to the right. *Coin toss,* she thought, and decided to slip to the right first. She guessed the one leading straight ahead might move directly to the center of the building, where people might be . . . and she wanted to move around them rather than fall straight into their laps.

The hall was dark, but Christy's eyes were adjusted to low light from walking outside, and she managed to see enough shadow to avoid tripping over a chair and a table set in a corner where the corridor took an abrupt left. There was light at the end of that tunnel, and she stepped carefully the closer she got to its end.

The end was a wide-open lobby-style room, a handful of couches and coffee tables scattered about. The room wasn't lit, but there was a bright source of light from farther down the way to the left, where Christy imagined the main offices of the asylum were housed. She opted to avoid that area, and crossed the lobby, coming to another branching corridor. But this one didn't just wind on. It passed a narrow stairway on the right, and Christy hurriedly crossed the heavy carpet and walked up the first few steps. The stairway turned in an L before she reached the top, and found herself standing at the end of a long, empty hall.

Jesus, she thought. *Doesn't this place ever fuckin' end? One hall after another!*

But this one had a series of doors—hotel suites—breaking the pin-striped wallpaper of its inside wall. She began to walk down the corridor, watching the numbers go up—2015, 2017, 2019, 2021.

And then suddenly the old number plates stopped, and a new one appeared, this one simpler . . . and out of sequence. In a simple white-on-black sign, the room was designated as "13."

Christy tried the knob, and it turned easily. She looked around the hallway, and, assured that nobody was coming, she pushed the door open and peered inside. It was dark, but starlight filtered into the room through the thin gauze curtains, enough that Christy could see that the room was empty. One perfectly made-up bed pressed against the left wall, while an old bureau took up the opposite. The room felt pensive in the blue twilight . . . as if it was only waiting to be filled. Waiting impatiently.

She eased the door shut, and tried the next room, also newly labeled, "12."

There's something about the aura a human being exudes. Maybe it's just the rhythm of breath, or the animal faculties in our back brain that still instantly pick up the scent of prey. But this time when the door opened, Christy knew before she could even make out anything inside the room that it was occupied.

She instinctively began to ease the door closed, but then she remembered why she was here in the first place. Slipping inside, she eased the door shut behind her and stared at the figure on the bed, waiting for her eyes to adjust to the shadows. Female, light hair, young—in her twenties or thirties. She couldn't tell much else, as the woman lay sleeping beneath the covers.

Quietly she tiptoed up to the edge of the bed to get a better look at the woman's face. With visions of the sleeping woman coming to and screaming an alarm to the whole floor, Christy's heart was thudding like a jackhammer, but she forced herself to go ahead and lean closer. These patients were supposed to be pretty heavily sedated, from what the doctor had said the other day, and from the slow, deep breathing of this one, she supposed that was true. Plus there was a heavy white strap of gauze across the back of the woman's head . . . Apparently this woman wasn't just here for psych reasons; she'd had cranial trauma.

She snapped her fingers in front of the woman's face, *click, click,* but there was no response.

Stepping away from the bed, Christy found a string hanging from the ceiling in the closet, and pulled it, flooding the room with yellow light. She closed the closet most of the way, and then pulled out a folded wad of papers from her back pocket—the fax of missing persons she'd gotten from Oak Falls PD.

It only took a minute for a positive ID.

Carrie Sanddanz, twenty-nine, Oak Falls.

Reported missing just three days ago.

Christy's stomach contracted into a snowball. Why would this woman have ended up in an asylum supposedly for abused and pushed-over-the-edge women when she was just reported missing this week?

She looked back and forth between the picture and the woman's sleeping face, confirming again and again that this had to be one and the same person. Christy put her hand on the woman's forehead, and the woman sighed in her sleep.

Christy pulled back, and then stood over the bed, in conflict over what exactly to do now. She'd found one of the missing persons at a mental institution. An institution she had no warrant to be inside. Absently, her fingers wound together and Christy did what she always did when she was nervous and lost in thought.

She cracked her knuckles.

Oh crap, she thought as the sound snapped through empty air like a cap gun. The figure on the bed stirred and Christy backed away fast. She was almost out of the room before she remembered the closet light. "Oh come on," she moaned silently, and then hurriedly retraced her steps to pull the string to douse the light, before slipping back out of the room and into the well-lit hallway.

Christy didn't notice the hand that rose in the darkness from the bed, or see Carrie's eyes flicker open, to stare in blurry incomprehension at the shadows of the strange room. She didn't notice Carrie slowly roll to her side, clutching at her belly, and then roll to the edge of the bed, tentatively feeling the open black space with her leg for the floor. She didn't hear the closet light click back on.

After the door shut behind her, Christy's eyes blinked and teared at the sudden change in light from dark room to electric-lit hall, and nervously she looked back and forth as she wiped her cheeks and began to creep again along the hallway toward the next number, which she guessed—and was right—would be eleven.

Again the knob turned without issue, but as soon as she poked her head in, she realized that she didn't dare enter. The dark-haired woman on the bed tossed and turned, kicking sheets away and mumbling something in her sleep. Christy pulled the door shut and proceeded to room ten.

This room was again quiet as a crypt, but another young woman lay prone on the bed, hands tucked to her obviously pregnant belly. Using the closet light, again she was able to positively ID the woman as one of the missing persons on the Oak Falls list. Trisha Kacek, thirty-two, reported missing two weeks ago after a night at a bar.

Room nine held another missing Oak Falls woman, Alina Prus. And room eight hosted a former cleaning woman from Oak Falls—Becky Mills.

Christy's skin was crawling by the time she pulled the door closed on room eight. If she kept going down the rest of the hallway, she had no doubt that she'd find the rest of the names on the list that Oak Falls had sent her; some of them missing for more than six months.

But why were they all here? They certainly all couldn't be crazy, unless something was going on with the water in Oak Falls. And why hadn't the asylum been in contact with the families?

A room at the end of the hall was open—Christy

could see light pouring out onto the carpet. She stayed still and listened, praying that nobody was down there who would discover her here. But after waiting a minute with no sign of movement, she crept down the hall and pressed herself to the edge of the door frame. The lights were on in the room, but the room was empty. Not even the bed was there. Christy stepped inside, and noticed spots of something dark on the carpeting. She bent down and rubbed a finger across it, and blanched when her suspicions were met. The tip of her index finger was smeared a bright, warm red.

"Shit," she whispered. The screams earlier . . . they must have come from here. What was the doctor doing to this poor woman? And why?

The spots led out of the room, and then she lost them, but after searching around for a couple seconds, she found another drop of blood. And a few feet farther, yet another. They led to the end of the hallway, to a small service-elevator door.

She thought about it for a minute, but didn't touch the button. No, she was here to try to figure out what was going on, and walking right into the O.R. in the midst of an operation probably wasn't the best way to surreptitiously manage that.

Instead, she doubled back to the stairway she'd passed and decided to slip downstairs and see if anyone was about on the main floor. She wasn't sure where the operating suite was, but she guessed from the freshness of the blood, that the doctor was otherwise occupied. She looked down the main stairway and saw no one; it opened to a broad lobby area, so she hurried down the stairs and pressed herself to a wall on the close side, trying in vain to see who was running the floor. She was glad it was in vain, but she had no doubt that someone was close by.

Christy moved down the lobby to a hall, and

when she reached the end, recognized the evaluation room she'd been in with David just the other day. She stepped inside again, although this time, the room was a little different.

Oh it still had a stainless-steel sink and an adjustable bed covered with paper "body Kleenex." But this time, as Christy looked around, she realized there were other things of interest in the room. Clues, if you will.

Like the photo of Barry Rockford shaking hands with President Bill Clinton. She looked closer and noted the caption: AT THE NATIONAL SCIENCE COUNCIL 1998 GENETIC RESEARCH AWARDS CEREMONY. And framed on the wall beside it, a plaque from the event, which below Rockford's name read IN RECOGNITION OF YOUR PIONEERING WORK IN EMBRYONIC STEM CELL RESEARCH.

On the opposite wall, an article hung in a black wooden frame. It had a picture of Rockford, but the headline said this particular mention wasn't laudatory. As Christy read the first few paragraphs, the hair began to stand up on the back of her neck.

GENETIC DOC DEFROCKED IN ETHICS SCANDAL

Barry Rockford, PhD, once considered one of the nation's preeminent genetic researchers, was dismissed yesterday from the faculty of the Massachusetts Institute of Technology after it was revealed that for the past seven months, he had been engaged in forbidden experiments on the unborn children of more than three dozen women.

It's a shocking turn of events to members of the MIT Board of Regents, who were under the impression that Dr. Rockford's lab was currently being used to test the potential uses for adult stem cells. A $1.5 million grant from the National Institute of Health to the university was allocated to Dr. Rockford and his team for the purpose of developing a system whereby adults could bank their own stem cells for a future time when they needed the cells' recuperative powers.

For the past two decades, stem cells have been looked to by the science community as the fountain of youth; all that was necessary was the right key to unlock the fountain. Stem cells exist in all living creatures, and are the body's building blocks for the creation of new structures, whether skin, muscle or bone. Stanley Kooper, chair of the board of regents, explains, "The theory is that if a person banked their healthy stem cells, in later life when the body is diseased and decaying, those youthful stem cells could be utilized to regrow vital tissues and return the body to a healthier state. Some speculate that stem cells could replace surgery, essentially regrowing an old body to a youthful form from the inside out. Ailing hearts and wrinkled skin could be a thing of the past if the power of stems could be harnessed by medicine."

But the most powerful stem cells exist in unborn babies. Scientists discovered years ago that prior to birth, an unborn fetus can heal from in-uterine operations without scarring. However, when stem-cell research began to focus on this specialized genetic fountain of youth, ethicists from around the world demanded that such experimentation be banned.

When it was discovered that Dr. Rockford had provided a false plan for his federally funded research program and was, in fact, conducting stem-cell research on a parade of women who came to the MIT campus with the promise of a paycheck if Dr. Rockford could be allowed to extract stem-cell material from their unborn

children, the university board stated that it had
no recourse but to demand the researcher's res-
ignation.

Christy felt a chill across the back of her neck
and flipped around, but the shadows outside of the
exam room didn't move. As she looked out at the
empty hallway, however, she realized that the Dr.
Rockford depicted on the walls of this exam room
was not at all the psychiatrist she had met a few
days earlier. He set up this asylum in the middle of
nowhere to help "troubled women."

Troubled *pregnant* women.

Women who happen to have recently all been reported missing.

"He isn't a psychiatrist at all," Christy whispered
to herself. "And he sure as hell hasn't stopped doing
whatever the hell he was up to at MIT."

Somewhere far away, someone screamed.

"What the fuck *are* they doing here?" Christy whispered and crept out of the exam room and into the
hall. She turned a corner and saw the room with the
red *X* across the door, and carefully, looking from
side to side every two seconds, approached it. As
she put her hand on the doorknob, she heard the
scream again, and this time, she knew with certainty
that it was definitely coming from downstairs.

Carefully, she began to turn the knob, not really
sure what she was going to do if the door opened.

"Hey, Rockford, you around?" someone yelled
from the hallway she'd just left. Christy let go of the
door as if it were a hot coal and darted around
the corner, ducking behind one of the couches in
the darkened open lounge.

A man in blue jeans and a dark button-down shirt
stepped into view. He was whistling . . . "Summertime
Blues" she recognized.

He passed the door with the red *X*, the whistle receding. Christy stood and started toward the hallway she and the man had both come from, but before she got to the door downstairs, she heard the whistle returning.

"Shit," she said under her breath, and ducked back to the couch.

"Hey, Rockford man, where are you!" the man shouted again. A few seconds later, the door Christy had been about to open, opened. Dr. Rockford's chiseled features poked through the frame looking around.

"There you are," the whistler proclaimed, stopping from his ambling pace in the outer hall and heading toward the door with the red *X*.

"Not now, Carl," Dr. Rockford said. His voice was hard, and the hand he held out to stop Carl was stained red. "We've got an emergency situation right here."

"Yikes, Doc, what's going on?"

"Birth," Rockford said simply. "The samples are in the fridge. They're marked with today's date. Please just take them, and leave the payment in the office. I'll talk to you Tuesday night."

"No problem," Carl said. "Good luck."

"Thanks." Rockford nodded, and pulled the door closed with a bloody hand, leaving a smear on the outer edge. Christy watched Carl disappear down the hall, counted to ten, and then followed.

She tiptoed down the hall, hanging tight to the wall, and saw the man step into a room at the far end. She ducked into the main exam room again, and waited until she saw him come back out, now holding a small plastic box. He didn't look back, just walked straight back out, the way they had both (she assumed anyway) come in. Again she counted, this time to twenty, and followed.

As Christy opened the door to the back drive of the asylum, she saw a flash of red lights, and then the side panel of a van as it spun around and headed toward the front of the old hotel. The insignia on the side was the same as the one she'd seen just a couple nights before.

INNOVATIVE INDUSTRIES.

"What exactly is he running here?" she mumbled under her breath, while she carefully opened and quietly pulled the back door closed behind her. She ran along the back wall of the asylum, stopping just once to peer into a window well where orange light leaked out from the basement. But a shade of some kind blocked her view, and she couldn't see anything but the glow.

The red lights of the van were on 190 heading back toward town when she slipped inside the tree line at the edge of the asylum's entryway. The air was hauntingly silent, as Christy opened the driver's door and slipped back into the Olds. The noise of it slamming felt like a gunshot, but she didn't turn the key right away to start the car and get away. Instead, she stared at the wavering lights of the hotel turned asylum below. What was she going to tell the chief? He'd kill her if she admitted to what could get her slammed with a breaking-and-entering charge. But she had to let him know that there were missing persons inside. All of her suspicions had been true.

Still stumped on how to approach it, Christy shook her head and started the engine, easing the car out onto the highway. She didn't notice the ghostly white figure behind her, stepping slowly up the gravel path from the asylum toward the road.

But the figure didn't care. The woman held the pain in her middle and put one foot in front of the other.

She only knew that she had to keep walking. Something warm and wet coated her thighs. She had to keep moving.

Walk, Walk, Walk, was all her mind said.

And soon she was on the gravel shoulder of 190, staring at the red taillights of Christy's Olds, cotton gown flapping in the slight breeze behind her, and showing the ghostly white of her thighs and back as she plodded forward.

The ride would have been nice, a distant part of her cried. But the rest of her just focused on walking. And singing a little song to keep her going. She didn't really know the words so she just hummed until she got to the chorus. "Because hell, hell is for children," she whispered in a voice that disappeared like smoke on a bitter wind.

CHAPTER NINETEEN

Sometimes the scenery got old. Sometimes being a cyclist felt terminal. In the best of times, the feeling of the summer breeze slipping down the back of his neck to riffle through his shirt, cooling the sweat and pushing him on toward a new track record . . . or just an enjoyable training sprint, made him feel good to be alive.

But other times, like today, David cursed himself for ever involving himself in the sport. He gasped with every press of his foot to the pedal, struggling to keep the bike in motion as he pumped his way up the steepest curve on the 190 just a mile or so outside of town. *This is what chain gangs feel like,* he thought, imagining the whip coming down on his back to force him to one more effort. He wondered if he'd ever really get the feeling back again. When he'd first started out, almost every ride was magic, a secret place where he went in full view. It was him against gravity, and he sometimes felt at one with the machine he rode as he struggled to escape the chains of physics.

But ever since he'd washed out of the Olympic team, riding had felt different. Truth be told, it had felt different before then, which was maybe why he'd faltered on that last important ride. He hadn't gotten into riding to win, he'd gotten into it to ride.

But it didn't feel like riding right now . . . it felt like he was being punished. The bike finally reached the top of the ridge, and David stifled the urge to leap from the bike and lie down on the gravel at the side of the road. "C'mon, man," he prodded himself. "This is the payoff."

Because with that, he spurred the pedals a couple more times and then pulled his feet back, letting the wheels have their head. The bike careened down the long, winding road, which thankfully remained empty of traffic. He kicked his feet into it a couple times, increasing the breakneck speed until the air whistled in his ears. The rush almost felt like the old days, and he took a couple of deep breaths as he let the bike go.

The turnoff for the asylum was just ahead, and David had set that as his training mark point. It was ten miles from here back to town, so a twenty-mile round trip. Not a lot of miles, but when the hills are steep, it was a solid workout; better than any you'd get at the gym.

He skidded to a stop at the front of the asylum entry road and paused. There was a sign at the front of the drive that hadn't been there the other day.

OUTDOOR HANDYMAN WANTED.
CUT GRASS, TRIM BUSHES, PAINT.
1–2 DAYS PER WEEK.
SUMMER ONLY. INQUIRE WITHIN.

"Hmmm," David mused aloud. "I could use some pocket cash. And I'm already riding out this way every day. Some more exercise could only help the training . . ."

He punched foot to pedal and rode in toward the asylum.

"Chief, we need to get a warrant for the asylum."

Christy shook her head, paced across the room and tried it another way.

"Chief, you were right. That Dr. Rockford is dirty. We need to do a bust on the asylum."

No, that isn't right either, she thought.

"You know, whatever you've got to tell him, it'll be easier if you just go in and get it over with. He doesn't bite, not usually. And anyway, you're making me dizzy pacing back and forth like that."

"Sorry, Matt. I know I'm being ridiculous, but after the screwup last time . . . I just want to do this right."

"Go in and just say what's on your mind," Captain Ryan suggested. "I find that always works best."

"You're right," she agreed, and took a deep breath.

Chief Maitlin was hidden behind a tall newspaper front page, and Christy stood in the doorway for several seconds waiting to gain his attention. Finally she cleared her throat and he jumped, just a hair. Well, really the newspaper jumped . . . Chief wasn't the type to move much. The newspaper slowly lowered to the desk and two scowling eyes met her own.

"Aren't you supposed to be on the street?" he asked.

"Yeah," she said. "But Chief, I've gotta talk to you about the asylum. I think that you were . . ."

Just then the phone rang and he put up a hand as he answered it. "Castle Point PD. Yeah. Yeah. When? Okay. Yes, yes we'll send somebody. Don't do anything until we get there."

With a groan he eased his bulk from the chair as he dropped the phone back in its cradle. He stepped right past Christy but motioned for her to follow.

"C'mon, you can tell me on the way. There's a nutcase from your mental hospital walking around on Main," he said.

"Chief, that's what I wanted to talk to you about," she said. "They're not nut jobs."

"Well, this one's wandering around wearing nothing but a robe and a bandage on her head in the middle of the day. I'd call that a little left of center, wouldn't you?"

"Not if you've been kidnapped by a Dr. Frankenstein," Christy shot back. "Chief, we have to help her. We have to help *all* of them."

He opened the door to the back parking lot to let her through and pointed to his cruiser. "Get in. And let's hear it. Let's hear it quickly."

As he eased the car out of the lot, she told him about staking out the asylum the night before. He flinched when she talked about using her key to gain entrance to the back of the old hotel, but didn't say anything. When she was done, he still stayed silent. Christy felt her stomach turning to ice as she awaited his verdict. But then he was pulling over just outside of Smythe's Grocery, and as he put the car in park, said only, "We'll talk back at the station."

Then he was pulling himself out of the car, and Christy followed, noting the small crowd of people standing just a few yards away. She saw a white-clad figure in the middle of the throng, and groaned as they reached the people. She knew who it was. She'd stared at the woman's sleeping face the night before. Hell, she'd used finger snaps to try to wake her. It was Carrie Sanddanz. And she looked awful. The bandage around her head was stained a brownish red in back, and her eyes looked wild and unfocused. The group of people contained her as the woman walked back and forth, trying in vain to find an exit. She was barefoot, and Christy could see the stains of dried blood between her toes.

"Chief," she whispered. "I saw her last night. She walked all this way barefoot?"

"And wounded," he said. "Help me get her into the squad."

"All right," he called and broke into the circle. "Let us get this woman some help."

An older man clapped the chief on the shoulder. "Thanks for coming so quick, Chief. I saw her walking down the side of the road out here when I pulled into the lot to open the store, and knew something was wrong."

The chief nodded. "I'm guessing she's from the new asylum outside of town."

"Well, something for sure's not right with her." The man shook his head so fast his jowls wagged. "She ain't said a word since the bunch of us came over here to try to talk to her. We thought we should try to keep her from walking anymore, but she wouldn't go inside the store."

Christy took the woman's arm near the elbow. It felt thin and cold. The pale, naked skin of Carrie's back and butt was exposed for all to see through the loosely tied gown, but the poor woman didn't seem to notice her indecency. "C'mon, hon," Christy said softly. "We're going to get you some help."

Just then, a black car pulled up in the supermar-

ket parking lot and came to a stop right next to the
group. Two doors popped open instantly, and a
man and woman got out and ran to the woman.
"There you are, Carrie," Dr. Rockford said, pushing
his way into the mob of people to take the woman's
arm as Christy still held the other. "We've been
looking all over for you."

The doctor surveyed the group of people and
nodded perfunctorily at them, including the police.
"Thank you for trying to help," he said. "We'll take it
from here."

Rockford started to pull Carrie away, and his nurse
reached out to take Carrie's arm away from Christy.
But the chief set a beefy hand over Rockford's arm.
"Just a minute," he said. "Who are you, and what
makes you think you can waltz in and take this
woman out of my custody?"

The doctor's eyes widened, and then he gave an
"aww shucks" grin and apologized. "I'm sorry, Officer," he said. "I should have told you right away. My
name is Dr. Rockford, from the Castle House Asylum down on 190. Your officer here—Christy, is
it?—came out to visit us just the other day. She can
vouch for me, isn't that right?"

He looked at Christy, who nodded, but still didn't
release the woman's arm. Carrie only stood still,
eyes blinking in disorientation. She looked as if
she'd simply fold up and collapse at any moment.

"Carrie is one of our patients," the doctor continued. "Somehow she got out last night, and after we
searched the grounds, we came looking for her in
town. We need to get her back in her bed and on her
medications. Please help us to help her."

The chief released his hold on the doctor, but
didn't break his gaze. "I'm a little concerned about
your security, Doctor. I don't want to start seeing a

parade of mental patients roaming around this town—both for their sakes, and for the safety of my people."

The doctor nodded. "It won't happen again. We're going to change our lockdown procedures today."

Then he grinned at Christy, as he pulled the limp girl away from her grasp. "Nice to see you again, Officer Sorensen."

In moments, they had stuffed the woman into the backseat of the sedan and pulled away, and the small crowd dispersed, murmuring among themselves a variety of anecdotes about crazy people.

"Chief," Christy said finally when they were all out of earshot. "How could you let him take her?"

He shrugged, staring after the black car as it rounded the block to head out of town. "What grounds did I have to keep her? She's hurt, and he's a doctor."

"But he is not helping her," she insisted. "I don't know what he's doing to her, but it's not about making her better."

"We're going to see about that," he answered, and pointed at the car. "Let's get back to the station. I think we need to have a short review of police procedure, Officer."

She didn't like the way he elongated the pronunciation, awwww-ficer. "Yes, sir," she answered, and hurried around the car. Christy didn't think she'd ever had such a long drive back to the station. The chief could make five minutes feel like an hour when he was angry. And the car ride was only the start of it.

CHAPTER TWENTY

TG rolled the keg across the dirt to the steps of the mountain shack. As he muscled it up the steps and pushed it in through the bent aluminum screen door, he thought that there was maybe nothing better in this life than a cold beer. And anyone taking a cursory look at the kitchen would quickly grasp the depth of that infatuation.

Empty beer bottles sporting a variety of brand logos lined the faded yellow countertops, though they all shared one trait in common—a six-pack of any of them would set you back less than six dollars. A Budweiser beer light glowed bright red on one wall. TG and Billy had broken into a bar in Oak Falls after hours to get that light, and they were damn proud of it—kept it lit twenty-four/seven.

But the capper was the next stop for the new keg. TG had found an old beat-up refrigerator at the side of the road one day and drafted Billy into getting it onto the back of a pickup and up the hill. Then they gutted its insides and rerouted the ice water spigot line to a plastic hose. TG now tapped the keg, hefted it into that fridge and hooked up the hose to it. When he closed the door, he pulled a mug from the freezer and pushed it into the water spigot on the outer door of the unit. In seconds, the mug was full of frothing golden goodness.

Yeah . . . there was nothing better than a cold beer.

In fact, as he thought of that, he called out to Billy. Then he stomped fast on the floor and grinned as he ground the green guts of an inch-long cockroach into the stained white linoleum.

Billy called back from the other room. "In the middle of a game," he complained.

"Nothing better than a cold beer, is there Billy?"

"How about a hot woman?" came the disembodied response.

TG scratched his balls at that and grunted. "Hmmm. Tough call," he finally decided. "Be perfect if you could combine the two."

There are times when you can almost see the thought balloon appear above somebody's head, and if anyone had been standing in the run-down shack's kitchen right then, they would have seen a big, electric neon sign pop into life above TG's head. Truth be told, he was bored. He and Billy had spent the summer picking up chicks to deliver to the asylum, and while the first few had given him a rush—hell, be honest, a hard-on—he'd started to wonder what could come next. TG wasn't the kinda guy who sat still.

Oh sure, he drank a lot of beer, and sat up here at the cabin day in, day out watching game shows on the tube and fast-forwarding through the slow parts of his porn collection. (He hated it when they tried to tack a plot onto the sex. "Show me the MILFs," he'd complain.) But at night . . . TG always had a new game plan. Over the years he'd gone from robbing convenience stores while wearing a Bill Clinton mask to busting dope dealers while pretending to be a cop. He got away with some good cash AND a lotta weed on those gigs, until the word got out on the street about the false shakedowns. Billy and he had hot-wired cars, burned down buildings and forced housewives to strip naked and walk down the center of the streets where they lived (a favorite ploy of TG's for months running). It's amazing what people will do when you hold a gun to their kids' heads.

So when Dr. Rockford had come to them with the offer of kidnapping a few women and dropping them at the old hotel for a thousand a pop, TG hadn't blinked. It was the job that was made for him . . . or he was made for the job, whatever. Point was, he didn't do it just for the money. He enjoyed stalking the girls, watching that first glint of fear in their eyes when they realized that they were being snatched. When the first tears came, it was all he could do to keep it in his pants. And actually, on the last run, he hadn't bothered to, had he?

Of course that had led to one pissed-off employer. But he didn't care too much anymore. He'd gotten all the kicks he could out of kidnapping, and now he needed a little more. It'd felt good knocking in that split tail's skull a few days ago. Maybe it was time to hire out as a hit man. Hell, he'd done just about everything else. You could get real creative in how you disposed of a body. And TG even had an old meat grinder tucked away in the back of the shed, something he'd nicked back when the grocery in Oak Falls was going under. Gave him a way to make all the iffy parts of the deer and cows they shot usable. 'Cuz when you're living on a mountain in a shack with virtually no cash, you don't waste shit.

Now maybe, he could use the damn thing to get rid of the evidence. Knocking someone off had to pay better than kidnappin', right? A couple bodies run through the grinder and then he and Billy could probably finally afford to open up that bar on the edge of town they'd been talking about since the first dope dealer they rolled. Had a good $15,000 in the bank at this point, but TG figured they needed double that. And once they owned their own bar, they'd get the kegs for the fridge a lot cheaper, he speculated, pushing his glass to the door to fill it up again.

'Cuz what was better than cold beer?

Billy poked his head around the corner, finally. "Doc called," he said. "Wants us to do another run."

"Pussy run?" TG laughed, tilting back the beer. "Did you tell him we'll be happy to when he pays us for the last one?"

Billy shook his head. He didn't smile. TG was getting worried about the boy. He always had had a bit of a stick up his ass, but he'd gotten into the game a lot more not so many months ago. These days, he never wanted to do anything off the charts. It was getting old.

"He asked what we did with the car and I told him. Then he said he'd pay us for that chick and the new one when we brought her in tonight."

TG pulled a switchblade from his pocket, and thumbed it open. The blade slipped free with a thin swish. He poked the tip of the blade between his teeth and picked at something left over from lunch.

"Doc better not stiff us," TG said. "I'm in a mood. And I don't work for free."

Billy shook his head. "He sounded all right," he said. "But I gotta tell ya . . . I'm not feeling so good about doing this anymore. I mean, what's he doing to those girls? What if he's shooting 'em full of weird chemicals and shit, like lab rats? He's gotta be doing something to 'em that makes sure they're never coming out again."

"Yeah, so what?" TG asked, now using the blade to make a thin paper-meets-brush sound as he scraped at the stubble beneath his chin.

"He's gotta be killing those gals," Billy said, his

voice rising an octave. "It's like we're ack-cess-tories to murder."

TG shook his head. "You got a problem with that?" he asked. "You didn't care when we rolled that pimp into a tarp of gasoline and set it on fire before we left the room."

"That was different," Billy whined. "That guy was bad news. These girls haven't done nothin'."

"Yeah, well I'm about ready to cut out the middle man and have some end-of-the-line fun with these bitches myself," TG said. He held the blade out at arm's length and then flipped it, smiling as it made a satisfying twang when it stuck in the dirty floor.

"Time for us to get serious about having some fun," he said. "You ready to head up to Oak Falls and find us some?"

Billy's eyes were downcast. "I guess."

"You want to buy that bar or what?"

"I guess."

"You're really starting to piss me off, pansy ass," TG said, retrieving the knife from the floor. The next twang it made was when it embedded in the wooden door frame a foot from Billy's face.

"I'll load the car," Billy said.

Amelia jabbed the needle into Carrie's arm and pushed the plunger down. She didn't worry about the finer points of finding a vein, or making the pain minimal for the patient. This little vixen had caused them enough trouble, and she hoped the damn injection *did* hurt. Either way, Carrie was going to be sleeping soundly for the next twenty-four hours at least.

They were so close now to everything. Amelia could barely sleep at night. For years she had planned, hoped, dreamed of being where she was now. Finding Barry Rockford had been the ultimate coup. Without him—without his connections and money—she could never have pulled this together on her own. And the fact that he was a world-renowned scientist—if a little tarnished—was perhaps the best piece of the pie. But here they were, just a few weeks from the moment that would change everything. Some had spent their entire lives waiting for such an opportunity. There were books on their experiments and failed attempts. Not books in wide circulation, obviously. But Amelia had read widely in places most had never dreamed to go.

There was a reason she had arrived at this moment. It was not an accident.

She closed the door on room twelve and walked the silent hallway slowly. No sound came from any of the patient rooms; she'd seen to that before they had left to pick Carrie up from town. It helped to have a police band scanner; that's where Barry had first heard that Carrie was wandering around like a true loon in the middle of town. Thank God he had. Amelia had shot up the rest of the patients with a sedative so they wouldn't add to the trouble and headed into town like a bat out of hell to reclaim their patient. Amelia liked to think of her as simply "Number Twelve."

She opened the door to the basement and descended the wood plank steps feeling warmly pleased with herself. When she found Barry fiddling with a test tube at the far end of the cement-walled room, she placed her palms on either side of his face and wrapped her body around his from behind, pressing against him like a boa.

"Amelia," he complained, but she only craned herself up to nibble at the lobe of his ear, breathing warmly against his neck.

"Now?" he said, his voice no longer sounding quite so annoyed. She didn't answer, only slid one hand between the buttons of his shirt to press cool nails against the hair of his chest. Her pelvis ground against his ass and she moaned, just a little, in his ear. That was all it took for Barry Rockford to lose his cool, and setting down the test tube in its stand, he turned to give Nurse Amelia his full attention.

Her lips were already flushed and full of wanting, and her eyes bored into his with an intensity that many would have found frightening. Rockford, however, found it sexy, and he wrapped an arm around her, crushing her thin body to him. She ripped open the front of his shirt, slipping her arms all the way around him to dig nails into the flesh of his back as she inhaled the subtle scent of him while burying lips to his chest.

Some would have called her a witch, but there were times that she preferred being the word that sounded similar.

"You're a pushy bitch, aren't you?" Barry whispered, slipping a hand down the back of her jeans.

"And you like it that way," she answered. "Where would you be if you hadn't found me? Still moping in a research lab, wishing you could keep doing the shit they wouldn't let you do? With me, you can do whatever you want. And I won't tell."

She dragged him over to a bed against the opposite wall. A woman lay there beneath heavy white sheets, an IV bag hung at the head of the bed with tubing disappearing into her arm. Amelia held on to Barry with one arm, but with the other, she pulled down the sheets, exposing the naked breasts of the woman beneath. She took Barry's hand and guided it to the unconscious woman's chest, helping him massage the full, creamy breasts. She matched her thumb and forefinger to his and rolled the woman's thick nipple between their fingers before turning to kiss him, tongue forceful between his lips.

He was out of breath when she pulled away, and she laughed at his excitement. "Without me, you'd still be a pawn," she said. "Now, you're a king. And when you're a king"—she yanked the sheets off of the bed, exposing all of the woman—"you can do anything. What do you want to do, Barry?" she whispered, while pulling her shirt over her head, and unbuttoning her jeans. "What do you want to do?"

Then she lay down naked on the bed next to the unconscious woman and waited for his response. At the risk of a bad pun, it wasn't long in coming.

Chapter Twenty-one

For a place that perched on the outcrop of a mountain, Castle House Asylum sure had a hell of a lot of grass to cut. And the killer was, since so much of the lawn crawled down steep slopes, it wasn't a very smart idea to sit on a riding mower while doing it. You could pretty easily find yourself unbalanced and flipping over hundreds of pounds of steel with a big, deadly spinning blade.

So that's why David was huffing up a storm as he pushed the hand mower up a hill back toward the gabled windows of the asylum. Oh, the mower was self-propelled, naturally. That just didn't count for much when the incline was about 160 degrees!

He consoled himself that at ten dollars an hour this was great money for a part-time job while at the same time serving as great training. But that didn't make the sweat streaming down his cheeks any sweeter.

The job was simple. He had an acre or two of

grass to cut each week (which might take him two days, from the feel of today's attack), and a bunch of wild rosebushes to trim. And a handful of topiary gardens to bring into civilized check. At the moment, the bases of all the bushes on the property were completely overrun in crabgrass and thistles.

David figured he could put in three afternoons a week and still have plenty of time to work on the projects around Aunt Elsie's place. But he'd be pocketing probably $150 a week, instead of simply spending the money he'd arrived here with.

Apparently, he'd been the only one to apply for the job, because Dr. Rockford had hired him on the spot, with the promise that he not get into any more accidents on the grounds. Now he was feeling a little sorry he'd taken the job.

The rules were pretty simple. Show up after lunch, check in with Rockford or the nurse to see if they had any special jobs to do, and then hit the yard for four or five hours. He had a key to the gardener's shed out back, and access to a small bathroom near the asylum's back entrance.

Today there had been no special jobs . . . just get the yard cut. It was hard to believe that there was any grass left on the hills around the old hotel to cut, after decades of neglect, but while there was plenty of clover and weeds interspersed, there was still some remnant of what had probably once been a five-star-resort lawn of rich emerald grass. Each time he pushed the mower back up the steep hill toward the old hotel he stared at the old building, trying to imagine what it must once have been like. He knew people had come here from all corners of the world to enjoy the pampered life. But he also knew that something had cut that heyday short. He remembered some tiny fragment of a rumor about a bloodbath that had killed guests and ended the hotel's attraction. No amount of promotion had ever managed to overcome that, and so the hotel had slipped through poorer and poorer hands until it had been left to rot into the hillside, vacant and empty.

Now the ivy crawled up and around nearly all of the front brick, cascading over the upper-story windows in mystery and stirring shadows. The glass of most of those rooms remained dark even in the daylight; ciphers that showed and promised nothing. Except in one window . . . David stared as he pushed hard to crest the top of the hill. There was someone in that window just to the left of the main entrance, on the second floor. He thought it was a woman.

Though his cutting pattern called for him to turn left and go back down and around the hill, he kept pushing the mower forward, steadily approaching the asylum. He could make out the face of a girl now, probably a patient, he realized. She had dark hair that hung in a strand across her face, and her mouth seemed to be hanging partially open, as if she was calling out. If she was, he'd never hear it over the mower. It looked like she'd bleached a bit of her hair; there was a lighter strand that slipped out from her temple. As he reached the edge of the grass and the start of the entry drive, he realized that that lighter strand of hair wasn't just light . . . It looked . . . pink. Like Brenda's hair . . . Just then, the girl suddenly disappeared from the glass, and a hand reached up and pulled down a shade ensuring that David wouldn't see in anymore.

What the hell? he thought, turning the mower and heading down the hill again, but not without a couple glances over his shoulder at the now-shaded window. Had he really seen what he thought he had?

No way, he told himself. Brenda may have been wild, but she sure as hell wasn't crazy.

Nevertheless, the image troubled him as he finished his last half hour of cutting, before finally tucking the mower back into the shed. He didn't bother to wash up inside, just got on his bike and began the arduous journey back to Aunt Elsie's. He'd almost forgotten about Brenda over the past few days, and now she was right back in the center of his head again.

The thought about what might have happened to her only spurred him on to pedal harder, and for once, he didn't even notice the steep slope on the way back into town. His frustration gave him all the energy he needed to climb the mountain.

CHAPTER TWENTY-TWO

"I bet I can get one to come back to the car with us before you can," TG pronounced, as he tilted back a stiff shot of Jack Daniel's. He nodded at the crowded bar, and then slammed down the shot on the counter, instantly gaining the attention of the bartendress, a well-tattooed brunette in a loose tank top. TG had already made it a game of making sure he set their glasses just far enough away from the back of the bar that she had to bend over. They'd been at the Last Look in Oak Falls for an hour now, and after a couple beers, an ice water and three shots, he was feeling ready to go to work.

But tonight, TG had decided the game was going to be a little different. Knocking a bitch over the head and stuffing her in the trunk was easy. Where was the sport in that? Naw, tonight he wanted to win the pussy fair and square, and that meant breaking out the old bad-boy charm. He grinned an expanse of yellowed ivories as he considered his array of pickup lines.

"You in?" TG prodded, nudging Billy, who was staring across the room at a blonde. She was hunched over the bar, deep in thought. Or deep in drunkenness, he couldn't be sure. She seemed to be alone.

"In for what?"

"You get a filly back to the car without a lead pipe or a dose of ether before me, and you win."

"And you're going to try to win over a chick yourself?" Billy asked. He sounded doubtful.

"Yeah, you think I can't do it?"

"What are the stakes?"

TG scratched his chin a minute. Then his eyes lit. Well, *lit* might be overstating it. Let's just say you could see the red capillaries crisscrossing the whites of his eyes a bit clearer. Midnight is pretty late when you start drinkin' at three in the afternoon.

"Let's say whoever gets a girl to follow him to the car first gets to keep her."

"And the loser?"

"Whoever comes outta the bar last has to turn his gal over to the doc."

"Not much in the way of stakes," Billy mused.

But TG was already off the stool. "I'll be waiting for you in the Mustang," he promised, and set off across the bar to hit on a dark-haired girl who was already in the midst of a conversation with two other guys. Billy saw the one, a needle-thin preppy dude, fade back as soon as TG approached, but the other just kept talking, his brow twitching a bit in annoyance as the flannel-clad hick approached.

"Why do I do this shit?" Billy mumbled, and slipped off the stool himself. Picking up his beer, he headed across the room to where the blonde sat. If there was one thing he knew about bars, it was that the lonely girl there in the corner was just waiting for someone to show. And if Billy put on a good face, that someone could be he.

Tonight, that lonely girl was Mary Jane.

Mary Jane hadn't had a very good week. Her dad was currently hooked up to a respirator thanks to a forty-year chain-smoking habit, and her boss had announced today that if sales didn't increase in the next month, she and a handful of others would be on the street. No foul on their part, and really nothing they could do to change their fate . . . but business was business. And business sucked. She hoped they carted all the Republicans out of Congress on sharp sticks in the next election, that's all she could say.

Billy listened, and bought more drinks, encouraging the bartendress to pour the vodka heavy in her vanilla vodka and sodas. A couple extra bucks in the tip always helped with that gambit.

Mary Jane had a head start, so he didn't need to prime the pump too much, and she was more than willing to talk about her woes, so he didn't have to make up too much about himself. (He figured that mentioning that his only current employment involved kidnapping young women for some kind of medical experiments and that she could be next if she didn't give it up fast probably wasn't the right way to approach a pickup.)

He liked it that there was a white line across the fourth finger of her left hand instead of a ring. Easy story to coax there, he figured, if her tongue slowed down. And he liked the way she grabbed his wrist for emphasis when she talked about her asshole boss, and got misty-eyed over the likely impending death of her dad.

When she excused herself to go to the bathroom, she wobbled a bit getting off the stool. And when she came back, she didn't seem to be moving in anything resembling a straight line.

"I need to get home," she slurred. And he made the natural move.

"Let me drive you home," he said. "You're in no condition right now."

She only hesitated a minute, and then leaned on his proffered arm. "Okay."

Billy led her through the jam-packed bar, getting jostled and elbowed with every step. He didn't see TG, but figured he was still in the back somewhere.

But when they got to the parking lot, he saw the Mustang's windows were steamed up, and Billy had a sinking feeling that was quickly answered. Before he even reached for the handle, the driver's-side door popped open, and TG's stubbled mug peered out. His hairy chest was bare, and a naked foot slid up and over the black hair on his shoulder. Red-painted toenails waved at Billy, as TG grinned.

"Hey buddy. We're kinda busy back here right now, so I'd say you've got the wheel. Looks like you'll be contributing to the doc's stash tonight, eh?"

Billy felt like crying, but instead, he helped Mary Jane into the front passenger's seat and heaved a sigh of relief when her head lolled back between the headrest and the window as soon as he shut the door.

When Billy started the engine, there was a giddy squeak from the backseat, and Mary Jane blinked her way to semiconsciousness for just a moment, and put a hand on his wrist. "Thanks," she said.

"Don't mention it," he said, and pointed the car back toward Castle Point. In another few hours, he guessed she wouldn't be thanking him at all.

As the moaning escalated from the backseat in al- most exact proportion to the increased action of his

foot on the gas pedal, Billy couldn't help but wonder
what in hell TG was going to do with his prize, now
that he'd won it. TG hadn't had a girlfriend since he'd
known him; so that wasn't what this was about.

Somehow, he knew that whatever it was about,
was *not* going to be good. Not for the girl, anyway.

CHAPTER TWENTY-THREE

Billy took the turn up the hill to the shack slowly. He
didn't want to wake Mary Jane, who had closed her
eyes as soon as he'd pulled away from the bar in
Oak Falls. If he had to deliver her to the doc, he'd
like to do it with a minimum of fuss. Kinda pissed
him off though to lose the bet. He'd been starting to
actually look forward to waking up next to this little
piece. She wasn't bad . . . and she hadn't told him to
take a hike like most of the bitches he hit on.

In the rearview mirror, he could just see the hairy
back of TG. *Asshole,* he thought. As if to counter-
point it, TG moved just then, displaying the crack of
said ass in the mirror, and Billy looked away. There
were some things that could haunt your dreams,
and he didn't relish the idea of waking up to the after-
image of *that.*

Finally, the Mustang pulled up to the dark house
and Billy killed the engine. "We're here," he announced
softly.

TG's head popped up over the seat. "Stay here,"
he said. "I'll dump her inside and then we can make
our run to the doc's. But I wanna get back fast to the
shack. The *love* shack!"

"How are you planning to keep her here?" Billy said, nodding at the backseat. "Do you want me to stay here and watch her?"

"Oh she'll wait for us nice and quietlike." TG grinned, holding up a strip of black cloth that once had comprised part of a woman's T-shirt.

Billy looked over the seat, and saw the girl's eyes bugging out of their sockets. She was whimpering behind the improvised black cloth gag, and Billy guessed that was because in addition to being gagged, her hands and ankles were hog-tied behind her back with more strips of the black cloth.

"Doesn't look too comfortable," Billy observed.

"Naw, I'd guess not," TG agreed. "So let's dump your bitch at the asylum, get our money and get the hell back here to let her loose. Who knows, I might even get generous and let you have a piece of her tonight, seeing's you're losing yours."

"Take a swim in your sloppy seconds?" Billy said, wrinkling up his nose. "Thanks, but I'll pass. I know where you've been."

"Don't knock it 'til you've tried it, friend," TG said, and opened the back door. He pulled his shirt on and then yanked the naked girl out of the backseat by her armpits. She struggled a little, but just before he reached the house he stopped and slugged her with the back of his fist upside the head, and then she visibly relaxed. Her feet bounced up the stairs to the shack's kitchen door, and Billy wondered if TG had knocked her out. Would make the wait a little more bearable for her, he supposed. Though she'd wake up with a hell of a headache.

Billy glanced at Mary Jane, relieved to see that she was solidly out as well. Then he lit a cigarette and, for the first time all night, relaxed. He hadn't realized how tense the whole scenario had made him . . . first just the pressure of abducting someone, but then the added insanity of trying to sweet-talk the victim into the backseat beforehand . . . He took a deep drag on the smoke and stared at the sprinkling of stars just above the tree line in the black richness of the night sky. In some ways, this was the time he was happiest—at night, alone, with a warm buzz of nicotine sliding in and out of his lungs.

"I need a new life," Billy said to himself, sliding deeper into the seat and closing his eyes. He knew the perfect feeling of this solitary moment wouldn't last long.

And it didn't. Before the cigarette was out, TG slid back into the Mustang and slapped Billy in the back of the head. "Let's go, bubba," he laughed, and pulled his door shut. The drunk girl barely stirred.

"Did you call the doc and let him know we were coming?" Billy asked, guiding the Mustang back down the rutted road to the highway.

"Yeah, called him from the house. He'll be waiting with the cash."

The asylum was just a mile down the road, and this time, Billy didn't slow down at the front entrance, but pulled immediately around to the back. TG didn't hide how eager he was to get back to his trophy at the shack. Before he'd even thrown the car in park, Billy's partner hopped out to the gravel drive. Then he opened the passenger-side door and grabbed Mary Jane's limp head and pulled it upright by a hank of hair.

"Wake up, bitch," he said sweetly. "Doc wants ta give you a little examination. I think you'll like how he's gonna take your temperature."

Billy was already out of the car himself, and he stepped around TG and grabbed the girl by the elbow as she blinked herself awake. She tried without success to stop TG from pulling her hair, struggling to evade Billy's grasp while slapping at TG. "Let go," she complained.

"Leave her," Billy hissed. "I'll handle it."

"Where are we?" she asked, staggering as she stepped out of the car.

"A friend's place," Billy said. "We're staying here for tonight."

"You were supposed to be taking me home." Her voice trembled, and she looked around wildly, trying to figure out where she was, and whether she should try to run.

"For now, this is the best I can do," he said, and turned the knob on the asylum's back door. TG stepped behind her and gave a push. Mary Jane fell through the door, landing on her hands and knees in the dark foyer.

"Welcome home," TG growled.

Dr. Rockford walked into the room before the woman had gotten off the floor. He didn't hesitate, but knelt down next to Mary Jane.

"Hi there, hon. I'm gonna give you something to make you sleep tonight."

Before she could protest, he stabbed a needle into her upper arm and pushed the plunger down. "Sweet dreams," he said.

"What the hell is this?" Mary Jane moaned, and scrambled up from the floor. The doctor didn't try to stop her. The three men watched as she staggered down the hallway, clutching at the wall, and then stumbled. She pulled herself up against the wall again and got in a couple more shaky steps before slipping to her knees.

"Why?" she asked, as the floor came up to meet her face.

TG walked over to her, and answered.

"Money." Then he pulled her limp body up, hefting her over his shoulder like a sack of potatoes.

"Where do you want her, Doc?"

"Upstairs," he said, and led them down the hall and around a corner to the wide, grand staircase to the second floor. Billy trailed behind, a lump inexplicably thickening in his throat. He couldn't explain why; he hadn't minded turning the other girls over to the doc this much. But he just thought of all the shit that Mary Jane had gone through over the last few days—the conversation they'd had at the bar playing over and over in his head. And he felt, well, kinda like a big plop of horseshit to be adding to the list.

"Right over here," Rockford pointed. "Room thirteen."

"Lucky number," TG laughed.

Rockford smiled as TG laid the limp body down on the old hotel bed. "Yes it is," he said. "A very lucky number."

The doc led them back downstairs to the front office, where Nurse Amelia was waiting. "Thanks to the boys, we have our Number Thirteen," Rockford said, a pronounced smile on his face.

The nurse grinned as well. "That's great news," she said. "And great timing, since the clock is now ticking."

TG showed his impatience without embarrassment. "Doc, you owe us for two now," he said. "I'd like to get our money and split. You know where to find us if you need another job."

Dr. Rockford nodded at Nurse Amelia, who reached into a drawer in the desk. "Here you are, Doctor," she said, and Rockford leaned over to take something from her. She stood then and came around to Billy from the other side of the desk.

"Actually," Dr. Rockford said, "this is the last job I think we're going to need you for. We needed thirteen women, and that is all we needed. I appreciate all that you've done for us, and I trust you'll keep your mouths shut about the nature of your work for Castle House Asylum?"

TG was disappointed to hear that the money tree was drying up, but he hastened to agree with the doc. "Our lips are sealed," he agreed.

The doctor put a hand on TG's shoulder, as he swung the other arm up quietly to connect with TG's arm. The needle entered cleanly, and he had pressed the plunger before the lowlife even registered the sting of the penetration. Then TG was swinging his body around intending to punch the doctor, but Rockford dodged easily, noting from the corner of his eye that Amelia had executed her half of the needle ballet with equal success. Billy was flailing in place, trying to grab hold of the nurse as she dodged away, spent needle in hand.

Amelia dove away from the men to hide behind the desk, while Rockford backed out of the doorway to wait in the hall as the two men slapped at the injection points on their arms and cried out in irritation.

"What the fuck?" TG complained. "What did you *do?*"

Billy didn't ask. He only closed his eyes as the wave of cold swiftly spread from his arm to his chest. "Fuckin' bitch," he mumbled, just before his knees lost their ability to hold him upright.

"So," Amelia said moments later, when Billy and TG had both stopped fighting the drug and lay motionless on the floor. "That's done. But now what do we do with them?"

"I think the coup de grace can always use a couple more bodies," Rockford said. "We'll keep them in the cellar for now. In a couple weeks, one way or the other, it won't matter."

He grabbed TG by the wrists and began to drag the heavy man out of the room.

"Give me a hand," he huffed. "We'll come back for the other one."

Amelia grabbed TG's ankles and helped the doctor wrestle the body out of the room and down the hall to the elevator.

"Then we need to dump their car back at their place. I don't think we need to worry about them being missed anytime soon."

Amelia laughed. "No," she agreed. "I can't imagine who would ever miss these two."

Amy Lynn rolled back and forth on the dirty kitchen floor of Billy and TG's shack. Every now and then she felt the tiny legs of an insect kiss the back of her neck, or run across her cheek. She screamed each time it happened, not that much sound escaped the gag. But it was enough to send the roaches back to their holes for a minute or two. She pulled at the bonds that kept her limbs in pins and needles, and cried as she flipped from lying on one side of her body to the other. She'd been repeating these futile efforts now for what seemed like hours.

Her tears only smeared the mud and roach droppings that coated the floor onto her face. Cleanliness wasn't one of TG's virtues.

Outside, she heard the loud rev of an engine. It had the throaty growl of a sports car, and she prayed as it cycled off that Billy was back in the black Mustang. She was afraid of his return too . . . but she didn't know how long she could stay tied up like this without losing it completely. She had screamed herself hoarse in the hours since they'd left, and not managed to make a sound that anyone could actually hear. She waited for the sound of feet on the steps, and the creak of the door, but minutes passed, and there was nothing, though she did hear the sound of another engine pull away from the house outside.

Amy Lynn shifted and thumped her legs and arms on the floor, like beating on a drum. Someone had to be outside. She tried to scream again, and thwacked the floor. Then she stopped, and listened.

Still, only silence.

There was one person in the world who missed Billy and TG.

Amy Lynn tried to control her wracking sobs, head thudding softly on the floor. She missed them very much indeed. And the night wasn't nearly over.

Chapter Twenty-four

Officer Christy Sorensen slowed the squad down to fifteen miles an hour and crept along the side of 190. The call had come in just as the chief had started to bawl her out for endangering herself and the department on a breaking-and-entering charge. When Matt had stuck his head into the office to say that a car had been reported as crashed off the road just a few miles outside of town, Chief had had only one more thing to say to her:

"Go check it out," he growled. "I was thinking of busting you down to traffic patrol anyway."

Traffic patrol in a town the size of Castle Point was a cruel sentence of boredom. The department didn't bother with it unless there were reports of teens drag-racing in a particular area, because basically all it meant was sitting in your squad on the side of Main or 190 and watching the dust blow by most of the day.

The tip had come in from someone on a cell phone while on the way out of town, so Christy only had an approximate location to go on . . . but if someone else had spotted the crash from the highway just by seeing the sun glinting off the silver of the car's chrome, she figured she ought to be able to find it if she was looking hard.

The gravel crunched beneath the tires in a low, steady rhythm, when suddenly Christy hit the brakes. Something reflected in the late-afternoon sun like light in a mirror. *That must be it,* she thought and pulled off the road.

She walked along the shoulder until she saw the source of the light. The tip had been correct; a car lay at the bottom of the hill, half buried in the brush and small trees. But standing here, it was easy to see the tracks where it had gone over—the grass and bushes had been broken and ripped from the car's passage, and the trees below were singed from an apparent fire. She stepped carefully along the rocks, zigzagging her way down the hillside to the wreck, holding on to tree trunk after tree trunk for support so that she didn't stumble and land in a heap on top of the wreck herself.

Christy was winded by the time she reached the bottom; at times she felt like if she let go of the tree she was holding that she'd plummet!

But once down, she circled the wrecked car, noting that its entire outside was scorched and blackened, and the interior was charred beyond recognition. While the front windshield was a mess of spiderwebbed glass, one of the passenger windows was completely blown out, and Christy was able to peer inside to assess the cab.

She steeled herself for the horror she knew would

be inside. There was no way the driver had walked away from this one, and her stomach turned a little as she peered in through the open window.

She saw the long strips of rubber hanging in hardened teardrops from the steering wheel, where the flames had melted it. She saw the springs exposed beneath the blackened seats like a 3-D picture of how a car was put together.

But nobody was inside.

She pushed back, and walked around the car again, staring hard at the matted grass for some evidence of a wounded driver. Blood spots. A severed limb. Something. Maybe the driver was trapped beneath the car, she thought, but a closer investigation negated that theory quickly. She walked in a widening circle, and then stood still, staring up the rocky hillside to try to see any color that didn't belong there; evidence of ripped shreds of clothing . . . or perhaps an intact body that had been launched far from the impact. She cringed at every step, expecting the grass to part on a bloodied, blue-tinged hand.

Nothing.

She spent more than a half hour poking around the hillside, and finally decided that this was maybe a job for a search dog. Or someone with better shoes. She almost left the scene without performing the most important task. But thankfully she remembered just as she'd begun to climb back up, and pulled the notepad out of her pocket to scribble down the license plate number.

Wouldn't do to confirm a report of a crash without being able to look up whom the car belonged to, would it?

Back at the top, Christy walked around the area where the car had gone over. If you knew what to look for, you could just barely see the displaced gravel where the tires had ground through it. She paced the shoulder for a couple minutes, not knowing what she was looking for, but looking just the same. That's how she found the screwdriver. It was just lying there on the gravel at the side of the road, not far from where the car had plunged to its fiery death. She reached down to pick it up, and then thought better.

Unreported accident, car burned to ruin, no victim in sight? Christy walked back to the squad and retrieved an evidence bag from the glove compartment.

You never know when you just might need to dust for prints, that's what her instructor in the academy had drilled into her class, over and over. Laughing at the unlikelihood, she scooped the abandoned tool into the bag and got back in the car to call the station.

"Hey Matt," she said. "Can you run a plate for me?" She read him the numbers, and waited for his reply. As he looked it up, he asked if it was an abandoned vehicle.

"Yeah," she said. "Pretty burned up, and nobody around."

"Is it a Nova?" he asked after a moment of silence.

"Yeah," she said. "Older one, I think."

"License says it belongs to one Carrie Sanddanz of Oak Falls."

"No way," Christy breathed.

"What's a matter?"

"Matt, Carrie Sanddanz is the woman that was wandering around town the other day after escaping from the asylum. She's been reported as a missing person by her family."

"Weird," Matt said.

"More than weird," Christy agreed.

"Christy?"

"Yeah?"

"Chief's standing here at my desk. Says to tell you not to even think of heading over to the asylum right now."

"Wouldn't think of it," she said sweetly.

From the background she heard Chief's voice: "I mean it, Sorensen. My office, fifteen minutes."

She pulled a U-turn on the highway and headed back to Castle Point, only slowing a little bit when she passed the cutoff for the old Castle House Lodge.

"I promised I wouldn't go there right now," she said. "But I made no promises about later."

CHAPTER TWENTY-FIVE

David finished cutting the seemingly endless grass around the asylum at dusk on Friday. He honestly only knew it was Friday because, for the first time in weeks, he was actually looking forward to a paycheck. And payday was Friday.

He put the mower away in the gardener's shed and let himself into the asylum through the back door. Sweat ran down his back in steamy rivulets and he could feel the heat radiating from his face. It didn't get that hot in the summer at this altitude, but when you're pushing a mower up a hill, it quickly started to feel like a one-hundred-degree day.

He started the water, let his soggy clothes fall to the floor and stepped into the tiny shower and pulled the curtain closed. He was tilting his head back, letting the hot water run over the knotted heat of his shoulders when he heard the scream.

He wasn't sure it was a scream at first; maybe it was a rusty pipe that just whined for a minute? But as he rinsed his hair, he heard it again. And again. Short, guttural complaints of pain from somewhere close.

He remembered the zombielike patients he'd seen in the front foyer the day he'd been brought here after the accident, and frowned. His impression was that the patients were all kept pretty well dosed up.

David finished rinsing off with a renewed speed, and toweled off quickly, stepping into his underwear and clean jeans without pause. He stuffed his dirty laundry in the duffel bag that the clean clothes had occupied, and stepped out into the hallway. Leaving the bag in the hall near the exit, he walked down the dark corridor to the center of the old hotel, listening for the screams. They didn't come again.

"Hmmf," he said, standing in the middle of the open lobby near the front reception desk. Nobody was there. In fact, nobody seemed to be around at all.

Not inclined to leave without the paycheck he'd been looking forward to, David decided to check the second floor to see if Dr. Rockford or his nurse were up there, dealing with a difficult patient. He walked up the long staircase, whose thick carpet seemed to absorb his footfalls instantly. He was a ghost on the landing, gliding upward to uncover a mystery . . .

The long hall was empty at the top of the stairs, and all the doors seemed to be shut. All but one. He stepped over to the entry to room two, where the door was ajar, and peered inside. A small table lamp was lit next to the bed, which was unmade—a rumple of sheets and comforter were tangled together in a heap halfway down the mattress. Other than that . . . it looked like any other empty hotel room.

He stepped back out and walked down the length

of the hall, passing the corner and turning to see that the door numbers ended with thirteen before reverting to an older numbering designation.

On a spur-of-the-moment thing, David reached out and turned the knob of room thirteen, and when it turned, he eased it open a crack.

On the bed, a woman lay sleeping, black hair cascaded over her breast like garland. Feeling like a Peeping Tom, he quickly eased the door shut.

He rounded the corner and peeked inside room twelve. Another woman dozed inside, but no doc. He moved to room eleven and paused. Should he check all of these rooms for the doctor?

David reached out for the knob, but then thought better of it. The last thing he needed was to wake up a bunch of mental patients and start a new batch of shrieking. He pulled his hand back and decided to go back downstairs.

Inside room eleven, Brenda Bean shifted and moaned slightly on the bed. In her drug-enhanced dreams, she saw a beast with horns and a leering grin advancing on her with a club. She laughed and pointed at the weapon suggesting, "I hope you know how to use that thing."

David descended the stairs and again looked in the office. The asylum seemed abandoned. Now and then the dull whir of an air-conditioning unit broke the perfect silence, but that was all. He paced back and forth, stopping in an alcove where a bunch of old paintings were hung. The images were predominantly of pastoral scenes and hillsides, but one, obviously newer creation struck him. The artist displayed far less skill than most of the paintings, but the picture was striking nevertheless. In it, a tiny baby lay in a wicker basket. The style was almost cartoonlike, but the impact of the art was striking. The naked child stared at the onlooker with wide black eyes. And in the center of its chest, a circle was drawn. Within the circle was sketched an upside-down cross.

David got a chill just from staring at those dark eyes and the dark tattoo. He backed away from the painting and shook his head, willing the image to go away. He stepped down a side hallway, on the way back to the main office, he thought, but then realized that no, it had been a wrong turn when he exited into a waiting lobby. He almost turned back to retrace his steps when he saw the door at the end of the corridor.

A door with a faint, but distinct red *X*.

From somewhere deep within the bowels of the building he heard the faintest hint of yet another scream. Not hesitating or stopping to think, David stepped forward and grasped the knob of the strangely marked door . . . and turned the handle.

The stairs that led down were shadowed in darkness, and David stepped carefully to avoid having them creak and give him away. In seconds, that fear became moot, as from beyond the stairwell, a woman began to scream.

The horrible shriek sent the hair on the back of David's neck to standing. He paused, and waited for the cry of pain to diminish, but instead it seemed to only grow more intense, wavering and holding in the air like a terrible, suspended spray of the darkest, deepest blood. Finally the horrible sound quieted, but the woman continued to cry out, harsh, grating sounds of anger and pain.

David held the wall with one hand and stepped down another wooden stair, and then another. When he came to the cement floor at the bottom, he held his body tight to the wall and slowly edged his way to the corner, holding his breath as he did so.

Finally, he got a clear shot of the room, and he almost choked trying to hold in a gasp.

An old steel hospital bed was set against the long wall of a room lit by dim bulbs hung from the rafters. A ring of guttering candles surrounded the bed, set on small tables and a wall shelf. Above the bed, a crucifix hung upside down. But the shocking part was not the candles and the antireligious iconography. David's throat caught when he saw the woman thrashing around amid white sheets stained a wet, deadly red.

Dr. Rockford was at the bedside, and when he lifted a hand in the air to accept a shiny instrument from the rubber-gloved hands of Nurse Spellman, David could see that the doctor's hand and forearm were smeared in the woman's blood.

"It's time," Rockford said, as he slid the bloody arm forward, back between the legs of the woman on the bed. The silvery spatulalike instrument disappeared between her thighs, and David saw the woman writhe and buck on the bed as it did. Her wrists were tied to the head of the bed, and her feet were likewise strapped into a set of stirrups extended from the foot of the frame. She could bounce her head and back as much as she wanted, but she couldn't move from the center of the mattress.

Nurse Spellman stepped back from the bed and picked up a black bound book from one of the candlelit tables. She quickly leafed to a ribbon-marked page in the center of the book and began to read in a strange language.

"Ei' mi lord Ba'al," she said, as the woman on the bed screamed. *"In du Astarte, est ei' no hebarti'l sem'jen. A la virgo d' daemon er' Ba'al incorpus."*

Next to her, Dr. Rockford echoed her words, raising crimson hands in the air to call out "Hail Ba'al" and "Hail Astarte" at moments where Spellman paused.

"What . . . the . . . fuck," David whispered to himself.

Spellman's voice ascended, spreading a stream of dark words that to David sounded like a strange mélange of church Latin, guttural German and exotic Egyptian. Whatever language, it sounded cruel the way she pronounced it.

As her voice reached a climax, so did the voice of the laboring woman. And then with a final yell, the patient fell silent. As the echo of her voice faded, Dr. Rockford held a small, bloody body up in the air, umbilical cord trailing to a mass of crimson meat spread out on the sheets between the woman's legs.

"I baptize you in the name of Astarte," Rockford said. "Let him be named after the day on which he was born."

Spellman grinned. "His name shall be Friday. And by the time his day of naming rolls around again, he will be a child of Ba'al."

"And we will finally offer him the Thirteenth," Rockford agreed.

Acid boiling now in his stomach, David pulled back from the room, and carefully stepped up the stairs, setting his feet down as if he were walking on glass. When he reached the top stair, he stepped out of the basement and carefully closed the door with the red *X*. He leaned his back against the wall for a moment, heart beating like a machine gun in his chest.

What the hell should he do? Who could he tell? Who would believe him?

From the basement, he heard the tiny cry of a newborn infant, and taking a deep breath, David sprinted away from the door and down the hall of art, barely slowing to pick up his backpack of dirty clothes before exiting the back of the asylum.

Suddenly getting his weekly paycheck didn't seem terribly important.

Chapter Twenty-six

Amelia sponged off the infant and took it to an empty crèche on the other side of the basement. The warmth of the heat lamps above the row of empty baby cribs felt good against the top of her scalp, and she laid down the tiny baby wrapped in soft cloth.

Running her fingers across its tiny red cheeks she smiled and cooed. "You're a sweet one, Friday, aren't you?"

Next to the crèche, a wail began, and Amelia reached her free hand into the small plastic bed next to Friday's. "Feeling jealous?" she murmured. Amelia rubbed her hand across the thick black hair of their firstborn, and clucked.

"There, there, Wednesday's child. Don't be so full of woe. Next week you'll be ready to join your mother. And you can get out of this bed finally. But until then, we'd better get you some milk, hmmm?"

She stepped away from the babies to a small counter and pulled a canister of formula powder from a cabinet. Then she measured out scoops of the powder into two plastic bottles and filled them with warm water from the tap. After capping and shaking them, she brought them back to the infants and plugged a nipple into each tiny mouth.

"You know, Barry," she called across the room. "This is going to get difficult to do in a couple more days when these beds start filling up."

He stepped away from the now-quiet mother, and came to the sink near her to wash his hands.

"I know," he agreed. "But it won't be for long. Most of the kids are too young to induce until the day we need them. I think we can probably get Janie and Sarah in three and four to go this weekend. They're both near term. Then we've got Chelsea. But she's just seven months. I'm worried about taking any of the others until the end of next week after her."

"That's a lot to do all at once," Amelia said, shifting an arm to follow the head of an infant. "Maybe we should wait a few more weeks."

The doctor shook his head. "No way. You said so yourself—the birth of the first starts the thing moving. It's our own fault that we took so long to get things moved out here and set up. We should have found a dozen women at the same time as we grabbed Angela so that they'd all be due at the same time. But it doesn't matter. Babies are babies, no matter how old. We'll cut them out when we need them." He shrugged. "Or we'll just use them right where they are."

Amelia nodded. "I suppose."

She held up a half-empty formula bottle, and then slipped it back in the mouth of the newborn baby. "And I sure as hell don't want to be doing this a moment more than I have to. There's not a mothering bone in my body."

"Maybe not," Rockford said, sliding a hand up her leg to cup her ass. "But I could put a bone in your body."

She slapped his hand away and laughed, a wicked, knowing sound. "You're a greedy bastard," she said. "Aren't a dozen women enough for you?"

CHAPTER TWENTY-SEVEN

If he had been timing his ride, David would have been elated to know that after weeks of cycling the crossback on 190, he had finally just broken his all-time speed record for the five-mile sprint. And a good chunk of that was spent pumping uphill.

But the image of Dr. Rockford's bloody hands kept appearing before his eyes, and he imagined the doctor and his twisted nurse would suddenly appear behind him on the road in their black sedan at any second.

"C'mere, son," they'd call from behind the tinted windows. "We just want to talk to you a minute about the grass." But if they got their hands on him and pulled him inside that sedan he knew that he would never see the lawn mower or the grass or his bike again.

"We know you were downstairs," Nurse Spellman would say, pointing at him with the spine of her black book.

"And we don't like what you saw," the doctor would follow up, pulling out the silver birthing instrument and running it slowly up David's thigh. "We need to make sure you don't remember it anymore."

"I promise I'll never say a word to anyone," David would say, as the car's rear tires shifted across the gravel and evened out again, pointing steadily back toward the tall ivy-covered walls of the asylum.

"I promise you won't too," Dr. Rockford said, moving the silver instrument up David's chest to rest at his mouth. He could feel something sharp, like a tiny forked blade pressing against his closed lips.

"I will make sure of it."

David shook the image from his head but pedaled even harder, desperate to get as far from the asylum as possible before the night fully fell. Already the horizon betrayed the deep hues of purple, and the stars were out overhead.

He rounded the curve and sped through the center of town in a blur of sweat and panic, and in moments he was back at Aunt Elsie's, ditching his bike in the garage without any thought for protecting it from scratching. He hastily kicked out the kickstand and let it settle on its own . . . but the bike instead overbalanced and fell to the ground. He didn't look back.

"Hey, sweetie, how was your day?" his aunt called, as he practically ran through the kitchen and up the stairs to his room.

"Okay," he mumbled. "Gotta take a shower."

He didn't really, since he'd taken one at the asylum, but he ran the water anyway, deciding that he might as well wash off the sweat of the ride. And truth be told, he wanted to enjoy the comforting hot rain on his face. Maybe that would make him feel clean . . . because after what he'd witnessed, he didn't feel very clean. Not at all.

As he soaped up, he replayed the basement scene again in his mind. Obviously the doc and his nurse were not there just to help poor psycho pregger girls. But what the hell did they want with the babies? Something bad, judging by the weird candles and strange language in which Nurse Spellman had spoken. They were into ritual, and a ritual carried out in a basement—with blood and candles—was not the white kind, he surmised.

They'd repeated the same names over and over as the woman gave birth. Ba'al. And Astarte. He could still hear the two repeating those names over and over. David ran his fingers through his hair quickly, pushing out the last of the soap, and then turned off the water. He toweled off quickly and then walked to his bedroom, turning on the computer before he searched for clothes.

As the machine booted, he got dressed, and then sat down and hit the AOL icon. He cringed as he logged on and then listened to the digital pong sounds as the computer accessed the phone line and dialed in. His aunt didn't own a computer, so he was stuck here with dial-up for the summer. He didn't know how people had ever lived this way. You could leave the room and have dinner by the time the damn machine actually got online and accessed anything.

Still, it was all he had, and he tried to be patient as he waited for the image blocks to load. Finally he typed in his query, and it returned a long list of references for Ba'al and Astarte. He'd typed in "demon, Bail, and Astart," but saw the listing for "goddess" next to Astarte, and clicked there first.

When he skimmed down the page and found the reference to "cultic" worship, he whistled. The page suggested that Astarte was worshipped through ritual sex, and was the mistress and mother—as well as lover—of Ba'al. He flipped over to Wikipedia and found Astarte was connected with fertility, sexuality and war. The listing connected her to symbols of the lion and the sphinx, as well as the planet Venus. It also noted that she was frequently portrayed as naked. He laughed silently. Pornography of the ancients.

He read further and found a photo of a statue of Astarte sitting on a throne. The listing noted that the statue's breasts were pierced, so that "a hollow in the statue would have been filled with milk through the head and gentle heating would have melted wax plugging the holes in her breasts, producing an apparent miracle when the milk emerged."

"Damn." David shook his head. "People have always been fucked up, haven't they?"

He read further and found a reference to Ba'al, son of Dagon, whom Astarte kept from attacking other deities.

He followed more links and learned that both Ba'al and Astarte were worshipped throughout the Old World in various ways, but always with the idea that they were fertility symbols. Men and women staged ceremonies on crop fields that culminated in ritual intercourse to encourage the god and goddess to spread their mystical seed in similar fashion across a couple's crops, blessing their harvest for the year.

There were dozens of entries that discussed the licentious worship of Ba'al and his mother, as well as his sister and lover, Anat.

But what did these have to do with Dr. Rockford and Amelia and the nut farm? David wondered. He read entry after entry of innocuous worship and then found one page that chilled his heart.

"The cult of Astarte and Ba'al on the island of Cieran believed that only through the sacrifice of their firstborn children could the land of heaven be opened to those on earth. Every year the Cieranites staged a magnificent feast in the center of the town, and after an evening of eating the best harvest of the year's crops, drinking the last year's vintage wine and dancing with all of the women in the town, the women of age would pair off with a man of their choice and lie with him in the street, asking for the child of Ba'al to be seeded in their loins.

"After the orgy was completed, all of the town would gather again, and the firstborn children would be brought to a sacrificial altar in the center of the square. Mothers were said to surrender their babies readily, knowing that the offering pleased the god Ba'al, and they would thus be guaranteed good crops in the coming year, and more babies that they could keep."

David rolled his eyes up at the ceiling as he leaned back from the screen. "What the fuck is wrong with people?" he said. "People are idiots now, and they were idiots then. We haven't evolved at all."

He skimmed down the page a bit further, finding notice of another ritual that apparently had not remained in vogue long.

"There was a period where it was believed that the ritual copulation on the night of Ba'al could result in the incarnation of Ba'al to a woman who had been properly prepared as the vessel of Astarte. The ceremony of the Thirteenth was only documented in the writings of Monsieur Getty in the 1600s, and has widely been debated for its veracity."

The words "the Thirteenth" were a hyperlink, but when David tried to follow them, the hourglass came up on his computer.

"God damn this thing," he said, slamming a palm on the desk. He hit reload on the browser, and this time the page came up quickly. But it was mostly white, because at the top it simply read PAGE NOT FOUND.

"Oh, that figures," he said.

He tried running a search for "The ritual of the Thirteenth" but most of what came up seemed to revolve around dark metal rock bands.

He tried a couple more variations on the phrase, as well as for "Monsieur Getty," but at last gave up, not finding anything applicable. On a whim, he plugged "Dr. Barry Rockford" into Google, and his eyebrows raised when the return list came back.

There were dozens of links and entries about the Castle House Asylum founder, but none of them mentioned psychiatry as his expertise. Instead, he saw lots of references to stem cells and genetic mutation and some kind of President's Award for Research.

David sat back and scratched his head absently. The guy wasn't a psychiatrist, but he was running an asylum. He was famous for genetic research on fetuses, but today he'd been arm deep in a new baby delivery, and calling out the names of ancient gods and demons as he did it.

Exactly what kind of medicine *was* going on down at the asylum?

CHAPTER TWENTY-EIGHT

The night seemed to go on forever. David's mind would not shut down after the events of the day, and after lying in his bed for an hour or two tossing and turning, he did what he usually did when insomnia struck. He got up and paced the house. He slipped downstairs to the kitchen and blinked at the brightness of the fridge bulb when he opened it. A tear wet his cheek from the intensity of the glare—his eyes were adjusted to the dark, and the light was almost painful.

He pulled the milk from the fridge and poured a

glass before putting the carton back. A good glass of milk always seemed to weigh down his body and encourage sleep. He drank it down and then wandered the downstairs for a while, idly staring at the knickknacks his aunt had accumulated through the years. Statuettes of giraffes, and coffee mugs with a variety of sayings and logos on them like "I (heart) My Attitude Problem." He grinned at that one; Elsie had never had much attitude that he knew of. She was always helping someone out.

Presently, David returned to his bed. He pressed his face into the pillow and willed away the images of bloody hands and babies from his mind. But in their place, he saw the photo of the statue of Astarte with holes where her nipples should be. While the holes were intended to be used in a fertility rite—cow's milk would be piped through the cavities in the statue's chest so that the local farmers could drink of the goddess's goodness and enjoy productive harvests for the season—David imagined a more sinister use. In his waking dreams, the statue changed to a human woman. But where her nipples should have been were instead ragged red holes, blood leaking down her torso. It was an abomination of the archetypal fertile woman whose breasts leaked life-giving milk. Instead, this woman leaked her life, and a throng of people lined up before her, each of them eager to swallow the ragged flesh that gave up her very life's blood. One by one they suckled her ruined breasts, and walked away with faces painted crimson, each of them stealing a small bit of her life.

David rolled to his back; but the shadows of the trees moving outside his window reached for him from the ceiling, as if they were demons ready to rip the soul from his heart. The milk sloshed in his stomach as he rolled from side to side, and finally he curled into the fetal position and tried to instead fill his head with images of something good. Something happy. His summer hadn't really been filled with good things; the frustration of training wasn't really something he wanted to think about. There was the night at the Clam Shack with Brenda . . . though that too hadn't ended well. There was one good part though, and he worked to remember the warm touch of her hands on his back, and the intoxicating taste of her tongue in his mouth as they clutched each other on the trail behind the bar.

That image did push some of the horror from his mind, but it brought with it a whole new set of worries. He felt that somehow her disappearance had been his fault, and yet he had let his own investigation of the cause dissipate. He'd gone to the bar, and talked to a couple of old lushes there, but he'd not pursued any of the rest of the people on the list he'd gotten from Joe the bartender.

Instead he'd started the job at the asylum and let the work and his training take over the needs of his conscience.

He thought of his aunt and the bric-a-brac downstairs that served as the mementos of her life—all of them gifts from people she'd touched. She wouldn't have given up trying to help someone as easily as David had abandoned trying to track down Brenda. He vowed that in the morning, he'd try to pick up the trail again.

It was after two A.M. when David finally drifted into a troubled sleep. In his dreams, he heard Brenda calling for him, and every time she did, her plea for help was punctuated by a scream of pain.

The morning came far too quickly after the long night, but David woke oddly refreshed. He showered and ate a couple pieces of toast with his orange juice.

"Are you working at the old hotel again today?" Elsie asked.

His heart jumped at the question, but he nodded. "Yeah, but I want to do some solid riding first. So I'm heading out early."

Truth be told, he wasn't sure that he was going to the asylum to work. He couldn't imagine showing up there again after what he'd seen. Yet . . . they did still owe him money, and despite his dreams, he knew that they didn't know that he knew about the activities in the basement. He didn't want to be drawn into whatever hellish shit they were involved in . . . but he was curious to learn more about what was going on.

Those thoughts were still in mind as he climbed on his aunt's old Huffy and kicked the bike down the drive and across town. There were very few cars on the road and the morning air was sweet, and he marveled at the clots of fog that still hugged the edges of the low spots in town.

He made his first stop the supermarket, where Joe had mentioned a handful of people worked who had been at the bar the night of Brenda's disappearance. But just like the old lushes he'd spoken to at the bar, the store was a dead end. He did get a glimpse of the town's transvestite though, which gave him a good chuckle. He/she was walking down an aisle in a short skirt and panty hose, but David guessed you were not supposed to notice the stubble on his/her face.

"Hard to be a woman with that kind of beard," he mumbled to himself, and ducked out of the grocery.

His next stop was somewhere along the 190. The bartender had mentioned two other guys who had been at the bar that night—the "Terror Twins." From the vague directions, it seemed like the two were on one of the gravel roads that cut off 190 near the asylum. He wasn't crazy about the idea of visiting two guys that far out of town who had earned the nickname "Terror Twins," but, on the other hand, they were also his last lead. His conscience wouldn't rest until he at least gave it a shot . . . and hell, they were near his work. When they slammed the door in his face, his conscience could feel vindicated that he'd tried, and he could go try to collect his money from the psychos at the insane asylum. And actually, maybe he could walk the patients' floor and find the girl who'd appeared the other day in the upstairs window who'd reminded him of Brenda. He didn't believe that Brenda had ended up in the asylum, but he supposed he could rule out that last idea too while he was on a fool's errand.

Sounded like the setup for a perfect day.

Christy chewed on the inside of her cheek as she guided the police cruiser around the curves of the 190. She'd been enjoying the scenery around here a lot lately. Except, she couldn't really say she'd been *enjoying* it. The academy hadn't really prepared her for this one, and she could tell the chief didn't quite know what to do about it after forty years as a small-town cop. She'd asked him to apply for a warrant to search the asylum, but he'd only shaken his head.

"On what grounds?"

"On the grounds that they're holding people there against their will."

"And your proof?" he prodded, settling his weight back in the leather chair. It groaned under the attention.

"I know, I know—my proof implicates the department in a breaking-and-entering charge. But there has to be another way to get one."

"You tell me what it is," he grumbled. "Probable

cause. How do you think the courts look on the idea of an insane asylum holding people against their will? That's really kind of the *point* of an asylum, isn't it? To hold people whose mental faculties are suspect. In other words, to keep people in a safe place, most likely against their will?"

"But Chief . . ."

"Look, I don't know why the girls you saw are there, but until we've got something more to go on, we're watching and waiting."

She'd left his office in a huff, and proceeded to drive her shift around town, not seeing anyone doing much of anything this early in the morning on a Saturday. After a couple spins through the little town she had turned and headed out toward the asylum. She didn't know what she hoped to see out there—and she certainly couldn't bang on the door again. But the place had become her private obsession.

The radio squawked when she was just a couple miles out of town.

"Cruiser 103 come in."

It was Glenna, their weekend dispatcher. Nobody else used the car numbers when calling. It was kind of ridiculously formal in a department of three.

"Yeah, Base, whatcha got?"

"Captain said to let you know that the fingerprint report came back on that screwdriver. Thought you might like to know whose they were."

Christy impatiently thumbed the talk switch. "Of course I would. Spill it!"

There was a burst of static and then the stentorian-voiced dispatcher clarified. "They matched the prints to a Billy Walker. Five previous offenses, all of them robbery related. He's got an address outside of town, if you want to pick him up for questioning."

Christy shook her head and laughed. Fuckin' Terror Twins. How did they figure into this? Or did they?

"Nah, Base, I know right where he is. On my way there now. Out."

Christy put down the radio set and frowned. The screwdriver had been found on the road near the wreck, and the woman the car was registered to was in the asylum. Was there really a connection? Billy and TG were habituals, but she didn't see them wrapped up in a kidnapping scam. They were just a couple stupid local thugs who tried every scheme to get ahead . . . and generally failed miserably.

Still, if there was any connection to be made between Billy, the car and the woman she'd seen in the asylum . . . she intended to find it.

Christy stepped on the gas and sped down the 190, trying to establish the line of questioning she'd begin with when she got to the twins' shack. Or should she even ask a question there? Maybe she should just bring Billy in for questioning . . . though once she did that, they had to make it pay off, or he went back out scot-free—and knowing that the cops were watching his ass.

When she neared the turnoff for the Terror Twins' shack, Christy took the turn slow. She wanted to approach this one quietly.

As it turned out, it was a good thing she didn't barrel around the corner. Because as soon as she turned, she saw a familiar set of tires ahead of her.

David Shale.

Was that fuckin' kid EVERYwhere?

She hit the brakes and pulled up next to him, rolling down the passenger window.

"Can I ask just what the hell you are doing here?" she said after he pulled off his helmet.

"I'm riding up to see the Terror Twins," David answered, narrowing his eyebrows at her gaze. "Is that a crime?"

"No crime," Christy said. "I'm just getting tired of you turning up every time I have a job to do."

"Yeah, well, the feeling's mutual," he said, and slipping on his helmet, he kicked off from the gravel and started pedaling up the hill.

Christy let out an exasperated groan and kicked up gravel as she punched the gas, passed by the biker and then headed him off with a hard swerve to the right. This time when she rolled down the window, it was David who was angry.

"What's the big idea?" he yelled. "I have just as much right to ride this road as you do."

"Look, I'm here on police business, and I'd appreciate it if you don't interfere."

"I thought your only official business was to try to run me over."

"Wise up, brat, or I'll throw you in the back of the car too."

Christy hit the gas and left David behind. She could see him shaking his head and yelling something at the back of her car in her rearview mirror.

The twins' shack looked quiet in the late-morning light. Christy had only been out here once before. During her first week on the force she'd had to drive out here after a public indecency charge had been leveled at TG. Seems he'd mooned a couple of old ladies in broad daylight after they'd called him a hooligan. Christy had slapped him with a warning and gotten out fast. He *was* a hooligan, after all!

Nothing much had changed since her last visit. The old place looked as if it sagged under the weight of a hundred years of winters. Its tin roof had a sway to its center that she was sure it hadn't had in the early days of its installation, and the small windows on either side of the old wooden door looked crooked. The gray paint on the four stairs leading to the small wooden porch was all but gone, though the wood underneath was almost the same weathered color as the remaining paint.

Around her the wind whispered through the thick stands of trees, but the shack itself stood silent, seemingly vacant.

The first step creaked under her foot, and Christy hesitated. She couldn't explain why, but she felt nervous about this visit in a way she hadn't the last time she'd been here. Not that she necessarily thought Billy would get violent and resist her, but . . . something just didn't feel right. Shaking off the feeling, she stepped up the next couple stairs, and then paused on the landing, again getting a chill up the back of her neck.

She stood there, just inches from the door, and listened. The breeze whispered by her ear just above the sound of silence and then she heard the telltale sound of gravel clicking gravel. Christy turned and there was David, still astride his bike, stopped just in front of her squad. He held his helmet to his side and stood there, watching.

"I told you . . ." she began, but her reprimand was interrupted by a muffled scream. It came from inside the shack.

Christy held a hand out directing David to stay where he was, while she drew her gun and stepped to the side of the door frame. With her free hand, she reached out to turn the knob. It turned easily, and with a quick motion, she pushed open the door, at the same time putting both hands on the gun and holding it above her head, ready to come down and fire if someone stormed out of the shack.

But instead, the door simply swung inward, revealing the shadowed entryway to a dilapidated kitchen. She dropped to a crouch and pirouetted to face the entrance, gun at the ready, but saw nobody.

"Ewwwwahhhhhaaaiii!"

The scream was loud and unmistakable this time. It was high-pitched, a woman's voice. It was close by.

Christy stepped on the stained and yellowing black-and-white tile of the kitchen and slowly began to rise from her crouch. It didn't seem like this was going to turn into a hostage/gunfire exchange. She instinctively reached out to push the door shut behind her and stopped.

"Aiiiiiieeeaaaiiiii!"

The noise came from the floor behind the kitchen door.

Or, more specifically, from the naked woman bound and gagged on the dirty floor behind the kitchen door. Her long black hair tangled in knots all around her neck. She shook it away from her eyes, which bugged open wide, bloodshot and filled with desperation. The woman's arms and legs were tied behind her back, leaving her exposed breasts and tummy to thrust forward in a terrible display of helplessness. Her whole body was smudged and smeared with dirt from the floor, and blood caked the edges of the bindings around her wrists where she'd struggled to break their hold to no avail. Her cheeks displayed the trails of a river of dried tears, and the floor in front of her still held a pool of yellowed water, where she'd apparently scooted forward to pee before inching back away from the mess. As Christy registered the scene in front of her, the woman let out another long wail behind her gag—a sad and horrible cry of anguish—and tried to bring her legs up tighter to hide her nakedness, but she only succeeded in yanking open the wounds on her wrists again, resulting in a new round of whines from deep in her throat.

"Holy shit," David said from behind her.

"I told you to stay *outside,*" Christy hissed.

"Again, it's a free country," he said. "Are you going to cut her loose, or should I?"

Christy stifled the urge to punch the cyclist right in the mouth, and knelt down by the bedraggled captive. She untied the gag first, gently pulling it away from the woman's face. She took a deep, gasping breath when the material left her mouth, and whispered, "Thank you."

"Is anyone here?" Christy prodded, nodding toward the inside of the shack.

The woman shook her head. "No," she gasped. "They left me here the night before last. Nobody's been back since."

Christy stepped behind her and began working on the knots at her wrists and ankles. David reached into his pocket and pulled out a pocketknife. "Here," he said. "She might want to get out of that, um, today."

She took the knife without comment, and in moments, the woman lay limp on her back. Her whole body began to tremble, and she started to cry.

Christy put her hand on the woman's forehead. "Shhh," she said. "It's okay now. We're here."

"I . . . can't . . . move my arms," the woman gasped. "Pins and needles."

David knelt at her side and began to massage a shoulder and elbow.

"I think you should . . ." Christy began.

"Rub her other arm," David insisted. "She's been lying here for like thirty-six hours. We need to help the circulation come back."

"What's your name?" Christy asked.

"Amy Lynn," the woman whispered. Her voice was raw as chopped meat. After a few minutes, she pushed herself away from their massage and sat up, slowly pulling her legs up in a crouch and crossing her arms over her bare chest. "Will you take me home, please?" she asked.

"Yeah," Christy promised. She stood, and caught David's eye. "Stay here with her a minute?"

He nodded, and pulled his gray T-shirt over his head. "I can't say it's totally clean," he said, offering it to Amy Lynn. "But it's better than nothing."

The pale skin of her dirt-streaked face betrayed the hint of a blush and she whispered a thanks. Christy nodded at them and stepped through the kitchen, gun in hand, to investigate the rest of the house. Again, she was trespassing without a warrant. But this time, she had cause, and she wasn't going to pass it up.

After she left the room, David put his arm around the girl, who now wore his Boston U shirt. It settled loosely over her middle, and she pulled its edge to cover some of her thigh. "It's all right," he promised. "It's all going to be okay now."

Amy Lynn started to say something, but then her eyes welled up, and she simply collapsed into his arms, hoarse cries coming fast and hard. He held her and tried to give comfort. But in his head, he had only one thought.

Was this what had happened to Brenda? Part of him grew cold at the idea of her naked and tied up in a basement somewhere. At the idea that she was just waiting, somewhere, for him to find and help her.

Christy returned to the kitchen a few minutes later, shaking her head. "Nothing," she said. "C'mon, help me get her out of here."

"Now it's okay that I'm here?" he poked.

"Do you WANT me to bust your balls?" she asked. "There's a woman who needs help and we're here to give it. Shut up and help the girl up."

Amy Lynn leaned heavily on both of them as they walked to the car. David helped her slide into the backseat, but as he stepped away, Christy nodded.

"You can take the other side."

"That's all right," he said. "I've gotta get to work. I've got my bike."

"I need you to come down to the station and give a statement," Christy insisted. "We can put your bike on the rack." She pointed to the silver struts on the car's roof.

David opened his mouth to protest and Christy put up a hand. "Look, just do this, okay? That girl in the car needs our help, and she needs an ironclad case whenever we find the guys who did this to her. Which means I need you as a strong witness to what just happened, and the best way to establish that is a statement immediately after the event. So take a ride with me and let's get this girl a shower and some clothes faster, huh?"

He somehow couldn't argue with that one. Christy helped him strap the bike down, and then the gravel was crunching behind them as they pulled away from the shack.

"Where are you from, Amy Lynn?" Christy asked, looking at the girl in the rearview mirror. The woman clearly was in shock, eyes wide, arms tightly crossed at her chest.

"Oak Falls," she answered. "These guys . . . they picked up me and another girl at a bar there . . . They seemed really fun, you know? Kinda redneck, but good for a night, you know? I was making out with the one, he was a big guy, in the backseat while his friend drove. He had a girl in front too."

"Do you remember his name?"

Amy Lynn shook her head. "No. Tom or Tim, or . . . T something. He had a black Mustang."

In the front seat Christy smiled sourly. "After they brought you back to the shack, what happened?"

"They were taking the other girl somewhere else," Amy Lynn said. "She was passed out in the front seat and T . . . TG! That was his name. TG said he wanted to hurry up and get their money so he could get back to me. Then he dragged me into the house and dropped me there on the floor. But he never came back."

"Did he say where they were taking her?"

"To the doc's, he said a couple times. And once he mentioned an asylum."

David's stomach turned to ice as he pictured again that girl in the upstairs window of the asylum. Meanwhile, Christy's foot increased its pressure on the accelerator. Maybe *now* the chief would process a warrant.

CHAPTER TWENTY-NINE

Something cold interrupted the warmth between her thighs. There were voices, whispers outside. She could hear them. But as much as she tried, Brenda couldn't open her eyes to see the speakers. Her world swirled with a hum of dark violet and sinister shapes slipped between the curves of silver clouds. Brenda floated in a sea of sensation; her arms and legs tingled with the touch of a thousand tiny pinpoints. A feather's kiss of touch on every part of her. She seemed perfectly free, and yet somewhere inside she knew that she was trapped here. Now, as she heard the voices just outside, she knew she had to escape.

"Open your eyes," she whispered to herself.

"Open your eyes."

Again the coldness between her legs, as the buzz of a vacuum grew inside her ears.

"Open your eyes."

"She won't be fertile for a couple more days," a woman said. "That's really cutting it close."

And a male voice.

"It will be enough. She only has to have conceived for her to serve as the Eleventh."

"What if it doesn't take?"

The man laughed. "C'mon, Amelia. We'll make sure it does. And you'll enjoy every minute of it."

CHAPTER THIRTY

"Can I talk to you a minute?" David asked. He was gritting his teeth as he said it, but he couldn't hold back any longer. He'd been thinking about it throughout the morning as a police captain took his statement. Christy had disappeared to procure some clothes for Amy Lynn and get her statement. Now the blonde officer had come back to escort him from the station, and he knew he needed her help.

"Sure," Christy said, raising an eyebrow. "What's up?" They were standing near her cluttered desk in the middle of the station; Captain Ryan was just a few feet away, typing at his computer; probably keying in things about David's statement.

"In private?" David asked softly.

Again, she cocked an eyebrow—well tweezed, he noted—and motioned for him to follow.

Outside the station, she led him around the back to the parking lot. Resting her butt against the hood of her squad, Christy looked him in the eyes and held empty palms out in front of her. "Okay," she said. "What've ya got?"

"Something's going on at the asylum," he began.

"What do you mean?"

"The doctor . . . He isn't really a psychiatrist."

She nodded, but didn't interrupt.

"And I don't think they've got those women there to help them with mental illness."

Christy shifted on the hood and looked toward the front of the station. When she looked at him again, she said, "What makes you think that?"

"I work there," he said. "And yesterday, I saw what they were doing in the basement."

"And that was?"

He told her about witnessing the ritual in the basement of the old hotel, and as he did, Christy looked toward the front of the station, as if waiting for someone. When he finished, she slid off the hood of the car and put her hands on his shoulders. David found his stomach went just a little weak when she did that. Her eyes were intensely blue as she leaned closer to his face and whispered, "Look, David. We're looking into what's going on at the asylum. That's why I was out there the day we first ran into each other."

"Well, actually you ran into me."

She rolled her eyes at that. "Whatever. Look, I want you to stay clear of that place for a while, okay?"

"But my job . . ."

"Call in sick."

David shook his head. "I can't," he said. "Somebody's got to do something. I don't know what they're doing to those women, but it can't wait. And, there's one other thing . . ."

"What's that?"

"I'm worried they've got Brenda Bean in there somewhere. If those guys have been tying girls up and taking them to the doctor to experiment on . . ."

"We don't know that."

David grew insistent. "C'mon. They tied up the girl we found today. They took someone else to the asylum that night. And Joe, the bartender at the Shack, said they were in the bar that night that Brenda disappeared. If she's there, I have to help her."

"How do you suggest we do that?"

"We go there tonight after dark, when everyone's asleep, and we look for her."

Christy nodded, as if impressed. "Brilliant plan. I love it. Just one problem. How are we going to get in? I don't think the front door is open after-hours."

David reached into his pants pocket and held out the answer. "I have a key."

Christy shook her head. "Look, David, I know you want to help. But you're just asking for trouble that way. If Brenda is there, I promise you, I'll find out. There are things going on that you don't know about. And for once, I'd like you to not turn up in the wrong place at the wrong time, okay?"

She put a finger under his chin and forced him to meet her eyes. And again, David felt himself tremble just a bit at the intensity of her gaze. For an irritating cop, she sure was gorgeous!

"Promise me?" she insisted. "Go home to your aunt's, and stay there?"

Christy watched David pull his bike off the car rack, and ride away in silence. He looked unhappy, but what could she do? Nothing with him. But she could do something with a little help from the chief. Steeling her courage, she marched back into the station, determined to get the chief to get a search warrant issued. Today.

But when she went inside, the chief instead grabbed her first. He stood at Matt's desk with the girl, who was now dressed in a pair of sweatpants and a T-shirt that the chief had commandeered from the grocery. Her hair was still damp, and up in a ponytail; while they'd procured her some clothes, she'd taken a shower in the station's locker room.

"Sorensen," he called. "I've talked with Oak Falls, and they know Amy Lynn's story, here. I want you to give her a ride home. Oak Falls will keep an eye on her for the next few days, at least until we track down TG and Billy."

Christy's heart sank. Now she was a taxi service?

"Chief, can I talk to you before I go?" she asked.

"After." He patted Amy Lynn on the shoulders paternally, and then gave a curt nod to Christy before lumbering back to his office.

Christy forced a smile for Amy Lynn's sake. "Two rides in a squad in one day?" she joked. "Better be careful this doesn't become a habit."

The girl gave a weak smile in return. "I hope this one will be my last, for a while anyway."

By the time she delivered Amy Lynn to her apartment back in Oak Falls and then answered a shoplifting call at Smythe's Grocery, the afternoon light was fading. As Christy reached for the door of the station, it opened, and the chief came out.

"Chief," she started, but he held up a hand.

"I know what you want, Sorensen," he growled. His face looked more lined than usual, the silver in his hair a sign of weakness right now, not wisdom. "But you don't have enough evidence. I can't pull a warrant on a crazy house just because some girl said a couple of thugs were headed there with some-one else. It'll never stand up."

He moved past her and shook his head. "Stay alert," he said, repeating his police chief mantra. Then he added something to it. "And stay away from the asylum."

Christy stood there holding the door open, as she watched him slowly lumber toward the park-ing lot. He looked exhausted in a way she'd never seen him. She was furious. Her mouth hung open as she followed his slouching figure until it turned out of sight. Taking a breath, she finally went in-side the station, and noted that Matt was already gone too.

Wasn't the captain supposed to be the last man on deck? she thought, as she sat down at her com-puter to file her paperwork for the day. But no, in-stead, it looked like in Castle Point, it was the rookie who manned the last station.

Or womanned it, she thought.

It was after six by the time she hit print and gath-ered the last forms to drop in Chief's in-box. As she dropped them off, something on his desk caught her eye. A small card folded and tucked under his desk calendar. With the edge of a photo sticking out. Glancing behind her to make sure nobody had walked into the station, Christy stepped around the chief's desk and slid the photo out. She knew why it had caught her attention before she even got to the face. It was the high school photo of Chief's daugh-ter, Stacy. A larger version was there in a frame on his desk; she'd seen it virtually every day since she'd started with the force. Slipping the card out from under the calendar, she read the handwritten words inside, and her heart leaped.

If you'd like to see her again, don't think about any warrants for the next few days. I think you know what I mean.

The card was unsigned, but Christy knew instantly whom it had come from: Dr. Rockford. But how? Why would he even know about her push for a warrant? She racked her brain, trying to think if she had mentioned it on the police band when she'd called in from the Terror Twins' place this morning.

What the hell is going on out there? she thought. Carefully, Christy tucked the photo back into the card and slipped it back under the calendar. Then she left the station and took a drive over to Stacy's neighborhood. She slowed when she saw the squad in front of Stacy's house. That's why Chief had been in such a hurry to leave when she'd tried to talk to him. He'd been on his way here. And as she made a left turn to avoid passing directly in front of the house, she saw that he hadn't found anything. The chief was sitting on the porch of his daughter's house, hands wrapped around his knees, staring off into space. Christy thought that for as big of a man as he was, the chief suddenly didn't look very large at all.

Chapter Thirty-one

David wasn't sure if he could watch one more episode of *Cheers* with his aunt. It was a ME-TV marathon, and they'd been listening to canned laughter since dinner. He didn't mind the first half an hour, but after that, sitcoms really got on his nerves. It was almost as if they inserted the laugh tracks to tell the sheep watching the programs what was funny. He could hear the studio executives editing the programs: "Here, laugh, dipshits. It's funny. Trust me."

His gaze began to wander around the room, resting on old photos chronicling Elsie's life, from a recent one of her neighbor's chubby kids wearing Santa hats last Christmas to a faded one of his late uncle Bill holding what looked to be at least a twenty-pound fish on a line. Over on the table near the front door, a more recent photo showed a woman with chestnut hair on her tiptoes, exaggerating a kiss with a man whose mouth was curled up in a stifled laugh. David remembered when that photo had been taken, not long before the fire. His eyes grew wet at the memory of his parents, and he forced his gaze away to the pile of mail on the catch-all table. He saw the *People* magazine and a handful of catalogs stacked there, beneath what looked to be a couple of bills and an invitation of some kind. She'd opened that and in simple red block letters the card's front read YOU'RE INVITED. He wondered whose yard party he'd be dragged to. On the TV, Norm put up his hands when Sam answered the phone and said, "It's Vera." "No way, Sammy," the rotund barfly hissed and pushed his empty mug forward across the bar. "I'll need at least two more of these before I can go *there*."

David rolled his eyes as he brought his attention back to the television. That settled it. He put a fist to his mouth and exaggerated a yawn. "Think I'm going to turn in," he said.

"But it's not even ten o'clock," Elsie said.

"Yeah, but . . ."

His excuse was cut off by the doorbell.

"Now who could that be?" Elsie said, and started to pry herself out of the easy chair.

"I'll get it," he said, and motioned for her to stay in her seat. When he opened the door, and saw who stood on the stoop, he could only think of one thing to say.

"You again!"

Christy Sorensen brushed a moth from fluttering in front of her face, and smiled grimly. "Yeah, I knew you'd be having withdrawal by now, so I decided to stop by."

She was wearing worn, faded blue jeans, and a black T-shirt with the logo of a bar called Red-Eyed Fly. Instead of the police squad, there was an old boat of a car parked on the curb. Clearly this wasn't an official visit. "You want to come in?" he asked.

Christy peered around him and saw Elsie craning from her chair to see who was at the door. "Why don't you come out?" she countered. "And bring that key you were bragging about this afternoon."

David grinned. "Give me three minutes."

"So what changed your mind?" he asked, as the car pulled away from the curb. He'd pulled on his other jeans, grabbed his keys and told Elsie he had to help a friend. Christy already had the engine running when he came out.

"I shouldn't tell you, because it's police business," she hesitated. "But I suppose it doesn't matter since if we get caught I'm going to be fired anyway."

She pulled to a stop at the light on Main, and caught David again in that look. Instead of feeling uncomfortable this time though, he decided he liked it. Liked her, actually. She might be a cop, but she was all right. Didn't hurt that she was a total fox either. He almost laughed out loud at that thought.

"Look," she said, staring hard at him, as if it was very important that he understood what she was about to say implicitly. "The chief has had a hunch that something was going on out there at the old hotel since the day these asylum people moved in. I was out there trying to figure it out, but you blew my cover. Still, I got inside one night and got a glimpse at some of the patients, and I found out that most of them are missing persons."

"So they're not crazy at all," David interjected.

She shrugged, and then looked back at the road as the light changed. "I don't know, but I'd bet against it. I saw some of the doc's stuff on the walls and in his exam room, and none of it talks about him being a head doctor. He's some kind of big-shot genetic scientist. I don't think he's worried about whether they're schizoid, I think he's doing some kind of experiments on them."

"It's worse than that," David said. "I told you what I saw yesterday. The guy's doing some kind of rituals in the basement using these women."

"Jury's out on that," she said. "But he's doing something there that he doesn't want the world to find out about. And here's how I know for sure."

She told him about the blackmail note she'd found

with the picture of the chief's daughter. David whistled.

"So that's why we're going out here on our own tonight," she concluded. "The department isn't going to get a warrant. And something's going on there *now;* they wouldn't grab the chief's daughter to hold indefinitely."

David nodded. "Just so they don't grab us."

Christy pulled the Olds off the road just before the cutoff to the old hotel. When they got out of the car, the cricket song was loud as locusts. Stars lit the ground with a steady glow; it was a warm, clear night.

"Nice out," David said.

"Yeah," Christy said. "Not sure that's a good thing. We don't want to be seen out here."

"Just stay close to the tree line," he suggested and stepped off the gravel road and into the brush. She followed, and a few minutes later he led her across the back patio to the rear entrance of the asylum.

"Think they've got a night alarm?" he asked, only half joking as he pulled out the key. Christy held the screen door.

"Shit," she said. "If they do, you better be as fast on your feet as you are on that bike."

He turned the key in the lock and it clicked. The door whispered open, the light from the summer sky illuminating the dark foyer just inside in long shadows. Christy put her hand on David's chest and eased past him, taking a flat stance against the hallway wall and slowly easing her way forward. *All she's missing is the gun,* David thought, admiring her precision steps. He carefully pulled the screen and inside doors shut, and tiptoed after her.

In moments they had crept down the hallway to the main reception area. Just as the last time they'd each been here, the main floor was silent, and empty. When they reached the second floor, Christy grabbed David by the arm and pulled him against the wall near room one. For just a second, his pulse quickened as he thought she was about to kiss him. But instead, she dug a hand into her jeans pocket and slid out a photo of a pretty young woman, golden-haired and freckled. She handed it to David.

"I got this from Oak Falls PD today," she whispered. "She was reported missing yesterday, and was last seen at the bar where Amy Lynn was picked up. Name's Mary Jane McCarthy. I'm betting she's the girl who was passed out in the front seat of the Mustang. The girl they brought here after they dropped Amy Lynn off at the shack."

David tried to commit the photo to memory, and nodded. Christy took it back, and reached out to try the doorknob of the first room. It opened easily, but the pounding in David's chest as she pushed it open was for naught.

The room was empty. Just a bed and a dresser.

The same as the next room. And the next.

When they pulled the door shut on an also-empty room five, David hissed, "I thought they had patients in this whole wing."

Christy's lips turned down. The creases at the corner of her eyes betrayed her concern. "They did," she said.

Finally, when she pushed open the door to room six, their luck changed. Christy held up her hand to caution him as soon as the door let light into the room and she saw the sleeping form on the bed. They slipped inside and closed the door. "Is this Brenda?" Christy whispered in his ear. He shook his head no, and she pulled him back out to the hall.

"I didn't bring the mug shots of all the patients I saw here last time, because it doesn't matter at this point. I know they were here, and as the Law, I can't do anything about it at the moment. But if we see Brenda, or can confirm this other girl . . ."

There were women in rooms seven through ten, all of them sleeping deeply. Several were obviously pregnant. None of them stirred as they slipped in and out of their rooms.

"This is creepy," David whispered as they left room ten. "It's like they're dead."

"Sleeping with Prince Valium," Christy said. "I recognize a couple of them from the missing persons mugs. And I'm pretty sure the Terror Twins brought them here."

Christy turned the knob on room eleven as she talked to David, and pushed open the door, expecting another dark room with a sleeping woman inside.

While that's exactly what she opened the door into, she hadn't expected David's reaction. He pushed past her, running to the bedside of the sleeping patient inside.

"Oh my God," he cried, and put his hand on the woman's cheek. "It's you. It's really you. Brenda? Brenda, wake up, please."

Christy stepped up softly behind him and put her hand on his shoulder as he pleaded with the unconscious woman. "David," she said. "She's drugged. She's not going to wake up right now."

Brenda certainly didn't look likely to wake. She lay flat on her back beneath dull white sheets, dark hair mussed over her left eye, a strand of hot pink spread like anemone on the pillow. But David wouldn't give up so easily. He took the sleeping girl by the shoulders and shook her, and then bent to hiss in her ear, "Wake up, Brenda, wake up!"

He shook her again by the shoulders, harder this time, and Christy pulled him back. "Stop it," she commanded.

When he turned to her, his eyes glistened. "It's my fault she's here," he said. "We have to get her up."

Christy nodded. "We will. But she's probably not going on her own power."

David shrugged off her hands and returned to the bed. He folded down the blanket and reached an arm beneath Brenda's head. He lifted her to a sitting position, and her face promptly slumped forward, hair hanging across the faded blue hospital gown like a shield.

Somewhere in the asylum, a woman screamed.

David jumped, nearly pushing the poor girl off the bed. Christy reached out and caught her, and the two of them laid Brenda back to the pillow.

The scream came again, this time more faint, yet somehow, more bloodcurdling.

"We've gotta get out of here," David whispered.

"No," Christy answered. "Someone needs our help."

"Yeah," he said. "Brenda."

Christy shook her head. "She's not going anywhere. We'll come back for her. But right now, somebody is in pain."

She walked away from the bed and opened the door. "You can stay here until I come back if you want. That's probably best."

The door closed and David stared down at Brenda's face. She was beautiful still, lit only by the faint light of the moon through the window. He ran the back of his hand up the side of her face. Her skin was velvety smooth and warm. Her body seemed to respond, taking in a deep breath and then settling heavily into the mattress.

Again, a horrible shriek echoed into the room.

David bet that it came through the ventilation ducts, and he knew where Christy would have to go to find its source.

"Shit," he moaned, and bent forward to kiss Brenda's forehead. A strand of pink hair caught on his lip. "I'll be back in a little while," he promised.

Christy closed the door to room eleven and slid silently down the long hall past the patient rooms they had already looked into. Then she tiptoed down the wide staircase to the main floor. The scream came again, and the hair on the back of her neck stood up. Someone was being filleted alive, or so it sounded.

She stepped carefully across the carpet at the base of the stairs. The floor was quiet. Too quiet. A light shone from the front office just down the hall, but the rest of the place was cloaked in shadow. It seemed far more like an abandoned hotel at midnight than a fledgling medical institution. Who was on hand to watch over the patients?

The door to the basement was not hard to find. She rounded a corner, and there it was, the red *X*.

As if on cue, another scream sounded from someplace not so far away. This time though, it didn't just end, but sort of quavered and quivered and lingered in the air, as if someone was having their intestines slowly reeled out from inside, one foot at a time.

Christy flinched from the mental image, and just then, someone grabbed her by the shoulders.

"Wait," came a familiar whisper. "I'll go with you."

She turned to face David, whose eyes betrayed a glint of both concern . . . and fear.

"I told you I'd come back for you."

"And I told Brenda the same thing. I couldn't let you do this alone."

"Then let's get it done." She grinned and started

to turn away. But David put a hand on her shoulder to stop her.

"Wait," he said. "Do you have a gun?"

"I'm off duty," she hissed and pulled away.

"Great," he mumbled, following her to the door. "Just great."

The stairs creaked as Christy stepped down them, and David took in a deep breath as he followed. Dead. They were dead meat here. The doc and his dominatrix butchered pregnant women down here . . . What the hell were a chick cop with no ammo and a college kid going to do to stop them? He waited for the screams to echo painfully through the narrow stairwell, but there was no sound. Just the labored breath of their fear.

Christy reached the bottom first, and he grabbed her arm as she started forward. "Wait, they'll see you."

She slowed but didn't stop. Instead, she moved to the entryway and cautiously peered around the corner at the room beyond. David could see she was trying to flatten her body so as not to be seen, but in the end, it didn't matter.

"There's no one down here," she whispered.

David slipped around her and stepped into the long basement room. The fluorescent lights overhead flickered occasionally, but outside of that, everything seemed quiet.

And then a baby cried.

Christy jumped. But the sound didn't surprise David. He knew where it came from. He tapped her on the shoulder and nodded his head as he walked into the room and headed immediately toward the far end.

She followed, and in seconds they were standing in front of four plastic crèches, each inhabited by a small infant. One of them, a child with long curly black hair, cried out again.

"This is what they're stealing from the mothers," David said. "But what happens to the women after that . . ."

Christy opened her mouth to say that they were probably just waiting for their babies upstairs and then remembered the handful of empty rooms they had seen. She closed her mouth. The babies were cute, and tiny and helpless. And Christy knew that the people who kept them here couldn't be far away. David was peering through the glass at one of them, and making wide-mouthed smiles at the baby, who only stared back with enlarged blue eyes.

"We can't stay here."

He nodded. "Let's find them."

They left the infants behind and crossed the long room, which led to a hallway at the other end. In between, they passed two empty hospital beds, and in his mind, David saw the ghosts of a woman with red spattering her middle, and Dr. Rockford holding crimson hands toward the sky.

Christy paused at the entry to the hall, and put up a hand, motioning for David to stay behind. "You're kidding, right?" he said, and followed her in.

That's when the lights went out.

Ahead of them, a woman screamed. But somehow, the sound didn't scare David like it once might have. He'd gotten used to it in this creepy hotel. What was making his skin crawl was the darkness. He reached out for Christy, and his hands only met air.

"Christy," he whispered.

"Christy?"

When the lights went out, Christy moved. Her training told her this wasn't a power outage . . . this was a trap. And traps only sprung if you were around to get caught. So she darted forward to where she had seen a long wall, and when her shoulder slammed into it, she dropped to a crouch and squinted into the darkness.

There was no light source down here, whatsoever. No windows to let in the faint illumination of the stars and moon, and the hall was disconnected from the main room where maybe, just maybe, a slight wisp of light might fade down from upstairs. Christy didn't know if her eyes would ever adjust to make out anything.

She heard the scream, and moved, heading toward it. Wherever the pain was, she would find the doctor, she knew. And where the doctor was, the answer to this whole mystery lay.

With her hands she followed the rough texture of the stone wall. It was cold to the touch, and damp. She shivered as she felt her way down the corridor. The air moved around her, and her neck felt like a thousand spiderwebs were slipping by around her, a haze of clinging death hanging in the dark.

The scream came again, and Christy tried to move faster . . . She didn't know what she was going to do, but she had to do something to stop whatever they were doing to that woman. It sounded as if they were drawing her lungs out through her vagina . . . the horrible gurgling, wet sound she uttered with each scream made Christy's skin crawl.

Ahead she saw the faintest hint of red light through the blackness, and she moved toward it. She'd forgotten David with the urgency of the chase upon her, and didn't think twice as she crept forward. The light grew stronger, and then she was at the opening to another room. In the shadow she could make out the archway of the space. She put her hands on the cold rock and tried to peer inside. She could just make out in the twisting crimson shadows two figures standing over the silvery glint of a table. Their hands moved over a figure on that table, and candles flickered and glowed in the space just beyond. A man's voice called out the words *"Astarte dumei e' DesCrat!"* and a woman's voice quickly answered, "Ba'al we serve you."

Christy entered the room, creeping quietly toward the two figures, trying still to make out exactly what they were doing to the woman on the hospital bed before them. She recognized Dr. Rockford now, and her stomach only clenched tighter as she realized that there was no way the chief was going to believe her when she explained what she'd seen this man of science doing. Because right now, instead of injecting someone with drugs, or expeditiously slicing through the skin to excise or salvage an organ, the doctor was instead carving the woman. It wasn't an operation, she saw, as she drew closer and closer to the operating circle. It was a flesh tattoo. Or more specifically a flesh scarification . . . or ritual evisceration. She couldn't tell how deep Rockford was cutting with his scalpel, but he clearly had drawn a ring of blood around the perimeter of the woman's distended belly. Bisecting the circle were an array of long, sharply cut lines, each bleeding tears of red down toward the center of the design. Her belly button.

Again the woman screamed as Dr. Rockford bent forward, and Christy could be quiet no longer. She stood up to charge the doctor, and that's when she felt the hands on her shoulders again. Only this time, they weren't David's hands. When she turned to see who had grabbed her, she found herself staring into a pair of eyes so red, they could have

been hot coals in the grill of a Fourth of July bar-
becue.

But she didn't stare at them long. Because just as
a toothy grin broke the darkness beneath those red
eyes, something swung audibly in the air and came
to a rest on the back of her skull.

Christy came to rest on the dirty floor. And then
her thoughts were as dark as the hallway she'd just
left.

CHAPTER THIRTY-TWO

David heard the second scream in the darkness
and felt his skin crawl. "Christy!" he called desperately again, struggling to keep his voice just above a
whisper. There was no answer.

The air down here was cool, and wet, and it
stuck in his throat like algae. He felt like he was
drowning in the darkness. After calling Christy for
the third time, he decided that standing still in the
dark was not the best strategy. Sooner or later, the
lights might come on, yes. But by then, he might
be dead.

So David began to inch his way along the wall to
his left. He moved like a slug . . . slow and gentle . . .
careful not to run into anything that might give
away his position. Like Christy, he didn't believe the
lights had gone out accidentally.

Which meant, of course, that they knew someone
was in the asylum that shouldn't be. Which meant
they were looking for . . . him.

David moved. The wall suddenly gave way to

open air, and he almost fell as the rock he'd put pressure on disappeared. He gasped, but recovered quickly and stepped to the left, into another trail of empty darkness. He wondered if the world had seemed so cruel and filled with potential pain to Helen Keller. Every step of his feet brought a pain of tightly drawn breath to his lungs.

The wall dropped away again, and he followed it, not knowing what else to do. He could get lost following corridors into darkness, but the other alternative was simply to crawl back up the stairs and slink back home. And he hadn't come here to lose.

The wall that slid roughly beneath his hands in the dark suddenly became smooth. David slid his hands along it, tracing the invisible surface until he came to something cold and metallic. And round.

A doorknob.

He had found a doorway to someplace else, and David didn't hesitate to try to turn the knob.

But it didn't budge.

As he twisted the knob, trying repeatedly to move it, something moved beyond the door. Someone was inside!

"Hello," he hissed. "Is someone there?"

A thud.

"Hello?"

"Open the door," a voice demanded. A man's voice, tired and lost. "Open it, hurry."

"I can't," David said truthfully. "It's locked and I don't have a key."

"Then get the hell away before they throw you in here . . . and come back when you have the key," the voice concluded. David had the impression of a vocal cord twisted around a fence post.

"Who are you?" he asked.

"Just fuckin' go!" the voice inside demanded.

David tried the knob again, but it didn't budge. Shaking his head, he moved past it, but in seconds came up against a stone wall. Dead end.

Okay, he thought, Christy hadn't come this way. He began to head back the way he had come, when without warning, the lights came back on. Blinded at first, he dropped to a crouch against the wall, and shaded his eyes with his palms.

As the stars fell away and he could make out his surroundings, David realized that he was in a short, stubby hallway. The room he'd just tried to enter was the only thing here. But ahead, in the corridor he and Christy had been walking down, he could see that it continued. He began to head that way, assuming that she had simply gone forward when he had turned left. But then he heard voices and froze.

"I knew she was trouble the first time she came in here," a woman's voice declared. "Fuckin' cops."

And then a man: "Not trouble at all," he said. "Opportunity. The time for trouble is over. Tomorrow, we will use all of our resources."

The corridor in front of David suddenly was filled with the owners of the voices. Dr. Rockford. Nurse Amelia. And dangling between their arms, blonde hair trailing along the rock floor, Christy. Officer Christy Sorensen.

So much for cop training.

"Fuck, fuck, fuck," David mumbled to himself.

After they passed, David slipped down the corridor and turned in the direction they'd come from. In moments he found the room that Christy had seen, or not seen, in the dark. It was a small room, and smelled of iron. The floor was speckled in dots of rust, and the walls looked painted in crimson. As David looked, he swore he could see the paint crawl.

Shit, he realized. *That's not paint.*
That's blood.

The room smelled in a way David couldn't define. It reminded him of mortality. Of life and hurt and earth and loss. As he watched it move and shift on the wall, his throat clenched. Someone had died in here. Deep in the darkness, someone had screamed and begged for mercy, and instead . . . her blood now flowed in slow, sluggish rivulets down the walls.

He didn't want to see what the body that had been left behind looked like. And his quick survey of the room didn't reveal it. David backed away before he was forced to process the source of the blood.

He backed away until the wall pressed against his back, and this time, he headed back toward the main room of the basement without caution. He wanted out, and out now. When the baby cried, he didn't even slow. Deep inside him his conscience cried out, "I'm sorry little guy," but David's feet were already on the stairs. This time, he didn't listen to see if they creaked. He vaulted up them, and turned the handle on the door at the top without worrying about whether someone was there.

As it happened, they weren't. And David didn't stop to see where they might have gone. He bolted straight to the back hallway, where he knew a safe exit was. He didn't believe that anyone who stayed within these walls would have the free will to leave for long, and he sorely wanted to leave. When he came back the next time, he'd rescue Brenda from her drugged stupor, he swore. And he'd find Christy.

But he clearly couldn't accomplish either rescue

on his own. He needed help, and he needed to be free to get it.

So he pushed his way out the back door and ran, not looking back.

Behind him, the Castle Point Asylum watched in silence. And waited for his return.

CHAPTER THIRTY-THREE

The Innovative Industries truck pulled into the circle drive at Castle Point Asylum at its usual time on a Wednesday. Late. After dark. Near midnight.

Greg Sackobit parked the truck and stifled a yawn. He'd been cranking the tunes from WCIG—*your goth connection*—for the last half hour . . . but at midnight (plus or minus fourteen minutes) it was hard to stay focused on anything for very long, even the repetitive heaven of Ministry's "Everyday is Halloween." He stepped up the stone walkway to the door of the classic old asylum and reached up to ring the bell, but the door was already open before he could complete the action.

Amelia was there in her white nurse smock . . . but he noticed that it was buttoned up wrong, leaving an open lip to expose her navel. And near her ribs, the outfit was smeared with something red, as if a patient had grabbed and pulled at her with bloody hands.

Greg ignored the evidence. He'd been to plenty of bizarre places to pick up what he needed, and a little blood was certainly not a deterrent. Maybe she'd just finished a procedure to fill one of those vials he'd come for. Innovative Industries couldn't continue its under-the-counter research into gene cloning and limb replacement growth without the embryo stems he gathered here. Maybe it was bloody business. He didn't know, and didn't really care.

"Hey, Amelia." He grinned. "Got a dose for me?"

She didn't even smile at his playfulness. She motioned him inside and then almost ran down the hallway into the shadows to retrieve what he needed. Greg knew the asylum lived off the money his pickups brought in to them, so he didn't even question whether the material she handed him a minute later was what they needed. Innovative Industries paid good money for these stem cells, and had the ability to shut down Dr. Rockford's operation in a heartbeat if he crossed them.

As he took the box from Amelia, the devil himself loomed up behind her.

"Hey, Greg," the doctor said. "Tell Monty that this one is it. After tomorrow night, I don't think I'll have any other material for him. So please tell him . . . good luck. And use it wisely."

"What about next Wednesday?" Greg asked.

"I'll let you know if I have anything," Rockford said from the shadows, as Amelia already began to close the door.

"But don't count on it," his voice finished, as the door joined with the frame in a definitive *click*.

CHAPTER THIRTY-FOUR

The Castle Point police station looked quiet in the morning, David thought, as he pedaled down Main and turned to park his bike outside its white frame walls.

He walked down the sidewalk with far more confidence than he wished he had; confidence built from having been here before, and knowing the ins and outs of the local cop shop was not exactly what David had in his mind as a life goal. Nevertheless, he knew this place, and he stepped inside and pushed through the glass doors hoping to find Christy there ahead of him. But when he looked out at the floor and saw her desk empty, he knew he had to continue with his plan.

The detective he'd dealt with briefly yesterday came up to him as he stood in the foyer staring around.

"Hey," Captain Ryan said, smiling widely at David. "What can I help you with today?"

"I'd like to report a kidnapping," David said.

"Who?" the cop said, hair falling across his face in a faint halo of silver.

"One of your own," David said, waiting for the glint of interest in the cop's eye. It didn't come.

"And who's that?" Captain Ryan said. His voice sounded terminally bored.

"Detective Christy Sorensen."

"Hmmm. What makes you think that she's disappeared?" Ryan said.

"Because I was there when they took her," David said.

"Where is that, and who's 'they'?" Ryan asked, looking slightly interested now.

"The people at the asylum," David said.

"I see," Ryan coaxed. "The folks at the funny farm came and took one of our officers right off the street, did they? Was she directing traffic at the time?" There was no mistaking the sound of scorn in the older officer's voice.

"No, they didn't *come* to get her. *We* were at the asylum last night," David clarified. "I saw them carry her away in their arms, limp as a rag. I think she was unconscious, and they were probably taking her to one of their rooms."

"What makes you think that they locked her up? Couldn't they have been helping her, and she's back at home right now?"

"Why don't you call her and find out?"

Ryan raised an eyebrow at that, pausing. Then he reached for the phone on his desk. "I'll do that," he said. He hit the speed dial for Christy's house, and didn't take his eyes off David as the phone continued to ring in his ear. Nobody picked up. After ten rings, he put it back on its receiver.

"She may have gone out for a run," he said.

"Officer, I was there. I saw them carry her away last night, and it wasn't because she fainted or something. Two minutes before that, she'd been just fine. I was talking to her."

"So how did they come to be carrying her?"

David explained that they had gotten separated when the lights went out.

"So maybe she fell and bumped her head in the dark."

David shook his head adamantly. "They've got all kinds of people there who don't belong there," he said. "Including Brenda Bean, who disappeared a couple weeks ago from the Clam Shack. That's why we were there last night," he admitted. "To find her."

Captain Ryan stared hard at David, and then finally nodded, and wrote something down on a piece of paper. "What's your number?" he asked. "Where can I reach you if I need to?"

David gave him Aunt Elsie's home number and Ryan stood.

"Thanks for reporting this," he said. "I'll handle it from here."

David stood, but hesitated. It seemed like there should be something more. "Are you going to go out there now? I'll go with—"

"Go home, David," Captain Ryan said. He tapped the paper. "I'll be in touch."

David turned and walked toward the door with more than a hint of dejection. He didn't know what he'd expected, but it shouldn't have been a surprise that the cop didn't ask him to ride shotgun. Still . . .

"And David," Ryan called from across the station. "Stay away from Castle House Asylum."

CHAPTER THIRTY-FIVE

There was a time when Barry Rockford hadn't been able to stomach the sight of blood. A minor cut could bleed and make him queasy, his head spin with alarming lightness.

That time was before he and Amelia had moved to Castle House. Once he had been totally immersed in the study of cells—really the study of subcellular structure—and how to rebuild that structure in a lattice that would unfold its new blueprint across the body, enacting wholesale change from the tiniest particle to influence the entire body.

Now . . . he only wanted to destroy that body. He slid his hands inside the open belly of the woman on the table and reveled in the heat of her uterus in his hand. It pulsed and trembled at his touch, and with one quick motion he sliced through the meaty membrane to expose the amniotic sac inside. Here, *here* was life, he thought. The ultimate beginning. A smile slid unconsciously across his face as he pulled the fetus from the ruined womb. "I give you the ultimate end," he said, and handed the small, wriggling creature to Amelia, who voiced something in Arabic and invoked Ba'al.

"I would never have believed just a year ago," he said. His nurse laughed, and licked at the lobe of his ear before taking the baby to an incubator across the room.

"If we hadn't come here, you might never have believed," she agreed. "But here . . ." The shadows on the wall seemed to move in answer to her unspoken words.

"I hear them every night," he said, slipping his arm inside the woman up to his elbow, resting his body half inside hers. She felt so good, oozing around his forearm like hot jelly.

"Astarte is here with us now," Amelia whispered. "Listen."

Rockford listened, but could hear nothing except the woman on the table's labored breathing. If he didn't close the wounds he'd inflicted soon, he'd lose her. And that wasn't the plan. He needed twelve mothers for the ceremony tomorrow night. And then, of course, the Thirteenth.

"You're still more sensitive to them than I am," he admitted. "Come help me stitch her up." His voice grew deeper, more uncontrolled. Beneath his bloody doctor's gown his cock was painfully erect. "I want to bathe in her now."

Amelia was back at his side then. Her arms caressed his cheek. One finger slid across his lip and then inside his mouth before she trailed his saliva down his chin. He sucked the iron taste from her fingers greedily before her hands grasped his arms and followed them into the gore. Gently her hands gripped his wrists hidden deep inside the woman on the table, and began to pull him back from the edge.

"Not yet, love," she said. "Just a little while longer. And then we will bathe in all the blood you can imagine. All the blood you can ever desire. Just a few more hours."

She produced the sutures, and both of them began to stitch the unconscious woman's womb and belly back together.

Rockford's breath continued to hitch and sigh

with every stitch. Amelia only smiled and licked her dry lips with anticipation. Around them, the shadows pulled together, an oily cloud that strained from the walls to leer over Rockford's shoulders at the ravaged woman on the table. The room filled with the whisper of anxious breath.

CHAPTER THIRTY-SIX

David heard the front door open downstairs, and the murmur of voices trying to be quiet. He didn't think Aunt Elsie had been expecting anyone; usually she'd tell him if she was having company. He pushed back from the blurry photos on his computer monitor and cocked an ear to try to recognize who might be downstairs. He had spent the past hour surfing the Net, trying to track down some more history on both Dr. Rockford and the Castle House Lodge. Rockford had a thousand write-ups, but they all seemed to be the same. "Famous genetic scientist gets in Dutch with medical ethics over embryonic stem-cell research." Castle House had been a little more difficult to pull information on. Many of the search returns were simply ghost-story mentions in blogs or irrelevant connections to Stephen King and his "Castle Rock" mythos.

But David had found one report that detailed in bloody clarity the mass murders that had occurred inside the old hotel a quarter century before. The screen ran red with the horror as he scrolled down the police blotter–like pictures of a dozen dead women. He recognized the room in which they lay in varying states of dismemberment—he had been in that basement just yesterday with Christy.

The article said that E. E. Morgan—a rich, but militantly private businessman—had purchased the hotel in the late '70s with the intent of returning it to its former glory. The man had been in failing health and reportedly planned to recuperate in the country, while at the same time founding a new luxury hotel. Yet, after years of renovations, the only guests who were ever allowed on the grounds of the revived Castle House Lodge were those who were part of an elite monthly social club that met there.

That is, until the bloodbath.

There were photos of some of that "social club" running wide-eyed from the hotel, blood speckling their faces like freckles. The photo reminded David of one of those "end of the world" book covers where a frenzied mob is dashing pell-mell away from a giant lizard, or away from a city with a mushroom cloud blast behind them. A newspaper clipping about the murder bust was headlined: DEN OF DEVIL WORSHIP DISCOVERED; DOZENS DEAD AND DISMEMBERED.

Clearly the newspaper editor had been feeling just a little too jaunty with the alliteratives that day. David grinned.

But now he pulled his attention away from the carnage on-screen, and listened instead to the tone of the voices downstairs. They seemed to be moving closer. David stood and walked to the window and looked at the street. It was the kind of deep dark out as it can only be in a mountain ridge town. The glow from the streetlight three doors down faded into the velvet black of night as fast as an ice cube dissolving in a McDonald's coffee. Most of the street remained well hidden in cozy shadow, but David caught the slightest glint of chrome on the car parked on the street just outside of the house. And that silvery reflection helped reveal the quiet but official red and blue glass on top of the car.

There was a cop downstairs, David knew immediately. For the third time this month. Only this time, he knew it wasn't Christy.

This time, from the intense but whispered dialogue downstairs, he had an overwhelming sense that it was not a friendly visit.

David glanced at the story on the computer and on a whim, hit the print button. Just as the printer whirred up and into action, Elsie called his name. "David, could you come downstairs for a minute?"

The first sheet spit out of the printer and then he heard Elsie's voice from the bottom of the stairwell. "David?" There was a creak that he knew all too well; she was on the second step.

"C'mon, c'mon, c'mon," David whispered, yanking the second sheet out of the creaky printer before the last line had quite spooled out. The spindle whirred and a third sheet fed across the drum. In hindsight, David couldn't have explained why he did it. Some unconscious self-protective instinct. When he saw the dark cop car on the street, he just . . . knew. And so he didn't think twice when he pushed up the screen on the bedroom window above the garage, and then when the window was fully open, quickly dashed back across the room to yank the last sheet of paper printing out of the printer. He folded it with the other two pages and stuffed it into his back pocket. He had one foot over the window ledge in five seconds flat. His timing was right, because as he ducked his head under the bottom of the window, his aunt knocked on the door, again calling his name.

His feet dropped to the slope of the shingles and he steadied himself on the sill before letting go, just as the doorknob to his bedroom began to turn. Not waiting to see whom Elsie was escorting into his room, David slid down the slant of the garage on his butt fast enough to feel the heat through his jeans. At the bottom, he flipped over to rest on his chest and carefully let his feet dangle over the edge until they found the top of the giant green yard-waste container. Then he let go and launched himself from the trash bin to the ground. He ran around to the side door of the garage, let himself in and rescued the old Huffy from the dark. In the distance, he heard Elsie's voice, but didn't look back as he kicked the pedals forward down the driveway. In seconds he was flying down the hill toward Main, and on his way out of town.

If he had looked back, he would have seen the man in the second-story window, watching him ride away. The man didn't look perturbed at all. He only nodded slowly, as if he'd been expecting this.

CHAPTER THIRTY-SEVEN

The invitation had arrived two days ago. Even now, Alan couldn't believe he held it in his hand. How long had he waited for this? Half of his life. He'd barely been nineteen the last time someone had tried to invoke the Thirteenth. And that had ended very, very badly. He could still feel the warmth of the blood running fast between his fingers, the sensation of the guiding spirit running violent hands through his hair as he had laid the bodies of the Eighth and the Ninth to final rest on the floor of the old hotel.

The touch of those hands had never been far from his mind, ever since. All this time since.

Now he was forty-five, felt like he was going on sixty, and the invitation shook in his fingers. Actually, *he* was the one who shook; the invitation was neutral. It only said one thing:

THURSDAY NIGHT, 11 P.M.: THE 13TH.

Someone not in the know might have pointed out that Thursday was not, in fact, the thirteenth, nor, in fact, was any other Thursday this month or next. But to Alan, those words could only mean one thing: the hotel was alive again.

Alive with death. And life beyond death.

His groin ached at the thought. It had been years since he had been inside Castle House . . . but the memory never faded. There were events in your life that formed you, and events that broke you. Castle House had done both to Alan. It had given him his taste for blood, which never abated; when he saw an accident on the street, he didn't slow down to gape at the shocking site, he pulled over and knelt down at the scene, thirsting for just a taste of what the victims had left behind on the vinyl seats, and windows and asphalt.

Alan set down the invitation and decided to dress for the evening. It would be something of a walk down memory lane, he thought. But he knew his outfit still fit; he tried it on every few weeks, just to relive that night twenty-five years ago, when the blood flowed so fast you could taste it in the air like hot fog. It made him shiver to think.

He unlocked the door to the hidden room in the cellar and pulled the soft black leather pants from their wooden box on the shelf. As he smoothed the skin over his crotch, he studied the tiny spots that marred its perfect gloss, and felt himself stir. Blood secret. Blood sport. Blood evidence. Still here, more than twenty-five years later.

Then he pulled another box off the shelf, this one filled with long, shiny implements of torture. Files that tapered to razor-edged fillets. Curved needles that hooked once they were inside the flesh, making it easier to slip inside your victim and then pull them skin from limb. He slipped those into a small black leather pouch, and then held up one simple tool to study. Unlike the other twisted needles and multi-razor-edged tools he'd picked up before, this one was simple, unadorned. Just a silver staff, and a long, arced blade.

This was his favorite. There was no mystery to it, no false twists. There was a time for art, and a time for terror and a time for long, extended pain. But this was made to sever flesh, fast and easy, pure and simple. He slipped it lovingly into the breast pocket of the skintight leather vest that now covered his chest.

Alan lifted the long, bloodstained white bib from its hook on the wall, and slipped it over the black leather vest and pants. The leather repelled most of the blood, but it was always wise to protect the soft skin from at least some of the harsher sprays. His fingers ached for the touch of the matching gloves, and he rummaged around in the back of the tiny room behind a stack of paint cans until he found them. Secreted in a small nook within the wall.

He didn't know who had summoned him to the Thirteenth, but if they knew enough to call him, they did so for one reason, and one reason only.

He slipped the gloves on and thought of what that one reason was. Could only be.

In the years since Morgan had found and recruited him to help in the ceremonial bloodletting that was the Thirteenth, he had worked in a number of rewarding vocations. Coroner, dentist, and his favorite, which had stood as his nickname:

Butcher.

Eager to meet the sender of the invitation, he stepped quickly back up the house steps and into the deepening gloom of his kitchen. He still had two hours to kill before he dared start down the road toward Castle House. He thought of sharpening his knives, but knew there was no need. He had spent years sharpening and honing them for this moment.

Alan could already taste the flavor of the night.

And that bitter taste of iron was good.

Chapter Thirty-eight

. . . You are sacred, and soon you will be with us. The night is near. Be'wei ne sie' fo . . .

The voice told her that she was sacred. Brenda didn't know what that really meant. She certainly had been no angel in her life so far, and she didn't like the tone that the voice used. Lascivious. Hungry. It whispered to her familiarly in the darkness. Sometimes it laughed, a high-pitched crazy-cruel kind of giggle. It had spoken to her for days now, and she found it easier to ignore each time she awoke.

. . . Flesh of our soul, food of our thirst . . .

She knew now that she was a prisoner, though why, or where, she couldn't say. The days passed in a blur of foggy grins, and hands on her body and twisted voices. She knew she was being taken advantage of; her nightmares were filled with the leer of a granite-lipped man leaning naked across her to kiss and fondle her as he thrust between her legs. The image gave her chills, but also gave her a feeling of truth.

Now and then, she broke through the fog and understood that she and a number of other women were being held here, wherever this was. It seemed almost like a hospital, with a doctor and a nurse . . . but there were not the usual orderlies and astringent-scented hallways and emergency messages on overhead speakers. This felt almost like a resort, she thought.

Wherever they were, Brenda frequently woke from the mist to find herself sitting, not in her room, but on couches and chairs in a long room with other women who seemed as broken from reality as herself. They stared blankly at lamps and walls, or ran unconscious fingers up and down their waists and thighs, as if preening and posing for invisible suitors.

. . . Give yourself to the night . . .

Brenda could never stay lucid long enough to explore, to determine why they were here, or where here was. She would stand, perhaps, and stagger down the ornate Persian-design carpet for a few steps, and then, without fail, there would come a faint pinch on her arm, and a comforting voice in her ear: "There, there, hon. Let's sit down now, shall we?" And before she was even back on a couch the room began to fade from view until only a tiny light remained with her. A focus just before her eyes . . . Sometimes she stared for hours at her lap, forcing her fingers to fidget as she stared amazed at their movements. Sometimes she slid back against the soft upholstery of the couch and watched Jackie draw. She'd tried to make friends with the girl, in those rare moments when she could actually move her lips to form words, but had never received a response. The girl seemed to be able to escape the drugs enough to focus on her art, and sometimes mumble tearful questions about her son, but couldn't maintain a conversation.

. . . Forever we live, forever we wait, forever in you . . .

Amelia came every day and set her up at a table to paint with a small kit of colors and brushes. When Jackie wasn't painting, she stared straight ahead, oblivious to all attempts at speech. But when she painted . . . somehow she beat the fog and found a way to slip through into the real world again, if only for a few moments.

Brenda knew that her time in the real world was probably already slipping away. She'd been sitting up in her bed for the past few minutes, holding her head in her hands and willing away the cobwebs in the darkness. But will was not always as powerful as the somnolence instilled by whatever narcotics they were hyping her up on. The voice kept beating away at her brain, promising her sex and love and ecstasy and eternity, and she tried to stay away from that vortex, but already, she felt the clouds returning.

. . . Live in us and you go with a god. Blood is only a means to our end . . .

Brenda threw off the covers and promised herself that this time, she would not black out, would not succumb to the fog that threatened to leave her limbs listless and uncoordinated.

Promises don't bring coordination however, and when her foot caught in the lower reaches of the blanket, Brenda went over the edge of the bed, letting out a slight shriek as she fell and smacked her temple on the carpeted floor. She rolled her face away from the nap of the carpet and stared upward into the black shadows of the ceiling. Above her, hovering in the dark, she saw the woman.

Busty and barely clothed—wearing only a black strip across her breasts and leading down in a T to her waist, the woman looked like a dark angel. Her cleavage was laved in crimson, and her face speckled with weeping tears of blood. Above her, gray-blue wings gently fluttered in the air, veins bulging in muscles like blue worms on death.

. . . In the name of the nether and the scum and the syphilitic . . .

Brenda's heart froze at the sight of the angel . . . or demon. Yet, the medicines that numbed her from reality also seemed to save her from fear. She shook her head at the creature's whispering voice, and gasped only two words in answer: "Fuck you."

As the blue stars cleared from her head, Brenda crawled toward the faint light she saw slipping in through the bottom of the bedroom door. Above her, the demon continued to speak, alternating from words in some foreign tongue to simple declarations that Brenda could understand—and didn't at all like.

. . . Xudei' ah Siet du ven. I will lick the blood from you like a mother, and you will taste me like a lover . . .

Brenda slammed her head against the door as she scrabbled to stand up, but the pain helped clear some of the fuzz, and she used the moment to slap her hands on the door and wall and pull herself up to the knob.

. . . You will open your veins to me, and I will drink your hate forever . . .

With a trembling unsure hand, she grasped the knob and turned. Ever so slowly, it began to follow the lead of her fingers.

. . . Every sin I will share . . .

"Go fuck yourself," Brenda hissed, and slipped between the jamb and the half-open door to lie under the glare of the lights in a long hallway.

Behind her in the dark, the voice continued.

. . . I will suck dry every child you bear . . .

Brenda pulled the door shut behind her, silencing the demon. She pressed her back to the door and took several long, deep breaths, willing the fog to clear. The light from the hallway made her eyes water, and the patterns in the long stretch of carpeting blurred and twined in her head. She blinked and blinked to straighten it (and herself) out, and then slapped her cheek with the palm of her hand three times in rapid succession. The hall echoed with the cracks, but after the bright flashes cleared from behind her eyes, Brenda felt more in control. Holding the wall for support, she rose to a standing position, and cautiously moved down the hallway.

She didn't know why she was awake now. There was no way of knowing how long she'd been here, but she had the feeling that it was a long time. Regardless, she was awake, and she intended to get out of here.

Wherever here was.

Brenda fought the vertigo and crept along the hallway, one hand on her belly, the other on the wall for support. She counted down her progress with the numbers of the rooms: ten, nine, eight . . . She toyed with the idea of opening one of the doors to see what or who was inside, but the thought of having to grasp the knob, and turn it, and push the door open . . . made her opt to simply stagger forward, curiosity unheeded. When she neared the stairwell at the end of the hall, she began to move even slower. The buzz of voices wafted up from below.

Brenda dropped to a crouch, and crawled across

the carpet to rest her head against the cool metal of the stair railing. She tried to see whom the voices belonged to . . . but the stairs wrapped around, and the landing was invisible from upstairs. It sounded as if there was at least a dozen people down there . . . maybe more.

Good, she thought. *If the doctor is occupied, maybe that will make this easier. Of course, going down this way isn't happening.*

Brenda pushed away from the railing and started to turn around to go back down the hall the way she'd come. Her stomach began to feel queasy as she passed rooms nine, ten and eleven. It had probably been days since she'd walked more than a couple steps, she guessed. And the drugs couldn't be doing her guts any good. Biting her tongue to give her the pain jolt she needed to keep going, Brenda steeled herself and passed room twelve and turned the corner.

The hand came out of nowhere, and clamped around her mouth. Brenda's eyes went wide and she bit down hard on the skin of the hand that held her, but instead of letting go, a hand yanked on her hair, and pulled her out of the hallway, and out of sight.

Into room thirteen.

Chapter Thirty-nine

"The guests are arriving," Amelia announced. She stepped around the corner from the stairway, two-inch black heels clicking on the stone floor of the basement as she came.

Rockford looked up from his study of the baby in crèche two and grinned. "It's almost time. I can hardly believe it. It seems like we've been getting ready for this forever."

She sidled up to him and licked a lobe of his ear as a hand caressed his back. "Everything is ready in the chapel," she promised. "The candles are lit, the food is ready . . . there is wine and rum and every other liquor under the sun."

Rockford laughed. "Let the orgy begin!"

Amelia stepped between him and the baby. She took his hands into hers and stared up into his eyes. Even now, more than a year after she'd first met him, those eyes still made her thighs tremble. So hard, so powerful. And she had won that power for her own. Tonight was the proof.

"This is the best place, the only place we could hold this ceremony," she said. "Thank you for bringing me here." Her voice betrayed the seriousness of her intent. "They failed here, twenty-five years ago, but they were amateurs. We are more prepared. We are ready. And the residue of the souls they spilled still permeates the walls of this very building like blood. It will bolster our own effort, to help make our offering a success."

"They did something right last time," Rockford said. "Because whatever they called through, never completely left. We've been seeing ghosts since the day we walked into this place."

"Lower-level devils," she agreed. "But not Ba'al or Astarte. Not the incantations of the Thirteenth."

He pointed at the row of baby incubators against the wall. "Well, we're ready to call Astarte and Ba'al to incorporate all the way this time. We have the blood, and the wine, and the excess. We have the mothers, and the babies. And the Thirteenth. Now all we need are our guests."

Amelia's eyes sparkled in the dull candlelight. "I'll send them down," she promised.

When she walked away, Rockford couldn't help but follow the shapely curve of her ass through the black satin fabric of her ceremonial robe. It trailed low to her ankles, and even had a hood in the back, which she still wore down. But what made it really work for Amelia was the way she draped it around her. She didn't just wear the robe, it wore her. She'd tied a sash tight around her waist, accentuating her curves. From the thick golden rope that rippled against her belly hung a half dozen small white pendants. If you'd looked closer, you would have seen that they were actually skulls. Human skulls.

And if you'd looked even closer, you'd have seen that they weren't simply replicas of human skulls, they were actual denuded bone. They were not fully formed, and ranged in size from a pebble to a shot glass, yet each one hung and jangled against each other at her hips like a ghastly wind chime.

Rockford shook his head, as he remembered

harvesting and helping her cure each tiny head for her ceremonial outfit. These were no ordinary ornaments of death.

These were the skulls of fetuses, taken from their mothers while still alive.

Of course, by the end, neither mother nor fetus had lived to tell tales. Each one of them lay in waiting just down the hall, their bodies acid-washed, but their souls ready to be released in calling.

Rockford turned his attention back to the babies who waited for the night. He reached in a hand to one of the cradles and thumbed the infant's chin thoughtfully as it gurgled and stared at him with wide dark eyes.

"Tonight's the night, little guy," he said. "Goo-chi-goo-chi-goo."

CHAPTER FORTY

David pulled the hand brake and slowed the bike as he approached the turnoff for Castle Lodge. Traffic tonight had been heavy for the ridge, and the last five cars that had passed him had turned onto the gravel road that led to the asylum.

Something was up tonight.

Peering behind him to make sure no cars were approaching, he turned onto the narrow road and stared down the lane. Through the protective screen of the trees, he could make out the glow of brake lights ahead. After a moment, they went out, and the path turned to unbreachable shadow again.

He preferred the shadow. The red light only meant that Brenda and now Christy were in trouble.

Something was about to change. There was a gathering here tonight. And David didn't like the import of what that could mean for the women behind the thirteen doors.

Women that included Brenda. And now Christy.

Cautiously he pedaled down the lane, cringing at the crunch of the wheels on gravel. He imagined they could hear his approach inside the doors of the asylum. And then the beams of another pair of headlights out on 190 filtered through the trees to light the way ahead of him, and David swore. He leaped off the bike while it was still in motion and pulled it down to hide in the tall grass of the ditch beside the gravel road. His groundskeeping work hadn't extended yet all the way to the highway, and he thanked God for that as he lay flat on the earth, hidden by a two-foot-high stand of grass and weeds. The headlights had turned onto the lane and shivered and bounced as the car crunched down the narrow rutted road toward him.

Was it his imagination, or was the car slowing as it approached? He hugged the ground tighter, willing his body to sink into the warm earth. His breath caught as the car reached his hiding place, headlights blinding as twin suns in the pitch of night. His heart stopped for a moment as the car seemed to slow further, but then it was easing past, and as David looked up, he recognized the black-and-white panels of a police squad.

Straining to see inside the car as it passed, he just barely made out that there were two heads in the front of the squad, and the one in the passenger seat, closest to him, looked disturbingly familiar.

A woman's curly gray hair shone briefly in the light reflected off the forest leaves, and David bit his tongue from calling out, "Aunt Elsie?"

And then the car was gone, and pulling into an

empty space amid a row of cars now lining the front entryway of the asylum. In a moment, the echo of two car doors slamming shut filled the air, and David could just barely make out the silhouettes of two figures walking up the steps of the asylum. For a moment the front columns of the old hotel were bathed in light as the door opened, and then with a snap, the two figures were gone, and David's eyes struggled to adjust again to the subtle shades of night.

He pulled his bike out of the weeds and slowly pedaled a few more yards along the gravel path before stopping again. The unkempt weeds changed to mowed grass, and the forest retreated from the edge of the road as the path opened to the circular drive of the entry gardens of the old hotel. Realizing that he couldn't exactly ride his bike right up to the front door, David stepped off, and rolled the bike down into the ditch a second time, laying it down in the first stand of uncut grass.

There were at least a dozen cars parked in front of the asylum, more than he had ever seen. They filled the open space that ringed the topiary garden in the center of the circle drive. David slipped away from the visible entryway though, and stole around the back of the hotel past his gardener's shed to the back door. There were more lights on than usual inside, he noticed, and the wells that protected the basement windows glowed.

What the fuck was going on in there tonight? The image of Dr. Rockford's bloodied hands raised into the air after reaching inside the womb of a woman in the basement flashed across the back of his eyes and David cringed.

His hand shook as he pressed the key into the back door of the asylum. He held his breath as he turned the knob and eased the door open.

But he needn't have worried about making noise. As soon as the door opened, the din of voices spilled into the night around him. Still, David was careful as he pulled the door shut behind him.

He stole along the wall of art toward the center of the asylum, and the pictures seemed to leer at him with the echo of conversations ahead. One in particular caught his eye. The new one, with its garish color splash, a crimson wound that looked something like a baby . . . and something like roadkill.

Its distorted eyes shone like black marbles in the dim light, and the skin of David's neck crawled when he looked at it.

There were people milling about in the center reception area of the old hotel, just at the base of the winding stairs that led to second floor. The floor where Brenda was. There was no way he could reach her now, David realized. All he could do was wait.

Slipping down to a crouch, he leaned against the wall and bit his tongue. In front of him, people milled about, sipping from wineglasses and filling the room with the din of excited conversation. It looked like it could be a long wait.

Heart pounding, and stomach clenched with concern, David wondered how long he could stay secreted here, before he couldn't wait any longer. He *had* to get to Brenda . . . but the only way was through a crowd of people. He supposed he could just join the mob and pretend to be one of them . . . but to walk up the stairs in full view of a couple dozen people? No way.

Frustrated, David pursed his lips, and leaned against the wall to wait.

But he didn't wait long.

A shrill whistle cut the air. The hall suddenly quieted. David looked up for the source, and there was the granite-faced doctor himself, standing at the railing of the second-floor landing.

Rockford.

The fraud wore his white doctor's coat, and his face beamed as he looked out over the crowd. Nurse Amelia stood at his side, a vision in black. Where Rockford looked austere and upstanding, dark pants sheathed in the trustworthy garments of the physician, Amelia was decked out in the raiment of a goth queen. Her raven hair slid down the black lace that edged a midnight dress. The lace slid across her neckline to plunge across highly visible cleavage. The body-hugging fabric clung to and accentuated the curve of her ass, and outlined the flare of her hips. Her waist was ringed in the homemade belt of baby skulls, which rattled and shifted with her every move.

The dress barely crept lower than her ass, where it gave way to a tantalizing meld of white thigh and black fishnet.

David caught his breath in spite of himself. He'd always thought she was attractive in the times he'd seen her in her nurse's smock, but now, with eyes smudged in dark shadow and hips hugged tight, he realized that Amelia was not just cute . . . she was smoking hot.

"Thank you all for coming tonight," Rockford called out over the crowd. As Rockford began to talk, a girl decked out in a skintight skein of black even racier than Amelia's cycled through the crowd, retrieving wineglasses and placing them on a circular plastic tray she balanced high in the air. David thought her lips looked coated not in lipstick, but in blood.

"It has been twenty-five years since Castle House Lodge lived. You all know what happened then. Morgan attempted to stage the ceremony of the

Thirteenth, and while he certainly succeeded in spilling plenty of blood here, he ultimately failed to complete the ritual. Tonight, what failed here then, will succeed. Amelia and I have followed every letter of the ritual up to now. The women in our asylum all carry children.

"And tonight, their blood will provide the passage for Ba'al and Astarte. At last, after thousands of years, the mother and the father, sister and brother, will be joined as one, incorporated in our child.

"The Thirteenth."

The throng below him began to applaud, and David realized then that he recognized many of them. Not all by name, but he'd seen most of them in town over the past few weeks.

Erin, the druggist from the pharmacy. Mr. Cleary, the manager down at the grocery. And . . . it pained him to recognize, when he thought to look . . . Aunt Elsie, standing in the midst of the throng, tilting back a glass of amber wine and laughing as she spoke to a tall man in a white butcher's apron.

David realized the man wore a belt beneath the apron, and the glint of steel implements hanging from a sheath on his belt shone as he joined Elsie in laughing at some shared jibe.

"And now," Rockford continued, "it's time for us to begin. Over the next hour, we will make our twelve offerings to Ba'al and Astarte, and at thirteen o'clock—the stroke of one A.M.—we will consummate the creation of that which you have all dreamed of for half of your lives. We are ready to bring them into the world, at last, to share in the flesh that they have celebrated since the dawn of time. Please, let Angeline lead you downstairs so that we can begin. After far too long, I'm pleased to tell you now . . . it is time."

The waitressing girl set down her platter of empty

glasses at the reception window of the main office, and then strode through the crowd like a minx, shifting and bouncing her hips provocatively as she stalked straight toward the door marked with an unmistakable red *X*. In moments, the crowd began to follow her lead, and a stream of bodies disappeared from the main foyer of the asylum to its hidden depths.

In minutes, the entire throng had left the main room of the asylum, and David found himself alone, crouching in silence.

He hadn't noticed when Rockford and Amelia had joined the throng, but he assumed they had gone through the red *X* as well. After all, the action was clearly slated to occur downstairs . . . Which led David to wonder if there was anyone left to rescue upstairs.

"Shit, shit, shit," he mumbled, and forced himself up from his crouch to tiptoe through the center room and up the stairs.

As he cautiously placed his foot on the first step, a noise interrupted the sudden quiet and he froze, sweat breaking out instantly on his brow.

The noise rumbled louder, and then broke. Then it happened again—almost like the sound of a faraway crowd at a sporting arena.

Below the stairs, the throng was cheering.

David reaffirmed his haste and instead of tiptoeing up the stairs, he kicked into gear and took them two at a time.

He wasn't surprised when he threw open the doors to rooms one, two and three and found them empty. But he moved faster down the hallway then, and grew more nervous as four, five and six also lacked a woman in the rooms' beds. After he discovered room seven was empty he skipped straight down the hall to eleven.

Empty.

They'd already taken her downstairs, along with all the rest of the women. David didn't want to think about what they were going to do to her. What they might already have done.

Below the floor, another cheer reverberated.

Shit, David thought. He couldn't just walk in front of a mob of bloodthirsty devil worshippers and steal away their victims right before their eyes. He'd been hoping to slip her out the back door without notice. But now?

Maybe they would have robes or something, he hoped, imagining a druidic rite. After all, they were down there to worship demons, weren't they?

He slipped quickly down the carpeted stairs, and then stepped more slowly down the first steps to the basement. When he reached the bottom, he took a deep breath, and then stuck his head around the doorway to look into the open room.

Getting through the crowd unnoticed was going to be more difficult than he'd thought.

They weren't wearing black robes and hoods, like demon worshippers in some dark Hammer horror movie would.

They weren't wearing anything at all.

The floor near the entrance was piled high with discarded shirts and shoes and pants. And the room was filled with naked or nearly naked people, in various states of carnal excitement. He pulled his head back and considered his options.

He wasn't going to doff his clothes to join the crowd, but he couldn't walk through them fully dressed.

The stairwell echoed with another cheer and David's stomach quailed. Not from the cheer, but from what came before it.

A woman's scream.

David knew without a doubt that it was just the first of many. And sooner or later, it would be the screams of Brenda and Christy.

"Raise your glasses to the sky," called out a voice from somewhere around the corner. "Speak his name: Ba'al!"

David peered around the wall again and saw the crowd following the command, wineglasses glittering with ruby and gold sloshing and dripping on the bodies below as they raised their hands as one, swaying together and calling out again and again: "Ba'al."

There were still some women and a couple men in the throng who wore shorts and sandals, and David made up his mind. With a silent gulp, he pulled his T-shirt over his head, and balled it up in one hand. Then he steeled himself and slipped into the room, carefully positioning himself in the back of the crowd, behind the hairy buttocks and back of a fat fortysomething man who was far too busy pawing the equally naked (but most oppositely non-hairy) ass of a younger woman at his side. She slid her free hand through the fur of his apelike back and knocked her hips to his as she steadily tilted and emptied her glass of red wine.

When it was empty, she put her mouth to his ear and whispered something, and his mouth met hers in a wet animal kiss before he showed a swath of wide yellow teeth at her and relieved her of the empty glass.

He disappeared to their left, leaving David with a clearer view of the front of the room, and he instantly regretted the clarity.

To the left of the basement stairs stood Rockford and Amelia. Both remained dressed, though the doctor's white coat was already smeared with blood across his chest. The reason struggled in his hands.

She was dark-haired, with skin of almond ... breasts were full but small, and the shiny black thatch of her pubic mound glimmered in the uneven light of the flickering candles. But the beauty of her nakedness was not what drew David's eyes.

It was the blood streaming from the many slashes on her nakedness that he stared at.

And the knife in Amelia's right hand.

"The first one is mine," she announced to the crowd. "Death by a hundred cuts. We will bathe in her life, warm as the wine settling in your stomachs, and then it will be your turn," she promised.

With that, Amelia held the long silver blade beneath the woman's left breast, touching its edge to the pendulous flesh like a gentle kiss ... before she pulled the knife back, fast, opening a slash of red.

Again, a scream. But this time, David was the witness, and he quailed at the sight as the crowd surged forward slightly, again celebrating the violence with a communal shriek of delight.

Amelia brought the knife to bear again, this time defacing the woman's other breast, and soon both bled slow rivers of red down her belly, joining the already opened slashes on her ribs and hips.

Something tugged at his belt, and David's gaze returned from the front of the room to see a hand on the front of his pants, long kinked hair hanging over the woman's arm as she worked to undo his jeans. It was the same woman who'd sent away the naked bear man for more drink.

"No, that's okay," David said awkwardly. He put a hand on her naked shoulder to push her back, but instead was met with a surge of sultry flesh as she raised her head from its attention to lean all of her flesh against him. Reaching up with her mouth she planted a warm, wet kiss on his lips and whispered, "I want you to be one of my chosen tonight."

David didn't know what that meant, exactly, but if the outcome was anything like what was happening to the bloody woman up front, he wanted none of it.

"Not now," he said again, and pulled her hand away from his crotch.

"Soon?" she implored, blackened eyes beaming like cat's in the shadow.

"Yes," he lied. "I'm just a little shy."

"Wine." She grinned. "We'll get you going in no time."

"I'm sure," he agreed, as her hands slipped up his chest. She pulled herself to him in a body hug, and the press of her silky, sumptuous breasts was almost more than he could bear. But then the focus of the show changed from demonstration to interactive.

"Come and feel her life," Amelia called out to the room. "Taste her, breathe her, wear her. Make her blood your own." She pressed her own palm to the woman's side, and held up a glistening hand to the crowd in evidence.

An old man approached first, shriveled genitalia hanging useless as chicken jowls beneath his silver-haired liver-spotted torso.

He pressed his face between the woman's cleavage and shook his head slightly, as if burrowing into her bosom. Then he turned to face the crowd and grinned, white teeth gleaming evilly from a face dripping with blood. With his fingers he rubbed her life away from his eyes, and then smeared it in turn across his wiry chest and belly.

"At last, we can begin," he cackled.

David hadn't recognized him without his clothes on, but with the voice, he recognized the man as Mr. Tamarack, from the post office.

Next, one of the managers from the grocery ran his thick hands up and down the poor victim's body, smearing her blood equally across her flesh and his own. He pressed his privates against hers, and then backed away, to display his sickly white skin spackled with glistening gore.

The crowd surged forward, eager to be the next in line to bathe in the woman's pain. A raven-haired woman was next, licking the blood in long rakes of her tongue from the woman's breast like an erotic vampire.

Then a man grabbed her as she turned from the dying woman and instead of taking the blood from the source, he ran his tongue across the vampiress's lips as he massaged the globes of her bloodstained breasts.

She grabbed him by the growing leash between his legs and led him off to the side of the room. David couldn't see what happened next as the crowd closed ranks, but he did see who the next person was to christen himself in the victim's blood.

Captain Ryan.

David couldn't watch the cop feel up a dying woman as if she were some kind of sensual hors d'oeuvre.

Instead he looked around to see where his own seductress had gone. He quickly located her by the long-nailed fingers slipping around and up and down the hairy beast's back, who'd apparently returned with more wine.

But now at the front of the room, a line was forming, to bathe in the blood of the moaning, dying woman.

Amelia held up a crimson hand and held back the crowd for a moment, so that she could carve a fresh font of blood, this time sliding the knife across the woman's belly, opening a deep gash, which bled fast and dark. "Oops," Amelia giggled, as the woman bleated briefly, incoherently, before her eyes rolled back to whites, and she slumped unconscious against Rockford.

"Quick, my loves," Amelia called, as the cut woman mewled and shook in Rockford's locked hands.

"She will go fast now," Amelia said. "You must all taste her before she's gone."

One by one, the people in the room wrapped their arms and legs and lips around the dying woman as if she were just a piece of meat for the taking.

David slipped back from the crowd, before he could be drawn into the line. He knew there were rooms in the corridor behind him, and he prayed that in those rooms were the rest of tonight's planned victims. He managed to disappear into the hallway at the back of the large room without being noticed, and breathed a heavy sigh.

Maybe this would go easier than he'd thought.

From behind him, the sudden shriek of the woman and the answering roar of the crowd brought a shiver to his spine. The end for her was no doubt near. And that meant the next victim would be brought out.

He didn't have much time to find the "holding pen" where Rockford had hidden the women.

David turned down the dark passageway and found his way back toward the room in which he'd seen Rockford butchering another woman the day before.

He found the room quickly, but this time, he couldn't simply slip in the back. Because this time . . . the door was locked. He had no doubt that the women were on the other side of the heavy wooden door, but there was no way he was budging the door without a key.

From behind him, the crowd screamed out again, and this time, it lasted longer than before.

David knew without question that the woman was dead. Which meant that Dr. Rockford would be back in the catacomb of hallways any minute to retrieve his next victim.

Again he wrestled with the doorknob. It was cold and hard and didn't budge a centimeter. Finally he admitted that there was no way it was going to move through brute force, and David slipped back down the short hall.

Just in time.

He heard the footsteps from just a few feet away, and his heart leaped. He had to get out of this hallway, or there was no way that they would miss him.

David ran in the dark, praying that he could find the other hall without stumbling and falling. He'd hidden there when he'd been here the day before; it was where he'd seen them take Christy away.

Voices carried like smoke in the darkness, and he heard someone say, "The next needs to die faster. We only have an hour."

David pressed himself to the wall at the edge of the main hall just in time. The black of the night got blacker as Amelia's lace passed, followed by the white and red slash of Rockford.

David waited until they passed, and then slipped back into the hall to the torture room behind them to see what they did.

Rockford paused at the door, and pulled a key from the pocket of his doctor's coat. In seconds the heavy door creaked open, and Amelia and the doctor slipped inside. David stole to the doorway to see where they went, and saw a room more disturbing than the one he'd just left. Torches guttered from six steel holders spaced around the room, throwing a flickering orange light on the skins of the prisoners David had known would be there. Tied to the walls all around the room were a dozen women, as naked as the victim in the previous room, but unlike her, this group all seemed drugged or already dead.

They hung from the ropes tied around their wrists and attached to spikes in the stone walls without complaint or struggle. Most of their heads hung down, hair draping at least some of their body in the shadow of privacy.

David's eyes searched the room quickly for a girl with a single pink strand in her hair, but didn't see her on first glance. He didn't have time for a second look as Amelia was already leading a slumped figure with brown hair and stumbling feet back toward the exit. He backed away from the door and then turned and softly ran back to his hiding hall again until the deadly duo passed.

After they did, he slid to the floor and put his head in his hands.

He couldn't get into the room without the key. He couldn't get the key without Rockford. Or at least Rockford's coat. Unconsciously he moaned.

"Hey—who's out there?"

The voice came from farther down the hall. David stood and walked back into the dark. He remembered that there had been men locked back here when he'd found this hall the day before. "Who's in there?" he answered in a whisper.

"TG," came the answer. "You want to let us the fuck out of here?"

"Don't have a key."

"Excuses, excuses. Hey, weren't you here yesterday with the same cock-and-bull story? Who are you?"

David leaned into the small grill opening at the top of the dark wood door. He could only see the glimmer of light off the eyes of the man who harangued him from inside.

"I'm here trying to find my girlfriend," he whispered back. "They've got her locked up down the hall."

"Yeah, her and a dozen others," the man replied.

"If I can get you out, will you help me get her?" David asked.

"Sure, what the fuck. But you gotta get us out first."

"Working on that," David said. "I'll be back."

"Yeah, we've heard that before."

"Shut up and wait." David wasn't sure where that last bit had come from, but somehow it felt right.

"Fuck your mother and the donkey she had you with," the man answered.

"At least my mama had a donkey. Yours fucked a cockroach. So shut up already. I'll be back."

David grinned at the rude interplay, in spite of himself, and slipped back down the hall toward the main assembly room. He had no idea what he was going to do, but whatever he did, he had to get his hands into Rockford's coat.

It occurred to him that this may have been the first time he'd ever wanted to get into another man's clothes.

He hoped it would be the last.

Chapter Forty-one

Brenda tried to scream but the hand tightened across her mouth. "Shhhh," a woman's voice hissed in her ear. "I'm a friend."

She struggled to answer, but only succeeded in gumming her captor's palm.

"Promise me you'll stay quiet and I'll let you go," the woman whispered.

Brenda vigorously nodded her head up and down.

After a second, the hand slid off of her mouth and Brenda turned around to see who'd grabbed her. Even in the dark, she could tell her abductor was slim and blonde, probably about her own age, maybe a little older.

"Hi," the woman said, offering a thin hand to shake. "My name is Christy. And if we don't get out of here, I'm pretty sure we're going to be killed."

Brenda couldn't argue with that. "So how do we leave? There's a mob of people downstairs. And I don't think they're inclined to let us leave."

Christy shrugged. "We'll think of something. First thing is to get out of the place where they're sure to come looking for us."

"I'm all for that," Brenda said. "Seems like I've been here for weeks."

"Three weeks," Christy affirmed. "I'm with the police. We've been looking for you. So has your boyfriend."

"My boyfriend?"

"Yeah, David?"

"The guy from the Clam Shack?"

Again Christy shrugged. "That's where he said he lost you."

Brenda laughed. "Wow. That's pretty cool that he looked. I mean . . . we didn't even do anything. I just met him that one night."

"Yeah, well, for whatever reason, he'd like to see you alive again."

"Then let's get the hell out of here."

Brenda could have sworn that someone in the room laughed quietly at those words. But before she could look around, Christy reached out to open the door. "There's a back staircase," she said. "From there . . . I don't know where to go, but once we're off this floor, we at least have a chance."

She pulled open the door and the light from the hall splashed into the dark room. So did a familiar voice.

"Going somewhere, my angels? I don't think so."

Barry Rockford held up a syringe and smiled as Amelia, no longer decked out in nurse's whites but in a black form-fitting goth dress, grabbed at the arm Christy had used to open the door. She held it steady just long enough for Rockford to plunge in the needle, and thumb down its plunger.

"We've been looking for you, my dear," Rockford said. "You see, our previous candidate for the Thirteenth turned out, unfortunately, to already be pregnant. And you, ironically, have resisted my best attempts to put you in that state. So I'm afraid you'll be switching roles this evening."

Amelia laughed. "Tonight, and for the rest of your life."

Brenda ducked beneath the nurse's arm and bolted toward the hallway, but Rockford didn't miss a beat. He simply stuck out a quick foot, and Brenda—still unsteady from the weeks of drugged bed rest—went down like a sack of rocks.

"Knock her out for a bit," she heard the doctor say, just before a cold pinch stuck the back of her thigh. "We have a ritual to perform. And our star performer can sleep through the first act."

CHAPTER FORTY-TWO

There were few things that TG respected in life, and a smart-ass sure as hell wasn't one of them. "Billy," he said. "You hear that twerp? Tell'd me my mama fucks roaches?"

Billy didn't budge from his slump against the wall on the floor. He'd rarely moved since the doctor threw them in the cell a couple days ago. "She smoked roaches," he mumbled. "Maybe that's what he meant."

"T'ain't what he meant and you know it. When he gets back here and gets us out, I'm gonna ram one up his gut good."

"Serve him right for rescuing us," Billy slurred.

TG thought about that one a minute, and an eyebrow crept upward on his forehead like a spring caterpillar. "You sarcasming me, po' boy?"

"Naw, TG, ya know I love you like an illegitimate brother whose mama—"

TG kicked his partner in the ribs and Billy shut up.

"When we get outta here, I'm gonna give that doctor all the love he's been givin' those women we brought him."

Billy stirred and groaned. "You turning homo on me, TG?"

This time, when TG's boot headed toward Billy's ribs, he was ready. The taller man went down hard, and offered a colorful—and astonishingly multilingual—stream of curses to commemorate the fall.

"Don'tchoo ever pull the rug out like that again," he hissed, once he'd regained his feet.

"Keep your toes away from my rib cage, and we'll get on just fine," Billy grumbled. It didn't even occur to him that this was probably the first time he'd stood up to his partner in crime . . . even if it hadn't involved actually standing up. The effect of the meds the doc had shot him up with still lingered, which was why he'd stayed crumpled on the floor all this time. His head alternated from feeling light as a helium balloon to heavy as a block of wood with an ax gouged into its center.

"Point is," TG said, "we given that doc a bunch of fine women to play with, and you know what he's done with 'em."

"I don't have a clue," Billy said.

"You've heard 'em screaming down here. He's roughing 'em up. When we get out of here, we're giving him exactly what he's given our girls."

Billy shook his head. "You ain't pissed off about what he's done to those girls," he said. "You just wanna get at his liver for what he's done to you."

"Same thing."

Billy laughed. "You just focus on Rockford and leave the kid alone if he ever comes back, and we'll be just fine."

"I'll let him walk us outta here. I'll let him take us to Rockford. But after that . . . Well, if he loses a couple feet of gut, I hear you can live without that."

Billy felt the world swim again, and didn't answer. He suddenly found he didn't care who lived or died in this ridiculous mess. Including himself. Leaning to his side, he proceeded to allow the bile that had been gathering in the back of his throat to release, and the smell filled the tiny cell in a heartbeat.

"You stupid fuck," TG raged, and raised a boot to kick Billy in the ribs again. But even in the throes of puking, Billy's sixth sense of paranoid fear protected him, and his hands were ready.

CHAPTER FORTY-THREE

Amelia had not always been evil. And maybe there was a part of her still that was not. But since she had first felt the whisper of the voices in her mind, and the touch of their ethereal, yet still-powerful fingers on her breasts, on her ankles, on her belly, inside her crotch, teasing and slicking and seducing, she had surrendered any pretense of goodness. She didn't believe in a God, but she believed in gods. There were forces—call them elementals, call them devils or dark angels—that still cavorted invisibly in the affairs of men. And she had been sensitive to their touch for years. She had felt them in the room when her father had taken his time while spanking her, making sure to pull down her panties to her ankles, and making sure to feel the red swelling after he'd slapped her bare ass with the palm of his hand to make sure that he hadn't hurt her too much. "Does this hurt?" he'd say, palming over the heat of the back of her ass after a beating. Then he'd run his fingers down her thigh to where the flesh grew cooler, and more private. "How about this . . ." She endured his touch by leaving the room, at least in spirit. And that's when she felt, somehow, that there were others who were there for her. Others who reached out to hold her as her father slipped his fingers around that special place as he mouthed in her ear, "You were a bad girl, you know . . ."

She'd just been a teenager the first time she heard the voice of one of the invisibles. She'd been making out with a Valley High basketball player in the woods near her house, and he'd gotten just a little too pushy for her liking. But when she'd pushed back and told him to cool it, he'd instead simply pulled her hair and pressed her to her knees in front of his crotch. "C'mon, baby," he implored, yanking down his jeans to expose a blue-veined and pink-capped sausage of growing meat. "Just do me."

That's when she'd first heard the voices. "He can't hear us anymore," they said. "But he can feel us, if you help. Don't you want to help? It's time to show him a lesson."

She had shown him a lesson. One that would last a lifetime. When she spit out the shriveled lump of his cock at his feet, blood drooling like thick red cum from her lips, she had grinned, just a little bit, while he grabbed at the stump of his dismembered orifice and complained, "How can I play now?"

"Should have thought of that before you forced it in my teeth," she laughed, and behind her a chorus of voices laughed in unison. She heard them and felt warm, throughout her belly and breasts and mouth.

The boy heard them, and curled into a bleeding ball as he cried, and cried and cried.

She still heard him from near the doors of the old venerable hall.

But for the first time in her life, she didn't feel threatened, or cornered, or unhappy. The taste of the iron from his cock in her mouth lingered. And Amelia realized she liked the taste better than cum. A lot better.

Her tongue flicked like a cat's across her lips, and instead of spitting out the last of his blood on him, Amelia swallowed.

Then she stepped naked across the bleeding rapist and took the long way home.

She never looked back.

Amelia had studied the occult since high school, and she'd grown to know that those voices who'd been her only friends in the darkest hours of her life could be reached in the brightest rays of daylight, with the right intention. She had dedicated her life to knowing of them, enrolling in a university with the deepest research base on spirituality and religion, which is how she'd come upon the rituals of incubation for the mother and the father, Astarte and Ba'al. Among the stacks of protected "historical" documents, she'd found numerous references to the cults of the two ancient demons of fertility and hedonism and violence of the flesh.

In an age when all belief was fading, she had become a dark light of faith. She knew the spirits were there; they had seen her through the darkest scenes of her life. And now, she only wanted to do what they needed from her . . . that which she could give.

"I am your handmaiden," she'd promised one night on her knees in the dark. She'd been naked in the forest, and had felt their hands caress her with the softness of the wind, and the sensuality of the most tempestuous of lovers.

"Help us then," they had whispered in her ear. "Bring Astarte and Ba'al into the world once more, so that we can make you our first witch of the new century. You can be she who is the mother of all darkness, the whore of a god."

She had leaned back and felt their feathery

touches ripple through her hair, and across her chest, pinching and sucking, before other touches slipped to the velvet skin of her nether regions and the sensitive hair of her sex shivered in a vibrating breeze that oscillated in a frequency no mortal ever normally enjoyed.

Her orgasms wet the forest with pleasure.

Her orgasms made her their instrument.

Her orgasms eventually won over Barry Rockford to the cause.

Her orgasms were tonight to be baptized in the blood of a dozen mothers and their babes.

After years of subjugation, whatever humanity and empathy had existed in Amelia, had bled away. She relished in the death of the women she cut. She would relish in the death of Rockford, when it was time.

Her fingers found the only pleasure that mattered to her anymore, and pinched. Hard. She licked blood from the knife she still carried and grinned, red speckles fading slowly from the whites of her canines.

"Let Ba'al come," she begged, loins parting and trembling in anticipation of his incorporation. "Let him be mine, as Astarte allows."

She laughed as the taste of metal filled her mouth, and closed her eyes as she swallowed.

CHAPTER FORTY-FOUR

The basement stank of the iron of blood mixed with the offal of spilled intestines and the smoke of candles burned hours to their core. The perfume evoked something primal, ancient. And the room's inhabitants echoed that sense of secret history, dark history, in their Bacchanalian aesthetics. Nude, but clothed in a dead woman's blood, they kissed and rubbed flesh indiscriminately. Old fat banker with young coltish girl, young frat boy with swarthy hairy man. Grandmother with greasy mechanic.

David saw the bob of an old woman's gray bun in the lap of Captain Ryan and felt his gorge rise as he realized that the wrinkled shoulder and old-woman ass he saw across the room belonged to his dear, sweet aunt. That woman who'd laughed naively just the other night at the kooky antics on *Cheers* and who had so lovingly cooked him the ultimate cure for a hangover not so long ago.

Amelia and Rockford had decked the space in hundreds of burning candles, and hung purple curtains at the edges of the front of the room to enclose the line of infant incubators along the wall there. A wooden platform had been raised before the children, draped with black sheets, and it was here that the victims were to be killed. The basement had become a twisted church, and hung from their wrists on either side of the altar were two women. Both were nude, but untouched. Thick, corded rope ensnared their wrists and held their arms high. Their heads lolled back while gravity stretched their chests taut. David hated himself for admiring the curve of the girls' bellies and the tight, yet outthrust breasts. One of the women was a natural redhead, and he didn't have to get close to her to verify that. Her eyes were closed and she didn't move as the throng rutted before her on the floor, against the walls, on the step to the altar. The other, a brunette, hung on the opposite side of the altar, and appeared equally oblivious to the scene before her, though her eyes were open as her head lolled against a shoulder, and long lengths of raven ringlets streamed down her ribs like sultry feathers.

On the back wall of the room hung the totem of the god or demon David supposed they were here to worship. At first glance, the statue appeared to be a vandalized woman, face of thinly chiseled white stone, with stylized curls draping across naked shoulders and teasing at the start of full, heavy breasts that poised above a rounded classical belly pierced with a thin belly button. But the breasts did not end in tips, as they should in life. Instead, where the areolae should have capped were deep black holes in each.

To make matters worse, the cleft of her thighs were adorned not with simply a patch of carven pubic thatch, but with a spiked penis, its mushroom head also excised and hollowed. She . . . it . . . was a hermaphrodite.

David had slipped along the wall of the back of the room and up the side, trying to keep in the shadows of the guttering candles so that perhaps nobody would recognize that he still wore his pants and had not painted himself in the blood of the sacrificial lamb.

Amelia and Rockford were attaching the new victim's arms to rope that hung from the ceiling, and so David slipped closer to the altar. It grew harder to walk, albeit slowly. Whether it was the sight of the naked bodies, or the smell of their sex, or the influence of the evil that simply lived in this old hotel, David's hard-on was painful against his belt. The room felt fogged in his mind, as if he were looking at it through a prism of sexual smoke. Primal need filled his mind, pulsing through his veins like a fifth of X-rated liquor. He was losing himself in the invisible power that held the room in thrall. As he slipped around and behind a tall golden post that held a candelabra of white flaming candles, his hand moved to massage his crotch absently. He had unzipped his jeans and slipped his fingers inside before he realized what he was doing.

"Fuck," he whispered, and yanked his hand back out as if electrocuted. He knocked the back of his head against the stone of the basement wall to clear his head, and for a moment at least, the thickness that had been growing in his lips abated, and his vision sharpened. After the stars behind his eyes cleared anyway.

"What are they burning in these candles?" he murmured to himself. He didn't expect an answer, but there was one.

"It's not in the candles," a purring voice whispered in his ear. "It's in us." A hand slipped again inside his pants, and he felt something cool grip him with a slow turn of fingers. He almost let go and closed his eyes, but again he caught himself and looked down, expecting to see the hippy chick from earlier taking advantage of him.

But instead, when he stared at his crotch, he saw nobody. In fact, there could never have been anybody, he realized, because the candleholder imme-

diately in front of him would have toppled if anyone
had tried to wedge between it and him.

"Whoa," was all he could say.

As he looked at the throng writhing together and
apart on the floor, he realized that he wasn't the
only one to have felt phantom hands. There were
several people standing and lying down on the floor
who were twitching and moving as if in full copulation, or fellation . . . but they were, in fact, alone in
their own space.

The new victim at the front of the room was ready.
Rockford and Amelia stepped back from where she
thrashed helplessly from the ropes, which ascended
to a metal bolt on the ceiling. Standing next to the
woman, they began to undress each other, Amelia
casting Rockford's coat to the victim's feet, and then
unbuttoning his shirt. Rockford stopped her at his
belt and instead helped her to shimmy out of the
devilish dress she'd worn for the special evening.
When their privates both dangled in the warming
moist air of the room, they knelt face-to-face at the
feet of the new victim, and kissed with abandon.

Amelia's hands slipped around Rockford's back
and traced passionate trails of white in his skin as
her nails gouged and gripped him as she moved
against him. Her moans could be heard above the
grunting, gasping sighs of the throng that copulated
throughout the room, and when she at last broke
the kiss, it was Rockford's breath that gasped loud
and hard in the air.

David couldn't help but murmur, "Get a room."

Dr. Rockford stood then, apparently unashamed
at the prominence of the promontory of his nakedness, and addressed the crowd. With a bobbing
pointer below his midsection accenting each word.

"What we have begun here, you must finish. The
ceremony of the Thirteenth is not my ceremony, it's

not Amelia's. It is all of ours," he said. "We have gathered the mothers . . . we have birthed the children . . . and we have sacrificed the first offering. But now, we turn the night over to you. The offering of the second mother is yours. Who will take the knife?"

With that he held up the long silver blade in the air, and the noises of passion from the floor disappeared. The room slipped to silence. And then a heavyset man stood up from a tangle of bodies on the floor, and walked to the side of the room where he shrugged on a white apron over his bare flesh. Nobody spoke as he walked back across the room.

When he reached Rockford, the doctor held out the knife, but the man waved it away, holding up his own silver staff capped by a long, arced blade. "I brought my own," a gruff voice announced.

Amelia ran her hands across the pendulous breasts of the second mother, who struggled to keep her eyes closed. Unlike the last woman, this one seemed resigned to her fate . . . or perhaps she was simply still drugged. She stood before the crowd, nude and limp, making no attempt to hide or protect her body. Her eyelids fluttered open and then closed, as if she was fighting sleep—or perhaps fighting being awake!

David stayed still behind the candle as the man raised a blade quietly, smoothly high above his head, and then brought it down cleanly, without wavering.

The woman lurched backward as if electrocuted, and the reason bloomed instantly from her left breast down to her left knee. Her executioner's blade had carved a long, steady cut all the way down her body from point to point, and as David watched, its edges turned from a sliver of red to a river.

The woman began to shudder and cry . . . but still

she held her eyelids shut. "Puh-puhlease," she moaned. "Don't hurt me anymore. Please don't hurt me anymore."

The Butcher—David had begun to think of him as a thing, not a man—put a gloved hand to her cheek and stroked it. The second mother's pleas changed, and instead of asking for her life, she began to lean her face forward to rest on the hand, taking comfort in the strength of her torturer. "Please don't hurt me," she said over and over.

The hand did not show mercy. The Butcher slid a finger across her forehead, tracing the line of her scalp, before slipping his other hand around her to hold her lower neck. The knife haft pressed against her throat as he held her. Without warning, he slipped two fingers into her moaning mouth and moved them around a bit. His face betrayed the struggle within, but then his fingers reemerged, the pink flesh of her tongue held tight between them.

That's when the other hand with the knife left her neck and in one swift stroke, severed the tapered front half of her tongue in a flash of silver and red.

The mother's whimpering turned to claustrophobic gurgling cries, and the Butcher wiped his blood-stained glove off on the pale flesh of her breast before making his next move. It was no mystery to anyone what that move would involve. The Butcher drew the tip of his blade from the curled hair of her pubes to the hollow of her throat in a slow dance of razor danger . . . and then he dragged the tip back again. And again. And again. The crowd had ceased all amorous attentions and instead began to inch closer and closer to the front, anticipating the first spray of blood.

When he struck, the blood flowed fast.

David closed his eyes and swore silently. He didn't want to watch this. But he couldn't interfere.

To try to stop the murders now would only mean his own death . . . To try to free at least some of the women—including Brenda—meant waiting here until there was an opening to retrieve Rockford's coat—and more to the point, the keys that it held.

As the Butcher raised his knife to draw another cut down the body of the trembling blood-drenched woman, David looked away and instead located the doctor and Amelia. The crowd was edging around them, moving closer to the murder in progress, as Rockford and Amelia stayed in place, fingers tracing the flesh of each other's bodies in a private, twisted orgy with bloodstained nails and long, bloody kisses.

David saw the Butcher raise his long red-tipped knife in the air again, and this time he looked forward to its down swipe. Not for the pain of the woman, but for how he could use it. If this woman had to die, at least her death might pay for someone else to live. He tensed and stole a look at the white coat on the side of the stage as the mother let out one horrible, quavering cry.

"Peeez s'oppp," she begged, red saliva spilling across her lips like a grisly fountain. Her blood and spit coated the floor at the Butcher's feet, but he took no notice. Arm like a derrick, he lifted the knife again.

When the candles glimmered on the silver of the killing blade, and the knife's edge began to fall, David eased forward. He ducked low to the ground, and stepped closer to the impromptu stage, as the bodies around him surged forward at the same time, intent on seeing the stroke of the blade as closely as possible. He used their perverse interest to move past the Butcher along the wall. Praying that Rockford wouldn't notice that he'd advanced beyond the throng, he stepped on the coat and then eased back toward the crowd, dragging the white coat with him.

The Butcher's amorous attention to his prey shielded David, just as he'd hoped. The man had stopped his live fillet to take the bleeding, shuddering form into his arms. Her wrists remained shackled but still she tried to pound on his back. Her reaction didn't slow the Butcher, who only leaned in closer to her until the pale carmine of his lips pressed hard against the glistening blood sheen of her own.

David saw her eyes shoot open when the Butcher's tongue invaded her mouth, touching the horrible wound of her amputated tongue.

"Stop," Dr. Rockford yelled.

David's heart stopped. He'd been discovered. Frantically his eyes searched first one side of the room and then the other, trying to decide where to run. There was certainly no exit—only a rock wall at the front of the room, and a solid mass of bodies between him and the stairway.

Assured of defeat, he looked for the doctor, and saw him pushing his way through three or four rows of the crowd that had surged closer to the stage. The Butcher held the mother close, pressing the cuts in her flesh against his own chest, opening her wounds to bleed faster against his skin.

"She is an offering, not your whore," Rockford said, pushing the Butcher back from his bloody kiss. "Give her to Astarte. Feed us her screams."

David almost gasped with relief. He was still safe!

The Butcher's thin features seemed to broaden and crease . . . as if he was about to cry at the reprimand. But then he steeled again, and with a grin uncoiling across his face like an unstitched wound, he lifted the knife to strike again.

David took the opportunity to bend and pull the white coat closer. He searched with his hand and found the pocket, and then while staring ahead at the Butcher and the doctor, his fingers slipped in and felt around to look for a metallic ring of keys.

"For Ba'al!" Rockford proclaimed, as the knife came down again.

"For Brenda," David whispered in his mind as his fingers closed on something cold and metallic.

"Ahrraaaawhhhh!" screamed the poor, bloody woman as the Butcher stabbed his blade into her throat, and then dragged it across her neck and down the slope of her chest to peel back the skin of her breast like a slab of chicken.

David dropped the coat while holding on to the metal. "I'm sorry," he whispered, as he saw the woman convulse with the last pumps of her heart. The crowd only pushed closer, as if she were a rock star they needed to touch. Those in the front row were quickly slick with the dying woman's blood, and moans of excitement began to rise again from the crowd.

"Drink her life and taste the sin!" Amelia's voice called from somewhere behind him. But David didn't stop to see from where. He had already wound his way through four rows of demonic nudists and was headed toward the back hallway. He hoped that he had the right keys.

He couldn't afford to go back.

As he slipped into the dark hallway in the back of the room, David heard the doctor call out five words that would haunt his nightmares for the rest of his life:

"And now for her child."

CHAPTER FORTY-FIVE

The corridor felt cool and smelled wormy dank after the cloyingly heavy scent of bodies and heat and candles in the main room. David breathed it in like the purest drink of air ever.

He made a left when he reached the corridor branching, figuring that it would only help to have the assistance of the guys trapped down here when he went to rescue the women chained in the other room. Call it "David's Gang." He laughed. Better than chain gang, anyway.

He only hoped they really would help.

He found the key to the lock on the first try. The guys within hadn't even time to heckle him before the door was creaking open.

"Told ya I'd be back with a key," he announced.

"Took you long enough," a dirty voice growled from inside.

"Ungrateful bastard, aren't ya?"

"You want to keep using those lungs, or wear them?" This time, the owner of the voice strode into the dim shadow just bright enough to allow David to see him. He stood a full head taller, and probably a whole person wider than David did, but oddly enough, the smaller man was not intimidated.

"Gimme a fuckin' break," he said disgustedly. "I just let you out of the goddamn cell, which, I'll point out, you and your behemoth muscles were unable to accomplish. So quit giving me shit and give me a hand so we can all get out of this hellhole."

Billy stood behind TG and at the start of those words he was convinced that the little guy was going to be the flattened guy in about thirty seconds. But instead, a slow grin crept across TG's face. And his hand clapped David on the shoulder.

"Yeah, little man," TG growled. "I gotcha. And I'm still gonna rip your lungs out. But not until we're all topside, right?"

"Whatever," David said. "Just help me get my girl out of here and you can do whatever you want to me."

"Thanks for the offer," TG answered. "But I don't do guys."

David just shook his head and started toward the prison of the thirteen mothers. "C'mon."

He led them down the dark corridor and across the hall leading back to the main room. The echo of screams and ecstasy bled down the shadowed bricks to meet them.

"Someone's having some fun," TG said. His face lit up when a woman's scream rose and fell.

"You wanna beat up on some chicks, or you wanna beat up on Rockford?" David asked, as he fumbled for the keys. They stood in front of the door to the prison room.

"Can't we do both?"

Billy punched TG in the shoulder. "Conserve your energy," he cautioned. "We can always beat on some chicks."

Somehow, despite the vileness of the comment, David got the feeling that the other man was arguing on his behalf, and he silently thanked him as the door swung open.

"Holy shit," TG announced as the three stepped inside the prison room. Naked women seemed to be chained to the walls everywhere, most of them with ragged black stitching across their lower abdomens. Some of those stitches still leaked blood from the struggles of the women against their bonds.

"Are you here to help?" one of the women asked as they entered the room. "You're not the doctor," said another.

"Not the doctor," agreed TG. "Here to help, is another story."

Billy elbowed him.

"One more time with the elbow, buddy, and yer gonna be using that beer-tap contraption back at the shack as a die-ally-sis machine."

"Impressed that you know the word 'dialysis,'" Billy answered, and quickly dodged a fist.

"Help me get them off the walls," David said, staying out of it. At the same time, he was again scanning woman to woman to woman, looking for a dark-haired sylph with a lock of pink hair. While none of them were looking themselves—most hadn't probably bathed in days, most were discolored and bruised across their midsections from surgery and most hadn't used makeup or a hairbrush in weeks— David was sure he'd recognize Brenda at her worst if she were here. And he was convinced that she wasn't.

His heart sank.

"What do you want us to do with them?" Billy asked.

David was tempted to say, "Nothing." What did he care about all of these anonymous women? He was here for a reason . . .

"David!" a voice called weakly from the farthest corner of the dark room.

"Help them down," he answered Billy, and turned in the direction of the voice.

He almost didn't recognize her naked. Her arms

were bound above her head in thick, rough knots of rope, and the darkly trimmed finger of her pubic mound was not the color he would have expected from the sun-blonde knotted hair that streamed from her head to lick at her shoulders, but there was no mistaking the upturned tease of her pert nose or the deadly bright blue of her eyes.

"Christy!" David grinned. He left TG and Billy and ran to her, throwing his arms around her as if they'd been intimate for years. She was the only hint of the world as he'd always known it that he'd seen in hours.

"I'd blush, but I'm too fuckin' worn out to care," Christy whispered in his ear.

"I'd get excited, but I'm too freaked out right now," he answered, eliciting a slight laugh from the young cop.

"They're killing all of the women, aren't they?" she asked.

He nodded. "I saw them kill two so far," he said. "And I think they're going to work their way through this whole room. They say they are performing some kind of ceremony of the Thirteenth."

Across the room, TG and Billy were working on the ropes that bound some of the women to hooks dangling from the raftered ceiling.

"This ain't easy," TG declared.

"It was pretty easy when you decided to hit me up in a bar and drive me home," a voice came from the opposite wall. "Oh, *that* was easy as pie."

"Hair pie is always easy," growled TG. "Shut up, bitch."

David stayed out of it, and worked on Christy's knots. "Brenda's not here," he said, as he leaned closer, straining to unthread the heavy rope. The touch of her cool, but velvet soft breast slid across his arm like an evil tease.

Christy fought to ignore the touch, as much as desire for more vibrated through the wracked wreck of her physique at that moment.

"No, she's not," she agreed. "I haven't seen her since we left her room."

"Where else could they be holding her?" he asked.

"There's another room I saw, when they brought me in here," she said. "You'd think it's a closet, but it's just another entry behind the door over there."

She tried to point with her free arm, but it didn't budge. Pins and needles swallowed her up in an ocean of sensation, none of it pleasant.

"Why isn't she here with the rest of you?" David asked, undoing the other rope.

Christy shrugged. "I'd guess they have something special in mind for her."

"Like what?" he asked, pulling the last loop from around her wrist.

Again she shrugged.

"Something worse than death?"

CHAPTER FORTY-SIX

Brenda had never really been afraid of the dark. If anything, she embraced it. The dark was a walk down First Street at midnight, savoring the taste of heavy rain in the thick night air, sensing more than seeing the wave of the trees along the railroad line. Dark was the place she lived in after her parents were asleep, and she felt an itch, no, a drive that couldn't be denied and so her hands dragged wet, sticky ecstasy across her thighs as she writhed alone on her bed. Dark was the moments she lived in alone, and alone was a feeling she knew and felt safe in.

"Safe" wasn't a word you could have used to describe Brenda's emotional landscape right now. Rope chafed painfully against the soft skin of her wrists and ankles. The bindings held her back to the cold, rough stone wall. The doctor had brought her here and disrobed her with a cold efficiency that was frightening in its speed and complete lack of emotion.

Now the dark was a palpable force of evil around her, not a friend at all. Brenda tried to break the pall by forcing her mind to relive the time down at the Clam Shack a couple weeks ago when a woman billing herself as "Johnny Cash with titties" sang a set and alternated between a raspy feminine contralto and a damned-impressive deep-voiced rendering of the Man in Black's "Jackson." There was something just so wrong in seeing a broad-shouldered, red-haired Irish girl singing in a range below where most men could reach, that the show had left an indelible mark in Brenda's brain.

But the novelty of the singer's meandering through an eclectic catalog of Allanah Myles, Billy Idol, Janis Joplin, The Style Council, and the aforementioned Cash didn't ease the atmosphere in the dark for long. Pretty soon Brenda was back to feeling the air swirl around her without a body to move it. And from there came the touches, feather soft on her neck and breasts. And after that, the more demanding pinches on the inside of her thighs. Brenda would have chalked it up to . . . mosquito or spider bites . . . if it hadn't been for the laughter.

And the voices.

They whispered in the air like the scratching of leaves on a shutter. Or the gentle tapping of branches on glass.

Only . . . she wasn't near a window. She was locked in a tiny, dark, damp room in a basement, and the air shouldn't have been moving at all. And it certainly shouldn't have been colored by the sighs and moans of spirits in flight.

And the whispers of leaves on windows didn't usually translate in your ear to the faintest encouragements of "Soon, you'll be with us" or "Soon, I will be in you."

But that's what she heard.

The voices made Brenda shiver, and for the first time in her life she was petrified of the dark. At the faintest stir of air in the tiny room, her skin goosebumped and crawled. When the soft, fluttery touches reached her lips she hissed, "No," in answer, but the pressure only grew more intense until she felt as if her lips had met the pull of a vacuum.

Once she would have welcomed the kiss of the dark; it had been her lover through so many months and years of emptiness. She had never been the popular kid in Castle Point, and life after graduation hadn't improved her social standing.

But now . . . those midnight touches filled her with fear. There was something out there. And that something now was . . . here.

"You will be ours," the voice whispered in waspwing scratches in her ear. "You will be the Thirteenth."

Brenda pulled against the knots on her wrists until she felt warmth dropping down the inside of her forearms. She pulled in vain.

Around her, she could hear the echoes of laughter, though there appeared to be nobody else in the room.

CHAPTER FORTY-SEVEN

TG could only take so much shit. He was in the business of doling it out, not taking it. And for the past few days, he'd been on the receiving end entirely too much. First, Billy started cutting him crap, and then the damn doctor had shot him up with something raw and tossed him in the fuckin' basement. But the capper was when this little twerp turned up to act like his rescuer and mouthed off at him over and over again and expected to get away with it.

Now the goddamned sluts on the walls were pissing in his face when he was trying to cut them free.

"You're the asshole who . . ." one of them had the unfortunate audacity to say at this particularly inopportune point in TG's train of thought. TG didn't even think twice. The back of his hand shot out and cuffed her across already bruised lips. His hand came away wet, and he didn't bother to see if it was from saliva or blood. He thought the perfect followup would be a left hook to the jaw, and after the satisfying crack of that action against her jaw, her tits seemed to hang even more slack as she relaxed against the wall, supported solely from the ropes around her wrists.

"Nobody calls me an asshole," he pronounced. "In fact . . ." He turned to pick out David across the room. "Nobody gives me shit. Not now, not ever."

Tapping one thick fist in an open palm, he sauntered across the room to where a naked blonde was wrapping two pale arms around the bare and equally pale skin of David's back. TG considered doling out his lesson on the little prick with just his bare hands . . . but then saw a better option. Stepping over to a segment of the wall that had obviously seen some recent repair, he picked up a brick from a pile of masonry and debris on the floor. Then he turned toward David.

Billy staggered over then with a trembling woman wrapped around him like a leech . . . or an octopus. Her legs scissored around his waist as if she was trying to fuck him while he walked. She slowed him down, but Billy didn't seem to mind. After all, the woman was naked, and pressing everything she had against him.

"What are you *doing,* man?" Billy asked his partner in crime when he finally shuffled close enough. The woman kept her face buried in Billy's shoulder and refused to look up.

TG shrugged. "Takin' care of business," was all he'd say.

When the brick connected with the back of David's skull, Billy raised his hand from the woman's back to interfere. "What the fuck?" he complained. In a flash the smaller man was lying on the floor with the leechlike mother finally scrambling to get off of him. The mark of TG's fist glowed on Billy's cheek like sunburn.

"No more shit," TG declared, as he grabbed the blonde who seconds before had been hugging David. Still stunned by the sudden collapse of the man she'd just been embracing, Christy was easy prey for TG, who reached out to yank her by the hair before she quite grasped what was happening.

The final look of comprehension in her eyes was filled with hatred. "You!" she spit before his meaty fist clogged her mouth.

TG yanked her hair toward the ceiling to keep her in place, and the punch she'd been aiming at his face instead raised skyward. She went up on tiptoe to ease the pain of her hair pulling out of her scalp by the roots, and as she did, her body stretched provocatively in front of TG. An unintended, but still sensual result. Her breasts pulled tight to her rib cage as she scrabbled to grab at TG's fist to ease its hold on her hair.

"Nice rack," TG commented.

"*Ass*hole!" Christy screamed.

TG shook his head in disgust, and raised the brick over her head. "When will people learn?" he asked nobody in particular. He didn't wait for Christy's response, and a moment later she lay prone on the floor, the gash on her forehead looking more black than red as the heavy blood swelled to the surface.

TG dragged both Christy's and David's bodies to a small closet door in the back of the room, and thrust them inside. Then he pulled the door shut, refastened the hook latch on the outside, and returned to where Billy still sat on the floor rubbing his face. The girl who'd formerly been attached to him like a growth was cowering in a corner.

TG nodded his head toward the exit. "Now get up and let's take care of some more business. I think we owe the doctor a house call."

The thing about TG was that he was direct. He didn't screw around. While David had spent a half an hour easing his way up and around the room in an attempt to remain "invisible" to the ritual killers, TG didn't waste any time with subterfuge. He strode right out of the locked room and down the hallway,

exiting into the room full of naked, bloody cavort-
ers. TG walked straight through that throng as if
they were a room full of flies.

The doctor and his whore were standing on the
stage, overseeing the flaying of some other helpless
chick.

"Y'all like to tie people up, don'tcha?" TG asked.
His voice, though quiet, seemed to boom through
the room.

The doctor looked up from drawing a razor across
the woman's tits. The line of blood ended just before her right nipple as he acknowledged TG's unexpected presence.

"I have some things I'd like to talk with you about,"
TG continued.

Rockford's face didn't hide his surprise. "I locked
you up," he began, but his lips never finished the
sentence. Instead, TG's four knuckles broke against
the doctor's cheek with a crack that echoed through
the room.

"Yes," he agreed. "You did. That was your first
mistake."

TG slugged the doctor again in the stomach, and
then brought up a knuckle sandwich for good measure to Dr. Rockford's lips. They swelled faster than
collagen injections, and the man crumpled instantly.
But that didn't leave TG alone in his victory.

No. The wrath of a woman is always worse than
the fury of a man. And Rockford's bitch was suddenly
all over TG. A flurry of pounding arms and kicking
feet assaulted him. Nails gouged painfully at his face.

TG laughed at the attack. He reached out one calm
hand in the middle of the storm of the century and
popped the bitch one right between the eyes. Just
like that, she went down like a sack of quarry rocks.

TG rubbed sore knuckles in his free hand and
stifled a small moan of pain. Bitch was made of

coral. The flesh across the back of his fingers had marks. Still, the warmth that always swelled his groin after giving a good thrashing filled him, and a grin began to split TG's face. He began to turn to see what other victims he could put the hurt on; the room was full of 'em. For the first time in his life, TG figured he had a license to pretty much fuck up anyone and everyone within arm's reach. Hell, he'd be doing a service, probably get decorated for it—his name'd be in the papers and all that shit for single-handedly bringing down a dangerous mob of devil worshippers. And it would be fun . . .

"Look out," Billy warned from behind.

TG turned just in time to see the glint of steel in the air. He was not in time to dodge it though, and the sharp bite of death whispered its victory in his head even before the pain arrived.

A strangely tiny voice bleated from the body of a mean-looking heavyset man wearing a bloodstained apron and black latex gloves. In the cusp of those gloves, the man clenched the haft of the foot-long blade that was buried in TG's throat.

"Asshole," the ironically feminine voice pronounced.

TG's unibrow twisted in anger, but all that came from his lips was a gurgle of red, red blood. His hands fumbled at the blade where it entered his throat, and then something like confusion swam across the anger in his eyes, and TG began to collapse, as if in slow motion. The Butcher held on to his blade, which slid back out of TG's neck with a gentle glide in exact opposition to the force by which it had entered.

Billy had backed away at the attack, not having a weapon handy. Now the Butcher advanced on him, and the smaller man's feet tangled and tripped over the rutting bodies on the floor, most of them still oblivious to the turnabout battle going on near the altar of their worship. Once in the trance of ecstasy, the townspeople appeared completely absorbed in their degradations, and barely looked up as Billy fell backward over their twining hips.

When he at last was cornered against the back wall, the Butcher smiled grimly at him. "You could have joined us," he suggested, as he drew a thin line of beading blood from the tip of Billy's chin all the way down to the base of his cock. Then he drew a transverse cut across the shaking man's belly button, effecting an upside-down cross on Billy's torso.

"I will," Billy promised. His voice trembled.

"No you won't," the Butcher guaranteed, and aimed the tip of his blade at the center of the cross.

At the front of the room, Dr. Rockford and Amelia had recovered, albeit with already purpling faces. Still rubbing his cheek, the doctor called out to his followers, "Let us continue. It's time for mother number five."

CHAPTER FORTY-EIGHT

The night wind whispered warnings to Chief Maitlin. He ignored them as he sat on the porch of his daughter's empty house and argued with himself about the best course of action. Could he trust her abductors to keep their word and leave Stacy out of this, so long as *he* stayed out of it? And how could he allow so many other people to suffer in exchange for his daughter's life? Wasn't it his job to protect them all, not just his daughter?

After acting like a wooden Indian on Stacy's peeling wood porch for hours, Maitlin finally stood up, joints creaking and moaning at the long inactivity.

He shambled toward the cruiser like a zombie, still unsure about his plan. But once the keys were turned and the engine dragged the car slowly down the street, the chief felt the pall of desperation upon him even more than before. Castle Point appeared deserted as his cruiser slid slowly down its subdivision and then business streets. There were no longhairs leaning against the outside wall of the Clam Shack on this, a perfect summer night. There were no dog walkers patrolling the sidewalks near Main, pooper-scoopers in hand. Normally the Canine Fecal Ballet was a prime activity at this point in the evening, just before bed.

In his heart, Maitlin had known all along that the new proprietors of Castle House were tapping into the same demonic cult veins that had slathered the house in blood two decades before. He'd had a pretty good idea of what the reports of disappearing women over the past six months meant. What he hadn't known was how much of the town Dr. Rockford had recruited. The last time this had happened, Maitlin guessed that a couple dozen townsfolk had been lured into the blood-drenched rituals of the Castle House basement.

But this time, he feared that it was even more. After he watched an empty potato chip bag roll and skate across the empty asphalt of Main, Chief took a deep breath and closed his eyes. When he reopened them, the bag had disappeared into the weeds at the side of the road. And Chief Maitlin gunned the engine of the cruiser and flipped a U dangerously close to it. In seconds he was doing sixty down the hairpin curves of the 190. After an Innovative Industries van passed him going the opposite direction, Chief killed the lights and began to slow down.

The entrance to Castle House lay just ahead.

The entrance to hell.

CHAPTER FORTY-NINE

"It's working," Amelia hissed in his ear. "Can you feel it?" She waved her hand in the air around them, where shadows seemed to coil and writhe like heat pockets.

Rockford nodded, spilling a lopsided grin spattered with gore as he looked up from the latest sacrifice. He found it difficult to focus anymore on his partner, despite the fact that she was dressed only in blood he had spilled. It was difficult to focus on anything now but the blood. So much blood. So much more needed. The voices were loud now. Insistent.

The air around them smelled of slaughter. Tasted of flesh. Moved like water. Whispered like dirty lovers.

"Yes," he said, as he drew a knife across the belly of Elisabeth, an Italian woman they had held captive for the past six months. Rockford had impregnated Elisabeth and then kept her quiet in the fog of drugs, allowing her consciousness to swim to the surface only rarely in the past weeks and months. Still, she had grown to know, with the depth of feeling that only a mother can know, that she was pregnant. In those brief periods of lucidity, Elisabeth had loved and feared for her baby. She had rubbed her abdomen and whispered to it over and over in her locked room until Amelia had rendered her comatose again, "Don't worry, little one, I'll protect you."

But Elisabeth's world had mostly been a blur of shape and color with no meaning until this morning, when she had woken from the bad dreams to find ragged stitches across her abdomen. Then she had screamed herself hoarse.

Rockford and Amelia had let her go on and screech her lungs out, because for this part of the ceremony, she had to be at least somewhat conscious. The old hotel had been awash in spine-twisting cries today as Rockford and Amelia made their way through the rooms on the second floor, freeing child after child from unripened wombs.

So as Rockford cut into the stitches he had put in just hours before, Elisabeth wailed with rare cognizance.

"Where is my baby?" she cried. "What have you done to my baby?"

Amelia knelt at Elisabeth's side and pressed both hands against the woman's waist. She leaned in to kiss the mother, who responded by spitting. Amelia wiped the white foam from the blood on her naked chest and flicked it to the floor with her palm.

"Your baby is in a better place," she whispered.

"I want to see my baby," Elisabeth demanded.

Amelia looked at Rockford, and the whites of her teeth showed through the blood on her face. She looked vampiric. "Shall I?"

He nodded.

Amelia stepped away, but Rockford didn't stop tracing his knife across the thin flesh of the woman. "Would you like to hold her?" he asked.

"It's a girl?" Elisabeth gasped.

He nodded. "Yes, though she won't live for long outside of the incubator."

Amelia returned then, and held a tiny red-blotched baby to the mother's chest. The infant twisted in her hands and let out a thin wail. "Here she is," the nurse said.

Elisabeth couldn't hold the child with her arms tied up, but she tried to curl her body to the babe with a mother's protective hug. Its body twisted between her breasts. "Put her back," Elisabeth begged. "She needs to be in the incubator."

Amelia shook her head.

"She would have joined you quickly anyway. Now . . ."

Rockford touched the edge of a long silver blade to the infant's back. The tiny baby began to cry, its face against her mother's heart.

"Now . . . she will go *with* you."

The basement of Castle House suddenly trembled with the gut-wrenching force of a mother's scream that, just as suddenly as it began, was silenced.

CHAPTER FIFTY

The light from the open door blinded her for a moment, despite the fact that the room beyond it was lit only by candles. Brenda squinted and remained mute as a brawny man dragged in the body of a naked man. Seconds later, he was followed by a bony guy lugging an equally bare woman. The men dumped the two bodies unceremoniously on the ground and slammed the door behind them, apparently never noticing the fact that there was a girl in the back of the small room chained to the wall.

After a moment had passed and she was sure the

men weren't coming back, Brenda called out to the newcomers on the floor in front of her in a loud whisper.

"Who's there?"

The room remained silent. But their bodies were so close to her feet, she could hear the slight intake of their breathing.

"Getting crowded in here," she said to nobody in particular. Around her the air stirred. Hands seemed to slip in close to cup her breasts, as if someone had snuck up on her from behind. It felt as if the intruder had just come from a long, cold bath. Something brushed the hair on her arm in an icy caress and her skin goose-bumped.

"Get OFF!" Brenda yelled at the air. "I may be naked and tied to a wall . . . but that doesn't mean I'm easy!"

She laughed, a little, at her own attempt at bravado, but the quiet of the room after her words died only made her insides clench harder. And they didn't have any impact on the being in the room. The persistent cold hand slid up the inside of her thigh and Brenda shook and struggled to clench her legs together. But it was no use. When Rockford and Amelia had tied her up, they had left her spread-eagle; unable to touch her knees together. Now the invisible fingers capitalized on that, and gripped the tender flesh of her thighs without gentleness.

"Ow," she complained as the fingers squeezed her, and then she screamed out as an icy finger poked and pushed its cold way inside her.

"Get OFF!"

Brenda squeezed with every internal muscle she could control to expel the thing, but it slipped inside her like a steel spike, gouging up and in and sliding within. Its touch was hideous . . . She could feel the black ice spread through her groin and belly like some kind of bitter, nether anesthetic. It hurt and numbed her at the same time.

"What the fuck," Brenda moaned, and closed her eyes, as the world began to spin. She had been conscious now for the longest she'd been in weeks . . . and suddenly she felt unable to hold her eyes open any longer, despite the prodding at her insides by the cold prong, or the fact that two people had just been unceremoniously dumped naked and unconscious at her feet.

"I feel like I'm going to puke," she whispered. Inside, the coldness spread and spread until it overcame even her nauseated stomach, and then she shook her head and struggled to stay conscious . . . but the fingers reached her heart. And with one lone tear trailing down her cheek, beside the dirty pink lock of hair, Brenda—or that spark that thought of itself as Brenda—left the room.

"I didn't dump them here."

"Yeah, well don't look at me."

"Doesn't matter. Get her down. It's time."

Hands felt along her sides, and through a haze of fog Brenda struggled to open her eyes. The fingers on her wrists and ankles were not cold, as the last touches she'd felt had been. This was different. She recognized those voices.

A hand slapped her cheek and her eyes fluttered open instinctually.

"Wake up, baby girl," the male voice said. And as that granite chin swam into focus, Brenda's stomach sank.

"Dr. Rockford," she whispered.

"At your service," he said, and then she was in his arms, as Amelia cut loose the final bonds. She tried to kick away from him, but her legs wouldn't answer. Instead, there was a strange heat in her calves, and then behind her thighs . . . and then the pins and needles hit. She toppled and Rockford easily caught her, slipping a hand to cup her buttocks. Brenda could feel the hard, moving bone that could only be his penis pressing against her belly as he shifted and supported her. His arms pulled her to him and his lips touched her forehead before he lifted her by the ass to stare into his eyes.

"It's you," he breathed, his lips centimeters from her own. She could taste the blood on his breath.

"After all this . . . it's you."

"C'mon," Amelia said, running a cool hand up Brenda's bare back. "Let's not lose the momentum. We have three more, and the hour is nearly done."

Rockford nodded at the nurse, and then bent his head to capture Brenda's lips in his. Her eyes widened and she tried to block him out, but his tongue was thick and forced its way to the back of her throat before she could stop it.

When he drew back, she stifled a gag and spit his taste back at him.

Rockford only laughed. "Is that any way for the mother of Ba'al to behave?"

Amelia answered for her. "Get used to it," she said. "Ba'al and Astarte may spit all over you, and you better like it."

"You promised they'd do more than spit on us," he laughed.

"Oh, they will." Amelia grinned, rubbing blood-slick tits against his arm. "I just don't know that you'll be able to keep up."

CHAPTER FIFTY-ONE

David woke up with a boulder on his brain.

Okay, maybe it was a brick.

Okay, maybe just an ice pick that had somehow slipped inside his ear canal, pierced through the flesh and burrowed around in his brain until there was a big bloody hole in the middle of his skull filled with blood and . . . pain.

Skip it. Maybe there was no boulder at all. Just a bloody hole in the middle of his brain.

"Damn," he moaned to nobody. Only someone answered.

"Seems like . . . every time I have a nightmare anymore, there you are," a female voice whispered.

David tried to sit up, but the pain intervened. "I never asked for a female cop to be my torturer."

"Torture you?" Christy asked, slowly propping herself up on an elbow. "You should be so lucky."

"Are you okay?" he asked, while gingerly exploring his scalp to find the steel pick that *had* to be protruding from it somewhere.

"Yeah," the cop said quietly. "What about you? I wasn't the one moaning like a dog in a bear trap."

"Been better," he admitted, pulling warm, wet fingers away from his scalp. "But I seem to be alive." He sat up, feeling the room spin just a bit even in the cloak of complete darkness. "Wow."

"What?"

"Drunk and clobbered seem to share a few things in common," he explained. Then he saw the faint sliver of light in the wall and began to crawl toward it.

"Like what?" Christy's voice whispered.

"Like the room spinning?"

There was quiet for a moment, and David's fingers found the gap in the wall where the faintest light crept through. They followed it along until the gap suddenly took a ninety-degree upturn. A door. Then from behind him, Christy gasped. "When the room spins for you, does it hold on to you too?"

"What the hell are you talking about?"

Christy yelled. "Back off, asshole. These hands are licensed in five states."

David pulled his hands away from the crack in the wall. "Christy, what's the matter?"

"Some asshole's trying to feel me up."

David turned around and crawled back from the door and in just four turns of the knee had collided with Christy's foot. He pressed forward until he straddled her body on the floor on all fours.

"Nobody's here," he whispered.

"Someone was." Her hands reached up to hold his shoulders and he leaned in to listen.

"His hands were . . ."

"What?" he whispered. His voice still sounded loud in the black room.

"His hands were inside me."

"Lucky hands," David answered, instantly regretting it.

"Pig. I knew I should never have told you."

David pulled back from her and crawled past. In three pulls of his legs, his shoulder met the wall. He turned right and repeated the action and in just a couple movements, had found a wall again. He repeated it again and found himself back at the crack near the floor.

"Look," he finally answered. "There's nobody in here. It's you and me. And I wasn't feeling you up."

Behind him Christy answered, but in a way he would have never expected.

She moaned. And not in pain.

She moaned like a woman in orgasm, with a tongue stuck way up her . . .

"Oh, yeah," she told the dark room.

"Is this a lost scene from *When Harry Met Sally*?" David asked. "I'd just like to point out once again that there's nobody in the room but you and me." His voice quavered, just a little. And he crawled from the door back to her feet. His hands found her ankles in the dark, and he could feel her trembling as she gasped and groaned.

"There's nobody here but us," he said again.

"Oh, fuck!" the cop in front of him screamed, her legs tensing and pressing against his grip.

He crawled over her until he could feel her panting breaths on his lips. "There's nobody here," he whispered.

"Oh yes there is," she gasped, her voice mounting the scale in hitching moans of increasing volume. "He's here and he's inside me . . ."

David considered the proximity of his penis, currently dangling somewhere about an inch or two above her crotch and found that normally easily erected appendage suddenly squeamish.

He slapped her gently on the side of the face. "There is nobody here but you and me," he insisted.

"Oh yes," she said. "Oh yes there is."

David moaned himself then, and collapsed on top of her, both in frustration and in response to a sudden stimulus.

Something cold had just slipped between his legs. Something cold had just touched his . . .

CHAPTER FIFTY-TWO

Chief Maitlin tiptoed through the black hallway of the old hotel and gritted his teeth. It had been a lot of years since he'd been in this building, and he hadn't missed it one bit. The last time he'd been inside, he had been just a rookie cop, following the captain on an emergency call and stifling the urge to puke at the warm smell of feces and blood that thickened the air like a foul perfume. He had walked through the foyer and gagged at the sight of dismembered arms lying broken, like old toys on the floor, as they'd slipped deeper inside the nightmare. Somewhere in the basement, he remembered, a horrible twisting scream had echoed so loud it raised the hair on the back of his neck . . .

Now things were different. The hotel had been silent for half of his life, and he hoped that its core remained so . . . He hoped that it was just some fool who had tried to recapture the evil that once before had painted the walls here with entrails, and not someone who knew what he was doing. Because there *was* an evil here, something ancient. Something that had driven men to kill and kill and kill over and over again. Every generation had a story about Castle House. The bloodbath that the chief had seen a quarter century before was not the first. But he desperately wanted to make sure it remained the last.

His black-booted feet stepped carefully across the thick old carpet, as if trying to hide from whatever lay ahead. He knew in his heart that if the evil had awakened, there was no hiding, no hiding at all.

From somewhere down below his boots, a scream erupted.

"Oh bloody hell," the chief whispered, his voice quiet in the shadow. "Why me?"

When he had walked through this corridor the first time, a quarter century ago, his daughter had been just a baby; blonde curly locks crowning her tiny head like wreathes. Her mother, Tricia, begged him to "Just do your job and come home." She thought that a cop could just go to the office and come home again, without ever involving his family. "Leave us out of it," she'd said once. But when you're a cop . . . your family is a cop's family. They can't hide from who they are. And he couldn't hide them.

He had done his best to keep them out of it, but in the end his career had caught up to Tricia. One August night while he was running the front desk at the station, an old con whom he'd sent up the river for ripping off the general store had come back to town after serving his term. The guy knew who the cop was who'd put him away. He knew who the cop's wife was too. And he'd shown Maitlin a thing or two about crime and punishment.

Maitlin's crime had been putting away the local who had broken the law. The criminal's punishment had been putting a steel pole through the belly of the cop's wife in the middle of a city sidewalk.

They'd found her body the next morning . . . a wild halo of blood surrounding her like a sainthood.

Maitlin had never really been the same. But in the two decades since, he'd done his best to shield Stacy from the danger of what he did. And so now he wanted to call out his daughter's name in the shadows. He wanted to hear her voice that he knew must be suffering in silence here somewhere. He wanted to grab her and just take her home, regardless of what the other people here might need.

But in his heart he knew he was sworn to protect. And while he first intended to protect his daughter, he also intended to protect his town. His fingers slipped inside his jacket pocket to fumble for the book of matches he'd slipped there before he'd left the office. He gripped the pack hard and gritted his teeth to steel his courage. There was one thing that would protect his town more than anything else, he thought. The destruction of Castle House.

CHAPTER FIFTY-THREE

Ba'al.

Amelia grinned. She could feel the demon in the air now . . . His touch permeated every pore. As she walked, his feather touches stroked her face, and hair and . . .

She had grown up dreaming of the satyr incarnate, fucking her to submission beneath soaking sheets. She had begged her dreams to make him real. She had traveled to Ireland and spent weeks studying in forgotten carrels of old libraries. She had studied every ancient myth and legend in handwritten tomes locked away in private collections to find out how. The things she had done to get access to those texts would make a whore blush.

And finally, tonight, with the cooperation of Astarte, he would be hers, at last.

Rockford was a prop, in the end, but a necessary

one. He provided the focal point. The fulcrum. The means.

And the people of the town—the energy. With every sacrifice they sent a dissonance into space; a rift in the very matter that held soul and serendipity in its hand. With the blood of mother and child, mother and child, mother and child spilled again and again in this room, the dissonance grew until it could not be contained any longer.

"I hate you," Amelia whispered at the doctor's hairy back, as he walked ahead down the shadowed hall, the girl struggling feebly in his grasp.

"When Ba'al comes, I will make you the first offering to his reign. And Astarte and I will serve the god as concubines."

In the main room, the townspeople groaned as one . . . It was as if the soul of the goat lived in them all, as one.

CHAPTER FIFTY-FOUR

"There's nobody there," David insisted. His fingers touched the cool skin of the policewoman's shoulder with trepidation. The faintest fear slipped through his brain and asked, would she arrest him for assault?

"It's just you and me. In a closet."

Christy sat up and pressed her face close to his. "There was *someone* here. Some *thing*. There was . . ."

David nodded. "I know." He shivered as he thought of the cold weight that had thrust at his back. "I felt it too. But . . . they're gone now. We should find a way out before they come back."

In the faintest light of the room, he thought he saw her face grimace.

"I didn't ask to be in your nightmare," he told her.

Christy laughed. "And I didn't ask to feel your nightstick."

She coughed. "Um . . . please get it off my thigh."

David laughed. Then he crawled back to the faint light creeping in from beneath the door. With a fingernail he traced the indentation along the floor and followed its unlit gap up to standing level. After a little work, he found the door handle with his hand, which didn't budge in the slightest. He said, "Right here. We need something to slip up and into the lock."

"Oh sure, let me just get my hairpin," Christy said. David could almost see her smirk in the dark.

"Just feel around on the ground for a piece of paper . . . I think it's just a latch on the outside. If we can slip something in here and flip it up . . . we're home free."

"Just crawl around naked on the dirty floor of a basement with the spiders and bugs feeling around for garbage . . . Is that what you're suggesting?"

"Exactly."

"Okay, just wanted to be clear."

Christy felt in the dust for . . . anything. Her knees scraped against tiny stones and grit as she crawled. David did the same, working his way around the small room. From a few feet away Christy let out a small scream.

"What's wrong?"

"I think a spider just crawled across my ass."

"Ugh. Hope you don't get pregnant."

"Hey, a kid with eight arms and legs could be useful."

"Yeah, especially in searching for needles in haystacks."

"Or scraps of paper in the dark. This is disgusting. I feel like things are crawling all over my skin now."

"They are. You just crawled across a lice pit."

"Fuck you. I'm going to make sure to give you a big hug and infest you with them just for that."

"Ha," David laughed. "You just want to get your hands on me. I knew it."

"You wish."

David didn't answer. His fingers had just slipped over something that wasn't cement. He traced its edge until the back of his hand touched the wall.

"Did you hear me, I said—"

"Shh," he cut her off. "I think I found something."

In a second a warm hand grasped his shoulder. "What?"

He caught the edge with his nails and lifted it from the ground. It wasn't large, but it bowed in the air instantly, the top edge bending to lightly brush his arm.

"Not sure. A piece of plastic I think."

David stood and crossed to the doorway. Carefully slipping the edge of the thin material into the crack, he moved the edge very gently up and then down, teasing it through the gap.

"Is it working?"

"Not sure," he said again. "I . . ."

They both heard the sound of metal clinking against the door frame.

"That's it," Christy enthused. "You did it! We can—"

"That wasn't me," David hissed, pushing her back as the door burst open.

CHAPTER FIFTY-FIVE

The stairs were original. While the doctor may have renovated everything else aboveground in the old hotel, the steps into the basement creaked and moaned like they were a hundred years old. And perhaps they were.

Chief Maitlin took them slow, listening carefully to the din somewhere below. There were voices, a lot of them, in the basement, and most of the words coming from them were unintelligible. But passionate. Moans and sighs whispered through the stairwell like forbidden perfume; invisible, deadly, but alluring.

Maitlin reminded himself that he was here for Stacy's sake. In his mind he could see her in their kitchen as a child now, clasping the brown matted fur of a teddy bear to her side and asking, "Daddy, is it time for bed?" He had scooped her up with the promise that "Yes, yes it is . . . and it's time for sweet dreams."

He had never imagined then that she could be sucked into a dream as dark as this one. He was supposed to protect her from shit like this. He swore at himself for that failure, and stepped off the last wooden step to the concrete below. The moaning was louder here, the crowd like a single organism, gasping and moaning and sighing all in unison. A gestalt of evil sexual release. As her father, he prayed that she was not witnessing whatever was going on just a few yards away. But as a cop, he knew in his heart of hearts that she was more than witnessing it. She was a part of the action. She had to be. Why else would they have taken her, if not to be a part of this . . . this . . . whatever it was.

He drew his gun and poked his head around the corner to see just exactly what *it* was.

The room undulated in red. Smoky red-orange light flickered and swam through air that seemed alive with shapes. In the air, Maitlin smelled semen. And lilacs. And iron. And something thick and intoxicating. It made his head dizzy from just one deep breath as he tasted and tried to identify what it was exactly that smelled sooo good. So good it made him want to disrobe himself and join the other aspect of the room—the herd of copulating bodies that swam and moved across the floor like the kitchen floor of a cheap motel at dawn. The shapes moved and quivered like cockroaches, tasting the air and diving in to suck one more crumb of life from their feast.

He was immediately embarrassed to see what he saw . . . but even as his face reddened, his crotch responded.

"Damn," he murmured. "I haven't felt like this in twenty years. I could . . ."

He didn't finish the sentence. Instead, he brought up one wide hand and slapped himself in the face, forcing the inexplicable feelings away with pain. The lust retreated, for the moment, and he squinted through the shadows to scan the forms before him. If Stacy was somehow out there on the floor . . . he didn't want to see. But he had to know. He couldn't help her if he couldn't see . . .

His stomach trembled as his eyes roved over the bodies on the floor. They were a mass of bony shoulders and fat, rippled thighs. And on nearly all of them rested a splatter, or a smear of something that could only be blood. But he knew without question that it wasn't their own. They were too involved in their rutting to have any mortal wounds among them. From somewhere a female voice called out in orgasm, "Oh yes, yes . . . Ba'al is here. Ba'al is in me."

The former exclamation made sense, though he wished he hadn't heard it. The latter however . . . seemed puzzling. Ba'al?

"Chief," a familiar voice said.

Maitlin pulled his eyes off the buttocks of one slender woman, and met the face of his captain. Castle Point's second-in-command was disturbingly . . . naked.

"What are you doing here?" Captain Ryan hissed. "I've been working at getting accepted here . . . They think I'm one of them. But if they see you . . ."

The chief's gaze had left the body of his bloodied captain to take in the rest of the room. It curved around a wall in an L and just at the edge of his sight he could make out a wall, and the flickering light of hundreds of candles. And an arm, with ropes around its wrist.

From somewhere nearby a male voice called out: "To Ba'al, a mother. The Tenth."

And then, a scream.

Maitlin started forward, but Ryan held him back. "Wait!" he hissed. "You'll blow my cover."

"Someone's hurt," the chief said.

"Lots of people here have been hurt. But if you just dive right in, all that's going to happen is you're going to join them."

Maitlin looked his captain up and down, noticing the glistening sheen of sweat and other substances he didn't want to consider coating the cop's hairy legs and chest. He shook his head.

"My daughter's here, Matt. I can't sit back and wait on this one."

"Chief, you've got to trust me on this one . . ."

Again the horrible scream, this time ending in a gurgle that could only be the drowning choke of blood.

Maitlin pushed Ryan aside and stepped into the room of flesh. Because that was what the room had become. Flesh copulating. Flesh bleeding. Flesh fellated. Flesh filleted.

The miasma of sex and blood hung like smoke, but in that cloud there was something else. Something dead that . . . wasn't quite.

Maitlin looked confused as he squinted through a fog that wasn't quite candle smoke to see the source of the screams. The air seemed to move around him like a living presence. In his head, he heard not only the moans and cries of the room, but something deeper. Something like . . . laughter.

At the center of it all, a man's arm raised high in the air, and then brought a flash of silver down through the thick air to stop with a wet thunk in the neck of a naked brunette. But even as the horror of the action registered on the chief's mind, something even worse blotted it out.

Just to the right of the sacrificial stage, a body hung from ropes tied to hooks in the ceiling rafters. A body that the chief knew only too well . . . but didn't want to be seeing like this here. Now.

Stacy.

"You bastards," he breathed, as he saw his daughter's body displayed like a pornographic bit of meat for the crowd, breasts spattered with the blood of the stage, pubes wild and damp in the heat of the hell that the basement had become. Her eyes were closed, and for that Maitlin was glad. But he panicked that her apparent unconsciousness might be death.

"Stacy," he called out without thinking. In a heart-beat, Ryan's hand was over his mouth, and the chief shrugged him off.

"Back off, Matt. I mean it."

"Chief, she's all right. I made them promise that they wouldn't hurt her."

"You made them promise?"

"A bargaining chip," Ryan said. "I told them if we held her here and warned you off as part of the deal, they'd be left alone for the ceremony. And Stacy would walk away free at the end."

"Are you mad?" Maitlin turned on Ryan, eyes blazing. "There's going undercover, and there's joining the gang. You had no right to drag my daughter into this. How dare you—"

The chief's words were cut short by yet another scream. And this time, the crowd responded with a chant.

"Ba'al, Astarte. Ba'al, Astarte. Ba'al, Astarte . . ."

"What the hell is going on here?" Maitlin whispered.

"'Hell' is a good word for it," a new, high-pitched voice whispered in his ear. At the same time, something cold and stinging kissed his neck.

"It's all right," Ryan warned the man off.

"I don't think so."

Something bit the chief then, and he spun away from the bite . . . but as his hand slapped at the pain in his neck, he found it instantly wet with warmth.

"What did you do?" he heard Ryan yell. But Chief Maitlin didn't look back. He couldn't turn his neck, didn't dare. It felt hot and bloody, and his hand struggled to hold the pumping life in as his legs struggled to move him away from his turncoat captain and toward his naked daughter, hung like sexual meat for the whole room to sample.

"Stacy," he called, but it came out in a hoarse gurgle.

He stumbled over a man and woman on the floor who rolled entwined as if they were joined at the elbows and knees as well as groins. His foot kicked the man in the face as he staggered toward Stacy, and the man responded with a punch to the back of his calf.

Maitlin stumbled, and sank to the floor, one hand on his neck, the other grasping through bodies for the cement of the basement. He felt weak . . . dizzy. Something warm rubbed against the hand that steadied him on the floor and he looked to see the ribs and heavy breast of a fortysomething checkout woman from the grocery writhing beneath the body of a tattooed stick of a woman.

"It's wrong," he gasped, and brought the hand away from his neck to steady himself on the floor, which seemed to spin away from his grasp. Again he heard laughter. From behind, he heard the captain's voice arguing with someone, and then the chief found his legs again. He staggered up, slapping a hand to the wound on his neck to hold his blood, some of his blood, inside.

"Stacy," he called again, and this time, her eyes fluttered open as he stepped over another body to arrive at her feet. The ungodly shrieks on the stage were slowing to infrequent cries, and the crowd in the room still chanted, "Ba'al, Astarte, Ba'al, Astarte . . ."

"Dad," she cried out. "Oh my God, Daddy . . ."

Maitlin staggered to stand at her dangling feet and grasped for her arm, tethered to the ceiling by heavy twined rope. "Don't worry," he whispered. "I'll get you out of here . . ."

"You're hurt."

"So are you."

"No, they didn't hurt me; they've just hung me out here . . . kind of like a bad load of laundry."

"I warned you to stay out of this," Ryan's voice came in his ear. "You've got about thirty seconds to get out of here, and then . . ."

From the stage, Dr. Rockford's voice boomed coolly.

"Chief, thanks for joining us. Your daughter is delicious, if I do say so myself. You should try her out while she's all trussed up. I'm sure you've always wanted a piece of her . . . or did you get some on your own?"

Maitlin lunged away from Stacy toward Rockford, but Ryan grabbed his elbow with two hands and jerked him around. The chief staggered and almost went down. His clothes were dark with blood now, and he found it difficult to see. There were shadows at the edges of his vision, and faces that seemed to grin with teeth too long for their mouths.

"You should have followed the deal," Ryan hissed. "I didn't want to have to do this."

"Stop them," Maitlin gasped, crimson gathering like frost on his lips. "Matt . . . stop them, please."

Captain Ryan shook his head slowly, sadly. Then his hand came up in a sudden, deliberate jab to the police chief's middle.

Only, the hand was holding a knife. The Butcher's knife. Twelve inches long if it was a millimeter. The captain twisted it back and forth inside the chief's gut as his old friend's eyes widened and his brows creased in confusion.

"Our time here is over," Ryan said. "Castle Point won't need the police anymore. Ba'al will guard us soon."

The chief's eyes only had a second to register their incomprehension when the blade connected with his neck from the uninjured side.

The man with the apron and long knife grinned like a schoolkid at recess as his giant butcher knife hacked into the police chief's neck, and easily brought it through the vertebrae to come out clean on the other side. The chief was still opening his mouth to speak when his head toppled to the ground, and was instantly gathered to the breast of an orgasming woman as if he were her lover. She kissed his still-warm lips and grinned, and her lover shook her from below, and the chief's neck dripped hot on her breast.

The chief's headless body wavered for a moment and then slipped in slow motion to the ground.

Ryan shook his head at the Butcher. "You could have let me finish it. He was *my* problem."

The Butcher grinned and said in a girlish voice, "Everybody needs a little help dealing with their elders . . ." He turned toward the woman hanging from the ceiling and crying in great, wet sobs. ". . . or their daughters."

"Not her," Ryan said, bringing his blade, still wet with his old friend's blood to the side of the Butcher's neck. "I promised that she would be okay."

"Promises, promises." The Butcher laughed. His voice was so high-pitched he could have auditioned as a '20s flapper, so long as you couldn't see the portly frame and deep shadow of beard.

"Would you rather I fuck her, or kill her?" The Butcher batted Ryan's blade to the floor and held his own at the cop's shoulder. "I fancy the bitch, and tonight's the night for whatever you fancy. Isn't that right?"

He nodded at Elsie, who still lay prone on the floor where Ryan had left her when he went to deal with Maitlin.

"Come back," her lips mouthed to him. They almost looked unreal . . . as if a shadow moved them while the thin, pale lips remained closed and dead. But Ryan only followed the call of the foggy words.

Ryan felt the fight drain out of him then, as the voices behind his eyes whispered to him to *fuck, fuck, fuck* and the wrinkled breasts of his one perverse lust rippled on the floor before him. He never gave a second glance at the perfect globes of the chief's daughter, who any man in his right mind would have paid a fortune to bed. The waves of demonic obsession rode over him, and in moments, he rode over Elsie, as the Butcher lifted a blade to trace the beads of sweat down the center of Stacy's chest.

"Yesss, my love," he whispered to her as she quavered and struggled to pull her arms from the nooses anchored above her head. "You only get to lie with your father's corpse once in life, I always say . . ." he told her as he cut her down and dragged her kicking and screaming to where her father's dead body still bled in a widening pool on the floor . . .

As the Butcher forcibly pressed her lips to the wound on the stump of her father's neck, behind them, the nurse called for the next sacrifice:

"To Astarte. A mother. The Eleventh."

CHAPTER FIFTY-SIX

Carrie Sanddanz felt something press against the back of her thigh. Something cold, like steel left outside on a winter's night. She jerked away, but it followed her, creeping like a frozen noose up her leg to encircle the topmost skin of her leg . . . and then it released her . . . and moved to the middle.

"No!" she screamed, and struggled to move away

from the cold that engulfed her most private parts . . . but she could not move. She could only lie there and accept the fingers that slipped inside her and pressed her flesh with a cold, dead speculum that she could not, from any vantage point, see.

"What the fuck!" she moaned, and stared at her middle, struggling to see the marionette strings. But they were inside her now, and she jerked and moaned to their rhythm, at the same time praying aloud for it to stop.

And then the door opened and she heard the doctor's voice. He had locked her in this tiny room just barely large enough to hold a cot. No windows. No light. It was horrible . . . but the threat of the darkness and its invisible creatures was still better than having to see the face of the doctor again.

"So. Ready to take it to the next level?" Dr. Rockford's voice asked. His body was a blur of shadow in the pitch-black of her cell.

"No," she said. "I don't even know what this level is."

"This level is the important one," he explained. "Here, we give it all." He paused. "Or, at least, you do."

A blade came up to freeze her neck, but in the meantime, something cold pressed between her thighs.

The bandage around her head throbbed as she moved to see him. "Haven't you hurt me enough?" she asked.

Rockford grinned a row of perfectly white teeth. "The only hurt that is enough is when there is no more possibility of hurt. You seem like you have plenty of capacity for more. Anyway, we're going to find out."

He took her by the hand and pulled her from the cot. His touch was warm, but she realized that she preferred the bitter attentions of the ghosts that had forced themselves on her before the doctor's presence. They could be trusted ... or, at least ... understood. They were predictable. She had no idea what Rockford was up to.

He led her out of the tiny room and into a dark hall ... but she could hear voices ahead. The din of a room filled with people. Only ... these people didn't sound like they were filling the place with a buzz from casual conversation. These were the kind of chaotic but insistent syllables that one expected from a porno movie ... yet the number of voices and their intensity seemed to go beyond simple night movements. At one point, a group of them cheered, and a few steps later, the voices drew a collective gasp.

Carrie's skin crawled as she heard distant moans change to chants and then to a faraway scream.

"What are they doing in there?" she asked her captor, who kept a grip on her hand tight as a vise. She could almost feel her bones bending.

"Waiting for you," he said.

She tried to pull away, but his grip only tightened. She felt as if the bones in her hand would snap in a dozen pieces at any moment.

"There is no place to run to," he warned. "If you go back, you'll only find yourself trapped in that room once more ... and I don't think you want that. Forward is how we're doing this now. Move forward."

The first thing that hit her was the smell. As they rounded the corridor and entered the main room of the basement, the heat and humidity hit her like a wall. And within it, a scent of fertility and death mixed together like sin. Carrie gasped as she saw the Bacchanalian rites on the floor, but it was the smell that scared her—the room stank of evil. She could almost see the devils flitting through the shadows in the dark air, as candles flickered suggestively along the walls. And at the front of the room, the nurse stood naked, engaged in some strange ritual with another woman.

As Dr. Rockford led her forward, Carrie recognized the girl as one of the hospital inmates she'd seen over the past few weeks. She had painted with her once in what the doctor liked to call "art class." But it was more like bloodletting class, as all of the patients—most of them semicomatose—had slashed their hands and fingers and bled onto parchment in Rorschach designs that the doctor had collected and framed.

"You will be remembered for your art," he'd said, as he took Carrie's halfhearted attempt to smear a picture of him on her paper. In the center of his stick-figure chest, she'd puddled a thick circle of blood with a point protruding.

"Right," was all she could say to answer him. The drugs left her barely able to mouth a single syllable. The same was true for all of the women . . . and so it was easiest to simply obey his orders—like, "Paint a picture in your blood for me."

Carrie had used her own deep humor to turn that command into, "Paint a picture in your blood OF me." Her stickman writhed on a pointed stake. If he had caught the meaning of her crimson smears, he ignored it.

The scene in front of her now resembled the intent of her stick drawing . . . only the victim was her former prison mate. The woman struggled to kick and punch at Nurse Amelia, but the defrocked nurse only grinned and pulled the woman closer to her in a twisted chest-to-chest embrace. A man in a butcher's apron stood behind the struggling women, holding the patient's arms in a vise grip so that her punches couldn't land. In a moment, those arms ceased to fight, as Amelia's hand plunged a long knife into the back of the other woman. She stepped back, letting the body slump into the Butcher's arms and turned to the crowd, pressing the red edge of the knife to her lips. When she pulled it away and let her arm hang at her side, her tongue traced the bloody halo from her lips.

"The eleventh mother," she pronounced. "And"— she brought the arm back up in an attack stance and turned back to the woman who moaned feebly in the Butcher's grasp, but otherwise didn't move— "the eleventh child!"

With those words, she plunged the knife into her in the opposite direction, this time straight through the belly.

The room lit with one electrifying scream, as the woman's eyes popped open, their whites so exposed that they seemed to pop out of her skull. Amelia pulled back the knife and a gush of fluid exited the wound behind it. Without ceremony, the Butcher dropped the body and with his foot, rolled it off the side of the makeshift stage.

The room filled with the chant of "Ba'al, Astarte."

And then Rockford pushed Carrie to the front of the stage. "The hour is late and the minutes few," he yelled. The throng around them hushed.

"The blood of the mothers flows heavy in this room. But our time for blood is nearly done. The hour of the Thirteenth is almost at hand. For our last gift to Ba'al and Astarte, I give to you the twelfth mother."

Strong hands suddenly closed on Carrie's wrists and yanked her up on the stage. Amelia ran one wet hand down her back as if in comfort as she took over from Rockford. "There are only minutes left in the twelve o'clock hour," she said. "And all of you must share in our last gift. The twelfth mother gives her life and her baby to all of us."

"But I'm not a mother," Carrie gasped. "I don't even have a boyfriend."

Amelia smiled and patted Carrie's tummy. "Dr. Rockford is your boyfriend," she whispered in her ear. "And don't worry, I won't tell him you slept through it."

Pulling away from Carrie, Amelia called out to the mob again, and this time pointed at the edge of the stage, where a scattering of thin silver rectangles lay.

"You all must draw her blood. Quickly now!"

Carrie's eyes widened as she saw all of the participants in the blood orgy stand, and line up to pick up razors—one each—from the edge of the stage. When an old lady stepped before her and opened a gash on her thigh, Carrie didn't even scream.

She was thinking of the baby she didn't even know she had.

As another wound opened like fire on her calf and one blade bisected her breast like an acid burn across her nipple, Carrie pictured a tiny face in her mind, sucking on a bottle.

Carrie cried.

CHAPTER FIFTY-SEVEN

The door swung open and David pushed Christy behind him. As he did, he smelled the flower scent of her hair, and realized with a pang that this, right now, was probably the last time he would see her. Even if, strictly speaking, he couldn't really *see* her. He could smell her though, and she was rich and sweet in the dark. And her side felt smooth and velvety where he held it. In two heartbeats David vowed that he would do anything to protect this smart-ass cop from the murderer he was sure stood before them, and with that he bulled forward like a linebacker.

He crashed into the man in the doorway with his right shoulder, and the guy went down like a feather, with a whoosh of breath and a feeble cry.

David hadn't expected it to be that easy, and he stumbled and fell to the ground outside the room as he recovered. He had thought that their captors would have sent more than one weak guy to collect them. In the faint flickering light of a candle, David crept back to the man who now lay moaning on the ground and holding his side.

Christy was already at his side.

"Always in the wrong place . . ." she accused.

"What?"

"It's Billy, one of the Terror Twins, you dope," she said. David couldn't help but notice her breast swaying over the downed man's face. Lucky guy.

"He was here to let us out," she said.

David knelt and saw the dark pool of blood on the floor near Billy's hands, which clasped and kneaded at his side.

"I'm sorry," he said. "But . . . did I do *that?*"

Billy turned a weak gaze his way and shook his head slightly. "They stabbed me. Left me to bleed. Not dead yet . . ."

A spasm convulsed his face. When it relaxed again, Billy wheezed, "If you're going to go, then go. They'll be back soon. Figured I owed you that much, after what TG did to you."

David felt a wave of guilt and thanks twist in his heart. He gripped Billy's shoulder and gave it a slight squeeze. "Thanks, man. Hang in here . . . We'll go get help and come back for you."

"Just get out before I kick your ass."

David stifled the urge to retort. Billy wasn't going to be kicking anything but the bucket in the next few minutes, looked like.

"C'mon," he whispered and pulled Christy's arm, urging her away from the man. Billy curled in the fetal position and moaned painfully. "Let's get out of here."

The room, which just a few hours before had been filled with a dozen nude women, chained to the walls in a scene resembling some mediaeval torture chamber from hell, now was strangely quiet.

David had his hand on the door to the hall when Christy stopped him, and made him look behind them. The candle flames still guttered along the walls every few feet, but the chains and ropes hung slack from their hooks. No women remained. The void was expectant. And eerie.

"They seem to be running low on victims," David noted.

Christy nodded. "Let's not fill out the list."

They stepped into the hallway as one.

CHAPTER FIFTY-EIGHT

Blood is music. It sings of life. It sings of death. It pulses and twists, dances and sways. Blood filled the room of Castle House, and the house sang.

Ba'al heard the call and answered its tribal beat.

Astarte heard the call and joined the dance . . . Her feet slipped on its love and kicked at its anger. Her heart joined in its demand and she sang in the clouds of *almost*.

Because Astarte was not in Castle House. Not yet.

She and Ba'al saw each other across the fog of *nearly* and kissed at the brink of *almost,* as a knife bled yet another mother, and a stab killed yet another infant in their names.

Ba'al slipped her an ethereal tongue and she laughed, biting down as hard as she could. Her teeth echoed like metallic tongs in the dark, and even past the *almost,* the people could hear her humor.

"I've missed you, dark lord," she teased.

"I've had better," he called back. Aloof to the end.

"You've had none," she laughed. "You've got no bone."

He shrugged, a ghostly flip of the shoulder, its backdrop lit by blood. "Maybe not. But I will soon." He pointed at the stack of women's bodies piled up on the floor in the Castle House basement.

"All this too shall be yours."

"I don't want wormwood," she complained. "I need flesh to milk." She flexed a handful of pointed fingernails as if to underscore her point. "I need to reave and suckle."

Ba'al nodded, his humor gone. "The game is nearly done. And the vessel is nearby. This time . . ."

"How many times have you said that?" Astarte spat, though nothing material ever touched the floor. "How many times have we been 'almost there'?"

Ba'al shot her a look that would have wilted milkweed. "And I get to spend eternity with you?"

He pointed at the crowd, lined up to draw blood, one blade at a time, from a blonde woman. The woman didn't even struggle as their razors ripped and tore at her flesh, until there was no skin unblemished, only a flesh canvas painted in pain. Aphrodisiac of the gods.

"If you want to be real enough to feel it again . . .

then help," Ba'al said, and with that disappeared into the ether above Rockford . . . like a ghost. His voice echoed in the *nowhere*. "Make them feel it. Make them need it. Tonight we *will* be born again."

CHAPTER FIFTY-NINE

Brenda heard the demons.

She'd never much believed in the afterlife. If she had, she might not have taken the bus to Oak Falls as much as she had on Friday nights. Because surely her exploits there qualified her for an eternity in hell.

But now . . . she thought . . . she might actually be IN hell. Things touched her in the dark. Things laughed at her from a place she couldn't see. No matter where she turned, the air seemed to roil and turn . . . but when she reached out a hand to feel, there was nothing there. Nothing except maybe a whisper of cold . . . or a faint scorch of heat.

The room was alive, with the sound of demons.

Brenda shivered. In her heart, she prayed to be back in her house, in that place she had tried for so many years and in so many ways to get out of. She begged forgiveness for all of the rude T-shirts she'd worn to spite her parents. She recited the Act of Contrition for all the boys she'd . . . Brenda shook away the memories of nights on her knees in the shadow of a bathroom stall. If she had just one more chance, one chance . . . she'd do better.

"God, I don't want to die," she whispered.

Around her, the air erupted in laughter.

"God?" a voice tittered. "Goddddd? Did someone invite him here? I don't think so . . ."

And then a door opened, and light flickered like the wave of a distant fire into the room. A soft and gentle voice said the words she feared to hear.

"It's time."

Amelia's hands took her arm, and Rockford's fingers gripped the long silk of her hair, and together they led her out of the darkness, and into . . .

"Hell" is a subjective term. For some people, hell is an eternity in an office building sitting in a cubicle day after day and churning out pointless letter after pointless report from eight thirty to five thirty every day. For others, hell was coming home after those days in the office to face a loveless marriage and a clutch of thankless kids every night. And still for others, hell was a traditional place of fire and brimstone, flames licking the blistered feet of all who suffered eternity there, in unrelenting physical torment.

Where Amelia and Rockford led Brenda, *that* was hell. As soon as they stepped into the room thick with the scent of blood and smoke and sex, Brenda knew she was going to be punished for all her sins. She would get no pardon from a God she called on too late. She saw the dead women stacked up along the side of the stage at the front of the room, arms splayed over each other and blood covering them all like a drizzle of torment on a human corpse sundae.

This was hell.

There was a mob of naked people clustered around the stage, and Brenda soon saw why. At their center they propped up a woman. She was blonde. Dressed only in her own blood. The blood that the townspeople were drawing. One by one they stepped forward and lifted arms high above their heads, before bringing them down to slip into the skin of the woman. She didn't scream, only shivered a little at each contact, which released a new river of her life.

"It's time," Amelia said, as they dragged Brenda onto the stage. "Have you all drawn her blood?"

The mob answered in a resounding "Yes," and Amelia abandoned Brenda's arm to step forward.

"Then I will finish it." She held her hand out for a razor, and metal glinted like steely fireflies as hands everywhere offered them to her. Amelia accepted one and approached Carrie, who by this point was barely conscious. The Butcher had first held her captive with his grip and now only held her up. She had become immune to the blades after the first dozen slashes. And now her spark drowned in her own lifeblood.

"Carrie," Amelia whispered. She said it again, louder. The woman's eyes flickered open and struggled to focus. When it registered on her tormented brain who was before her, who was calling her out of the blissful unconsciousness she'd retreated into, Carrie had just one word to say through shredded, broken lips.

"Bitch."

"Twelfth," was all Amelia said in answer. Her lips pulled back in a rictus of a smile as she said it. And then she brought the razor to Carrie's neck and whispered, "Your blood to mine. My blood to yours. Our blood to Ba'al and Astarte entwined."

"Fuckin' piece of shit," Carrie said for the last time in her life.

Then Amelia's razor drew deep across her neck and let out the last blood that her struggling heart still pumped. She still didn't scream . . . in fact, after the depth of the cut in her neck, probably couldn't.

Instead she simply slid to the floor. Someone in
the crowd began to chant "The Thirteenth. The
Thirteenth . . ."

And in moments, the whole room echoed with
the cry.

Brenda felt tears well up in her eyes. She knew what
"the Thirteenth" had to mean. It had to mean her.
Sliced to bits. And she really didn't want to be sliced
to bits . . . She may have had a goth thing going on
for a bit, but she was no cutter . . . She hated knives
and razors.

"What the fuck did I do?" she said to nobody in
particular.

But Rockford didn't miss the cue.

"You were born, just like all the rest of us. And
now it's time to—"

From the back of the room someone screamed.

"Stop!!"

Rockford held on to Brenda and laughed. "Do you
think so?" he said to the interrupter. "I mean . . .
we've come all this way, bought a monstrous property that, oddly enough, happens to have ties to the
otherworld, spent nine months cultivating and cap-
turing and impregnating a complement of twelve
mothers so that on tonight, the night of the Sabbat,
we could decide . . . eh, ya know, we don't want to
do this." The one-time famous geneticist laughed.
There was an edge of mania to it. "I don't *think* so."

Rockford pointed and the crowd turned toward
the two at the back of the room.

"Bring them up here."

Christy and David saw the mob turn toward them,
and backed into the hallway from which they'd entered.

Christy dug nails into David's arm and pulled him

backward. "I don't really want to die," she mentioned casually, backing up one step at a time.

"That's Brenda up there," was David's response. He didn't budge even though the mob had turned.

Something in the "We have to save another woman" response didn't sit well with Christy but she tried not to analyze it too much. If she'd had a gun at her hip, she would have pulled it, but circumstances dictated a different approach. She kicked him in the back of the knee, and he buckled.

"What the . . ."

"C'mon," Christy insisted and yanked him back into the dark of the corridor. Two of the naked throng followed them, but these kind of odds she could handle. Christy did a mental ". . . two, three, four," and KICKed with all her might at the jaw of the first man. He was tall and bald—shaven—and he really wasn't expecting the full-frontal-nudity assault on his face. When Christy's heel connected with his head, there was an audible snap, and he hit the pavement with a wet-sounding slap. The guy following behind him took one look around and saw that nobody else was hot in pursuit and reconsidered his own mission. He backed away.

"Remind me not to fuck with you," David mumbled.

"Fucking's okay," Christy said, and bent down to rub the ball of her foot. "Man . . . never got that kind of extension before."

"What, they don't practice naked karate in the police academy?"

From the main room, Rockford's voice bellowed. "It is time," he said, and anyone in the crowd who had taken an interest in Christy and David turned back to the reason they were there. The final sacrifice. But this one would not involve blood.

"It is nearly the hour of the Thirteenth," Rockford continued. "And it is time to plant the seed of the god. That piece which will transgress the gate of worlds to bring him fully among us. Ba'al is here now already. I can feel him."

Amelia grabbed Brenda's hand and held it aloft for the crowd. "The thirteenth mother," she exclaimed. Rockford directed Brenda, "Lie down."

She looked at him in askance. "Lie down?"

"Yes . . . the only way to bring Ba'al through to us is to make him through you. With the other mothers, I have created their children, my children, and then given them to the god."

"You murdered babies."

"Their innocence opened the way," Amelia interjected. She ran her hands over Brenda's shoulders and began to pressure her to the floor.

"Now it is your turn," Rockford said, grinning wolfishly. "Let's make a god together."

"What's in it for me?" Brenda asked, now on her knees with the force of Amelia's nails. The nurse would draw blood soon with her nails if she kept up the pressure.

"Well . . . you won't die, like all the others."

Brenda considered this. She'd had sex with guys she didn't want to be with before, but the side effect of incubating a god as a result of the act hadn't surfaced before.

"You people are crazy, you know that?" she asked before giving in and lying back to the floor. She had seen what happened to Carrie, and presumably to all of the other dead women lying near the stage. Sex hadn't been part of the ceremony that spelled the demise of Carrie, from what she'd seen, so maybe her penance was to be different. If she could fuck her way out of this . . . well, it kind of went counter to the promise she'd made just minutes ago, but . . . this was different.

As she stretched out on the floor, she felt something cold and wet cling to her back and legs. Brenda closed her eyes. She knew what it was . . . She'd watched the blood dripping from Carrie's torso like a faucet.

Brenda was lying in the blood of dead women. Newly dead women. What kind of traitor to her gender was she, to voluntarily lie down in the blood of her sisters—who had been bred and then killed— the ultimate blasphemy against women. What kind of traitor, to lie down in their blood and open her legs to be used for the cowardly purpose of escaping their fate?

Brenda thought these things as she lay back, but the guilt didn't stop her. In her belly, Brenda Bean was a pragmatist, and the reality was, she couldn't do anything to bring those women or their babies back to life. All she could do was try to hold on to hers. Even if that meant fucking crazy men on the floor of a sacrificial altar.

Something cold entered her and she clenched her eyes tighter. From above she heard Rockford blathering on about something. A god and an Astarte, whatever that was.

Amelia's voice whispered in her ear, much closer. "It's okay," the nurse said. "It will all be over quickly."

Brenda felt the warmth of the other woman slip away. But the coldness between her legs didn't leave. It pressed against her, cleaving her flesh to leave goose bumps on her thighs. If her sex was a flower, Brenda would have said she wilted. She could feel her very life sucked into the cold; her heart seemed to beat harder, as if every pump was an effort. Her eyes wanted to cry, but there were no tears when she squeezed.

Above her, she could hear Amelia chanting something; it sounded Latin. And then Rockford joined in the words, and the crowd echoed their evil prayers, syllable for guttural syllable. The room was abuzz in words, unintelligible, foreign words, but Brenda lay in the midst of them, totally alone.

Well, not totally. She had lifted her arms to see who was using her, and was shocked to find that her fingers found only her own belly after slapping at the air. She ran those fingers up across her breasts and down to the place where something poked inside her . . . but instead of hands or a body near her, she found only . . . herself. As her fingers passed her groin and slipped to her thigh, they came away wet.

"Ugh," she groaned, as something trembled and kissed inside her. Her body warmed and throbbed in answer and Brenda fought to control herself. "No. I won't enjoy this . . ." she hissed.

But despite her words, she *did.* Brenda arched her back to accept whatever was working its way around her secret spot of pleasure; it certainly wasn't Rockford, who still seemed to be chanting wicked prayers over her. She struggled between crying and moaning and then finally she forced open her eyes and for just a moment, she could see a face before her.

He was dark and full of shadow, but Brenda saw the thin lips and long mustache. A triangle beard trailed from his chin and his forehead looked gashed and crossed with the brands of a thousand burns.

He looked like the devil.

And then he was gone, and Rockford's face leered close. "Are you ready, my bride?" he asked.

Around them, the room began to cheer, and Amelia's voice rose higher and higher above them, chanting words that trembled and twisted the tongue like a cascade of lice and larvae; a wriggling horde of infestuous language. The words made Brenda's skin crawl, but not as much as the touch of Rockford, who lowered himself to a push-up position above her body.

"Now, we will pierce the veil between worlds," he promised.

Brenda gritted her teeth and closed her eyes tighter, ignoring the cold heat that remained inside her. She didn't think the piercing was going to have a whole lot to do with worlds, but rather, a whole lot to do with piercing her.

CHAPTER SIXTY

"We need a weapon," Christy said, pulling David deeper into the dark hallway.

"Who needs a weapon when they've got you?" he answered.

Christy's heart leaped just a bit when she heard him say that. There was something about this annoying biker kid that had gotten to her. Even if he'd screwed up her job by getting in the way of her car.

"Yeah, well, I can't drop-kick a couple dozen people all at once. And anyway, I think I bruised my foot on that guy."

"Want me to rub it?"

"I thought you were all hell-bent on rescuing the pink-haired chick? I don't give my feet to just anyone to rub. Especially someone else's anyone."

David felt like a fool. "You're right," he said. He didn't know why he was flirting with the cop . . . He was here for Brenda. Who, at the moment, was about to be sacrificed by a bunch of demon-worshipping freaks. "What did you have in mind for a weapon?"

Christy felt her stomach sink. He was still stuck on the barfly. "Well, I don't have my gun . . . but we ought to be able to find something heavy down here. It's a basement, for Christ's sake!"

She turned a corner David knew all too well.

"Not this way," he said.

She looked back at him, and David suddenly realized, even in the dark, just how brown her eyes were. Mentally, he slapped himself. What the hell?

"The Terror Twins were locked in the room down here," he explained. "If there'd been weapons . . . I know they would have used 'em."

"Good point," she agreed.

They turned the other way and found themselves back in the room where the twelve mothers had been held. The cattle-call room, David thought.

They stepped inside and David said, "There's not going to be anything here," but Christy ignored him, walking to one of the places vacated by a victim. All that remained from that captivity was a length of silver chain on the wall, but Christy pulled over a wooden box and stepped up to remove the chain from its hook. Then she stepped down and began to wave the heavy links through the air, narrowly missing David's face.

"Useful?" she asked.

He nodded.

"Then take it." Christy tossed the heavy links his way and stepped up on the box to remove its companion for herself.

She stepped down and twirled the iron links in the air with a nearly audible fan. Her eyes looked hard at David's, and even in the dull light of the flickering candles, he could see that she was drop-dead serious.

"Let's go get your girl," she said.

David gulped. It was damn hard to talk about going to rescue a girl you barely knew when there was a hot blonde standing naked in front of you, belly button and everything it flanked so tantalizingly just feet from your own stuff. A part of him wanted to forget about Brenda at that moment and reach his hands out to cup the gorgeous cop's . . .

"I don't think the gods are going to wait for you to make up your mind," Christy whispered.

David realized he'd been simply standing and staring at her. And the evidence of it was rising.

"I'm sorry," he stammered. "I . . . I . . ."

"Thanks," Christy said, and stepped forward.

His eyes couldn't seem to pull back from the bounce of her breasts.

"You've gotta take a side," she said. "I'll help you if you want."

She looked directly into his eyes then, and David could see what his indecision was doing to her. She wanted him. It was written all over her face.

"You can't have us both," she said. "And if you don't choose fast, you may lose us both."

She stepped past him and he watched the muscles working in her ass as she did . . .

Christy stepped through the door, chain swinging from her hand. David shook his head. He'd come here to save Brenda. He didn't even know if Brenda wanted him to save her. But they had had a connection. And he had to play true to that. Christy was amazing but . . .

"Let's break some heads," he said, joining her in the hall, swirling a chain to match her own.

Christy stifled the hot flood that threatened her eyes, and only nodded. "Follow me," she finally said.

The room had quieted since they'd left, and in their unclad state, nobody seemed to notice as David and Christy quietly paced their way around the thick of the crowd to arrive at the side of the stage. The townspeople were too enraptured watching the live porn of Rockford going down on Brenda.

David had to stifle the urge to run to the scene when he saw the doctor on top of "his girl," but Christy gripped his shoulder.

"You won't do her any good if you get whacked before you get to her."

He stifled the urge to break all heads, and instead focused on getting close enough to break one in particular.

"Argehnti, Eifel ast en higs' e' ti!" Amelia said, standing next to the couple on the floor and scattering some kind of herb or essence with one hand as she raised her other to the ceiling and called out foreign syllables.

"S' in puer de se ate in leg-see!" With that, Amelia held both hands out to the crowd. Her breasts streamed with the blood of the twelve mothers, and her thighs were equally smeared with the evidence of their former lives. "This is the moment," she called out. Her voice sounded almost orgasmic. "This is the moment that Astarte has dreamed of for centuries. This is the moment that our god is crea—"

Amelia didn't finish her sentence because a chain suddenly whipped through the air and cracked with a loud snap against the side of her face. Christy did not normally revel in violence, but this time, she felt no remorse whatsoever for slinging pain.

Rockford lifted himself up to thrust into the Thirteenth, but felt something press against his neck. He reached back to grasp at the distraction, and was suddenly pulled back.

"That will be enough of that, *Doctor* Rockford," David said, yanking hard on the chain looped around the doctor's neck. Rockford coughed and rolled away from the girl, gripping at the chain pulled tight around his throat.

Before the crowd quite realized what had happened, David and Christy had quickly overturned the ceremony of the Thirteenth, rolling both of the high priests to the ground. David grabbed Brenda's hand and yanked her to her feet.

"What the . . ."

"Not now," he said, and screamed at both women. "Upstairs, now!"

They broke for the stairwell, but the crowd surged forward.

"Just go," Christy said, pushing David forward. "Get her out of here."

He turned and began to argue, but a fat, naked older woman grabbed at his arm. Christy kicked the woman in the stomach, and then in a pivot turn took down a younger guy with a goatee.

"Just get the fuck out of here," she screamed.

David gripped Brenda's hand tight and pulled her toward the stairs.

"Where are we going?" Brenda asked, still slightly foggy from her ethereal experience on the floor.

"Consider this my version of taking you for a walk around the bar," he said, and dragged her up the first step. Behind them, a woman screamed. David tried not to think about whether the voice matched the profile of Christy's or not.

CHAPTER SIXTY-ONE

Leaves bit into their calves as they ran barefoot through the weeds. The mood shone overhead in an eerie spotlight that set the woods alight with spectral luminance. David wiped a tear from his face as he heard screams and cries from behind them . . . muffled, but still cries of pain. Who was going down in the hotel?

The wind picked up as they raced toward where he'd secreted his bike, and the trees swayed above them with their own groans.

"Here it is," David said at last, reaching down to pull his bike from the ditch.

"We can't get back to town on that!" Brenda laughed, but David didn't flinch.

"Get on," he said.

"Oh shit," she murmured, but she did as he asked, and in seconds, David could feel the bristle of her crotch pressing against the swell of his butt as he stepped hard onto the pedal. He couldn't think about the soft flesh that rested against his back. The flesh that, counter to every male fantasy he'd ever indulged, he now wished was clothed. Brenda was a distraction, but if she was going to live to be a distraction for a second date, he couldn't let the feel of her against him matter now.

"Hold on," he said, and they were on the road.

The first few meters down the gravel were tough,

but then David turned onto the asphalt of 190 and felt his legs at last get some response from the wheels. He pumped harder, and felt Brenda rise to press against him, not to tantalize, but rather to work with him to make his work easier.

Rise and fall, rise and fall their bodies went . . .

"Why?" a voice breathed in his ear.

"Huh?"

"Why did you come back for me?"

David didn't have to think. "Why did you walk me around the Clam Shack? Why did you get me a pitcher of water?"

"Hardly the same thing," she gasped, working to keep up with him. The road passed beneath them in a pale snake of asphalt and yellow lines.

"It's exactly the same thing."

Behind them, a light flickered on. In seconds, they could hear an engine, as the light drew closer.

"Maybe it's just someone on the highway from the Falls," Brenda whispered.

"Don't bet on it," he said. "You're supposed to become the mother of a damn demon . . . I don't think they're letting you just walk out of there, no sweat."

Brenda leaned in and laughed in his ear. Her voice made David's toes tingle—which was good, since the spikes of the bike pedals were now biting into the soles of his feet so hard he could feel blood begin to flow.

"And you came to rescue me on a bicycle," she said. "How sweet. Did you bring a cap gun by any chance?"

"Do you want to spend the night in a ditch?" he huffed.

"Only if it's with you."

"Now I remember why I fell in love with you," he said, closing his eyes as he pressed down hard on the pedals. The lights behind them were now almost blinding.

Brenda didn't say anything for a moment.

"You love me," she said at last. Her voice struggled to remain neutral.

"No," he said. The worst part of the uphill climb of 190 was now almost behind them. Just a few more yards . . .

"No, I just risked my life and got naked in front of half the town so that I could say I attended an orgy. Hate to miss out on shit like that. I mean, life's short and all . . ."

Brenda flipped one long pink strand of hair back and massaged his shoulders as his body rose and fell in front of her, trying to give him some kind of energy as he struggled to pull them up the hill. "Shut up and pump," she said, wrapping her arms around him.

"I've been dreaming of you saying that since . . ."

"I mean it. Shut up and PUMP!" she yelled as the headlights behind them grew blinding. The car engine revved and David knew that it was only a matter of seconds before the car clipped them. He was a good cyclist, maybe good enough after this summer of training to make the Olympics, but he couldn't compete with a car. Especially while pedaling uphill and barefoot.

"Hold on," he warned, and pulled the bike to the right, away from the drop-off to the valley.

The car barreled by, but instantly the air was colored in red as the brake lights lit. David pulled his own hand brakes and the bike slid to a halt.

"What are you doing?"

"We can't outrun them on a bike," David said. "We either fight or get away off-road on foot."

"Right," Brenda said. "I have my getaway shoes tucked right here in my . . . oh shit, I forgot my bag at the demonic orgy. Whatever will I do?"

David skidded out the back tire and cursed as he

put one tender foot to the asphalt. "One word," he answered. "Run."

All four doors of the black sedan opened a few meters ahead of them and several figures got out and wasted no time in thinking. Feet were in motion, and headed toward David and Brenda.

"Where?" she said, looking around in panic. The left-hand side of the road dropped into a gulley that would have killed a mountain goat, and the right wasn't much better; the rock face simply rose up instead of down.

"Straight ahead," David decided. He grabbed her hand and let the bike fall as they raced forward. He saw that Captain Ryan was one of the men to leave the car, as was Rockford. Amelia and the man he'd begun to think of as the Butcher had slipped out of the back of the car and both held long knives at the ready. The steel glinted dangerously in the moonlight.

"Straight ahead . . . Into the fire?" she gasped.

"Around it," he huffed. For a few seconds he led them almost straight toward the cliff, but then, just as the group had turned to intercept them there, at the rock wall, David gave Brenda's hand a harder yank and pulled her to slant left toward the valley. The deception worked and in a second the two were running hard past the car as the group behind scrambled to follow.

"They . . . will . . . just . . . get . . . back . . . in . . . the . . . car," Brenda gasped as they ran together hand in hand.

"Maybe," David answered. "But maybe . . . we'll be . . . in . . . a . . . better . . ."

Brenda yanked David's hand and then suddenly let go. He turned to look just in time to see the fist that met him in the eye.

The sky suddenly moved . . . and then flickered . . . out.

CHAPTER SIXTY-TWO

"You really should have listened to me," Aunt Elsie said. Her voice seemed to come from far away, afloat on a sea of voices and murmurs. As he struggled to wake up, David saw in his mind's eye a flash of disparate, yet connected images; *Brenda and her pink hair. The Clam Shack loud and blurry at midnight. The old hotel, Castle Point. A mob of townspeople sacrificing women in the hotel's basement* . . . Then he heard his aunt's voice again and felt her hand stroke his forehead. "Everything's okay," she murmured.

A grin grew on his face, as he struggled to wake. He must have tied some kinda drunk on last night, he thought. Hearing Elsie's voice, he knew that all those weird memories were somehow just a part of the delusion; he must've been drinking a LOT.

But then Elsie ran her fingers through his hair and said something else. "Everything's okay now that the Thirteenth is here again."

David's eyes popped open. The first thing he saw was Aunt Elsie's kind, wrinkled face above his, rheumy eyes staring down at his head lying in her lap. The next thing he saw was that she wasn't wearing any clothes, and before his mind could absorb every blue vein and age spot that ran from her throat across tiny, sagging breasts to her stretch-mark-scarred belly, he wrenched his face away.

But the view in the other direction wasn't much

better. A fat man's hairy back blocked his line of sight until he sat up, which he did almost as soon as he realized that his nightmares hadn't been dreams at all. Gingerly holding a palm over the raw, swollen left eye, David looked up at the stage and saw that all of his pedaling had been for naught. The Butcher held Brenda's arms to the sky as Rockford and Amelia ran their fingers up and down Brenda's ribs and flanks. They looked as if they were worshipping her every pore. They mouthed some kind of chant, but he didn't even try to focus on the words.

Elsie rubbed his neck and leaned over to whisper, "The hour of the Thirteenth was almost passed . . . but they brought you two back just in time. In a few minutes the god incarnate will be among us, entrusted to the womb of your very own girl. You should consider yourself lucky. If you stay with her, the god will surely be generous with you both."

David yanked away from his aunt, the woman who had cradled him as a baby and played catch with him in her backyard as a kid. He took one look at her, ignoring the wrinkled skin below her neck. He saw the face of a crone; the face of someone he didn't know at all. Where was the kindly old woman who'd cooked him a hangover breakfast?

"I was here the last time they tried the ceremony of the Thirteenth," Elsie said. "It's been a long wait for it to happen again. And this time, we won't let anybody stop it."

Something cold pressed against his neck, and before he could react, his aunt had pulled herself closer to him again. "Settle down, sport, or you'll join the bodies up there." She pointed at the dead women cast around the stage like gruesome props. "I don't need to do anything more than push like this . . ." She demonstrated with a little pressure how easily the pain could start. David felt something hot trickle down his neck. ". . . and you'll never be able to watch *Jeopardy* with me again."

Her free arm wrapped around his chest and David flinched for the first time in his life at a hug from his favorite aunt. He tried not to think about the flesh that was pressing itself to him from behind, and focused only on the scene on the stage.

"Bring us the blood of the twelve mothers," Amelia called to the crowd, and for the second time that night, they lined up at the front of the stage. "Kiss the Thirteenth, and press the life you've taken to her. The blood of the mothers will coagulate and transform in the one."

The first in line was an old man—Mr. Gordon from the supermarket. He pressed his entire body against Brenda as he ran his hands, sticky with the gore of a dozen slaughtered women and children, up and down her smooth body. Then he tried to kiss her, with an anxious, forceful tongue.

Brenda spit at him when he stepped back, but the man only spread two rows of yellowing teeth and laughed.

"Quickly," Amelia cautioned. "There are only minutes left and you all must give what you have taken to her before Dr. Rockford can finish it."

The line moved faster then, grandmother, trucker, coed and priest, bartender, auto monkey, receptionist, bum . . . each taking Brenda in their arms to enjoy their brief taste of her flesh.

She didn't spit again, but her face ran wet with tears. The taste in her mouth was sour and bitter and . . . gross, was all she could think to describe it. She closed her eyes and tried to bear it, because she couldn't begin to escape from the grip of the Butcher; his hands on hers were a vise.

It may have been the smoke from the candles, but Brenda didn't think so. It felt like the air around her grew thicker, heavier, palpable. As the murderous mob came one by one to embrace her in their bloody sweat, she could feel other touches against her . . . Feathery, cold ones. And when she opened her eyes, from the side she thought she saw movement, a fleeting glance of a face that disappeared in the air like smoke.

David saw the people touching his girl . . . He realized as the thought passed that he labeled her as "his girl." He was ready to die to make sure that she got out of this place. He considered his chances of turning on Elsie before she severed his jugular . . . If she went deep, before he'd gotten Brenda off the stage, then he had done no good at all.

Amelia whistled as if she were calling a dog. The mumbling ambient noise dropped off and she held her hands up to the crowd. "We have sent the blood of the twelve mothers to Ba'al and their babies to the mother, Astarte," she said. "And you have given it back to the Thirteenth through your hands. Now, we call Ba'al, and if our sacrifices were good, he will be among us . . . and we will be his."

David shuddered as he looked at Brenda on the stage. Her breasts glimmered wetly in the firelight, and the smears from dozens of hands left her body clothed in a chocolaty smear of blood. If nothing else, at least some of her nakedness was covered by the blood of the mothers.

"Fuck," David said. "How do I help you?"

His aunt turned to answer, digging in the knife just a little more. "Maybe you could start by helping her to meet her destiny instead of running from it."

Rockford took Brenda by the shoulders, and began to push her toward the ground. The crowd began to cheer, and someone started to chant, "Astarte, Ba'al, Astarte, Ba'al." The whole room took up the cry.

David began to move, forgetting the knife at his throat, but Elsie wasn't forgetting. It dug into his flesh and he cried out, at the same time as Brenda, who Rockford had finally pushed all the way to the floor.

For the first time in the whole ordeal, David finally felt truly, completely afraid. Not for his life, but for what was coming. As the townspeople milled around and chanted at the stage, the air seemed to grow murkier in the already-shadowy room. It was as if a cloud had passed overhead, but it didn't go away. While the flames on the side of the room continued to gutter and sway, their impact lessened as the inky blackness grew from the ceiling. It twisted and moved, and then David saw something emerging like a funnel from the center. Something that almost glowed black in the darkness. But in its center, there was something lighter. Two somethings. Somethings that moved in slow motion to circle the room until they came to rest on him.

Eyes.

The cloud had grown a head and eyes that found him. He tried to look away, but couldn't . . . The thing held his gaze like a magnet, and David felt tears begin to stream down his cheeks as it slid through the oily air to grow closer, so close that he could see the deep black holes in the center of the yellowed eyeballs. Holes that you could get sucked into, he thought, as his groin turned over inside him. Even as his stomach quailed, his groin burned at the gaze of the demon, and suddenly David knew that all was lost. In a heartbeat he had gone from crushing fear to burning desire at the look of the thing. If this was what Rockford and Amelia were calling, then no man would prevail against it. The thing was lust incarnate, and David strained against the knife to move closer. He needed it. Needed . . .

Elsie whispered in his ear, "Not for you. Not now."

And with that the demon's gaze flipped away, back to the stage where Rockford knelt between the legs of David's girl.

Amelia invoked the demons from her place on the stage and someone in the room screamed, "At last, the god, at last."

That's when the gunshot echoed through the room.

CHAPTER SIXTY-THREE

"Every time I run into you, you're a prisoner," the voice said. Christy struggled to open her eyes. Her head felt on fire. She couldn't remember exactly what the last thing was that she'd seen, but she remembered a lot of fists and feet connecting with her body after David and Brenda had escaped the basement. And then the lights had just . . . gone out.

Now they were back on, and she managed to make her eyelids flicker open, a painful act even in the low light of the torch-lit room. At a glance she knew right where she was—back in the same room that the twelve mothers had been hung in. Hung just as she was now. Like meat in a locker. Her eyes flickered up to take in the chains that connected to the cuffs on her wrists. There was pain in her arms, but only a little . . . Mostly she didn't feel a thing below the neck.

"Who's there?" she finally said. When she tried to look around the room, she didn't see anybody.

Chains hung from the bricks around the walls, but no other bodies were to be found.

"Down here," the man answered. "On the floor where you left me. I don't think you'll be bringing any help."

Christy struggled to scan the floor. She didn't see him at first.

"To your left," he said, and she twisted.

"Billy!" she whispered.

"Last time I checked," he answered. "But that could change soon if you don't get an ambulance out here. Aren't you supposed to be a cop? Bringing help to those in need?"

His voice changed at the last sentence as he struggled to contain a moan of pain. "I could use a little help here," he said finally. "That's why I let you out the first time."

"Yeah, well, things got a little complicated out there," she answered.

"Not here," he answered. "Just bleedin' going on here."

Christy didn't answer immediately. She took in the room, trying to ignore the growing sounds of excitement from outside.

"There's a key over there by the door," she said finally, picking out the ring that hung on a hook just inside the old wooden door. "If you could get it for me . . ."

"What, I'd be your *hero?*"

"Something like that."

"You'd drop all charges against me, from now until death do we part?"

"How about I promise to drop all charges against you up to now?"

"What charges do I have now? I haven't done anything."

"How about aiding and abetting a mass murderer."

"Good point," Billy said. "So you'd drop that?"

"If you get me out of here, Castle Point PD will not ever mention your name in regard to this case, except as a victim," she promised. Deep inside, she had a feeling the chief would kill her for saying that. But . . . if she didn't get free, it wouldn't really matter anyway, would it? She'd be dead, regardless.

Billy crawled toward the door and once at the wall, used its solidness to prop himself up. Inch by inch he levered himself upright against the cool masonry, until he could easily snatch the key ring. Then, taking a shallow breath (and gasping at the sharp pain that resulted) he shuffled slowly across the divide.

"The step that they used to hang me up here is still there," Christy said, gesturing with her face at the small step stool just a foot or two away from her feet.

Billy finally made it to her side, and then stopped, putting one burning hot hand against her bare thigh.

"You promise me that you'll come back for me?"

"Yes," she said. "I can't help TG, but I will come back for you."

"Okay," he whispered, and then grunted as he groped his way up the wall and stepped up on the stool. Then she felt his hand on her wrist. He groaned as he touched her and repeated, first in whispers, and then in louder more agonizing tones: "Fuck, fuck, fuck, FUCK!"

Something clicked and Christy felt her hand slide free so that she was dangling from one arm. And then Billy warned: "I can't catch you."

Fingers touched her other strangely distant hand and something clicked again, and Christy was falling.

The ground only hurt a . . . LOT.

Behind her someone hurt even more, as Billy lost

his balance from the step stool and collapsed right behind her to the rock floor.

The words he screamed are not printable in any intelligible sense, but aptly reflected an enormous amount of pain.

Christy still was blinking back the stars as she crawled over and touched the damp curls of his head with a needles-and-pins-tingling hand. "I WILL be back for you," she promised.

Billy only answered with a moan.

Chapter Sixty-four

The gunshot stopped the chanting like . . . a gunshot. The crowd turned away from Rockford and Amelia and Brenda on the stage and tried to find the source of the noise.

David grinned when he found it. There, at the base of the stairs to the exit from the ancient hotel stood Christy Sorensen. She wore a black T-shirt and a baggy pair of gray shorts, and in her hand, she held a black revolver.

Captain Ryan suddenly separated himself from a young woman at the front of the stage and moved toward Christy.

She didn't hesitate a second. The report echoed through the basement room so loud some people held their ears.

Ryan fell to the ground, grasping at his right leg. "You can't shoot a fellow cop and get away with it," he wheezed at last, looking up at her.

Christy only shook her head. "It's your gun, Captain. How do I know why you shot yourself? Maybe you just don't know how to handle it. Small town like this, you probably don't practice much."

"You bitch," he complained, but she only pulled the trigger again, and bits of Ryan's brain spattered against the people behind him. One heavyset man looked down and saw the policeman's eyeball glued to his belly with hot blood and a yellowish paste, and began to scream.

But Christy didn't waste time. She moved to the stage before the mob could decide how to react, and pointed the gun at Rockford. "Back off, asshole," she said.

The doctor turned away from Brenda and looked confused. "How did you . . ." he began, but Christy only shook her head and fired.

Bits of his shoulder colored Brenda's face, and the girl bellowed at the hot spray. "What the fu—"

Amelia moved fast. With the echo of the first shot she had faded from the stage and took up a torch from the back wall. She moved up the side, knowing that the source of the attack had come from the stairwell. As Rockford got plugged, she moved into position, grinning with a knowing look.

Rockford had always been just a tool, and now the voices spoke to her. They were here; the blood of the mothers had paved the way. She could taste their pleasure in her mouth, and knew their anger on her ass like a drill point. They kissed her and paddled her in equal measures, and she jumped to make sure that their will was carried out. The doctor was inconsequential now; they had created the twelve mothers and then sacrificed them and their offspring. Now . . . his contribution was ornamental.

Amelia slunk along the wall toward the source of the attack, a ninety-degree angle between her and the Thirteenth. She saw Captain Ryan go down, and shook her head. The captain had been useful.

Above her the ceiling roiled, as the shadows of a demon flickered and moved toward the source of the attack.

She knew where Christy was. She knew the basement of this old hotel as if she'd grown up there. Amelia shook her head and edged to the corner. There was no question about what she had to do; there were only moments left in the hour of the Thirteenth. No matter what, she had to get rid of this distraction.

Amelia turned the corner like a pole-vaulter, both feet in the air and hands leveraging the corner of the wall as she threw herself at the woman with the gun like a bullet herself.

Her right foot connected instantly with Christy's elbow, and the gun clattered to the ground like a broken plate, as the two women both went down beside it.

David saw Amelia's gambit. As he watched her steel herself for her attack on Christy, he made ready for his one chance to escape his aunt. A collective gasp filled the room as Christy and Amelia hit the ground, and David used the moment to roll out of the grasp of his aunt. Before she realized he was gone, he'd thrown himself across the floor and come up in a crouch near the stage. He sprang.

"Get up," he demanded when he reached Brenda, who lay still, eyes clenched closed. When they blinked open at his voice, her mouth opened in shock.

"Later," he said, and grabbed her hand. "Let's go. Now."

"Déjà vu," she whispered.

"Not this time," he promised.

Above them, a swirl of dark spirit coalesced and reached with dirty tendrils toward the ground, struggling to find a purchase in this place that could support whatever magic that a demon wielded in hell. David felt icy fingers at his back, and he leaped over a fat man who still lay on the ground of the basement, lusts apparently so sated that the glutton couldn't stand.

The air around them buzzed with hate and desire, and David felt the two at war in his mind, in his heart. The feeling bristled like electricity sparking in water; conductive and opposite. He wanted to explode with the sensation, but instead, blinking past the yellow glare that seemed to cascade over his brain, he grabbed Brenda's hand hard and yanked her forward.

She stumbled over bodies and blood and when they reached the stairs and saw Amelia, the nurse stopped in her tracks and laughed.

"You're ours now." Amelia grinned.

David shook his head. "Not on your life," he answered. He dragged Brenda past her, but the nurse didn't back down.

"The Thirteenth is ours," she said. "You're just a problem."

With that, Amelia grabbed at David's waist and then dragged a razor down his side. Christy launched herself from where she'd fallen seconds before and grabbed the nurse by the throat. The two collapsed in a kicking, clawing heap once more, and David pulled Brenda past them, just as the pain began to register at his side.

He was up three stairs before he turned back and saw Amelia straddling Christy, hand in the air above the policewoman's face.

From the room beyond came a chorus of wails, as the crowd realized both their priestess and their goat had gone, but David ignored them. He only saw the matted blonde curls stuck to Christy's face, and her worn but determined eyes as she forced her hand to grab Amelia's hair as the nurse tried to turn away.

"Do me first, bitch," Christy demanded, and then her eyes met David's for the last time. "I told you to get her out of here," she screamed.

Then Amelia's arm came down and blood zagged like lightning across Officer Christy Sorensen's neck. It cascaded across the hollow of her throat and down the dark shirt she'd found in a pile upstairs. It sprayed the cheek of her murderer, and painted the floor in the color that could only be described as the color of love.

David pushed Brenda up the stairs. "Go," he said, but as she took the first step he turned back to Amelia, who already had risen from the body of her latest kill.

"You fucking bitch," he said, and ignoring the razor she wielded in the air like a dare, he kicked out and connected with her cheek.

Amelia's eyes popped open wide as a game-show winner's moment of surprise, and she dropped. But even as she went, David followed, dropping on her body to follow his kick with a punch and another punch and then, picking up the razor that had fallen next to her, a cut.

And a cut.

And a long, deep slice.

Tears ran from his eyes as he saw Christy's motionless body inches away, and his hand came down with the razor again and again, as somewhere just a few feet away, a chorus of bodiless voices wailed and laughed in equal measure.

When Aunt Elsie grabbed him by the hair to pull him away from the bloody mess that Nurse Amelia had become, he instinctively punched out with a razor-adorned hand and stopped his aunt from ever speaking again.

She went down holding her throat and wheezing in crimson bubbles that began at last to clothe her old skin in something other than air once again. He felt no remorse.

A cool hand gripped him by the shoulder and pulled, and David almost whipped the razor around again.

It was Brenda, and the screams grew louder behind him as she screamed at equal volume in front. "David, we have to go! Now!"

He stood and saw the bloody bodies of the townspeople rising to move toward him with something warped between fear and rage and hate and disgust in their eyes.

"Yeah," he said, and ran with her up the stairs.

The air outside of Castle House Asylum was cool and crisp and somewhere down the mountain, a chorus of locusts sang about the dreams of night.

Inside the old hotel, the wisps of demon limbs faded like fog at noon, disappearing with the life of their invokers.

As fast as hell had begun to materialize in the basement of Castle House Asylum, so now did it dissipate, just like dreams in the light of morning. And with it slipped the violently erotic spell that had colored the basement in invisible red. Released from that unnatural grip, the screams of the night continued, as one by one the townspeople woke from a succubic nightmare, saw the blood coating their hands and bodies and realized where they were, and what horrible things they'd done.

Chapter Sixty-five

The townspeople who survived had exited the hotel like rats from a sinking ship; some held hands across their faces to hide their identities as they went, but the rev of engines and faces of fear filled the night outside the hotel just seconds after Brenda and David fled the scene.

The bodies left behind were . . . left behind.

Castle House Lodge again became a place outside of time or consequence. Dead men tell no stories. Down the stairs from the reception desk, behind the door with the red *X*, bodies began to rot; but nobody was there to smell them.

When the Innovative Industries truck pulled up outside the front door of the hotel a few days later, Greg knocked and when he didn't get an answer, shrugged.

"I guess Dr. Rockford meant what he said last week," he mumbled to himself. "Don't know how he could quit; stem cells are good money!"

But Greg got back into his truck and drove away. And after that, all that came to Castle House Lodge were weeds.

Epilogue

The best part of a nightmare is waking up.

And the best part of waking up, for David, was waking up next to Brenda.

For the past few days, every morning had beamed through the window like a light sent specifically to illuminate the pink strand of her hair that invariably sprawled across their shared pillow like a stain of bliss.

But this morning, that bliss was gone.

David rubbed a fist in his eyes and tried to focus. "Brenda?" he called.

Since the night that they had left the old hotel behind, she had stayed with him at his aunt's house. Elsie hadn't returned from the hotel; neither had a bunch of people. And considering that the entire police force of Castle Point had been wiped out there, nobody was booking suspects or pressing charges.

The two of them had come back here to the tiny house and pretty much held on to each other without askance. They were still, somewhat, in shell shock. She told him what she could remember about being held in the room at Castle House Lodge, and he told her about looking for her.

"You really looked for me?" she said, when he talked about going back to the bar and interviewing people at the grocery to find out where she'd gone after the night of their fateful meeting.

"Yeah," he confirmed. "I figured you owed me money. Wasn't I buying the Guinness that night?"

"You wish," Brenda said. "I think you owe me at least three rounds."

Something creaked at the far corner of the room and David pulled the sheets around his neck. The air streaming in through the screens from the backyard was crisp and cool in the summer dawn, and he took a deep breath as he craned his head to look for the source of the noise.

It was Brenda, stepping out of the tiny bath adjoining his room.

"Okay?" he asked, hardly even meaning it. But she didn't give him the easy answer.

"No," she said.

Brenda wore only a pair of panties; pink ones, which David totally appreciated. Her breasts sloped low and tired in the morning light, but all he wanted to do was kiss them. He thought of the night before, as she'd let him do just that, but then had begged him to stop pressing her for more and simply hug her tight.

"What's the matter?"

She held out a thin paper strip in her hand, and he looked confused as he saw two pink lines at its end.

"What are you showing me?" he asked.

"I'm pregnant," she said. Her voice was barely audible in the quiet of the room.

"But, it can't be mine," he instantly said, and instantly regretted it.

Her voice was sharp. "I didn't say it was."

"Rockford's?" he asked, a knife of jealousy coming out of nowhere as he pictured the doctor's body pinning hers to the bloody basement of the old hotel.

"I don't think so," Brenda said, sinking to sit on the edge of the bed.

"Well then . . ."

Brenda thought of the cold thrusting between her legs on Rockford's impromptu altar, as the air flamed around her like an explosion of lust.

"It's not over 'til it's over," she said.

"What do you mean?" he said, reaching up to press a hand on the cool flesh of her belly. It twined beneath his hand like a snake.

"I mean, that something happened at the hotel that I can't explain," she finally said. "Something horrible."

"What do you mean?" David asked, hands turning to ice as he held her waist and silently prayed.

"I mean something happened," she said. "Something that made me . . ."

"Made you what?"

Brenda put her hands on David's shoulders and closed her eyes as she leaned against his head.

"Made me the Thirteenth," she whispered. "The demon is here, inside me." She pressed his hand to her belly, and inside, again, he felt motion . . . which was impossible at this early stage. Only a few days had passed since they'd escaped the nightmare.

Brenda bent to kiss his lips, one long strand of pink hair falling over his cheek to tickle him, before she leaned away, tears coursing down her cheeks. His hand still tingled with the motion from inside her, a movement that was unnatural . . . but undeniable.

"Kill me, David," she begged. "Before it's born, kill me. Please."

She pressed the cold steel of a butcher's knife into his hands, and David felt his throat close as the tears of hopelessness welled up in his eyes. "No," he whispered, but Brenda grasped him by the wrist and pulled him closer, for a final, fatal embrace.

David closed his eyes against her shoulder, and prayed for a dream to wake him.

"Simon Clark has what it takes to be another Stephen King."
—Bentley Little

SIMON CLARK

The local children call it "the ghost monster," a disturbing mosaic on a mausoleum wall in the old cemetery. For centuries the grim portrait has imprisoned the spirits of the notorious Justice Murrain and his vicious gang of misfits. But now someone has taken the portrait, and the spirits of the sadists are free to enjoy the darkest of pleasures. Mayhem rules the town. The streets run red with blood. People are not merely insane. They are possessed. And even death will not stop them.

GHOST MONSTER

ISBN 13: 978-0-8439-6179-9

☐ **YES!**

Sign me up for the Leisure Horror Book Club and send my FREE BOOKS! If I choose to stay in the club, I will pay only $8.50* each month, a savings of $7.48!

NAME: _____

ADDRESS: _____

TELEPHONE: _____

EMAIL: _____

☐ I want to pay by credit card.

☐ **VISA** ☐ **MasterCard.** ☐ **DISCOVER**

ACCOUNT #: _____

EXPIRATION DATE: _____

SIGNATURE: _____

Mail this page along with $2.00 shipping and handling to:
Leisure Horror Book Club
PO Box 6640
Wayne, PA 19087
Or fax (must include credit card information) to:
610-995-9274
You can also sign up online at **www.dorchesterpub.com**.
*Plus $2.00 for shipping. Offer open to residents of the U.S. and Canada only.
Canadian residents please call 1-800-481-9191 for pricing information.
If under 18, a parent or guardian must sign. Terms, prices and conditions subject to change. Subscription subject to acceptance. Dorchester Publishing reserves the right to reject any order or cancel any subscription.